Caught in a Pickle

New Orleans Magicians
Book 2

C.M. Kane

COPYRIGHT

～

Editing & book design by Maggie Kern @ Ms.K Edits

Cover art by Dar Albert at Wicket Art Designs

Photographer: Jean Woodfin

Model: Jeremy Dacanay

BOOK TWO

Dedication

For my husband, who understands that book boyfriends are imaginary, and he's the only guy for me.

Prologue

Hailey...
"Shut up," Missy said. "You did not do this."
"Of course I did," I said.

We'd met at the gate for the flight, each of us making our own way to the airport. I was wearing a tee shirt that read *Maid of Honor,* and I had one for each of the bridesmaids that read *Bridesmaid,* and one for my absolute best friend that read *Bride.*

"Can't be walking around Vegas without proclaiming our reason for being there," I said, handing the shirts out.

"You're so fucking amazing," Missy said. "I'm so glad you're my best friend."

"Right back at you," I replied. "Now shut up and put your shirt on. Same goes for the rest of you guys."

We were plenty early for our flight, so they all had time to go to the bathroom and change while I wrangled the suitcases. I'd made three shirts each for us, so we wouldn't have to wear the same one the whole weekend. I was so happy for Missy and Kelton. They'd been together for all of college, having met at orientation. Honestly, we were all surprised they didn't go from graduation to the wedding

1

aisle, but they said they wanted to save up and have a good, proper wedding.

My idea of a good proper wedding was getting married by Elvis in Vegas, which was another reason I was happy we were going there. Nothing like scouting out the sites to see where I wanted to eventually get hitched. Of course, it would be helpful if I were actually dating someone. Seemed like every guy I ended up with just wanted a fuck buddy, which was all well and good, but I wanted something that would last a little longer than a few hours.

When the girls all got back, we had one of the employees at the gate take a picture of us all together, so Missy could post it on her social media page. She was just so fucking adorable I couldn't stand it. We were gonna have an amazing time, and I couldn't wait.

Chapter One

Hailey...

Waking up with phantom soreness from a fucking amazing dream was a new experience. The killer migraine and a mouth that felt like I'd been sucking on old socks told me that whatever I'd drunk the night before might not have been worth it. Stretching, I slid my ass back, bumped into a body, and froze.

"Fuck," I muttered.

Maybe it wasn't phantom aches and pains after all. I was naked, that much was clear, and the body next to me was as well. God, I hope we used protection, because fuck me if I ended up with some STI from a rando. Whoever it was, they were definitely not awake. Their even breathing told me that much.

Sliding out of the bed, I took my unhappy ass to the bathroom and looked in the mirror. My reflection told me everything I needed to know. I had been fucked good. My bladder screamed to be emptied, so I sat and let it go, the relief nearly as good as an orgasm. When I finished, I flushed and washed my hands, but something was wrong. There was a fucking ring on my finger. Not just any finger, though. No. I had a fucking wedding ring on.

"You have got to be fucking kidding me," I said, the water running over the very nice, very large yellow diamond set in a gold band with small diamonds trailing down either side and wrapped around my finger. "Fuck, fuck, fuck."

The shade on the window was open enough that I didn't need to use the light from the bathroom to see by. When I looked at the bed, there he was. A sexy-as-fuck guy, sprawled out under the sheet, one foot on top of it, an arm thrown across his eyes. He had a dark mustache, and some stubble along his jaw that was trying to be a beard, but I couldn't really see a ton of features on his face.

His body, on the other hand, was barely covered, and damn those abs were fine as fuck. No wonder I ended up with him. I mean, I wasn't exactly a slut, but I did hook up with some dudes from time to time. Never, though, when I was out of town. Missy was gonna fucking murder me. This was her bachelorette party, or at least it had been, and the trip was all about celebrating her.

Maybe it was just a joke, that we were just fucking around, and didn't actually do what I thought. If I fucking got married in Vegas, none of my friends would ever let me live it down. I had to figure out what the fuck happened, and how to get out of it, if that was even possible.

"Think, Hales," I said to myself, then began looking around the mess of a room.

I found my clothes near the door, which didn't surprise me. His were next to mine, so I grabbed his pants and pulled out his wallet. Not that I wanted to steal anything, but to see who the fuck I had fucked. It was small, one of those that doesn't really have that many pockets, just on the outside. There was quite a bit of cash in it, which I left, and pulled out a couple of cards until I found a driver's license.

Alejandro de la Garza. At least he was from Louisiana, my home state. Actually, his address was in Destrehan, which wasn't too far from my own town of Metairie. Both of them were on the outskirts of New Orleans, which is where you said you were from when someone asked, because no one knows anywhere else.

He was twenty-six, so a year older, and while most pictures on IDs tended to look like a mug shot, his was actually decent. Dark eyes that had a brightness to them, and a smile that I could definitely fall for. Yeah, it didn't surprise me that I hooked up with him.

I shoved the wallet back into his pants and continued my search of the room. On the dresser at the foot of the bed, next to the television, there was a bouquet of flowers. Nothing fancy, just a few roses, and some baby's breath wrapped up in plastic. Next to it was a piece of paper that kind of made me wonder. I pulled my panties on, my shirt over my head, so at least I was covered, and went to it.

"No," I said, and it must have been louder than I thought, because the guy moved.

He didn't wake up, though, thankfully, so I turned back to the paper. We had definitely gotten married last night, *and* we'd consummated it.

"Fuck," I muttered.

I went back and picked up my jeans, pulling my phone out of my pocket. I pressed the button on the side, but it wouldn't light up. I pressed it again, and it started that warmup thing it does when you've turned it off. Fuck, fuck, fuck. That's all I could think. This just wasn't happening.

"Hey, gorgeous," I heard, and whipped my head back to the bed. "Thinking of running away?"

Fuck.

"I'm just trying to figure out what the fuck happened last night," I said, hand on my hip, glaring daggers at him.

"Well, if you can't remember, it must not have been as good as I thought," he said.

"That's not what I'm talking about," I said. "If my memory is correct, and it wasn't a fucking dream, it was the best fucking sex I've had in entirely too long. No, I'm talking about this." I held up my left hand and pointed to the ring that was sitting on a finger it shouldn't be. "This is what I'm questioning. Why the fuck did you marry some chick you didn't know? And why did you fuck said chick when she was obviously drunk off her ass?"

"Well, now," he said, sitting up. "That's not exactly how I remember the night going."

The sheet was coming dangerously close to losing its ability to cover him. I was having a fucking challenging time keeping my eyes on his face, and not letting them dip down his chest to that tantalizing V he had going on right at the edge of the sheet. Like his chest, very well defined, those abs looked tantalizing, but the way his waist narrowed, the muscles dipping down to the edge of the sheet, damn near had me done in.

"Eyes up here, darling," he said, and I snapped my eyes away from everything I wanted to touch to see him smirking. Fuck, if that didn't just make my panties wet. "Shall I remind you of our night?"

"Can you put something more than just that fucking sheet on?" I asked, and the smile grew bigger.

"I'm thinking you should take what you've got on off," he said, and I could see he was having a hard time holding back a laugh.

"I can't have a conversation with you if you're naked," I said, doing my damn best to keep my eyes locked on his. "And I'd like to have an actual conversation."

"All right," he said, and went to stand.

I turned around and faced the wall behind me, and he chuckled. I could feel him as he got closer to me, his heat settling on my back as he stood there. Thankfully, though, he ducked down and picked up his boxers, after untangling them from his jeans, and disappeared from my peripheral vision.

"I'm about as decent as I'm gonna get," he finally said, and I peeked over my shoulder before turning all the way around.

"Thank you," I said, actually feeling relief.

"You called this meeting," he said. "You should be the one to start."

"Fine," I said, walking to the bed and sitting next to him. "My name's Hailey. What's yours?"

Chapter Two

Alejandro...

She'd woken up first, which was totally fine. But she'd been all kinds of confused as to what had happened. She said she was drunk, but she didn't seem drunk when we met, and we hadn't drunk anything after that. She was the one who suggested sex, but then said it would be better if we were married. I was hesitant because who the fuck gets married the day they meet someone? But she'd been kind of insistent and fucking cute, so I thought, why the fuck not? No big deal to get it annulled if it didn't work out.

There was this jewelry shop she found that was fucking expensive, but she was adorable, and I figured if I was gonna do this, I needed to do it right. When she saw the ring we got, she damn near cried, and my God, did she look beautiful when she had tears in her eyes.

"Please, baby?" she'd asked, and who could say no to that pouty little mouth I intended to fuck?

The sales guy had shown us that it had a matching band for the wedding ring, which was full of more diamonds, as well as a matching one for me. I placed my card on the counter, and he boxed them all up. I didn't even bother to look at the price. I could afford it. If nothing else, she'd have a great story to tell, and a ring that she could pawn, if the need ever came. Not that she looked like she needed money or anything. On the contrary, she'd been wearing very nice clothes, and her bra and panty set she had on underneath were top-notch.

"Alejandro de la Garza," I said in response to her question. "But you can call me Alej, or baby. That's what you've been calling me all night."

"Oh my God," she said, falling back onto the bed. "I can't believe I did this. My friends are gonna kill me."

"Call them," I said. "I gotta pee."

"Go," she said, sort of shoving my back.

I got up and went to the bathroom, not bothering to shut the door. She'd seen me naked, had sucked my cock, and had let me fuck her, so it's not like it was something she hadn't seen already. I finished my piss, flushed, washed up, and headed back out to the room.

She was sitting on the bed, her phone in her hand, just watching it. She was fucking stunning, and I was amazed that she had even looked twice at me. I mean, she was a fireball, for sure, and God, could she move. I had sat and watched her dance for entirely too long before I felt comfortable enough to go up to her group.

It was obvious they were there for either a wedding, or a bachelorette party, because one of the girls had a sash that had "Bride" on it, and the rest had shirts that had "Bridesmaid" on them, except for Hailey's. Hers had, "Maid of Honor" on it. I knew she would need to get back in touch with her friends, especially if it had been their last night. God, I hoped it wouldn't be the last time I saw her. I mean, she lived in Metairie, so decently close to me. That meant we would likely either run into each other or could meet up at the very least.

Ours was not a conventional thing, but we fit each other so fucking well that I figured we could make it work. I mean, my mom would be pissed that she hadn't been invited, let alone met her yet, but that was just not something I could avoid. I had wanted Hailey, badly, and she was definitely ready, willing, and able to make decisions on her own. Even though I initially thought we could get it annulled, I didn't really want that. Not after the night we had.

"Finally," she crowed, and I could see the illumination from the phone on her face as it booted up.

I grabbed the folder for room service and looked it over, trying to decide if I wanted to order in, or take her out. I'd be good with either, but ordering in seemed like an opportunity to have a little more married sex, if she was into that.

"Fuck," she said, and I looked at her.

"What's up?" I asked.

"I missed my flight," she said. "Fuck, fuck, fuck."

"No worries," I replied. "I can get you another ticket, or we can change yours, since you missed it."

"Well," she said. "I'm gonna have to figure something out. I gotta work tomorrow, so I really do have to get home by tonight."

"Anything from your friends?" I asked.

"Oh, yeah," she said. "Only like a million missed calls and a billion messages."

"Can you call them?" I asked. "Let them know you're safe, and that you're getting another flight home?"

"I have to wait until the incoming messages stop," she said.

"Hungry?" I asked, holding up the book with the menu in it.

"I'm fucking starving," she said. "But I gotta get to my hotel to get my shit before I can do anything. God, this is an absolute nightmare. I can't believe I did this."

She'd set her phone down on the nightstand, the sounds of pings coming from it in rapid-fire succession, and dropped her head into her hands. I didn't know if she was gonna cry, or scream, or what. I sat down next to her, put my arm around her shoulders, and she sort of just melted into my side and began to sob.

"It's all gonna be fine," I said, rubbing her back while holding her. "We'll figure this out. I got you."

She just kept crying, almost flinching with each ping from her phone, until it was finally silent, and she sort of just relaxed. It took a bit longer before she sat up again, looking up at me as if I were some abnormality or something.

"Why are you being so nice to me?" she asked.

"You're my wife," I said. "It's my job to protect you, to keep you safe, and to make sure you feel safe, even when you're falling apart."

She blinked at me, like she couldn't figure out what I was saying.

"You don't even know me," she said.

"I know you enough," I replied. "Sure, we don't know all the stupid trivial things you find out when you first start dating. But last night, we certainly learned a whole lot about each other. Honestly, that's all I really needed to know."

"All you need to know is if a girl can fuck good?" she asked, and I knew I'd walked into that one.

"Not what I meant," I said. "We actually did talk. About a lot of things. We both want kids, but not yet. You're a teacher, so you get your kid fix during the week, but take the weekend to have your adult shenanigans. Neither of us wants a big wedding of any kind, and didn't want a long engagement. 'Just do it already.' That's a direct quote from you, by the way. You said, 'Why the fuck should we wait? Let's just do it already.'"

"Sounds like me," she said. "Actually, all of that sounds like me."

"I didn't know you were that drunk," I said. "If I did, I never would have indulged you. I saw you dancing with your friends, all having a great time. When I walked up to your group, you came up to me and asked me to dance with you. Then you couldn't stop grinding on me, and my fucking God, you were a temptress. You pulled my head down and whispered in my ear to take you back to my hotel room, and fuck your brains out. Another quote, by the way."

"Dancing should have been a dead giveaway," she said. "I don't dance sober."

"Could have fooled me," I said. "Anyway, we were walking down the strip, and you said we should probably get married before we have sex. Then you begged me to buy you that ring, which was not inexpensive, truth be told. After, we found a little chapel that had an Elvis impersonator doing the weddings, and you insisted."

"Okay," she said. "Some of that definitely sounds like me, but marriage before we have sex? Yeah, that's not something I would insist on. Not that I'm a whore or anything, but I have no problem with premarital sex. Been there, done that, got the damn tee shirt."

"I wasn't gonna argue with you," I said. "Besides, you *are* adorable, so how could I say no?"

"Well, now I feel like I just pushed you into the damn thing," she said. "We should just go and get it undone before it goes any further."

"I'm actually not that upset about it," I said. "I ended up with a fucking gorgeous wife."

She blew out a breath, then picked up her phone.

"Shit," she said, and showed me a message.

Girl. Did you die? 'Cause if you didn't, I'm gonna kill you. Call me!

"Is that the bride?" I asked.

"Yeah," she said, and pressed a couple of buttons on the phone before pressing it to her ear. "Missy, I'm sorry," she said, but I could hear the other girl yelling on the other end. Yeah, this wasn't gonna be a good thing.

Chapter Three

Hailey...

"Hailey Nicole Truitt," Missy said when she answered the phone.

"Missy," I said. "I'm sorry."

"Sorry doesn't even come close to cutting it," she shouted, and I could hear the rest of the girls in the background. "Do you have any idea how worried we were about you?"

"I know," I said as Alej got up and grabbed his jeans. "I really am sorry. I'm safe, but I'm not gonna make the flight. I have to go get my shit from the hotel. Alej is gonna help me get another flight home."

"Who the fuck is Alej?" she shouted.

"Apparently, he's my husband," I said, then pulled the phone away from my ear, knowing she was gonna blow a gasket.

"What the fuck do you mean, your husband?" she shouted, and I could hear Kelsey and Emma freaking out in the background. "Bitch, switch to video, right fucking now."

I knew it was gonna happen, so I did what they'd asked, and switched to a video call.

"Okay," Missy said, Kelsey and Emma behind her. "You aren't dead, but you're not in our hotel. What gives?"

Alej had pulled his jeans on and was standing in front of me, looking more than a little bit delicious. Honestly, I could see why I'd gone for him. He hit all the things I wanted. Tall, dark, and handsome with enough color to spice things up. Add to that how nice he had been since I woke up, and yeah, I was seriously thinking about keeping him.

"Do you remember me leaving the bar?" I asked.

"No," she said, then looked to the others, who both shook their heads.

"So," I said. "You let me leave a bar, drunk off my ass, with some rando, and didn't think to stop me or anything?"

They all had a sheepish look on their faces, knowing that, while I was an adult and could make my own decisions, we were a team, and were supposed to stick together.

"We didn't know you were gone until this morning," Kelsey said.

"Really?" I asked.

"Okay," Missy said. "We are bad friends, and you can kill us when you see us again. But seriously, what are you talking about with this husband shit?"

Instead of talking, I just pulled my hand up and showed them the ring.

"Oh my God," Emma said. "That is fucking amazing."

"Yeah," I said, and Alej sat down next to me, but out of sight of the camera. "You wanna meet him?"

"Fuck yeah, we do," Missy said.

I looked over at him, then motioned with my head for him to scoot closer. He did, wrapping his arm around my back, and he smiled at the phone.

"Hello," he said, and that low timber rumbling against my arm made me shiver with delight.

"Well, hello," Kelsey said, batting her eyes at the camera.

"Fuck off, he's mine," I said, but had a smile on my face.

"Hello, ladies," Alej said, and I could see their eyes widen.

Yeah, we were all suckers for a nice deep voice that was so smooth you could melt butter on it.

"Satisfied?" I asked them.

"Not as much as you," Emma said, then slapped her hand over her mouth.

"I'll let you know when I have a new flight," I said. "Until then, don't tell anyone. I kinda need to get my brain around this before I go announcing it."

"Okay," Missy said. "You gonna get home tonight?"

"I hope so," I said. "Otherwise, I gotta call the school and tell them they've gotta get a sub. Not like it's a big deal, but definitely not what I had planned."

"Don't worry about it," Kelsey said.

"See you soon," I replied, then ended the video call before falling back on the bed and letting a sigh out.

"That wasn't too bad," Alej said.

"Oh, it was bad," I said. "You don't know them like I do, but trust me, it was bad."

"They seemed nice," he said.

"They are," I replied. "They're also sharks, and they smell blood. Fuck, what are we gonna do?"

"Take it one day at a time," he said. "First, we find food. Then, we get your stuff, and figure out a flight for you."

"When are you heading home?" I asked.

"Tomorrow," he said. "I'd love it if you stayed another night. We can spend the day getting to know each other, for real this time. If it's a money issue, I can cover anything you might be missing out on."

"What is it you do, actually?" I asked, having just realized that he remembered our conversations, but I obviously didn't.

"Baseball," he said.

I waited, thinking he would expand on what he said, but he didn't. Baseball didn't exactly explain anything.

"I don't know what that means," I said.

"It's a game, played on a field," he said, a cheeky grin on his lips.

"I know that, fuckwad," I said. "I meant, what does it mean in the context you used it?"

"It's my job," he said. "I'm a professional baseball player."

"For who?" I asked.

"The New Orleans Magicians," he said. "I play second base, but we got much farther than that last night."

"Is everything with you a sexual innuendo?"

"If I can make it that way, then yeah," he said. "I mean, you're my wife, so I should be able to be sexual with you."

"Speaking of which," I said. "We gotta undo this. Like, we really do."

"Why?" he asked. "You already married? Have another guy on the side? This soon into our marriage, and you're already looking for an out?"

"You don't think so?" I asked, very confused. "I mean, how do you know I'm not gonna take you to the cleaners and take all your money?"

"You're not, are you?" he asked.

"Well, no," I said, looking up at him from the bed.

Just then, my stomach growled, and he smiled.

"Let's get some breakfast," he said. "We can figure plenty of things out while we feed you. I'm not gonna have anyone tell me I'm mistreating my wife by starving her."

"Thank you," I said.

"For what?"

"Taking care of me," I said. "And for not killing me last night."

"I'm a lover, not a fighter," he said. "Now, get dressed so we can get food."

"Okay," I said, sitting up on the bed.

"And, hey," he said. "I do really want to try to work this out. If we can't, I get it. But will you give me a chance?"

"I mean," I said, stalling a bit. "You are kinda cute. And while I didn't have 'having a relationship with a professional athlete' on my bucket list, I'm not gonna turn it down."

The smile he gave me was fucking hot, and I could see how he talked me out of my pants, and my mind, while I was drunk. Oh, this could actually be fun. At least, I hoped it would be.

Chapter Four

Alejandro...

Hailey was beyond sexy. She was smart, funny, and full of fire. I was definitely looking forward to getting to know her better but was also worried that she was just gonna bail, and that wasn't something I wanted. I'd promised for better or for worse, and I intended to stick through it, come hell or high water.

We'd eaten at the buffet in my hotel before going out to hers to get her stuff. It was still early enough that they hadn't done house-keeping, thankfully, and we got in, and she packed her stuff up before we headed back to mine. I kept her close to me, my arm around her every chance I could. It was like she was a drug I couldn't shake, and that made me a little worried. What if she decided she didn't want to do this? Then I'd have to let her go, and I didn't want that at all.

"Let's look at flights," I said once we'd settled back in my room. "Unless you wanna do something else?"

"I'm gonna have to email the school," she said. "Let them know I had an unexpected thing happen, and I won't be back tomorrow like planned."

"Okay," I said, disappointed.

"Look," she said. "I get that you remember last night, but I don't, so this is still kinda weird for me. I do like you, at least as far as the little that I know about you, but that's the thing. We literally met less than twenty-four hours ago, so you gotta cut me a little slack."

"I get it," I said, because I really did. "Doesn't mean I can't be upset about it. We had an amazing night. I'm talking three condoms amazing."

"Oh, thank God," she said and I looked at her. "I didn't want to ask but was hoping you'd thought to use protection. It's not personal to you, just something I'm pretty careful about."

"You were pretty clear last night," I said. "Not that I would have argued or not suggested them, though. I'm pretty careful myself, so I had a box with me, thankfully. Not that you wouldn't look amazing carrying my child, but it's not the right time."

"Definitely not the right time," she said. "And three is all we could manage?"

"Well, you were willing to keep going, but I kinda was done," I said, only slightly embarrassed. "Not that I didn't want to, but biology can only go so far."

"Oh, yeah," she said, realization dawning on her.

"But we can go now," I said. "I've recovered. Might even be able to top last night."

"Let's figure out logistics first," she said. "I'm gonna call the airline and see if I can get moved to a different flight."

"Or I could just book a ticket for you next to me on my flight," I said.

"We might get there," she replied, then started working on her phone.

I let her do her thing, sliding her suitcase next to mine. I pulled my shirt over my head while toeing off my shoes. Pants came off next, along with the boxers and my socks. She'd gone quiet, and I turned to look at her over my shoulder. She was sitting on the end of the bed, just sort of staring at me, eyes wide, mouth open.

"What?" I asked.

"Sorry," she said, turning away.

"No need," I replied. "Maybe when you're done, you'll join me in the shower."

"Mmhmm," she said, still staring at me.

I walked into the bathroom and set the towel that was on the edge of the tub next to it on the floor so I'd have a place to step on after I was done. I pulled the knob to get the water running, turning it up enough that it was warm, but not too hot. I made sure there was shampoo and soap in the tub before I pulled the plunger to start the shower itself. I took one last peek into the room, and saw her studiously working on her phone, but did catch her taking a peek at me. Instead of chastising her or teasing her, I just winked, then stepped in.

The water felt nice running down my body, and I stuck my head under the spray to get my hair wet. I poured some shampoo into my palm, and worked it into my short hair, letting the suds build up before ducking under the spray again to rinse it out. As I was lathering my hands with soap, I heard the curtain shift, and looked over to see her standing there, completely naked, and absolutely breathtaking.

"Do you mind?" she asked, almost looking worried I'd deny her.

"Never," I replied, shifting, so she could step under the spray.

While the shower wasn't giant, it was plenty big enough for both of us to use it without being in each other's way. Not that it mattered, though, because I let her move past me, then moved next to her, my front to her back as she stood under the spray.

"Need help?" I asked, the bar of soap in my palm.

She turned and looked up at me, smiling, and said, "I think we should get dirty first."

Before I had a chance to react, she was on her knees in front of me, and my cock was in her mouth. By all the gods of the universe, was she talented at sucking dick. I dropped the soap, held onto the handicap bar on the side of the wall, and closed my eyes, just feeling her mouth moving up and down my length. I mean, she'd already sucked me off the night before, but apparently she was drunk, and didn't remember, so this was her first time, at least in her mind, and she did not at all disappoint.

Like the night before, she was very enthusiastic, her tongue swirling on the tip as she pulled back, then letting the head hit the back of her throat as she pressed her lips against my body. Over and over, she bobbed on me, and it was almost impossible to maintain my control.

"Baby, stop," I said, pulling myself from her mouth. "You can't keep doing that or I'll lose it."

"Thought that was the point," she said, smiling up at me.

"My recovery isn't as quick as yours," I said, helping her to her feet. "Now, turn around and let me return the favor."

I turned her away from me, pressing her forward so her hands hit the wall, her ass presenting itself to me like a gift, and I knelt at that altar and worshipped her as the goddess she was, tasting the nectar that I swore sustained my life. Sliding my tongue up her pussy, from clit to slit, delving my tongue into her, and she moaned, music to my ears, pressing herself back and into my face.

As much as I could, I worked her into that high place we all went to when we were ready to orgasm, but she just didn't seem to want to fall over. I didn't take it personally, but knew she needed something more to get her there, so I sat back and slid my finger inside her, getting a low moan from her. My thumb was on her clit, working it in circles, my finger sliding in and out of her, looking for that one spot, the rough patch of skin just inside, that I knew would push her all the way over.

One of her hands had come off the wall, and she was squeezing her breast, pulling the tight bud out from her body, pinching it between her thumb and forefinger, her body bucking against my hand, working hard herself to find that wonderful release. Finally, after entirely too long, she shoved back against my hand, and gave a loud groan, deep and guttural, as her pussy clenched around my finger.

"That's it, baby," I cooed. "Just let it all go."

Her hand went from her breast back to the wall, her legs shaking, as she came down from the clouds. I stood up and wrapped my arms around her, holding her to me as she collected herself.

"Holy fuck," she whispered, raising up to standing. "That was fucking amazing."

I moved her hair from one shoulder and scooped it over and around to the other one, placing my lips against her skin in a reverent kiss. She relaxed even more, her back pressing to my chest, my arms still around her waist. Her hands went along my arms, finally ending up on top of my hands where she left them, just the two of us standing in the spray from the shower.

"Should probably finish the shower," she said, and my cock flexed against her ass. "Oh," she said, turning her head to look up at me over her shoulder. "Should probably take care of that first, huh?"

"Not necessary," I said, and she pouted.

"It is," she replied. "It's not fair that I got to get off and you didn't."

"Trust me," I said. "Watching you orgasm at my hand is more than enough for me."

She sort of leaned forward, and looked around and behind me, so I followed her eyeline, and saw there was a condom in its wrapper on the corner of the tub. When I looked back at her, she smiled.

"Would be a shame to just let that sit there," she said. "Especially when we could put it to good use."

The sparkle in her eye told me she wasn't done with me yet, and I was totally fine with that. I reached back and picked it up, and she snatched it from my hand once it was close to her. She stepped away and turned around, tearing the condom open and removing the slippery disc from inside. I stood still as she slid it onto me, stroking me as she did it, then turned back around, leaning forward again.

"Fuck me like a good husband," she said, and I couldn't do anything but oblige.

Chapter Five

Hailey...

Shower sex was fucking amazing, and he was so damn good at it. I almost didn't want to get out, but we were both spent, both orgasmed, me way more than him, and it felt nice to just climb into bed, and snuggle up. I must have fallen asleep, because I heard my phone going off, and jolted.

"Hey," he said, his eyes hooded, but a smile on his face. "Want me to hand it to you?"

"Probably should," I said. "I'm sure it's Missy, and she's gonna wanna know when I'll be home."

"Have you decided on whether you wanna stay?"

"Not sure," I said as he handed the phone to me. Sure enough, it was my best friend, and I answered with a, "Hello."

"Don't you pretend like you don't know why I'm calling," she said, and I could hear enough noise from the background to know that she was still at the airport.

"I don't," I said.

"Bitch, please," she said. "You haven't even left that hotel. Did you get your shit? Or are you just gonna pretend the rest of the world doesn't exist anymore?"

"My phone was almost completely dead," I explained. "If I'd taken it with me, you wouldn't have known, because it would have died anyway. I got my shit, and we're working on figuring out how to get me home."

"You sound like you were asleep," she said, and I could just picture her folding her arms over her chest, one hip cocked out, the glare of death coming my way.

"I was," I said. "I didn't get much sleep last night, and I'm still tired."

"Well," she said. "You need to figure your shit out and get home. I can't keep this secret forever, you know."

"I know," I said. "But it's been less than a day. You gotta give me a little time to get my head wrapped around all this."

"Are you gonna get it annulled?" she asked.

"I don't know," I said.

"What?" It was almost a shriek the way she said it. "You can't be seriously entertaining the thought of staying with some dude that married a drunk girl he didn't know."

"We're getting to know each other, now," I said. "Besides, it has nothing to do with you. Like, at all. I'll let you know when I know what we're gonna do, okay?"

"Fine," she said. "But it better be quick."

I could hear someone calling her in the background, so she said a quick goodbye and disconnected the call without waiting for a response.

"Fuck," I said.

"Let's get you sorted," he said. "First, what airline were you supposed to fly with?"

I told him and he had his phone in hand, looking at his own flight. By some miracle of fate, we were actually flying on the same airline.

"Looks like I can get you on my flight," he said. "Are you okay with getting home tomorrow evening? Or do you want me to try to find something today?"

"Might as well wait until tomorrow," I said. "I gotta email my principal and let him know I won't be back to the school tomorrow as planned."

"What are you gonna tell him?" he asked.

"That there was an issue with my flight," I said. "It's only slightly a lie, so I don't feel too bad about it."

"Okay," he said. "Are you sure you're good?"

"Yeah," I said. "I have a ton of PTO, so it's not a big deal."

"Can you give me your license?" he asked. "I want to book this before it goes away."

"Yeah," I said and got out of bed.

Walking over to where I'd stashed my clothes, I pulled my wallet out of my pocket and grabbed my license, then turned to see him staring at me.

"What?" I asked.

"Just watching my beautiful wife," he said.

"You're a sap," I said, but I couldn't help but smile. He called me beautiful, and I don't remember the last time someone called me that, or anything even close.

He took my license, then plugged my information into his phone to get my ticket booked. After he was done, he checked us both in, because it was less than twenty-four hours before the flight, and handed the license back. I put it back where it belonged, then started getting dressed.

"What're you doing?" he asked.

"I'm not gonna spend a bonus day in Vegas in bed," I said. "I didn't get to see much of the town while we were here, so thought I'd go check it out. Wanna come with?"

"Do you mean, do I want to go with my wife, and walk around the city where we met, fell in love, and got married?"

"Have we fallen in love, though?"

"I sure have," he said, sitting up on the bed.

God, he was fucking gorgeous, and I couldn't stop my roving eyes from sliding down his body, over those amazing pecs, his right one covered in faint lines from an unfinished tattoo just barely visible. Then, lower still, to the abs that were taut as he flexed his body to sit. Finally, to the sheet that was covering what I was discovering was my favorite part of him. If it wasn't love, it certainly was its very close cousin, lust, that I'd fallen into, and damn, did I not mind that at all.

"Hailey?" he said, and I snapped my eyes up to his. There was something there, unspoken, that was almost like hurt.

"Sorry," I said, though I wasn't sure what I was apologizing for. "Got kinda dick-stracted there for a minute."

He laughed. Like, full on, belting out a laugh, and I was thankful he took it as the joke I'd intended. Question still remained, though. Was I falling for him?

"Let's go find you some tchotchkes to take home," he said, standing up, which did nothing but distract me further.

He came over to me, tilting my head up with a finger under my chin.

"No rush," he said. "I know it's new, and we barely know each other. Who knows, I might find out that you leave wet towels in the bottom of the tub, or something equally heinous in the next few days, and decide we need to go our separate ways."

"Yeah," I said. "I'm sure I'll figure out that you're entirely too good looking, and the entire world has seen you naked. That's not something I'm very comfortable with."

"I don't know about the whole world," he said. "Maybe the guys on my team, but that's about it."

"No girlfriends?"

"I mean," he said. "Sure, but they all pale in comparison with my wife. She's sexy as fuck, trust me."

"Does she know about me?" I asked, hoping the tone was light, but also worried that something else was going on.

"She'd approve," he said. "Besides, I think you might know her."

"Oh, really?" I asked, playing along with his musings.

"Let's go meet her," he said, then steered me into the bathroom, and turned me to look in the mirror. "See? She's sexy, right?"

He placed a kiss on my shoulder, and it just filled me with warmth. I had to admit that we really did look good together. Him, with his dark hair, dark eyes, and skin that looked like it was permanently tanned, and me with my blonde hair, fair skin, and blue eyes. We were vastly different in our coloring, but he felt right. His arm around my waist, his lips on my shoulder, the actual care I saw in his eyes as he looked at us in the mirror; it wasn't just something he was playing lip service to. No, it was genuine, and it made me wonder whether I'd won the biggest jackpot Las Vegas had to offer.

Chapter Six

Alejandro...

We spent the day walking the strip, looking in the windows of the many shops, going into a few of them to grab some souvenirs for the both of us, and just getting to know each other. She was more than just beautiful, she was smart, and a smart ass, but in the most delightful way. Her sense of humor was dry and sarcastic, but she didn't say anything with cruelty. No, her way of teasing was more self-deprecating, which I continually reminded her was not who she was.

When we stopped for lunch early in the afternoon, she insisted on buying, which I thought was adorable, but didn't let it happen, which just pissed her off.

"I don't want to be a kept woman," she said. "I know you're stupid rich, but that doesn't mean you have to pay for everything."

"And I know you have enough money to take care of things," I said. "But that doesn't mean I don't want to pay for things."

"We're gonna have to have a serious discussion about finances when we get home," she said. "I can't have you paying for everything.

It just makes me look like a gold digger, which I am most assuredly not."

"I have no problem with that," I said. "By the way, we have to figure out where we're gonna live."

"I have a house," she said. "I'm not giving it up."

"I also have a house," I said. "Would you like to live with me and rent your house out?"

"I don't know," she said. "This is all so weird. Like, why did we do this?"

"Because you wouldn't have sex with me if we weren't married," I said.

"You can't seriously have believed that, can you?" she asked.

"Hailey," I said, and she stopped her walk down the sidewalk to turn and look at me. "You can be very persuasive. Besides, I'm not at all upset about it. I think I found the best thing I could have ever thought to bring home with me."

"You know," she said with a smile. "I thought this morning that I may have won the best jackpot that Vegas had to offer. I guess we're both sort of on the same page."

I pulled her to me, and she came willingly. I bent down and kissed her, her arms going around my neck naturally, as she kissed me back. It was full of passion and promise, and everything that was right in the world.

"Get a fucking room," some guy said as he walked past us, but neither of us bothered to stop.

Finally, after simultaneously entirely too long, and not nearly long enough, we came up for air. Her eyes were hooded, a hand going to her lips as if she could hold the feeling there with them. When she did look at me, her eyes brightened, and she smiled, splitting her face, sparkling in her eyes, and showing just a slight dimple in one cheek. I kissed that spot, then leaned in further to whisper in her ear.

"Shall we go back to the hotel?"

She didn't answer me, just stepped back, grabbed my hand, and started to drag me in the direction of the hotel I had stayed in for this trip. It had been meant to be a time to clear my head before heading to Spring Training. Instead, it turned my entire world upside down in the most miraculous way, and I had to admit that I was not in the least upset about it.

We walked through the lobby, past the slot machines and tables set up for gambling, and straight to the elevators where she jammed the button so hard, I worried she'd crack the plastic covering. She was antsy, bouncing a bit on the balls of her feet with anticipation, and as soon as the bell chimed for the elevator, she nearly ran into a couple who was coming out in her rush to get inside, and get us to our room.

Again, she jabbed the button for our floor, then, as soon as the doors shut, she turned to me, and pulled my head down, crashing her lips to mine, forcing her tongue inside to dance with my own, driving the passion far faster than I could keep up with. I barely heard the chime when the elevator reached our floor, but she heard it, tearing away from me, and dragging me down the hall.

I had my key card out by the time we reached the door, and as soon as it was open, she pulled us inside, shutting the door behind me, and pinning me to it, climbing me like I was some sort of tree or something, until she had her arms wrapped around my neck, her legs pressing against the door to push me away enough to wrap around my waist.

Carrying her to the bed, I let her fall on top of it, then yanked my shirt over my head before pinning her under my body to kiss her senseless. She'd pulled her own shirt off in the time it took for me to do it, and was working on my pants as we kissed. My hands went under her to unhook her bra, and she let go enough to get the offending piece of clothing out from between us before resuming her task of removing my pants. I'd kicked my shoes off, and as soon as the belt, button, and zipper were undone, I slid the jeans down, along with my boxers, pulling my socks off when I stepped on my jeans to get them removed.

As our bodies were slightly apart, she undid her own jeans, shoving them and her panties down to her feet, but they got stuck on her shoes. She laughed, trying to figure out how to get everything off her, and I had to stand up, and reach inside the pant legs to pull her shoes off before everything else could be removed.

Looking down at her, at my wife, at this beautiful woman I had tied myself to, I couldn't help but be amazed she'd even looked twice at me. I mean, I would probably be considered handsome to some, but she was well above me in that department. I had a moment of insecurity, until she pushed herself up and sucked my cock into her mouth, shoving everything else out of my brain as I simply enjoyed the feeling of her.

One hand went around my thigh, the other cupped my balls, gently massaging them in rhythm to her bobbing up and down on me. My hands went to her shoulders, not wanting to put pressure on her to stay down too far for too long. She tilted her head, looking up at me with those bright blue eyes, and all I could think was that she was mine, and I'd do anything in my power to keep her.

"You look so fucking good," I said. "I love watching my cock disappear into your mouth like this."

She hummed, which just shot through me, vibrations seriously challenging my control, and I could tell that she knew, because she smiled as she continued.

"You on birth control?" I asked.

"Mmhmm," she hummed on my cock.

"Good," I said. "Cause I wanna fuck you without anything between us. You good with that?"

She paused, my cock nearly to the back of her mouth, but still not all the way in. Finally, as if she'd figured out whatever it was that she was thinking about, she shoved me nearly down her throat, swallowing around my head, and holding me there for so long I was worried she'd pass out. Finally, she pulled back, laid back on the bed, opened her legs, and smiled.

"Fuck me," she said.

"Not yet," I said, kneeling next to the bed, and pulling her hips toward me as she yelped. She was nearly hanging off the edge of the bed when I said, "First, I'm gonna make you come on my face. Then, I'm gonna make love to you. After that, we'll fuck."

I slid my tongue up from her pussy to the clit, and she moaned with pleasure. I pulled that bundle of nerves into my mouth, setting my teeth into them just enough to add pressure, and slid my finger into her pussy. She was so wet, and so sweet, and it was like I was drinking the nectar of the gods the way she tasted.

I made quick work of her, using my finger to rub that rough patch just inside, while I kept my teeth set on her clit, the combination working her into a frenzy so quickly she burst apart in moments, her hands clenched in the fabric on the bed, her pussy pulsing around my finger, as I continued my stroking until she was pushing me away with her foot on my shoulder.

"Too much," she panted as I eased back, pulling my finger from her. "God, that was fucking awesome, but too much."

"Should we stop?" I asked, fully prepared to let her get off and be without my release.

"No," she said, almost glaring at me. "I just need a minute. Come here."

She held her hands open, gesturing for me to join her on the bed. I stood up and pulled the blankets down enough for her to move onto the sheets before climbing in beside her. She was warm and sated, as I pulled her into my arms, her leg sliding up and over my thighs as she settled in. With one arm around her back, the other hand was resting on her thigh, stroking along it as she relaxed, and before I knew it, her breathing had evened out, and she was fast asleep. Not exactly ideal for me, but I couldn't help but be pleased that I'd worn her out so much. Instead of worrying about getting myself off, I closed my own eyes, hoping to just rest for a bit.

When I woke, she was stroking me, slow and steady, her eyes wide open watching my face. The way she was looking at me told me she was more than ready to start again, and I wouldn't be me if I didn't let her know I was happy about it. Instead of just letting her continue, though, I sort of rolled us so I was on top of her, sliding myself between her legs.

"You're fast," she said with a smile.

"Hopefully, not too fast," I said.

"Yeah, that would suck," she said.

"I'll try my best to be slow and steady," I said. "You let me know if you need me to do something different, okay?"

"Well," she said, that little dimple appearing. "You could stick your cock inside me. That would be a good start."

I laughed, sliding myself up and down her slit, feeling that she was more than ready for me to press inside her.

"You good with no condom?"

"Just fuck me," she said, and I slid a hand between us, lining myself up and slipping in. "Oh, yeah," she said with a sigh, her eyes fluttering closed, her hips lifting to meet mine.

Her head was tipped back on the pillow, her blonde hair around it like a halo, and the sun coming through the slit in the blinds just made her that much more of an angel, and my God, did I worship her. Slowly, ever so slowly, I slid out, not completely, but nearly there, then slowly back in, holding myself up with my arms as I watched her body flex in time with me. She held my upper arms with her hands, holding herself where she was as I pressed into her, then let out again. My God, she was beautiful, and I just wanted to stay right there, never leaving.

I continued my pace, slow and even, sliding in and out of her, her breasts thrust up with each deep breath she took. The further along we got, the more her grip tightened, her nails biting into my biceps as she concentrated on her body, and how it was feeling. It was amazing to watch her climb that mountain, me pushing her up the hill to the very top where I would watch her fall over the cliff, ready to catch her when she was completely spent.

My arms were starting to feel the strain, but I wouldn't give up until I got her to the top, and she finally let go with one hand, dipping it between us to work the bundle of nerves at the apex of her sex, her hand stroking in quick circles as her breathing increased.

"That's it, baby," I whispered, dipping down to take a nipple into my mouth.

"Oh, God," she cried, arching her back to thrust it further into my mouth. "Don't stop."

She repeated it over and over again, begging me to not stop what I was doing, and I obeyed my queen, suckling at her breast while impaling her with my cock, all the while she was working that bud furiously. Her other hand came off my arm, hooking behind my head as she held me to her, her breath coming in quick pants until she finally fell.

"Alej," she cried. "Oh, God, Alej."

I stuttered and faltered hearing my name on her lips as she came apart but was able to recover as she continued to writhe beneath me, her pussy pulsing around my cock, pulling it into her, and I finally had to succumb to my own weakness, letting her milk me of everything I had, spasming inside her, as I released my load.

I nearly collapsed on top of her, falling to my elbows to keep my full weight off her, my breath sawing in and out of me in time with hers, both of us spent in that moment.

"Holy fuck," she breathed out.

"Indeed," I said, shifting to roll off her and onto my back beside her.

"That was intense," she said, still breathless.

"We should always do it like that," I said.

"Definitely," she said. "I mean, not exactly, but definitely that intensely. You are fucking amazing in bed."

"Do you mean I fuck amazingly in bed?" I asked.

She turned to me, confusion on her face, and I couldn't hold back. I just busted out laughing and she joined me.

"That was funny," she said. "Now, let's get cleaned up. Sticky sex is swell, but the swelling's gone down."

"Speak for yourself," I said, and my God, we were like teenagers.

"Come on," I said, sitting up and pulling her with me. "Let's get a shower."

I got out of bed and helped her up, taking her with me to the bathroom. I turned the knob in the tub to get the water going, then turned to her, and kissed her. Her arms went around my neck, and she pressed her body against me. She was soft in all the right places, and I wrapped my arms around her, holding her to me.

"We keep this up, we won't have any water left," she said against my lips as I'd come up for air.

"Is that a bad thing?"

"Nevada is a desert," she said, and that dimple was back. "Pretty sure they'd be pissed if we just let *all* the water go down the drain."

"Get in," I said as I pulled the plunger up on the spout.

She waited a moment, then stepped in behind the curtain. I stepped in behind her and she was fiddling with the handle to get the temperature right for her. I didn't really care how hot or cold the shower was. As long as it wasn't gonna melt my skin or turn me to ice, I was good. Once she was set, she turned around to face me, then tipped her head back to wet her hair.

Looking at her, the water cascading over her body, I knew I was a lucky man. Whoever it was that set us on a path to meet, I would thank them many times over. Honestly, the only reason I'd come to Vegas was to get away from everything that was coming up. I had a couple of weeks before I had to head down to Fort Myers in Florida for Spring Training, and if I could make something fun of my time before going, that was what I was going to do. Getting married had not been on my to do list, but I wasn't upset it had been checked off, either.

Chapter Seven

H**ailey…**
I could feel him watching me, and I fucking loved it. I even pushed my tits out further as I wet my hair, hoping it would entice him to touch me again. God, it was like he was a drug, and I was as addicted as anyone could be to anything in this world. I also didn't plan to give him up.

Sure, I'd said we should get the marriage annulled, but honestly, I might have been jumping the gun. I hadn't actually remembered the wedding, because I was entirely too drunk. But I did remember bits and pieces, and he'd shown me the video and pictures from it, and he was right in that I didn't really look drunk.

Considering I drank my way through college, I was very much an in-control kind of drunk, always held my own, never ended up completely blacking out, and definitely didn't toss any cookies. I hated throwing up and did everything in my power to keep it from happening. Thankfully, my kind of drunk just saw me with a headache and dry mouth, of course, that was on top of doing stupid shit like getting married to a stranger.

When his arm went around my body, I went to him with ease,

loving that he liked touching me. He was warm, his body hitting every spot on me from my tits to my hips, and his cock was hard and pressing against my stomach. Damn, but I wanted him again. We had just finished, and it was fucking amazing, but I was ready for another round.

"How many times would this make?" I asked, looking up at him as my hands rested on his chest.

"More than I can count," he said, pressing his lips to my forehead. "But not enough. Not yet, anyway."

"I like the sound of that," I said, leaning into him.

"We should probably slow down a little," he said, and I pulled back. "Need to save some of this for the flight home, as well as when we get there."

"I am not fucking you in an airplane bathroom," I said. "There is no fucking way that's gonna happen. Not that I don't want to, it's just not logistically possible."

"I'll buy you a blanket at the airport," he said. "You can wear a dress, sit on my lap, and we can fuck underneath it."

"You're serious," I said, clearly seeing the intent on his face.

"Why not?"

"No," I said. "That's just not gonna happen. There is nowhere near enough room for that to even be a possibility."

"First-class seats are pretty decent sized," he said.

"First class?"

"Yeah," he said. "I won't let my wife fly in economy. Not if I can help it."

"I can't afford that," I said.

"You don't have to," he replied. "I bought the ticket, not you."

"I should pay you back," I said.

"No," he said, pulling me even tighter against him. "I paid for the ticket. I was the one who messed the weekend up for you. I wanted to do it."

"You didn't mess the weekend up," I said. "I mean, sure, you took a total stranger to a chapel, and married her, but otherwise it's been great."

"Good thing I wasn't some kind of serial killer or anything," he said.

"Yeah, thanks for that," I replied sarcastically.

"Glad to be of service," he said. "Speaking of service, shall I service you?"

"You make it sound so clinical," I said.

"How would you like me to ask you for sex?" he asked.

"Umm," I hummed. "I've never really thought about it. I guess it just sort of happens as it happens."

We were standing naked in the shower having a conversation about how to initiate sex when we'd already had it several times. It was an odd thing, honestly, and I'd never thought this would happen to me. I mean, the sex in the shower had happened, and likely would again, but the conversation was definitely odd.

"I'm very much into consent," he said. "It's sexy to me."

"But you haven't asked today," I countered. "Not that I can recall."

"I've asked," he said. "It's just been more subtle than simply asking it outright."

"Okay," I said, thinking back over the day.

Honestly, he was right. Every time he'd initiated something, he'd asked questions, clarification of things, or what I wanted. I guess he had been asking, and I'd been consenting. Words were weird, I knew that, but the fact that the questions had come in such unassuming ways made me wonder whether I'd actually always been asked, and never thought about it.

"You're thinking," he said, pressing his lips to my forehead. "So serious about all of this."

"Trying to figure out how I never really noticed, but always had been asked," I said. "It's weird the things you don't notice until they're pointed out to you. Then, you simply can't unsee them, unthink them, unknow them."

"I didn't mean to break you," he said.

"It's fine," I replied. "But all this thinking is kind of killing the mood. And I really do need to get cleaned up."

"Yeah," he replied. "We kinda did get a bit sticky, didn't we?"

"Messy sex is always good," I said.

"You sure you're good with me having not used a condom?" he asked as I stepped away from him, and further under the showerhead.

"I have an IUD," I said. "Plus, we're married, so it's kinda moot now, isn't it?"

"Not ready for kids just yet," he said. "But I wouldn't mind at some point."

"Yeah," I replied, pouring shampoo into my palm. "I've only been at this school for a couple of years. I'd prefer to be there a couple more before I try to have a kid."

"That's what you said last night," he replied, turning me away from him, and working my hair with his own hands.

I relaxed into him, letting his strong fingers massage my scalp as he worked the shampoo into suds. He spun me back around, and I tipped my head back, the water running over it as he stepped up to me, and worked the strands clean. When he kissed me, I started, not expecting it.

"Sorry," he said, but I pulled him back to me, saying, "Don't be. I love it."

The kiss was sweet and slow, like our lovemaking had been just a little bit earlier, and I could tell he was enjoying it as his cock stirred to life, and nudged against my stomach. When he pulled away, I opened my eyes, and the look on his face was one of reverence, like he was looking at some amazing piece of artwork or something.

"Why do you look at me like that?" I asked.

"Like what?" he countered.

"Like you're worshipping me or something," I said.

"Because I am," he replied. "You are a goddess and should be worshipped. From this day until forever, I plan to show you that."

I bit my lips together, trying desperately to hold on to my

emotions. No one in my entire life had said anything like that to me. I'd been told I was cute, pretty, even beautiful, but he was placing me so high on a pedestal that I was sure I'd fall before we even got out of the shower.

"What are you thinking?" he asked.

"How hard it's gonna hurt when I fall from the high spot you've put me," I admitted. "I'm not something special, just a girl who likes to get drunk, and have sex. Apparently, I also like to marry strangers, too, but that's beside the point."

"Hailey," he said, and the way my name fell from his lips was beautiful. "You are exactly who I believe you to be. I know you're not perfect, but neither am I. We'll probably fuck this up along the way, but as long as you promise to work with me, we'll make it all work out."

"I don't know how I lucked out in meeting you," I said. "But I'm glad I did."

"Me, too," he said, kissing me again, just a quick peck. "Now, if you don't hurry up, we're gonna run out of water."

I smiled, then grabbed the soap, and started lathering up my hands. Instead of using it on me, though, I reached out, and pressed my hands to his chest, going in slow circles along his body as I cleaned him from our earlier escapades. He was fucking beautiful, and he was all mine.

Chapter Eight

Alejandro…

The shower took way longer than it should have, but we finally finished, dried off, and headed back to bed. I ordered room service for dinner, and we spent the entirety of the afternoon and evening in each other's arms. We'd even run out of condoms by the time we finally drifted off to sleep.

When the alarm on my phone started chirping at me, I rolled over and slapped the snooze, wanting just a few more minutes, but when I rolled back over to pull her to me, she was gone.

"Hailey?" I called out, and she poked her head out of the bathroom.

"Hey," she said. "I woke up and wanted to get ready."

"Okay," I said, still not fully awake.

"Do you need me to do anything for you?" she asked, and I could see she was dressed, and had put some makeup on.

"Nah," I said, stretching.

I grabbed my phone and turned the alarm off, then set it back on the nightstand. Sitting up, I tossed the blankets back, and put my feet on the floor, rubbing my eyes to remove the sleep from them. When I pulled my hands away, I stood up, and looked to the bathroom, and there she was, staring at me. Or rather at my morning wood standing straight out.

"Want some?" I asked her, and she blushed, her eyes snapping up to mine, a smile crossing her lips.

"I do," she said. "But I don't think we have time."

"We could make it quick," I suggested, but she smiled a sad smile, then went back to finishing her makeup.

I walked past her to the toilet, kissing her on the neck as I went, and she closed her eyes and shuddered as I did it, so I knew she really did want to, but she was right. We didn't really have time, and we had to finish packing up, and check out, before taking the shuttle to the airport.

I did my business, flushed, and went to wash my hands. Once I was done and washed, I headed out and started getting dressed. She'd already packed her bags, and they were sitting by the door. Mine just had a couple of things I had to shove in them, then they'd be ready.

"You want to carry the marriage license?" I asked as I gathered the pictures and other paperwork from the dresser that held the television.

"I can if you want," she replied.

"I'll stick them into the front pocket of my carryon, and we can sort things out when we get home," I said, sliding them into the zipper pocket of my suitcase. "Speaking of home, how do you want to handle housing?"

"I told you," she said. "I'm not moving."

"That's fine," I said. "Do you want to just live apart for now?"

"Probably best to start with," she said, as she stepped out of the bathroom, and stuck her makeup bag into her carryon.

We each had a rolling suitcase, and another bag for our two allowed items, neither of us needing to check anything as we headed home. I took one more look around the room, checking the drawers and bathroom to make sure I hadn't stuck something somewhere without thinking.

"You're very thorough," she said.

"Never want to leave anything behind," I said. "Done it entirely too many times. Usually, it's the charger for my phone, and it can be a pain having to replace them all the time."

"I bet," she said.

"All done," I said once I'd made my sweep. "Ready?"

"Yep," she said, then pulled the door open.

We walked down the hall toward the elevator, then waited for it to arrive after pushing the button. I pulled my bag up, and stood behind her, wrapping my free hand around her waist and pulling her into me. I could stand next to her forever, and it wouldn't be long enough, which was really weird, considering we didn't know each other very well.

She was short enough to fit under my chin, but just barely, and I could smell the hotel shampoo coming off her. I wondered what she smelled like with her own shampoo. Was she a citrus girl, or lavender, or something else? Until we got home, I wouldn't know, but did look forward to discovering even more about her.

Tenacious didn't even begin to describe her. She was smart, funny, sassy as all get out, and a hurricane in bed, all of which I reveled in. I was also interested in what her home looked like, and what she drove. Was she this wild in her regular life? Or was that something she only let out here with me? Either way, I was excited to find out.

The bell chimed on the elevator and it opened. Since it was empty, she stepped into it, and I followed her. She pressed the button for the lobby, and I stood next to her as the doors closed, and we made our descent. They didn't have any music of any kind playing in the elevator, and that made me wonder what she listened to. Honestly, there really wasn't much I actually did know about her, and that made me a little sad.

"You're pretty quiet over there," she said, looking up at me.

"Just wondering what I will discover about you when we get home," I said. "I don't even know what kind of music you listen to."

"Mostly alternative," she said. "I like the indie type stuff."

"Nice," I said. "I'm more of an oldies kind of guy, myself."

"Oldies as in..."

She stopped the question when the elevator bounced at the bottom. We walked out, and I headed over to the front desk to get checked out.

"Did you have an enjoyable stay?" the guy at the desk asked.

"Definitely," I said. "Do I need to do anything but give you the key?"

"Unless you need a paper receipt," he said.

"Nope," I said.

"Then it'll be emailed to you," he said. "What's your room number?"

I told him, then handed the key card I had to him. He checked his computer, then told me to have a nice day.

"I ordered an Uber. Will that be out front?" I asked.

"Yeah," he said. "They usually pull up right under the awning."

"Thanks," I said, then turned to walk toward the door.

Hailey was waiting near there, looking at a couple of the fliers they had by the door with local attractions.

"Hey," I said as I came up to her. "Ready to head out?"

"Yeah," she said, but there was something in her voice.

"What's the matter?" I asked.

"I feel like as soon as we get on that plane, everything will fall apart," she said.

"Not gonna happen," I said. "I'm in this for the long haul. It's you and me, together. I'm not going anywhere. At least not for a couple of weeks, anyway."

"A couple weeks?" she asked.

"Spring Training," I said. "I have to head out to Florida in the middle of February, so like two weeks or so."

"Oh," she said. "I didn't realize you had to go anywhere."

"I'll be gone quite a bit, actually," I said as we stood in the early morning outside the hotel.

Just then, a car pulled up. I checked the app on my phone, and it matched the one I was expecting.

"You Alejandro?" he asked once everyone was off.

"I am," I said, my hand in the small of Hailey's back.

"Great," he said. "You want those in the trunk?"

"Thanks," I said, and opened the door in the back seat for Hailey.

I let her get in, then walked behind the car to put my own suitcase in the trunk next to hers, then walked around to the passenger side to get in. I'd put her behind the driver because I needed the extra leg room. When I climbed in, I realized she'd scooted over to the middle seat, and leaned her head on my shoulder as soon as I buckled myself in.

"Tired?" I asked.

"Mmhmm," she hummed.

"Looking forward to going home?"

"Sort of," she said. "I know the girls are gonna want the whole lowdown on what happened, and I'm not sure I'm ready for it."

"So don't answer the phone," I suggested.

"Not quite that easy," I said. "Right now, Missy is living with me until her wedding at the end of the month. She'll interrogate me as soon as I'm home."

"Want me to come with you?"

She rolled her head on my shoulder, looking up at me, and smiled.

"Would you?" she asked.

"Absolutely," I said. "I'd want to run home, and grab some clean clothes, but then I will happily come over. Do you need a ride home?"

"I was just gonna Uber," she said.

"I've got my car at the airport," I said. "I can take you to mine, grab some clothes, then we can go to yours. That sound good?"

"Okay," she said.

I kissed her, soft and slow, not pressing too hard. I knew we wouldn't be able to do much in the small back seat of the car, but I wanted to make sure she knew I cared.

"We should be there in just a few minutes," the driver said. "Which airline are you flying?"

I told him, and he started the car, and pulled out from under the overhang, and toward the street. Sure enough, it only took a few minutes, and he was pulling into the airport. He pulled up to the curb, and put the car in park, getting out and opening Hailey's door, then opened the trunk. I pulled our bags out, setting them on the curb.

"Enjoy your flight," he said.

"You, too," Hailey said, then cringed. "I mean..."

"It's fine," he said. "I hear that all the time. I'm used to it."

"Thanks," I said, then turned Hailey toward the doors that led into the terminal.

When we got to security, we both pulled out our licenses, handing them to the agent at the podium. Then it was off with the shoes, sticking our luggage into the little trays, and waiting to step through the machine. Thankfully, neither of us had anything that caused them to have to do the pat down, and we were picking up our stuff to sit and put our shoes on.

"Where are we going now?" she asked.

"Let me look," I said, pulling out my phone. "We're going to gate D22, but we've got about an hour before we have to board. Do you wanna go to the lounge and get something to eat or anything?"

"The lounge?" she asked.

"You know, first class," I said.

"Yeah," she replied. "I've never flown first class, so this is all foreign to me."

"Let me introduce you to the richer lifestyle," I said, guiding her toward the lounge for the airline.

We stepped through the door, and the concierge asked for our ticket information. I showed him my phone, and he let us in. It was nice, nothing super fancy, but she was awestruck, and it was kind of adorable. Her eyes were big, taking everything in.

"What do you think?" I asked.

"This is wild," she said.

"Come on," I said, giving her arm a little tug.

We walked over to the bar, and she sort of looked at me.

"It's entirely too early to be drinking," she said.

"Coffee," I said to the bartender. "Do you want one?"

"Oh," she said, blushing, and I kissed her temple. "Yeah, coffee would be great, thanks."

"Of course," he said, turning to pull a couple of cups down from their shelf. He poured coffee in each cup, leaving room for us to add anything we wanted, then handed them to us. "Supplies are over there," he said, nodding to a side table that had carafes of what I assumed were options for cream and sugar.

"Thank you," I said.

"Yes," she said. "Thank you."

We took our mugs and headed to the spot where the options were. She poured a generous amount of cream into hers but didn't add any sugar. I, on the other hand, added sugar and cream to mine, both of us taking up a spoon to stir them with. I walked her over to a big picture window that looked out onto the tarmac and helped her sit on one of the plush leather chairs, taking a seat next to her, our bags in front of us.

"This is weird," she said quietly.

"Why?" I asked.

"I've just never done this sort of thing before," she said. "I feel completely out of my element here."

"Better get used to it," I said. "You're married to a man who takes care of his woman, and make no mistake about it, you are mine."

"I'm not property," she said. "This isn't the 1800s."

"That's not what I mean," I said. "I consider you family, and I take care of my family. I take care of my parents, and help my sister if she needs it, not that she usually does, but I am generous to my nephew when I can be."

"I didn't know you had a sister," she said.

"I do," I said. "It's just the two of us, and my parents. Well, my grandparents, too, but they still live in the Dominican Republic. They visit us sometimes, but they like to stay close to home."

"Is that where you're from?" she asked. "The Dominican Republic?"

"I was born in Florida," I said. "My parents immigrated before I was born. They brought my sister with them to Florida, because my dad got a job, and could get a work visa. I was born about a year after they got here. They still live in the same house I grew up in."

"That's cool," she said, but there was something off about her.

"What's wrong?" I asked.

"Nothing," she said, turning her face away from me.

"Hailey," I said and she looked at me. "Tell me what's wrong. I don't want to have secrets between us."

"I don't have family," she said, and I could hear the sadness in her voice.

"What do you mean?"

"I was in the system," she said. "That's why I'm so adamant about making it on my own. I put myself through college with scholarships, and some small loans, bought my own house about a year ago, and am just really proud of what I've done on my own."

"That's amazing," I said. "You should be proud of what you've accomplished."

"I mean, I am," she said. "I just don't feel like it's all that much."

"Are you kidding?" I asked. "You went to college, got a career, and bought a house, all by the time you're what, twenty-five?"

"Almost twenty-six," she said. "How old are you?"

"I turned twenty-eight in November," I said.

"So, you're robbing the cradle?" she asked with a smile.

"Only if you're robbing the grave," I replied, and she nearly spat out her coffee.

"You gotta warn a girl, babe," she said.

"You walked right into it," I said.

It was nice to find someone who had the same kind of sense of humor I did. Most of the girls I'd dated while I was in school were more interested in looking good than actually having a personality. Hailey was both. She was more than good looking, and her personality wasn't wrapped up in what she looked like or who she hung out with. Her phone rang and she grabbed it from her bag.

"Hello?" she asked as she answered. "Yeah," she said. "We're at the airport now."

She paused. I assume to listen to whoever she was talking to.

"What flight are we on?" she asked me.

I showed her my phone, and she relayed the information to the person on the phone.

"Says it gets in at five," she said. "Yeah, he's giving me a ride."

Another pause, and I could hear someone going off on her, which kind of pissed me off.

"He's fine," she said. "Honestly, I trust him."

Again, there was a loud voice on the other end, and I reached over, and took the phone out of her hand.

"Hello?" I said, and the other person stopped their tirade.

"Who the fuck is this?" she asked.

"I'm Hailey's husband," I said. "And I'd like you to not speak to her in that tone of voice. She's an adult, has full faculty of her senses, and is capable of making decisions. If you don't trust her, then maybe you shouldn't be in her life."

"Why I never..."

"Exactly," I said. "You need to respect her choices. She's said she's fine. I promise you that she's fine, and if you have an issue with me, then bring it to me, not her. Do I make myself clear?"

"Look, jackass," she said, but I cut her off.

"If you're going to insist on being a jerk, I'm going to hang up," I said. "You can either choose to be a decent human, or you can end the call. It's your choice."

"Let me talk to Hailey," she said.

"Are you going to berate her for her choices?" I asked.

"I need to talk to her," she said.

"Like I asked before, are you going to berate her?"

"No," she said, and she sounded defeated.

"Good," I said. "If I hear you yelling at her again, I'm going to take the phone, and disconnect the call. Do I make myself clear?"

"Whatever," she said, but I didn't hand the phone off. "Give Hailey the phone."

"Not until you promise to be kind," I said. "It's something I'm sure she teaches the students in her class, and they're way younger than you. If that's not something you've learned, maybe you need to return to kindergarten, and relearn it."

"You're an asshole," she said, and I disconnected the call.

I looked at Hailey, and she was sitting there, mouth open wide, a look of bewilderment on her face.

"What?" I asked.

"I can't believe you talked to her that way," she said.

"Are you upset?"

"No," she said. "I'm just... I don't know what to say."

"I'm not going to allow you to be mistreated," I said. "Not by me. Not by my family. Not by your friends. You are a responsible adult, and you should be treated with respect."

Her phone started going off, but I just hit the decline button.

"She's gonna be pissed," she said, but she was smiling.

My guess was that no one had stood up for her, and that this friend was likely the alpha of their friend group, and wasn't used to someone standing up to her. She would learn, however, that I didn't allow disrespect. It was something my parents had instilled in me when I was very young. They had a shit ton of people who would bash them because their English wasn't perfect, or because they had darker skin, or because they were immigrants. They insisted that we were just as good as the rest of the world, and the way we allowed people to treat us was a testament to who we were. If we allowed it, it would continue. If we shut it down, we'd get the respect we deserved.

Thankfully, my natural ability to play a game at a high level kept people from treating me like shit, but it took a bit to get there. Now, though, I had much more in common with my teammates than with the world at large, and even though I was rich, people still tended to look at me with a bit of hesitation and reserve, simply because of the way I looked. I got over it a long time ago, though, so it didn't bother me nearly as much as it used to.

Chapter Nine

Hailey...

The fact that he literally hung up on Missy blew my mind. Then, when she called back, he just declined the call. Yeah, he was a hero, but I was worried about how she'd react when we got home. I didn't have to wait until then to know what she was thinking, though. She sent me a scathing text about getting my marriage annulled as soon as possible, and getting this Neanderthal out of my life for good. She didn't know that I'd planned on keeping him, though, so she'd have to adjust.

We finished our coffee and leisurely made our way to the gate to wait for our flight. When it came time to board, I was fine with just sitting and waiting, because that's what I'd always done, but when they started calling first class, he had me get up, and we went to board. I was in front of Alej, and when the woman at the door asked for my boarding pass, I turned, and looked at him.

"Sorry," he said, holding out his phone for her to scan.

"Welcome aboard, Mr. de la Garza, Ms. Truitt," she said, and motioned for us to go through the door.

"Yeah, about that," he said as we walked down the tunnel. "Do you want to change your name?"

"I haven't thought about it," I said. "But I kinda like mine. At least for now."

"That's fine," he said. "I'm not so traditional that I'm gonna insist, but it would be nice to have you have it."

"It's not that I'm overly attached to mine," I said. "I just... I don't know, I'd have to change, like, everything."

"That's true," he said.

"Welcome aboard," the flight attendant at the door said.

"Where are we sitting?" I asked him.

"Three, A and C," he said.

I stepped onto the plane and walked down the aisle to the third row. I went to pick my suitcase up, but Alej put his hand on top of mine, shaking his head. I slid into the seat and moved over next to the window. Alej took his and my suitcase, and shoved them into the overhead compartment, one at a time, then sat next to me.

"Did you want the window?" I asked, pulling my phone and charger out of my bag, along with the book I'd brought with me to read on the plane.

"Doesn't matter to me," he said. "I fly all the time, so I'm used to sitting wherever. Never really cared much about the window."

"I like the window," I said, getting myself comfortable in the seat.

"Then you shall always fly in the window seat," he said, as if he could make that happen no matter what.

He'd pulled his phone and charger out of his bag, then shoved the bag under the seat in front of us. Mine was already stowed there, my book in the pocket in the back of the seat. There were two boxed waters sitting between us.

"Would you like anything before takeoff?" the flight attendant asked us, and I was confused.

"Nothing for me," Alej said. "Do you want another coffee?"

"No," I said. "I'm good, thanks."

"If you need anything," she said, stepping back to let someone sit in the seat she was standing in front of. "You just let me know."

"Thanks," I said, and looked at Alej.

"You're so cute," he said, then pressed his lips to mine. "I can't wait to show you the entire world."

"Let's stick with getting home, first," I said, and smiled as he kissed me again.

Yeah, I could definitely get used to having him kiss me over and over. It was definitely something I wouldn't give up. Well, he wasn't something I was willing to give up, actually. Not just because he booked me a first-class ticket home, or because we were sort of stuck at the moment. No, he was kind, generous, and so sweet. We may not have started this marriage as friends, but I felt like we were getting there, and quickly.

He leaned his head back, and closed his eyes, and I just stared at him. Was he the most gorgeous person in the world? Probably not, but that didn't seem that big of a deal. He had way more to offer than just good looks. Not that he was ugly, or even average. No, he was definitely my kind of sexy, and I was really glad I did what I did, even if it did mean that things would be weird for a while.

"You're staring," he said, keeping his eyes closed. It was low enough that I barely heard it over the noise from the rest of the passengers getting on the plane.

"Can't help it," I said, reaching over, and taking his hand in mine.

"Just an observation," he said.

"Oh, yeah?" I asked.

"I like that you like to look at me," he said. He turned to look at me then, and said, "The feeling is mutual."

"I noticed," I said.

"You gonna sleep?"

"Nah," I said. "I have a book. I'll read, unless you wanna talk."

"Planned to sleep," he said. "If you don't mind."

"Not at all," I said.

He leaned over, and gave me another kiss, this one lingered a while, and I was getting all sorts of turned on by it, wondering whether he was gonna make good on the threat to fuck me on the plane. I didn't want to do that, but I wasn't sure I'd be able to turn him down if he started something.

"Mm," he hummed as he pulled away. "Gonna have to do something about that temptation you have going on."

"Not my fault," I replied. "You started it."

"That I did," he said.

The line had dwindled down, and the flight attendants were walking through the plane to make sure everyone had their seat belts on, and everything ready for takeoff. I hadn't done anything but put my phone and cord into the pocket, along with my book. Alej had done the same, minus the book, and we were both just sitting there, waiting for the trip to get started. He was much more relaxed than I was, but I didn't exactly like planes. I mean, they were a means to an end, and I could do them without having a major freak out, but if I could go without, I would.

I heard them shut the door to the plane, then heard the pilot come over the intercom to welcome us aboard, tell us how long it would take to get where we were going, and to introduce us to the rest of the crew. Then, the flight attendant who had offered us drinks earlier came on to give the safety briefing. I never really paid attention to them, but it was nice that they all knew what they were doing. Not my kind of job, but someone had to do it.

Finally, after we were moving along, the flight attendants went wherever they sat, and the lights dimmed. It was just beginning to get fully light outside, so the lighting in the airplane was interesting, and I looked over at Alej, completely relaxed, and wondered how he did it. I was watching out the window, waiting for that rush as the plane started going fast, and that weird thing my stomach did when it took off.

"Relax," he said, taking my hand. "I'm right here, nothing bad is going to happen."

"How can you be so calm?" I asked.

"Because I've done this hundreds of times," he said. "Now, hold my hand, look in my eyes, and know that we're just fine."

He was looking at me, and there was something in his eyes, something so profound I'd never seen it before. He was being honest with me, in that he'd protect me with everything he had, and it was a heady thing, knowing that he was that protective of me already.

"Okay," I said, turning more to him, focusing on the fluttering in my stomach that had nothing to do with the flight, and everything to do with the man sitting next to me. "I trust you."

"Good," he said, and leaned over, his other hand going behind my head to pull me to him.

His kiss was deep, long and slow, and all the best things a kiss could be, and before I knew it, he was pulling back, and we were in the air.

"How did you do that?" I asked.

"I wanted to distract you," he said. "Could do something else to distract you, too."

The twinkle in his eye told me he wasn't lying, and I had to press my thighs together, the desire was so much.

"Are you interested?"

"No," I said, way too loud, and could see the people across from us glare over at me. "Sorry," I said to them, but Alej put his hand on my cheek, turning me back to him.

"The rest of the world doesn't matter," he said. "It's just you and me."

"Rain check?" I asked, knowing I wouldn't be up to anything on an airplane, even in first class.

"I'm going to hold you to that," he said, then kissed me once again.

He let his head go back against the seat again, but held my hand tight, his fingers laced through my own. I looked down at them, the contrast in our coloring so distinct, and wondered what our kids would look like. Would they have his darker skin or my fairer kind? How about their eyes? I hoped they'd have his deep chocolate brown ones, the kind that was more milk than dark, but tended to change when he was passionate.

Then there were his lips. Man, did he know how to use them. They weren't thin, but weren't exactly thick, either. They were sort of in that in between range, full enough to be perfectly useful in all the right ways. His dark hair was shorter on the sides, longer on the top, but not that moppy long shit some guys had. Nah, he styled his, clean and precise. I kind of wanted to go see him play, and I would make sure I got the chance, because his hands were definitely talented, and I wanted to see him in his uniform.

God, it was like I was in high school again, when all us girls would go and watch the games, get all sorts of twitterpated by the boys in uniform, only to be ignored for the prettier cheerleaders. I was definitely not a cheerleader type. No, I was all about studying and making sure that everything I did in class was more than perfect. I needed to make sure if I was ever gonna make anything of myself.

At least at the end, I was in a decent enough foster home that I could stay at until after I graduated, even though I turned eighteen before that. I had enough friends that would have let me crash at theirs if needed, but I was thankful I didn't have to figure that out. Of course, college was a whole other thing. Missy, Kelsey, Emma, and I were all in the same dorm our first semester, so we were at least close.

We'd known each other since elementary school, and they were the few who were nice to me when I first showed up. I was the little kid wearing the same thing all week long, and a lot of the kids would tease me about it, telling me I stank or whatever. Thankfully, Missy would take absolutely no shit from anyone and defended me, even bringing me clothes to wear if I wanted to change. I never did, because I never knew if I would get in trouble for it or not.

God, how had those people been allowed to have a kid from the system in their house? You would think the government would check in on those sorts of things, but not this house. No, there were a bunch of us there, and we all had to scrounge to get anything to eat, and had chores that were more than anyone should ever have to do. It was like we were Cinderella, only we never got to go to the ball, and fairy godmothers didn't exist in our world.

"Hey," he said, shaking my hand, and I looked at him. "What's wrong?" he asked, taking a thumb, and wiping a tear from my face.

"Just remembering my past," I said. "Not sure why, but I'm on this historical journey, and not the fun kind."

"Well," he said, smoothing his thumb along my face. "I'm here now. I'll be your knight in shining armor, your Prince Charming, or whatever else you need. You just say the word, I'll be it."

"You already are," I said. "Just don't leave me."

"Never," he said. "You're gonna get so sick of me, though. I might smother you."

I smiled at that, and it was a genuine one. He really had rescued me, even though I'd been doing just fine rescuing myself.

Chapter Ten

Alejandro...

She'd been so confident when I met her, dancing her ass off on the dance floor. Now, though, as we were nearing home, she was looking more reserved. I wondered whether the persona she put out while we were in Vegas was something she wasn't in real life. Honestly, I guessed she was somewhere in between, but her reaction as we got closer made me a bit concerned.

When the pilot said we were heading in, I made sure that everything was tucked away, before taking her hand again, and making her look at me. I never minded flying. Not the takeoff or landing, but she seemed just nervous enough that I wanted to make sure she had a pleasant time, so I pulled her to me, kissed her forehead, then let my lips land on hers.

She was so sweet, in both personality and taste, and I couldn't get enough of her. I let my kiss build gradually, and she responded exactly as I'd hoped. She leaned into me, pressed her hand against my chest, and fisted some of the fabric, as if she wanted to hold on, and never let go. As I teased her with my tongue, she opened for me, and I delved into her mouth, sliding my tongue alongside hers.

When her hand slid from my shirt up, and around my neck, and she nearly climbed out of her seat, and into mine, I knew I had her where she should be, completely distracted from everything outside of the two of us, and when we bumped down on the tarmac, she didn't even flinch, just kept holding me, and kissing me.

Finally, once the plane was mostly stopped, just taxiing toward the gate, I pulled away.

"I'm gonna need you to fly with me wherever I go from now on," she said.

"Happy to oblige," I replied.

She took a deep breath, then let it out slowly as we pulled up to the gate. The crew made their announcements, welcoming us to the city of New Orleans, and telling us what time it was, as well as what we could expect as far as weather was concerned. When the door opened, I pulled my bag from under the seat, and she did the same. I'd already turned my phone back on, knowing I'd likely get some notifications, but when she took hers off Airplane Mode, it started going off.

I looked at her, and she smiled up at me, turning the sound down so that all it did was buzz from then on. I pulled our suitcases out of the overhead compartment and stepped back, so she could get out into the aisle before me. I handed her bag to her, and she tugged it behind her, as I followed her out of the plane, and up the jetway toward the terminal.

We headed out to where the parking garage was, and she held my hand as we walked. It was a nice feeling, knowing she was mine, and I could take care of her. After the little sadness I saw, I wondered what her life had been like. We had time to figure all of that out, but for now, I just wanted to get her home. I wanted to keep her at my place but understood her desire to return to her own home. I wondered whether it was a small house, or something bigger that she shared with someone else. As we stepped up to my car, I popped the trunk, and she stood looking at me.

"What?" I asked.

"I didn't know what to expect," she said. "But this wasn't it."

"Yeah," I replied. "I need to get something new, but this still runs, so I'm not in a hurry."

"How old is this thing?" she asked.

"It's a 2009," I said.

"I hadn't even started high school then," she said. "Are you sure you're a baseball player?"

"I am," I said. "And I keep it because it runs. No need to upgrade if you don't have to. I'll get a new one eventually. My parents have newer cars, though, if that's any consolation."

"I have a newer one," she said.

"I bought this one used," I said. "It made sense for me at the time. I didn't need anything flashy, just something to get me from point A to point B."

"I get that," she said. "I mean, I only have mine because it was Missy's, and I could pay her more than what she'd get for the trade-in value. It made sense for both of us, so I went ahead and got it."

"I'll probably end up getting a new one either this year or next," I said. "This one is just about on its last legs."

"I thought you'd have something flashy," she said. "But a Honda Civic? That was not at all on my radar."

"It's a really reliable car," I said. "It's been mine since high school, so it has some sentimental value, too."

"Oh, yeah, I get that," she said.

"Your chariot awaits," I said, opening the passenger door.

"Thank you," she said, sliding into my car.

I closed the door and went around to the other side, pulling my wallet out of my pocket, and sticking it into the door once I was settled. I started the car, and thankfully the radio was off, so she didn't get a blaring of my music first thing. I backed out of the spot, eased into the lane, and drove toward the exit. As we pulled up to the ticket box, I scanned the one I had in my wallet, then stuck my card in to pay for parking, taking the receipt when the machine spit it out.

"My house, first?" I asked.

"Yeah," she said. "If you still wanna come over."

"Definitely," I said. "Were you gonna answer your messages?"

"It's just Missy pitching a fit," she said. "She gets that way some-times. Especially when she's not in control. I don't think she liked you hanging up on her this morning."

"She needs to learn she can't talk to you like that," I said. "No one should talk to you like that, honestly."

"That's just the way she is," she said.

"I don't like her treating you like you're beneath her," I said. "You are an adult and have done a ton of things in your life that you should be proud of. No one is better than anyone else, so she shouldn't treat you like that."

"I've learned to ignore her," she said.

I let it go, because it wasn't worth the fight. I would, however, remind her any time Missy acted up that she didn't need to accept that kind of treatment. She deserved to be treated like the goddess she was, or at the bare minimum, like an equal. I didn't know the dynamic between them, but I was damn sure gonna see to it that Missy stopped acting entitled to my woman's time and patience and started treating her with the respect she deserved.

The drive to my house was quiet, and I think it was because she knew I was mad. Hopefully, she didn't think I was mad at her, because I wasn't. When we pulled up in front of my place, I heard her intake of breath, and turned to see her eyes wide as she looked at it.

"Not what you were expecting?" I asked.

"Not at all," she said.

"Come on," I said as I turned off the car. "Let me show you around."

I got out, went to her door and opened it, helping her out, then popped the trunk to take my suitcase out. I walked up to the door, and opened it with my key, pushing the door in to let her proceed me into my space. It had a homey feel, something my mom and sister helped to create for me. I knew jack-all about decorations, but they wanted to make sure it felt like a home.

"This is nice," she said, looking around.

"Thanks," I said. "This is the living room, obviously. Kitchen is over here," I said, turning her to her right toward that part of the house. "Dining room there, with a guest bedroom down that hall past the bathroom. That's where my mom usually stays when she comes up from Florida."

"Nice," she said, and I couldn't tell if she was genuine, or confused.

"I have a gym back there," I said, pointing further down the hall. "It's past the bathroom and bedroom, but it's decent sized. Laundry is under the stairs here, and upstairs is the master suite and my office. Wanna come check it out?"

"Definitely," she said.

I led the way up the stairs, my suitcase in my hand. I turned on the light as I crested the steps, then took the few steps to the actual door of my room. It originally had been three bedrooms, but I had apportioned two together for a master suite, then made the other one into an office of sorts. When I opened the door, she gasped.

"This is amazing," she said, stepping past me to look at my room.

It was spacious, for sure, with my king-size bed against one wall, set high on a pedestal. Twin-high boy dressers to either side of the bed, serving as nightstands. Across from the foot was another dresser, lower, with a television on it. The floor was high polished hardwood, throw rugs in bright colors on either side. To the right, past the bed, was a walk-in closet, and next to that was the bathroom.

She stepped into the space, marveling at it, and I watched as she took it all in. I had pictures on all the walls, some of my family, but others of the fields I played at. I always took my camera with me when we went on the road, and my goal was to be able to take a photo of every stadium. I'd hit most of them, and now that the schedule changed to where we played every team every year, I knew I'd hit the rest this season or the next.

"Who took these?" she asked as she stepped up to the collection on the wall next to the dresser at the foot of my bed.

"I did," I said, stepping to the closet to drop my bag.

She whipped around, and looked at me, confused.

"How?" she asked. "When?"

"Every stadium I go to," I said. "When I get there, I try to find the best vantage point to take the photo. I usually do it before batting practice, so no one is really out on the field, and the stands are mostly empty."

"They're beautiful," she said, her hand hovering over one of the photos. "Do you know which is which?"

"Oh, yeah," I said. "I recognize them, but I did make sure to put their names at the bottom of the photos in case I forgot."

Her eyes shifted, and she looked to the frames again, realizing, I'm sure, that the stadium names were printed there. She let her hand flutter over the names of the stadiums, taking in each one as she looked at them. I let her look and turned my attention to my suitcase and closet. I unloaded the dirty clothes and looked to see if I wanted to take anything from my closet with me, or if I wanted to stick with jeans and tee shirts.

I turned around to take my case to the bed so I could load it up with a few days' worth of clothes. She was still there, looking at the stadiums, and I smiled at her, knowing there were a few to look at. I hadn't taken a picture of all the stadiums I'd visited, because I'd just started doing it in the last few years or so, so I only had about half the stadiums, at most. Also, it wasn't always easy to get a shot. Weather or the timing of our visit had a lot to do with whether I'd get a shot or not.

"These are amazing," she said, turning to look at me. "Which one is your favorite?"

"New Orleans," I said. "Not just because this is home, but also because I captured a really great sunset in that one."

"How many stadiums are there?" she asked.

"There's thirty in the majors," I said as I walked to my dresser. "I should be able to finish the series in the next year or so. Hopefully this year, but maybe not."

"Some of these I don't recognize," she said.

"There are some minor league stadiums there, too," I said. "I went back to visit a couple of them when I was injured a couple of years ago, so I took the opportunity to snap those while I was there at rehab."

"What did you injure?" she asked.

"Nothing big," I said. "I broke my hamate bone. Fortunately, it was in Spring Training, so even though I had a fairly long recovery time, I didn't miss all that much."

"You broke a bone?"

"Just the little one here," I said, pointing to my scar from the injury.

"How in the world?"

"It's pretty common," I said. "Injured it swinging wrong. It's weird, 'cause it popped, and I felt it, but it didn't really hurt right away. I mean, there was a stinging, but it sort of just went numb."

"I've never broken a bone," she said. "I would imagine it would hurt, though. I don't have a very high tolerance for pain, though. I mean, I stub my toe and you'd think I'd had it cut off or something."

"Yeah," I said. "This was my first break. Actually, my first really serious injury. I mean, there've been pulls and shit, but nothing that was really bad. I was just happy it didn't mess up my whole season."

"That's good," she said.

"So," I said, walking up to her. "What type of clothes should I bring with me? Are jeans and tee shirts fine? Or do you want to go out somewhere that would require something a little fancier?"

"Umm," she hummed. "I'm not sure. It's not like you live that far that we can't come get something if we need it, but I think jeans are fine."

"I'll throw in a button-down," I said. "That way I have something a little nicer than just tee shirts."

"Okay," she said.

I set my suitcase up on my bed, opened it up, and headed to my dresser. I opened the drawer for my boxers and socks, grabbing a couple of each, and tossing them into the bag. Then I grabbed a couple of shirts, choosing ones that were fairly basic, and tossed them in as well. Finally, I pulled some jeans from the last drawer, and tossed a couple pairs in. When I turned to head to the closet for a button-down, she stared at me.

"What?" I asked.

"Everything landed into the bag," she said, looking between me and my suitcase.

"Well, yeah," I said.

"But, how?"

"I throw balls for a living," I said. "It's important for me to be able to throw them right where I want them to go. My job depends on it."

"But those are clothes," she said.

"Yeah," I said. "Same principle. Throw it where you want it to land. Besides, I've been packing like this since I was in high school, so it's not anything new. I've learned how to do it."

"Meanwhile, my suitcase looks like someone let a toddler loose in a thrift shop," she said. "All sorts of random things thrown in willy-nilly."

"I like your clothes," I said. "I mean, I prefer them on the floor, but still."

She laughed at that but was still shaking her head. I headed into the closet and pulled out a button-down from a hanger. I could do laundry when I came back. I mean, I would have to come back to pack for Spring Training, so it was a definite thing.

"Ready?" I asked once I had my suitcase packed.

"Sure," she said. "Question is, are you ready for the wrath of my best friend?"

"Exactly how pissed is she gonna be?" I asked.

"I mean," she said with a shrug. "She's pissed, but more at me than you. I think anything she directs to you will just be one of those collateral damage type of things."

"I think I can hold my own," I said.

"I'm sure you can," she replied.

I pulled her to me, wrapping my arms around her body as she wrapped hers around my waist. There was definitely a height difference, but it wasn't completely unsurmountable. She pressed up on her toes, and I leaned down, pressing my lips to hers. She deepened the kiss, sliding her tongue into my mouth, taking full advantage of my willingness, and I was not at all upset about it.

"Do you have any condoms here?" she asked.

"I think so," I said.

"Good," she replied, then stepped back, and tugged on the hem of my shirt, pressing it up as an indication for me to remove it.

Not wanting to disappoint my bride, I pulled it over my head as she worked my belt, button, and zipper on my jeans. I barely had time to realize what was happening before she was on her knees in front of me, taking me into her mouth, and, my God, did she feel good. Her hands were on my thighs, her head bobbing up and down my length. My pants were around my ankles, which had me trapped where I stood.

Watching my cock slide between her lips, her eyes turned up to me, a smile clear in their bright blue depths, just got me harder, and before I could even realize what was happening, I could feel that tingle, the tightening of my balls, and I was unloading in her mouth. Stream after stream came from me, and she swallowed it all, the motion around the head as she did so just that much more.

Finally, she sat back on her heels, smiling up at me with a wicked grin, and I wondered whether I had made a terrible mistake. This hellcat was feisty, and it had been more than wonderful to have her while we were in Vegas. Now, though, in my bedroom, I would never look at it the same, and if things didn't work out between us, that made me a little sad. Instead of letting my brain go on that train, I reached down, and helped her to stand, turning her toward my bed.

"Your turn," I said as I kicked off my shoes, then pulled the rest of my clothes off.

As she neared my bed, I was right behind her, pressing her toward the steps that were next to it. I had her walk a couple of steps up, just enough that her ass and pussy would be at the right height, then pressed her forward onto the mattress. Without giving her much warning, I reached around her, undoing her own button and zipper, then worked her jeans and panties down her legs, effectively trapping her as she had done to me earlier. She looked back over her shoulder at me, and the gleam in her eye told me that I had all the permission I needed to get her off, and I would work my best to make that happen.

Chapter Eleven

Hailey...

He had me up on some steps, his bed so high you couldn't get into it without climbing up them. His hands made quick work of my button and zipper, and down both my jeans and panties went, baring my ass to him. Looking at him, I couldn't believe we'd ever met. Yet, here we were, married, in just a matter of a couple of days. My life was crazy on its own, but add this in, and it was just beyond reality.

He smiled at me, then dipped behind my ass, and licked my slit, and I just melted into the bed. His tongue was magic, the way he moved it along my body, and when he pulled my clit into his mouth, I moaned. His nose was pressed against my opening, his teeth setting into the tender flesh at the apex of my sex, and it was just so good.

I wanted to separate my thighs, but the way my jeans were around my shins kept that from happening. No, I was trapped with them close together, unable to even shift even a little bit. His one hand was on the base of my spine, pressing me into the mattress, while he worked my pussy into a frenzy, but it wasn't quite enough. I needed some penetration, and as I was about to say something, he shifted his head and shoved a finger inside me, quick like lightning, and I spasmed around it, him scraping that rough patch just right to send me flying.

"Oh, God, Alej," I cried, my body bucking against the onslaught of pleasure he was wringing out of me.

It took a while to come back to myself, and he pushed me as far as I could go. Finally, when I was completely spent, unable to hold myself up, he eased back, placing his lips on my ass in a gentle kiss.

"I love hearing my name on your lips," he said.

His hands slid up my body as he leaned against me.

"You are very talented," I said.

"Thank you very much," he replied. "I take pride in my work, and this isn't exactly work, but I definitely take pride in it."

"You do not disappoint," I said. "A little help with my pants?"

"Sure," he said. "Just give me another minute to admire that fine ass of yours."

I could feel his hands run along me, over the globes of my ass, up to the small of my back, and then back down my legs.

"God, you're beautiful," he said, and I shuddered.

Finally, he slid his hand down my leg, and pulled my panties up, shifting me so that I could get them over my ass. Then he pulled up my jeans, letting me stand, and button, and zip them myself. I turned around and was way taller than him where I was standing, so I stepped down a couple of steps, so I was at eye level with him, and put my hands on his shoulders.

"Thank you," I said.

"You are more than welcome," he replied.

"We should probably head out, though," I said, not at all happy about having to leave.

"I should probably put clothes on," he said, and I laughed.

"I wouldn't mind, but I think it's sort of illegal to walk around outside without them," I said.

"Yeah," he said, leaning into me. "But if we could, I'd keep you here, naked, and under my spell for a long time."

"That sounds like both a threat and a promise," I said.

"Not a threat," he said. "I wouldn't do anything you didn't want me to."

"Definitely a promise," I said.

I leaned over and kissed him, pressing my body into his, and damn, he was good with his tongue. Didn't matter whether he was using it on my mouth, my tits, or my pussy, he knew how to work it. He pulled back, his eyes dark with promise, and I looked down to see that he was growing hard again, and I loved that I could get that reaction from him.

"You keep this up, and we'll never get out of here," he said.

"Yeah," I said, leaning back a bit. "I guess we better head to my place and face the music."

"You sure you're good with me coming?" he asked.

"She's gonna have to get used to you eventually," I said. "Otherwise, there's gonna be issues."

He pressed his lips to mine again, just a quick, chaste kiss, then he went to the pile of clothes, and started to get dressed. I closed my eyes, not wanting to distract him, or myself, until I heard the metal from his belt clicking into place. When I opened my eyes, he had his jeans on, but still had to put his shirt on. I took the last two steps down to the floor, heading toward the door to wait for him to finish. When he saw me, he smiled as he pulled his shirt over his head.

"Just gotta get my shoes on," he said. "Then we can head out."

"Okay," I said, waiting for him.

He went to the stairs by the bed and sat on one of the steps, pulling his socks, then shoes, onto his feet. Once they were tied, he got up, pulled his suitcase from the bed, and headed toward the door and me. His hand fell to the small of my back as he guided me out the door and back down the stairs toward the front door. I was nervous about him meeting Missy in person.

As he pulled up in front of my house, I worried that he'd be disappointed. I mean, it was plenty for me, just a three bedroom with a full bath for the guest bath, a three quarter one in my master bedroom. It wasn't nearly as fancy as his by any stretch of the imagination. Honestly, it was beginning to dawn on me how different we were, especially in our economic status. He had this beautiful house, and I had a little tinder box.

He reached over, and squeezed my hand, turning to smile at me after he'd pulled to the side of the street. Something must have been showing on my face, because he leaned over and kissed me, so sweetly it was painful, before pulling back just enough to look in my eyes.

"Everything's gonna be okay," he said.

"I'm just realizing how poor I am," I said.

"You're not," he replied. "I just have more disposable income. My pay is higher, but not because I'm more important. Simply because more people pay to watch me do my job. Honestly, you should be the one making six and seven figures a year. Your job is much more important."

I pressed my fingers to my mouth to keep the little sob that was trying to break free inside. We had only known each other for two days, and he was just so kind to me. I didn't deserve him, but I was glad I had him.

"Let's get this interrogation from your roommate over," he said, pulling back, and opening his door.

He walked around and opened mine, helping me out of the car, then went to the trunk to pull our suitcases out.

"Thanks," I muttered, as he handed the handle of mine to me.

Turning, I walked up the little walkway from the street to my door, praying that Missy would hold off on her anger, and let me just get inside. Unfortunately, I wasn't that lucky.

"It's about fucking time you got here," she shouted, standing in the doorway. "I've been waiting for you for hours."

"Missy," I said, trying to get her to calm down.

"No," she shouted. "And you, mister," she continued, turning her rage onto Alej. "What the actual fuck did you think you were doing, marrying her when you didn't know each other at all? That's some serious bullshit right there."

"Missy," I tried again, but she was just getting going.

"This is the most unhinged thing I've ever seen," she said, still shouting at us, and blocking our entrance into the house. "I just don't understand how they can allow this sort of fucked-up shit happen. Who the fuck thinks it's a good idea to put a million little chapels in the middle of a strip full of casinos and bars? Don't they know that people are gonna end up getting married to people they don't know?"

"Missy," Alej barked, and we both looked at him. "Would you mind if my wife and I came into her house? Because airing all this dirty laundry on the front stoop is a bit melodramatic, don't you think?"

"How dare you—"

"No," he said, and moved past me and up to her. "You will move your ass out of the doorway and let my wife enter her own house right this minute. If you don't, I will move you myself. Do I make myself clear?"

She stared at him, and I wasn't sure if it was shock or fear, but she stepped back, holding the door open for us to go in. He stepped back, and let me in first, then grabbed his bag, and followed. Once we were inside, he shut the door behind him.

"Thank you," he said to her, and she looked between him and me.

"Missy," I said. "I'd like to introduce you to my husband, Alejandro de la Garza. Alej, this is my best friend, Missy Kimball."

"It's nice to meet you," he said, reaching his hand out to shake hers.

She took it, shook it, but didn't break eye contact. Her face told me she was both confused and excited, but also that she was still pissed at me.

"Nice to meet you, too," she said, though it came out strained. "Now, can I have a conversation with my best friend? Alone?"

She added the last as soon as he went to answer, and I glared at her.

"Where would you like me to put your bag?" he asked me, clearly telling me that he was willing to give her this, since it was important to her, but also that he was going to be close enough to hear if anything shitty started to happen.

"Down that hall there," I said, pointing toward the bedrooms. "Mine's the last door on the right."

He leaned down and kissed me, letting it linger longer than would normally be considered polite, but in a show of dominance to my friend that we were, in fact, together, and there was fuck all she could do about it. I leaned into him, wrapping my arms around his shoulders, pressing up on my toes, and deepened the kiss as another fuck you to my friend who had been nothing but a bitch since the minute I showed up.

She cleared her throat, but we both ignored it, in another show of his dominance, I think, and then finally, when we felt we'd done enough, he backed off a bit, and I planted my feet on the floor. When I looked at her, she had that look that she got when she knew I was right, but was still pissed about it. Alej, bless him, walked past her, taking both of our suitcases down the hall toward the bedrooms.

"What the actual fuck?" she whispered at me. "Why did you bring him here? And where the fuck have you been since your plane landed?"

"We went back to his place, first," I said, moving to the couch in my living room. "After he got some new clothes packed, and we had a little fun, we drove here. It's not my fault you let me run off, and get married to a stranger, but now that I have, you're gonna have to deal with it."

"I did *not* let you run off," she said.

"Bullshit," I barked back. "You know what I'm like when I get drunk."

"And that's all I thought that was," she said. "I figured you'd go find a corner to fuck him in, then come back."

"And when I didn't?"

I had her, and she knew it, but she still tried to play the hand of the injured party.

"I was drunk," she said.

"So," I said. "It's okay for you to be drunk, and not be responsible for your actions, but I am responsible for mine, even if I'm so drunk, I can't think straight?"

"Okay, fine," she said. "But, still. Why did you bring him here? And aren't you gonna get it annulled or something?"

"I'm not sure," I replied. "I kinda like him."

"You can't be serious," she said, and looked like she'd swallowed a lemon.

"Can you trust me for one minute?" I asked.

"I don't know," she said. "Are you gonna get married to someone else?"

"Kinda can't do that," I said. "Already married."

"I just can't believe you did this to me," she said, and she was seriously upset.

"What did I do to you?" I asked.

"You made my bachelorette party about you," she said. "You went and had to get married before me. Every time I think I'm the special one, you go and ruin it."

"Hold up," I said. "You're saying that my getting married, in Vegas, was ruining your wedding? How did I ruin anything? I was out having fun with my friends, who we were all supposed to be looking after each other. You all let me wander off, and get married to a man I just met, and it's my fault?"

"You didn't have to drink that much," she said.

"Neither did you," I returned. "Look, I get it. This wasn't how you wanted this to go, and it didn't turn out the way you thought it would. That doesn't mean I did anything wrong. We had an amazing time, have some awesome memories, and my marriage has nothing to do with your wedding."

"I wanted to be the first," she cried, and she sounded like a whining kid at that point.

"Well," I said. "Not everyone gets what they want. I didn't plan this, didn't set out to make it happen, and I am not at all upset about the end result. It has nothing to do with you. At all. Now, if you don't mind, I need to go into my room, change out of my clothes, and maybe take a shower with my husband. Can you handle that? Or should you find somewhere else to stay until you get married?"

"Are you kicking me out?"

"No," I said. "But if you can't handle it, then that's something you need to consider. I'm not going to change my life to suit you. I am a married woman, and most people who are married live together."

"So, move to his place," she said.

"Missy," I said. "This is my house. I can live here for as long as I want, or I can move out if I want. You are a guest. You don't get to dictate who I can and can't have in my house."

"I just don't understand why you're being so mean to me," she said, her whining voice grating on my nerves.

"I'm not," I said. "I am not responsible for your emotions. You're an adult. You're about to get married. You should start thinking about that, about how you want someone to treat you. Then, act like that, instead of the toddler you're resembling right now."

With that, I got up and headed down the hall. She had always been needy, but honestly, it had started to build up in the last few months. I wondered whether she was getting worried about being married, or if there was something else going on. Either way, it wasn't my problem to solve.

"Is she okay?" Alej asked as I stepped into my room, closing the door behind me.

"She'll figure it out," I said. "If not, that's her problem, not mine."

"Good," he said, pulling me into his arms. "Now, I believe I overheard something about a shower with your husband?"

"That was more for her benefit," I said. "But I'm not saying I wouldn't enjoy it."

"Then, off with your clothes," he said, a bright smile on his face. "I shall unpack the rain gear and suit up."

I laughed, then pulled my shirt over my head, tossing it on the bed while kicking off my shoes. My God, we had had so much sex it was amazing we could still do it. Like, he had the stamina of a God or something. Not that I was complaining. My sex drive was pretty high as well, so it was nice to find that I'd married a guy who matched that.

Chapter Twelve

Alejandro...

It was a good thing I'd brought the box of condoms I had in my nightstand, because she didn't have any at her place. We'd fucked in the shower, and she was not a shrinking violet. No, my queen was a roaring Viking, telling the entire world how much she enjoyed me, and I was more than happy to keep her satisfied for as long as I could.

After we'd cleaned up, we changed, and decided to go out to eat. She wasn't sure what food she had in the house, and I wanted to take her to my favorite place. It was this tiny little hole in the wall place called Charles Seafood, and they had the most amazing options on their menu. My mom loved going there, and she really liked the variety. A few of the guys had gone with me once or twice, and even JP, who did not at all do seafood, found their pot roast to be over the top good.

When we walked out of her room and down the hall, her friend was sitting at the table, a glass of wine in front of her, and she asked where we were going.

"Out to dinner," Hailey said.

"Oh," she replied.

"Would you like to join us?" I asked. "Invite your fiancé to come, too? My treat."

"Alej," Hailey said, but I pressed her against me.

"Really," I said, looking at Missy. "I'd like to get to know you better."

"I can't believe you're asking me to come with you after how I treated you," she said.

"You were worried about your friend," I said. "I can understand and appreciate that. I'd like to help alleviate some of those concerns. Answer any questions you might have."

Missy looked between me and Hailey, trying to gauge the reactions of each of us. I did my best to remain calm and cool. She'd been pissy with me the entire time I'd been in her company, but she was just looking out for her friend, so I got that.

"Let me ask Kelton if he's free," she said, grabbing her phone from the coffee table.

"I'll have Hailey send you the name of the place," I said. "Just let her know if you guys are coming and we'll make sure we get a table big enough for all of us."

"Okay," she said, and she sounded at least a little bit contrite for her earlier actions.

Pressing against Hailey's back, I steered her toward the front door where she grabbed her purse before opening it. When we got outside, she let out a breath, and looked at me.

"You didn't have to do that," she said.

"I know," I replied. "But she's your friend, and if I try to get you to cut her off, she's gonna accuse me of being controlling. I'm trying to be the bigger person and offer an olive branch."

"You are entirely too good," she said and squeezed me.

I opened the car door for her and let her enter. When I climbed into the driver's seat, she was already buckled in and had her phone out ready to send the information. I told her where we were going, but didn't know the address, just how to get there. She looked it up, then sent the address to her friend as I started the car, and we headed out.

I knew it would take a while to get there, so I didn't bother to wait for her to get a response. When her phone chimed, she looked at it, then laughed.

"Kelton is telling Missy to back the fuck off," she said. "I love that man."

"Um, I'm right here," I said, hoping it sounded light.

"Yeah, but I'm married to you," she said. "I don't love you like I do him. I love him like the brother I never had."

"I don't think I want you to love me like a brother," I said. "'Cause, if you treat a brother like you treat me, I'm gonna be really worried about you."

"Yeah, no," she said, then laughed. "Okay, they're coming, and Kelton promised to keep her in check, so I think we're good."

"That sounds both ominous and awesome," I said.

"You're gonna love him," she said, reaching across the space between us to put her hand on my thigh.

"You keep that up, we're not gonna make it through dinner," I said. "Speaking of which, we should make a stop at a store. You know, to stock up on condoms. You tend to make me go through them pretty fast."

"Yeah," she said, squeezing my thigh. "We definitely need more."

We made it to the restaurant fairly quickly, and she texted Missy to find out when they'd be there. She said that it should be soon, because Kelton was already on his way to her house when Missy texted him, so they were only a few minutes behind us. We walked up to the restaurant and put our name on the waiting list for a table of four, then stepped back outside to wait for them.

It was still warm enough to stand outside, even though it was the end of January, so we weren't uncomfortable waiting for them. Hailey had her back to me, my arms were wrapped around her, and she was holding my hands. I was sure she could feel what her body was doing to me, but she didn't comment, or even move, really. When they pulled up and parked, she took in a shuddering breath.

"Hey," I said, leaning down to whisper in her ear. "Everything will be fine. I promise to be on my best behavior."

"It's not you I'm worried about," she said, then her face broke into a smile as she said, "Hey," to the newcomers.

"Girl," the man, who I assumed was Kelton, said. "Give me a hug."

She moved out of my arms and went over to him, hugging him around his neck as he put his hands around her waist. He eyed me over her head, and I wasn't sure if he was sizing me up or what, but it wasn't exactly a nice look. Her description of him being like a brother made me realize he was like the older brother, taking care of his younger sister. I could respect that role, as I played it with my older sister, too. Of course, she hated when I did it, but I still did. I waited for Hailey to introduce us, knowing it would happen eventually.

"Hailey," a woman said as she stepped out of the restaurant.

"That's us," I said, reaching out to my wife, which still felt weird, to hold her hand as we walked in.

The waitress or hostess, whichever she was, took us through the main dining area, and up a few steps to a small table set off to the right at the top. It wasn't a big place, but even though it was a week-night, the place was still full, hence our needing to put our name on a waiting list for a table.

"What can I get you to drink?" the waitress asked after we'd figured out our seats.

"White wine," Missy said, and Kelton gave her a look. "What?"

"Just one glass," he said, and I wondered whether there was more to this than just wanting to keep her reined in as he'd told Hailey.

"I'll have water," Hailey said.

"Same," I said, indicating that I wanted the same as her, not the same as Missy.

"And for you?" she asked Kelton.

"Water's good for me, too," he said.

"Be right back," she said, setting menus on the table in the middle, and going back down the stairs to get our drinks.

"I'm Kelton," he said, reaching across the table to shake my hand.

"Alejandro," I said. "But I go by Alej."

"Good to meet you," he said, and his shake was firm, but it wasn't like he was trying to out muscle me or anything. "So, how did this whole thing happen?" he asked after settling back.

"I was drunk," Hailey said.

"But she didn't look like it," I added.

"Yeah," Kelton said. "She can really hold her liquor. It's scary how well she can act while completely unaware."

"As demonstrated by the fact that we're married," I said, smiling at her. "Not that I'm complaining. At all."

"So," he began, but the waitress came back with our drinks.

"You guys need a minute?" she asked.

"Oh, yeah," Hailey said. "Sorry, we were just catching up."

"I'll give you some time," she said.

Hailey passed the menus around, and I took a look, but I was already sure what I wanted. Missy looked over the menu, then set it down, looking as if she was uncomfortable. She picked up her wine, and took a generous gulp, which caused Kelton to look at her. Setting the glass back on the table, she looked sheepish, and I wondered what the dynamic between them was. If he was abusive, that would explain her reactions, but if he was just annoyed that she was being childish, that was something different.

"What's the matter," he asked her.

"It's all seafood," she said.

"They make a really good pot roast," I said.

"It's not on the menu," she complained, and I was already growing tired of her whining.

"Trust me," I said. "I have a friend who comes here with me. Doesn't eat seafood, but loves when I suggest we come here. That's what he gets every time. I've tried it, and it's amazing."

She looked skeptical, but Kelton must have nudged her under the table because she turned her glare on him. I looked at Hailey, and she was looking between the two of them. I couldn't read her face for sure, but she was not at all happy with how her friend was acting.

"What do you recommend?" she asked me, turning the conversation away from them.

"I'm getting the stuffed crab," I said.

"Oh, that sounds good," she replied.

Her hand was on my thigh, stroking up and down, and it was doing all the right, and wrong, things to me. I had to shift a bit, and Missy gave me a look that would have struck a lesser man down, but I just shot it right back at her, not intimidated at all by her theatrics.

The waitress came back just then, and asked, "Ready?"

"I am," I said.

"Me, too," Hailey added.

"Yeah, we're ready," Kelton said, and the look Missy gave him kind of pissed me off.

"What'll it be?" she asked, looking at me since I was the first to speak.

I ordered, Hailey ordered, and Kelton ordered. When she looked at Missy, the girl sort of hemmed and hawed until Kelton said, "She'll have the pot roast."

"Oh, for sure," the waitress said. "It's so good."

She took the menus and walked away.

"What was that for?" Kelton asked.

"For treating me like a child," Missy said.

"You're acting like one," Hailey said, and Missy looked stricken, tears springing to her eyes.

"Why are you all being so mean to me?" she whined.

"Maybe because everyone is sick to death of this drama," Kelton said.

"It's her fault," she barked, pointing at Hailey.

"What did I do?" Hailey asked.

"You stole my thunder," she whined, big tears tumbling from her eyes. "You had to go and ruin everything. Now, my day isn't special, and it's all your fault."

She got up and stomped down the steps and out the door.

"Fuck," Kelton muttered, and went to get up.

"Stay," I said, and he looked at me. "Where is she gonna go?"

"Is this a safe neighborhood?" he asked, clearly concerned about her, which was good to know.

"It's fine," I said. "She'll either pout until she's done, or spoil the night for the rest of us. Sometimes you have to treat people the way they act, and right now she's acting like a spoiled toddler."

"She's been this way for a couple of months," Kelton said, looking at the glass of wine sitting on the table. "And she's been drinking more, too."

"What's going on?" Hailey asked, and the concern was clear in her voice.

"Her mom's being kind of a lot," Kelton said.

"Oh, God," she replied. "That explains a ton."

"Mom's extra?" I asked, and they both looked at me, nodding in unison. "So, then, she cuts Mommy Dearest out."

"Oh, no," Hailey said. "That isn't at all gonna happen."

"It should've happened a long time ago," Kelton said.

"Yeah," Hailey said. "But she won't do it. She has to prove herself to her mom. It's like this whole competition between the two of them, where one has to one up the other. I think she's getting way too stressed."

"Did she tell you what her mom did last weekend?" Kelton asked.

"What?" Hailey asked.

"Hang on," Kelton said, pulling out his phone. "Here."

He shoved the phone over to Hailey, and she gasped.

"She didn't," she said.

"Yep," he replied.

She showed me a picture of a dress that was cut to ribbons.

"Oh, hell, no," I said, and got up, walking down the stairs and outside.

"Go away," Missy said when I walked up to her.

"Not gonna happen," I said. "I saw what that bitch of an egg donor did to your dress. She's wrong, and you need to cut her the fuck out of your life."

"She's my mom," she whined.

"Don't care," I said. "If anyone did that to my wife, or my sister, I would throw hands. You are family because you're family to Hailey. I'm telling you, cut her out. If you want to keep living like a second-class citizen who will never measure up, fine. But if you think that you are worth more than what she's been treating you like, you've got my vote."

"I can't do that," she said, clearly distressed.

"Why not?" I asked, and she looked at me like I was an idiot. "Seriously," I continued. "Tell me why you have to be treated like that? If she wasn't your mother, you wouldn't put up with it, would you?"

"No," she said.

"Then why does it matter that she is?" I asked.

She looked at me, and I could tell she was really thinking about it. I don't know whether it was because I was basically a stranger, or because she hadn't looked at it the way I'd presented it, but she actually was thinking about it.

"Would you let your mother treat Hailey that way?" I asked.

"Absolutely not," she said.

"Then why are you letting her treat you like that?"

"I don't know," she said. "But what will people think?"

"I know that right now, I think you're not treating yourself very well," I said. "I know Hailey is worried about you. I can tell that Kelton is, too. They care about you. They love you. Let them be your family."

"Can I just not let her come to the wedding, though?" she asked.

"Who paid for the wedding?" I asked.

"My dad," she said.

"Are they still together?"

"Oh, God, no," she said.

"Then, why can't you just uninvite her?" I asked. "She's doing nothing but hurting you. She isn't going to be welcome, and I'm sure she will cause a scene if she's there."

"Do you know her?"

"No," I said. "But my best friend's mom was kinda that way. She was so gross it was awful, and he just couldn't see it. I asked my mom to treat me like his mom was treating him when he was over. Told her to just do everything I'd told her she had done to him. It took less than two minutes for him to call her out on her bullshit, and I looked at him and reminded him that his mom did that all the time. It was like a light went on for him. After that, he moved in with his dad and never saw her again."

"But she's my mom," she said, as if that made any difference.

"Honey," I said, placing my hand on her shoulder. "She gave birth to you. She's not your mom. A mom wouldn't ruin your wedding dress. A mom wouldn't make you cry. A real mom would want to make sure that everything about your day was all about you, and would fight anyone who got in the way of that."

She was crying now, and I was glad that she could see what was wrong.

"I'm sorry," she said, sniffling.

"Nah," I replied, pulling her into a hug. "You're grieving the mom you should have had. I'm sorry I had to point that out to you."

She actually let go, then, and really cried, and I held her, rocking her back and forth as she let go of what I was sure was years of grief. Finally, she sort of pushed back against me, swiping up under her eyes, and then looked up at me.

"Thanks," she said.

"Anytime," I replied. "Now, shall we go eat?"

"Yes," she said. "I'm starving."

I opened the door, and let her lead the way in, following behind her as we went. I was glad I was able to help her out, even if it was rough. Whether she'd actually listen to me and do what I'd suggested or not was something we'd have to wait to see. Hopefully, though, she would.

Chapter Thirteen

H**ailey...**

Dinner turned out to be really great, and Kelton and Alej were fast friends. Missy even seemed to be in better spirits. I had no idea what Alej had said to her outside, but she was more like herself when they'd come back inside. I was glad he was able to do something for her and wondered if he'd tell me when we were alone.

When the check came, Missy grabbed it before anyone else could, handing her card over to the waitress.

"I said it was my treat," Alej said.

"You did more than enough," she said. "You helped me more than any meal could."

"Glad I could be of service," he said, and I cracked up.

"What?" she asked me.

"Inside joke," I said, then slapped Alej on the shoulder.

"Not the same thing," he said, and I glared at him.

"Oh, God," Missy said. "Please don't talk about that in front of me."

I laughed again, because she hated it when I talked about sex of any kind. The fact that she understood what I meant, and what he'd said, just made me laugh even harder. We got up, and headed out once she'd signed the receipt, and she gave me a hug.

"He's a keeper," she said. "Seriously, keep him forever."

"Planning on it," I said.

She then hugged him, which was unusual. She wasn't one to hug guys, especially guys she didn't know.

"Thank you, again," she said.

"Anytime," he replied. "You need anything, you have Hailey let me know. I'll do what I can."

"Good to meet you," Kenton said, shaking Alej's hand.

"You, too, man," he replied.

"You gonna be around for the wedding?" he asked.

"Don't know," Alej said. "When is it?"

"February twenty-fifth," Missy said.

"I'll already be at spring training," he said. "Otherwise, I'd love to come."

"What's spring training?" Missy asked.

"Preseason," Alej said.

"He's a baseball player," I said.

"Oh, yeah," she said. "I forgot."

"No worries," Alej said.

"Goodnight," I said, taking Alej's hand.

"See ya," Kelton said.

"Are you coming home?" I asked Missy.

"I'm staying with Kel tonight," she said.

"Okay," I said.

We walked over to our car, and he opened my door, letting me in before shutting the door. He walked around the back of the car and climbed into the driver's seat.

"What did you say to her?" I asked when he shut the door.

"Just talked about how her mom was treating her," he said. "How she wouldn't let anyone else treat her like that and asked her why her mom should be different. It took a bit, but she realized how toxic her mom was. I don't even know much of anything about that, but just from the picture I saw, I knew the type. Had a friend who had a mom like that."

We'd pulled out, and were on the way home, and I knew it was only gonna be a few minutes until we got there, but it wouldn't be soon enough.

"You're amazing," I said.

"Just honest," he said, turning to smile at me. "Besides, I wouldn't let anyone treat you like that, so I'm not gonna let someone treat your friend that way."

"When do you leave?" I asked.

"In a couple of weeks," he said. "I have to be there by the twelfth."

"So," I said. "I only get a couple more weeks with you?"

"Sorry," he said. "I wish it was more, but it's just the time of year."

"Can I come down there to watch?" I asked.

"Absolutely," he said. "You can come see me anywhere I am. I mean, you can't travel with the team, but I can fly you to wherever we are, or you can come to the stadium and watch. I can get you as many tickets as you want."

"You can?" I asked. "Don't you have to pay for them?"

"They give us some tickets for free," he said. "But I can pay for them, too."

"That's awesome," I said. "So, you'd be able to get me enough to bring my kids if I set it up? I mean, we'd have the parents, and everything."

"I could probably swing it," he said. "I mean, it would take some doing, but yeah, I think we could do that."

"I'll talk to the principal tomorrow," I said. "I don't want to take advantage, though, but the school is in a poorer part of the city, so I know not everyone could come if they had to pay. Even if we got a discount."

"We could also come to the school to see the kids," he said. "We do that sort of thing all the time. Could even bring the mascot, Jazzy. He's wild, and lots of fun."

"You do that?" I asked.

"All the time," he said.

"I never knew that," I said. "Of course, I never had anything like that when I was growing up."

"We weren't here when you were growing up," he said. "The team's not even fifteen years old."

"I was in school fifteen years ago," I said. "But then again, so were you."

"True," he said. "But I wasn't really that interested in baseball until middle school."

"Why's that?" I asked.

"My dad wanted both of us to get a good education," he said. "He said that playing sports would take away from our studies. When I went to middle school, a friend of mine was playing for the school team. I mean, it wasn't much, just a game a week, a couple hours practice after school, but it was something I could do that would keep me out of trouble. Besides, if I didn't do well in my classes, I couldn't play. That's what sold my dad."

"So," I said. "You could play because you had to be a good student to play, so your dad let you?"

"Yeah," he said. "It was weird. Once I was out there, though, he saw how good I was, and that made him sort of push me toward the game. I still studied, even through high school. When I was drafted way down after graduation, he insisted that I should take the scholarship to Florida State."

"What did you study in college?" I asked.

"I just went for a couple of years," he said. "I did the prerequisites, but never picked a major. I got drafted after my sophomore year. I wanted to go to the Manatees, but the Magicians took me in the first round."

"I don't know what that means," I said.

We pulled up in front of my house, and he shut the car off. I went to open my door, and he grabbed my other hand, squeezing it.

"Let me," he said, then got out.

I'd never been one of those girls who needed a guy to fawn all over them, or to insist that they do everything for me. I didn't mind, but it wasn't something I needed. Of course, I wasn't one of those that insisted on doing everything myself, either. I could do it by myself or have someone do it. Either one was fine with me. I had to admit, though, that he was very attentive, and I kinda liked it.

When he opened the door, he held his hand down to help me out of the car, and I took it, getting a little zing running through me at his touch. Damn, I'd known him for just a couple of days and he was already affecting me like that. I was smitten, which was weird, but not horrible. We walked to the door, and I unlocked it and opened it up.

As soon as he was inside, he shut the door, and tugged me to him, kissing me hard and fast. I responded in kind, pulling myself up to him, wrapping my arms around his shoulders and lifting my leg to wrap it around his waist. He reached down, grabbed my ass, and pulled me up, holding me in his arms as he walked us back to my room. He was so strong it was mind-boggling. I wasn't exactly heavy, but I wasn't light, either, but he seemed to have no issue with my weight, which I liked.

He dropped me on the bed and kicked off his shoes while simultaneously working the buttons on his shirt. I kicked my own shoes off, one of them kind of going flying at his legs.

"Sorry," I said.

"No worries," he replied, having not even flinched as it hit him.

I continued undressing, not able to do it nearly fast enough, and he was already shoving his pants down and coming at me before I could get mine all the way off. He snagged them, and pulled, both relieving me of the clothing while also pulling me toward him.

"God, you're beautiful," he growled. Like, full on growl.

I didn't even have time to react when he dropped to his knees next to the bed, and shoved my legs apart, diving headfirst into my pussy, and God, was he good. It didn't take long for him to get my fire stoked, his tongue stroking my slit, then his finger sliding into me. I still had my bra and shirt on, but I didn't even care. All that mattered was his tongue, his finger, and my God, the explosion he sent through me.

"Alej," I cried as he worked that spot just inside.

I could feel myself pulsating around his finger, his teeth setting into my clit just enough to add that edge, and I rocked again, rolling over and over in the bliss that was my orgasm. Before I even came back to myself, he had a condom out and was rolling it onto his length. I tried to sit up, but he was over me before I managed it.

"Just lay back," he said. "I want to fuck you so hard you won't be walking straight tomorrow."

"Yes, please," I said, and did as he asked.

He slammed into me hard and fast, and I let out a little yelp. He stilled, looking at me, watching my face for any sign of discomfort or something, but I just reached up and pulled those luscious lips to mine, showing him with my body, the way my hips rose up to meet him, that I wanted this, needed this, and he did not disappoint.

Over and over, he pulled back, then slammed into me, his arm above my shoulder, holding me in place as he punished my pussy. My God, it was a heady thing to watch his eyes as they rolled back in his head, the smile on his face, and the way his body rippled as he worked his muscles to move. It was almost too much, the sight, the sound of our panting breaths, and the slapping of flesh against flesh.

Reaching down with his other hand, he lifted my leg, moving it up and over his shoulder, changing the angle just enough, so he could go deeper into me, and yeah, he was hitting every button I had.

"Come for me," he said, looking down at me.

His eyes were darker than normal, almost like he had shifted into something else, but I did not let him down. I obeyed that order, and let myself go, flying into the abyss, shattering into a million pieces as he spasmed inside me, filling the condom, while still punishing me, and it was glorious. Having let my leg slide from his shoulder, he bent forward, pressing his lips to mine in a punishing kiss, nearly as powerful as how he'd fucked me. My arms went around his neck, my legs around his hips, and I pulled him to me, as close as possible, relishing the feeling of us together.

After however long it took for us to find ourselves again, he pulled out, holding the condom against his body as he did, and pulled it off, tying it into a knot before looking around.

"Bathroom," I said, realizing he was looking for a trash can.

"Be right back," he said, leaning back, and pushing himself up to standing.

Watching him walk away from me was a beautiful sight, his ass more than fine. Of course, watching him walk back to me with a washcloth he'd wet, was mighty fine as well.

"Let me clean you up," he said, leaning down to press the cloth against my body.

I sucked in air, and he stopped, looking up at me.

"I think we probably need to take a break," I said. "How many times does this make it?"

"I've lost count," he said, smiling at me. "You good if I keep going?"

"Yeah," I said. "Just be gentle."

As if I were going to break, he carefully wiped my pussy, pausing anytime I made even the tiniest of noise to see if I was okay. It was amazing how well he was caring for me, and I didn't really even know him. The why and how of it still baffled me, but whatever gods were in charge of us finding each other did one hell of a job, because we were definitely meant to be.

He walked back to the bathroom, and I heard the sink turn on again. My guess was he was washing the cloth out, then washing himself. While he was doing that, I sat up and pulled my shirt off, undoing my bra to get out of it, too. When he came back out, he found me naked and sitting up against the headboard of the bed, covers down, and open for him to climb in with me.

"You wanna shower, first?" he asked.

"If you do," I said. "But it's not a big deal for me."

"Okay," he said, sliding between the sheets.

He pulled me against him, tucking my back into his front, his nose beside my ear as he inhaled, then hummed out in a sound that was definitely pleasure. I settled back, with his arm around my waist, and let my eyes close. We hadn't turned any lights on, except the bathroom one when he went in there, so it was dark enough that we could sleep without worry.

I drifted off, exhausted from travel and sex and full of tasty food, not really thinking about much of anything except that my life had somehow turned out pretty good. Tomorrow, I had to return to reality, and I wasn't exactly looking forward to that.

Chapter Fourteen

Alejandro...

The bed was empty when I woke up, and I was a bit confused, because it definitely wasn't my bedroom. Then I remembered the night before and turned to see if I could see her anywhere in the room. There was a note on the nightstand next to the bed, so I picked it up.

Alej,
I had to go into work. There's coffee in the bin next to the
maker, and I put a spare key next to it as well. Missy said she
wasn't coming back until after she got off work, so you're free
to stay there, or whatever you might need to do. If you want
me, text me.
Hailey

She had her phone number under her name, so I programmed it into my phone, then headed into the bathroom to get my morning ritual out of the way. After that, I pulled on my boxers and jeans, then headed to the kitchen for the promised coffee. The machine was one of those that you put the pod into, then pressed the button. She'd left a mug on the counter, and the machine was ready to go once I put the pod in.

As I waited for it to finish, I opened the fridge and saw that it was, as she thought, almost empty. I went to her cupboards to see if I could find anything that I could use to make some dinner for that night. There were a handful of staples, but she really didn't have much. By the time my coffee finished brewing, I had come up with a plan for the day. I'd go to the store and get everything I'd need in order to make my favorite dinner, then have it ready when she got home. I honestly wasn't sure when that would be, so decided to text her.

Walking back into the bedroom, I could hear my phone buzzing. I looked at it and saw that I just missed a call from my mom. I set the coffee on the nightstand and dialed her back.

"Alejandro Luis de la Garza," she said when she answered the phone.

"Mama," I said. "You're up early."

"Don't you mama me," she barked, and I knew something was wrong.

"What's the matter?" I asked.

"You know good and well what the matter is," she said. "Your *abuelita* is gonna die that you didn't invite her, let alone us."

"I don't know what you're talking about," I said, thoroughly confused.

My parents were fine with me living my life, and didn't tend to interfere in it at all, so this was confusing for me. And to bring *Abuelita* into it, there was definitely something wrong.

"You went and got yourself married," she said, and I closed my eyes, pinching the bridge of my nose.

"I was gonna tell you," I said.

"I have not met this girl," she said. "She looks like she's entirely too young for you."

"Mama," I said. "She's less than two years younger than me."

"When did you have time to meet a girl?" she asked. "And why did you go and marry her in some horrible little church? I have no idea where you were, or why you couldn't at least introduce us before you made this commitment. Have you no shame?"

"Mama," I said.

"No," she said, shutting any argument I had down with that one word. "You will introduce us to this girl. After we meet her, if we approve, then you will date her for a respectable amount of time. After that, maybe, if you are good about it, then you will get married the right way. In a church with a priest and all your family beside you. Do you understand me?"

"Mama," I said again, then waited, seeing if she'd go on another tirade. When she didn't, I continued. "Hailey and I are married. There's nothing you can do to undo that. We are adults, and we both decided we didn't want to have a big wedding."

"You are not married until you get married in the church," she insisted.

"Mama," I said. "The state of Nevada has given us a marriage license. It has been recorded. We are husband and wife."

"Don't you try to tell me what is right," she said.

"Mama," I said. "I need you to listen to me. Hailey and I are married. We are going to stay married. We will come see you and Papi at some point. I will also take her to meet *Abuela* and *Abuelo*, as well as the rest of the family in the off-season. For now, though, you need to get it into your mind that we are not going to do what you want us to do. I am a grown man and can make these decisions on my own."

"You're my *niñito*," she said. "What will your sister think? She didn't even get an invitation. What kind of an example are you giving to Samuel?"

"Mama," I barked. "I am not going to have this conversation with you. I have things I need to do. I will explain things when I see you in a couple of weeks. Until then, I need you to back off. We didn't announce it because we wanted to do it in person. I don't know how you found out, but..."

"It's all over the news," she said.

"What are you talking about?"

"Your sister showed me on her phone," she said. "Someone posted the picture from that horrible church of you and that horrible little girl you married."

"Mama," I said. "Do not call my wife horrible or a girl. She is a woman and she is wonderful. I need to call Isabella and have her send what she showed you. We did not release anything, and no one should know."

"You need to make this right, Alej," she said. "If not for me, then for *Abuelita*. She cannot know this happened without her consent."

"I'll talk to *Abuelita*," I said. "Now, I need to go."

"You will bring her when you come?"

"No, Mama," I said. "She is a teacher, so she'll be working. I'll let you meet her soon, though. Now, I will talk to you later, okay?"

"Okay," she said, but she didn't sound at all fine about it.

"I love you, Mama," I said.

"I love you, too," she said.

"Bye," I said and disconnected the call.

I dialed my sister, hoping she was able to answer the phone.

"Alej," she said. "Mama is mad."

"Yeah," I said. "I know. I just talked to her."

"I'm sorry," she said. "I thought she knew."

"Why would she know?" I asked. "And where did you find a picture?"

"It was posted on Instagram," she said. "Then, someone else shared it. It's kinda gone viral. I'm surprised this is the first you're hearing about it."

"I just got home late yesterday," I said. "Can you send it to me?"

"It's not very flattering," she said. "You guys look drunk. Were you drunk? Because if you were, you can get it annulled."

"I'm not getting it annulled," I said. "We're gonna make this work."

"When did you meet her?"

Oh boy, I was worried she'd ask me that question, and I wasn't exactly sure how to answer it. I could just tell her I met her recently, not expand on it, but my sister could sniff out a lie better than any bloodhound.

"Alej," she said, and I realized I'd been thinking too long. "You didn't meet her that night, did you? Please tell me you at least thought to get a prenup before you got married."

"Bella," I said. "I'm fine. We met and fell in love really fast. It was kind of a whirlwind, but we're home now, and we're gonna figure everything else out along the way."

"How can you be so casual about this?" she asked. "Don't you know that women out there hook up with athletes for the power it gives them? Not to mention the money they can get when they get a divorce."

"We're not getting a divorce," I said. "And we're fine. She's amazing. I can't even believe she looked at me, let alone agreed to marry me. She didn't know I was a player until after the wedding."

"She didn't know?" she asked.

"No," I said.

"What did you talk about before you got married?" she said, and I heard the skepticism in her voice.

"Bella," I said. "I'll explain everything when I bring her down to meet you guys. Just know that Hailey and I are fine. She's good to me, and she is more than anything I ever thought I wanted. She's a hard worker and is really smart and funny. I couldn't imagine my life without her in it at this point."

"I'll believe you for now," she said. "But I want you to know that if she messes you up, I will be the first one to tell you that I told you so."

"I know," I said.

"Be good," she said.

"I am," I replied.

She disconnected the phone, and I set it on the nightstand and fell back on the bed. I didn't know how I was going to explain our relationship to my family, but that was something I could worry about later. Right now, I needed to get dressed and get some food. My bride was at work, so it was up to me to make her something to eat when she got home.

Chapter Fifteen

Hailey...

I couldn't believe how much I missed my kids until I was back in the class. I'd taken Friday off, so we could fly out, but was supposed to be back with them on Monday. Missing that one extra day seemed like it was almost too much. They were also really glad I was back, mentioning how much they missed me as well.

The principal had asked that I stop into the office before I left for the day, so I had stepped in just after the buses left the parking lot. I didn't know what he wanted, but hopefully it wasn't any kind of reprimand for missing an extra day. It was completely unavoidable, unless you count the fact that I got married, and turned my phone off, therefore missing my alarm, and subsequently my flight home.

"Ms. Truitt," he said when I stepped up to his office.

"Mr. Olsen," I replied. "You wanted to see me?"

"Yes," he said. "Would you please come in and close the door?"

I didn't like to go into an office with someone and close a door, especially with someone of the opposite sex, and Richard Olsen was no exception. I wouldn't necessarily consider him a sleazeball, but he was not exactly known for his manners.

"I'd prefer to leave the door open," I said.

"Suit yourself," he said.

I sat on the edge of the seat across the desk from him, and waited for him to say something, whatever it was that made him ask to see me after school.

"I'm going to need more than just the fact that you had plane trouble," he said. "I had to scramble to get a sub in, and it wasn't easy."

I wanted to throw up, the way he said that.

"I'm sorry," I said. "I notified you as soon as I was aware of the issue. If it had been within my control, I would have been here on time."

"I checked every flight that left Las Vegas on Sunday," he said. "There were no mishaps or any delays that I could see."

Shit, I thought.

"It wasn't something with the plane," I said. "It was with the reservation. By the time I realized there was an issue, it was too late to get a flight out, and still arrive in time to make it in, and be an efficient teacher."

Was I lying through my teeth? Absolutely. Did I think he could tell that I was lying? I had no answer for that. I was fiddling with my ring, turning it around and around on my finger, hoping against hope that he wouldn't ask any more questions.

"I'm going to have to mark this as an unexcused absence," he said. "It will go against your record and could have an effect on whether or not you're asked to return next year."

The fuck it will, I thought.

"This sounds like it has turned into a disciplinary meeting," I said. "With that, I will need to end this discussion until I have a union representative with me."

I got up and moved to leave the room.

"You and I need to settle this right now," he said, getting up, and trying to intimidate me with his larger size.

"I need you to move," I said, as he was closer to the door, and had effectively blocked my exit.

"Sit down," he demanded, and I glared at him, holding my place. "I said sit down."

He was nearly shouting by this point, and I just looked past him, and out the door to see that the secretary was watching what was going on.

"You can either move out of my way," I said. "Or I will call the police."

To show I wasn't faking, I pulled out my phone, and began to dial 911. He slapped the phone from my hand, and it fell to the ground. I heard a crack, and knew that he'd broken it, and I about lost it.

"Mary," I shouted around him. "Will you please call the police?" I picked up my phone from the ground, and sure enough, the screen was cracked. "I am going to file a complaint against you for both harassing me, attempting to intimidate me, and for breaking my phone. You need to move immediately."

"Sit your ass down, right now," he shouted, shoving me back.

I tumbled, tripping on my own feet, and fell to the ground, hard. He followed me, stood over me, and yanked my phone from my hand, throwing it across the room where it broke even further against the brick of the wall. He was breathing heavily, glaring down at me, clenching his fists, and I was actually afraid at that moment. All I could think about was what would happen if he decided to be even worse. Like, if he wanted to, he could have stomped on me, and there really wasn't anywhere I could go. The office was small enough that I was effectively trapped.

When I heard the sirens, I had a moment of peace, but then he leaned down and slapped me hard across the face, my head whipping over, and my cheek smashed into the wheel on the bottom of the chair that was right beside me. Without thinking, I kicked my foot up, impacting him where it would hurt the most, right in his crotch. He doubled over, almost falling on top of me, and I had to scramble to get out from underneath him.

Looking up from where I was, I saw two officers come into the room, looking around, and trying to figure out what was going on.

"Arrest her," the principal said.

"He started this," I barked.

"She attacked me without cause," he said, and Mary, bless her heart, countered with, "He did start it."

"Come on," one of the officers said as they helped him to his feet. "Let's get you two separated, and we'll get it all figured out."

The two of them walked out of the room, leaving the other officer there with me.

"Wanna tell me what happened?" he asked.

I was sitting on the floor, my hand on my cheek where it had hit the chair, and when I pulled it away, blood gushed from the gash that was there. The officer called over his radio, and asked for an ambulance to be dispatched, and I sat there, not sure what to do.

"Here," he said, handing me the box of tissues off the principal's desk.

I grabbed a handful from the box, and shoved it against my cheek, trying to staunch the bleeding. Looking behind me, I saw my phone sitting on the floor, and I just broke down. I don't know whether it was a relief that I wasn't in danger anymore, or if it was because my phone, that I had just got a few months earlier, was now in a mess on the floor, but it all hit me, and I just let it all out.

There was a commotion behind the officer, and I didn't even look up, but sat there sobbing my eyes out at everything that had happened in the last few days. Then I started laughing. Full on, maniacal laughing. The absurdity of it all just struck me, and I couldn't help myself. The fact that I married a stranger was the least insane thing that had happened.

"Ma'am," someone said, and I sort of looked up confused. "Can I check your cheek?"

It was someone from the aid car or ambulance or whatever had come. She was squatting in front of me, gloved hands, looking very unsure of the situation.

"Yeah," I said, and kind of just relaxed.

There were enough people around now that I didn't feel like I was in any danger. I wasn't sure what had happened outside the office, but the door was now closed. I could hear some muffled voices, but decided to just focus on what the EMT was doing with me. She'd pulled the tissue from my face and sucked in a breath through her teeth. "Where did you land?" she asked.

"I think it was the bottom of that chair," I said, sort of gesturing toward where I thought it might be.

She turned to her tackle box that was beside her and opened it up, fishing around for whatever it was she was looking for, then came back with a bottle of some sort of clear liquid.

"This might sting," she said. "I just want to irrigate the wound to make sure nothing got stuck inside. You okay with that?"

"Yeah," I said, just sitting there.

I wanted to call Alej, but I didn't have his number. Even if I did, my phone was likely not in any condition to make that call. Then I wondered whether Mary had made a call to Missy. She was my emergency contact, considering I didn't have family, so it may have happened. Not that she could do anything, though. Maybe she could go to the house and let him know. If he stayed. Maybe he left. I hoped he hadn't left because I needed him.

"You wanna tell me what happened?" she asked as she squirted my cheek.

"He tried to have a disciplinary meeting without giving me a chance to have a union rep with me," I said, and even to myself, my voice sounded flat. "When I went to leave, he blocked me. Then he slapped my phone out of my hand when I tried to call 911. I picked it up, and he grabbed it, and threw it against the wall. Then he shoved me down, then slapped me, so I kicked him in the balls."

She'd finished her washing and was now pressing on the cheek. I wasn't sure if she was trying to push something out, or just prodding around to see if anything was broken inside. I didn't feel like that was the case, but honestly, I didn't really feel anything. I was completely numb.

"Sounds like you defended yourself," she said as she continued.

Just then I heard a shout, and there was a crash against the door. I flinched, tucking myself down, trying to become smaller somehow. The door flew open and I could see Richard, the dick, trying to get through it. He was shouting something, but I couldn't quite make it out. There was foam on his lips, spit flying everywhere, and two big officers were holding him back. They weren't the first ones that showed up, though, so I was confused.

"That bitch is fired," he shouted. "Termination immediate, and no severance. She'll never teach another day in her life if I have anything to say about it."

"Focus on me," the EMT said, and I looked over. "That's it. Just follow my finger for me, will you?"

I did what she asked, and everything else faded away. The noise lessened, the lights dimmed, and all of a sudden, everything went black.

Chapter Sixteen

Alejandro...

"Hey, husband," Missy shouted as she came in the door. "Sorry, I forgot your name."

"No problem," I said, wiping my hands on the towel next to the sink.

I'd picked up everything I needed to make my mama's famous enchiladas. Everything was ready, I just needed to wait for the oven to heat up so I could put them in. I had made two pans of them, figuring we could eat leftovers, or share with Missy and Kenton if they wanted to come over. It had been nice hanging out with them the other night, so thought I'd try again, this time at home.

"You gotta come with me," she said as she rounded the corner into the kitchen. "Whoa, what's all this?"

"Decided to make my mama's famous enchiladas," I said. "Was gonna have Hailey let you, and your fiancé know. Thought a nice homecooked meal might be what she needed."

"Oh, yeah," she said. "She will love this. But first, we gotta go."

"I don't know what you're talking about," I said.

"Didn't she call you?" she asked.

I grabbed my phone to check, but there were no missed calls or messages or anything. I had a problem sometimes with putting it on do not disturb if I needed extra sleep on a day off, but that hadn't been the case here. It was fully functional, so I was confused.

"Why?" I asked.

"Come on," she said, grabbing my hand. "I'll tell you in the car."

"Let me turn the oven off," I said, pulling away, and pushing the button to do that.

I grabbed the trays, and shoved them into the fridge, knowing they would be just as good if we waited to heat them. She was already out the door when I came back around, and when I pulled the door closed and locked it, she looked at me a bit confused.

"She left a spare key," I said, holding it up. "You want to drive, or you want me to?"

"You drive," she said, walking purposefully to my car.

I unlocked it, and opened her door, and she looked at me with wide eyes, then slid in. I shut it on her, and walked around the other side, climbing into my seat.

"Where are we going?" I asked.

"UMC hospital," she said, and I looked at her. "Hailey was attacked at school."

"I thought she worked in an elementary school," I said as I started the car.

"It was the principal," she said.

"Shit," I said, pulling out into the road and heading to the hospital. "Why didn't she call me?"

"I think her phone got broken," Missy said. "I got a call from the secretary. I'm her emergency contact. That should probably change, though, now that you're married."

"Not the biggest concern right now," I said, focusing on not freaking out. "What happened?"

"I don't know," she said. "I just got a call from the school. They told me she'd been attacked, the principal was arrested, and that I needed to get to the hospital. They said that Hailey had asked for me to come get you."

I stopped listening after that, because I knew my woman needed me, and I had to focus on keeping us safe on the road. Nothing else mattered but getting to her. It didn't take long, and we were pulling up to the emergency department. I found a spot to park, then got out, walking around to help Missy out of the car as well.

"Thank you," she said.

"No problem," I replied, then walked with her to the door.

"How can I help you?" the woman behind the desk asked.

"We're here to see Hailey Truitt," Missy said.

"Gonna need your ID," she said. "And the relationship."

"I'm her husband," I said.

"I'm her best friend," Missy said.

We both handed over our driver's licenses, and she plugged the information into her computer, then I heard the whirring sound, and noticed a small printer next to the keyboard.

"Put these on," she said, handing the stickers as well as our ID back. "I'll buzz you back. She's in bay four."

"Thank you," Missy said.

"Thanks," I reiterated.

I heard the buzz for the doors just to our left, and headed on through, pulling the back off the sticker as I went. I held the door for Missy to follow, and we walked through. It wasn't as noisy as I anticipated, and we found the bay the receptionist had sent us to. I whisked the curtain back and saw her, going immediately to her side.

She had a bruise on her left cheek that looked a whole lot like a handprint, and when she turned to us as we went in, I could see that she had a bandage on the right side of her face that was likely covering a wound of some sort. Her eyes filled with tears, and she reached out to me, and I gathered her to me, sitting on the edge of the bed, holding her head against my chest as she let sob after sob out.

"I got you," I said. "You're safe. I'm right here."

"And you are?" the nurse or doctor, I didn't know which, asked.

"I'm her husband," I said. "Please tell me the person that did this to her is in jail."

"I have no information on that," she said.

"They took him away," Hailey said. "I don't know where they took him, but he fired me. I don't have a job, and I can't do this if I don't have a job. He said he would make it so I couldn't teach anywhere ever again."

The words were so heartbreaking that I wanted to cry myself, but I had to be strong for her. Nothing I could do right now, but I would make this right. Whatever I had to do, I would do it. She was going to be a teacher, because that's what she wanted to do, and I was going to make sure she got to keep doing it.

"I'll leave you for a minute," the medical provider said. "The doctor will be in shortly with some discharge instructions."

"Thank you," I said, but never looked at the woman, who must have been a nurse.

"I couldn't get ahold of you," she sobbed in my chest.

"Missy came and got me," I said, reaching back to let her know she was welcome to come sit with us.

"I'm sorry," Missy said.

Hailey just reached over, and wrapped her arms around her, letting go of me in the process. I didn't mind, because they were best friends, and sometimes you needed that person to be there for you.

The doctor came in a short time later, after Hailey had calmed down some, and had finally stopped crying.

"Ms. Truitt," he said.

"Yeah," she said.

"I looked at the x-rays and didn't see anything structurally damaged in your cheek," he said. "Just the laceration. I want you to keep that bandage on it for tonight and change it out in the morning. I've asked the nurse to get you a packet of what you'll need to do that. I also want you to be monitored for a concussion. I don't know for sure that there is one, but the symptoms indicate it's likely, so I just want to be on the safe side. Do you have someone to stay with you?"

"We will," Missy said, and the doctor looked between the three of us.

"I'm her husband," I said. "This is her best friend and roommate. We're all living together until Missy gets married."

"I see," he said, though I wasn't sure he believed me. "I'm going to need you to watch her for any of the symptoms on the discharge paperwork. It'll be clear that there's an issue, so just be mindful of how she normally behaves, and watch for any irregularities. I've prescribed you some pain medication, but you can also just go with Tylenol or ibuprofen for the laceration. I anticipate she will end up with black eyes, and there may be swelling around them as well."

"I'll be with her for the next two weeks," I said. "After that, we'll make sure she has someone around."

"It shouldn't take that long for her to return to normal," he said. "If there are issues, or if additional symptoms arise, she needs to come back in and get additional tests. Have you dealt with a concussion before?"

"Not personally," I said. "But teammates have, so I've seen what needs to happen."

"I thought I recognized you," he said. "Didn't know you were married."

"Just happened," I said.

"Good to know," he said. "So, yeah, just watch her and make sure she's resting, and taking her meds. Watch for the symptoms on the list and bring her in if anything comes up."

"Absolutely," I said.

"Off topic, but," he said, then the nurse came in.

"I have the discharge paperwork," she said.

"Thanks," the doctor said, and took it from her.

She looked confused, and my guess was when she brought that in, the doc jumped at the chance to leave. When he didn't, she likely wasn't sure what was going on.

"Thank you," I said to the nurse, so she knew I knew she was the one doing the lion's share of the work. "Doc was gonna ask me something, so I think you just surprised him with your efficiency."

I winked at her, and she smiled, obviously taken by the charm I sometimes had, then turned and walked out of the space.

"So, anyway," the doctor said, and I could tell he was a bit annoyed. "I was wondering whether you or your team would be willing to come visit the kids in the pediatric unit."

"That would definitely be something we'd do with our outreach program," I said, knowing that wasn't what he was going to ask, but letting him get away with it. "I don't handle that kind of thing, though, and have no idea who to send you to. I would suggest you contact the team's main office and ask them about it. I'm definitely willing to come by if something is set up, for sure."

"That would be great," he said, then passed the packet of paperwork off to me, and turned, and walked out of the space.

"Was it just me or did he just change his whole attitude in the blink of an eye?" Missy asked.

"More like a wink," Hailey said, smiling at me.

"I think he's used to being the big dog, the one with all the answers," I said. "Being reminded that the nurses carry the ship probably knocked him down a peg or two, and he didn't like it."

"That, and your brushoff," Hailey said.

"Oh, yeah," Missy agreed. "That was a very polite way of saying, 'not my job.'"

"I've learned the lingo to use when dealing with people who think you're dumb because all you do is play a game," I said. "It's sad that sometimes the most educated of people forget that they once didn't know everything."

"And that they're not always the biggest fish in the pond," Missy said.

"Can we go home?" Hailey asked.

"Let me go ask the nurse," I said, getting up off the bed. "You stay here and make sure she's fine. Be right back."

I walked out of the space and toward the nurses' station and saw the doctor talking down to the nurse that had come into the room. He was heated, his face red, and she was standing there, just taking it. Nothing pissed me off more than someone taking advantage of their higher standing to attack someone, and I wasn't gonna stand for it.

"Can I help you?" another nurse at the station asked.

"I wanted to talk to our nurse," I said, looking directly at the two standing away from the main section.

"Yeah, she's gonna be a minute," she said.

"Is he always an asshole?" I asked, and I thought the nurse was gonna swallow her tongue, she was holding back a laugh so much.

"Yeah," she finally said, when she'd gained some composure. "Whatever you said to him really pissed him off."

"And he's taking out on her?"

"Don't worry about it," she said, and I looked at her. "Trust me, we all know how he is, and tend to ignore him when he gets his ass handed to him. How's she doing?"

"Concussion," I said. "Gonna baby her for the week, and hopefully she'll be right as rain this time next week."

"She's lucky to have you," she said.

"Nah," I replied. "I'm the lucky one."

Finally, after what seemed like an eternity, the doctor walked away from the nurse, and she looked in our direction. I raised my eyebrows at her in a silent question, and she just smiled and walked over.

"You good?" she asked.

"Question is, are you?" I returned.

"He's a blowhard," she said softly. "All bark, no bite."

"Either way, is there a place where I can lodge a comment?" I asked. "I want to make sure that the hospital knows you were amazing, and he was a dick."

Both the nurses looked at each other, then back at me, like I had said something completely unusual.

"You'd do that?" the nurse who had attended to Hailey asked.

"Why wouldn't I?" I asked.

"You'd be amazed," she said, but then pulled out her pen, and grabbed a sheet of paper from the desk, and wrote down a website. "There's an anonymous option where you can write whatever you want, and it won't be attached to any record."

"Thanks," I said, taking the paper. "Are we good to go?"

"Oh, yeah," she said. "The pharmacy just dropped off her prescriptions. Let me get a chair to wheel her out."

"A wheelchair?" I asked.

"Hospital policy," she said. "Stupid, but it's the way it works. Here are her meds. There are instructions on the bottles, as well as the discharge paperwork."

"I'll go bring the car around," I said. "Let me tell her."

I walked back into the bay and saw Hailey look up when I moved the curtain.

"Good to go?" she asked. "I just want to get out of here."

"They've gotta get a wheelchair," I said.

"I didn't break my leg," she replied.

"I know," I said. "They said it's policy. I'm going to get the car. Are you good to get her outside?"

"I've got her," Missy said.

"Thanks," I replied, then walked over, and gave Hailey a kiss. "Be right outside."

"Okay," she said, her hand sliding from the side of my neck as I stood up.

I walked away from her, out into the emergency department, and out the doors to the waiting area beyond and into the parking lot. While she wasn't sure how she was going to do whatever she needed, I knew that I'd be taking care of her. Both her physical needs, as well as any financial issues that might come up from this asshole's attack on her. Tomorrow I would call the team, and ask for an attorney recommendation, but tonight was going to be about taking care of my woman.

Chapter Seventeen

Hailey...

When he left to get the car, I turned back to Missy.

"Okay, now start again," I said.

"I came flying into the house," she said. "He was in the kitchen. Cooking. Like, full on meal. Nothing from a box, either. No, it was fresh, and it smelled amazing."

"I don't understand," I said. "He didn't need to cook. I was gonna get some groceries on the way home, and make dinner when I got there."

"Well, he beat you to it," she said. "He turned the oven off, shoved the trays into the fridge, and then went out the door and opened my door to let me in."

"Yeah, he does that," I said.

"It's nice," she said. "I mean, don't get me wrong. I don't need someone to do that, it's just..."

"Yeah," I said. "It took a minute for me to get used to it. I mean, not like I am, just, yeah."

"So," she began, but the nurse came through the curtain with a wheelchair right then, so she had to stop.

"All ready?" she asked.

"More than," I said as Missy got up off the bed.

I swung my legs over the side, then had to stop, and close my eyes. Except, as soon as I did that, the whole room swirled, and I had to hold on to the bed to keep from falling over.

"Easy," the nurse said, holding my arm as I steadied myself.

"Guess it's a good thing you have to use a chair," I said, trying to sound lighthearted.

"Now you see why we do," the nurse replied, though she was smiling.

I took a deep breath, then scooted closer to the edge of the bed, but my feet still didn't reach the floor.

"Hang on," the nurse said, moving to the control thing that was attached to the bed.

She pressed a button, and the bed started to sink, lower and lower, until my feet hit the floor and were set flat. I had to hold on because the movement was weird, and I didn't trust myself to not tip over.

"There we go," she said, coming back to where I was sitting. "Let's get you up and see how you do."

The chair was a bit away from me, and she was standing next to me. Holding my armpit, she let me hold on to her hand, and helped me to my feet. Again, the room went swimming, and I held on tight, waiting for the waves to slow to a roll. It was weird. This felt like we were on the water, and waves were undulating under my feet, so it wasn't what I was expecting.

"Okay," she said, easing a little bit away from me so I was standing on my own.

She brought the chair over, spinning it so it was to my side, then set the brakes on either side so it wouldn't roll out from under me. After that, she came around the front of it, and took my hand again, helping me to turn, so my ass was facing the chair, and I could sit down. She eased me down, not letting me fall back onto the seat, and when I was finally settled, she bent to flip the footrests around, placing each of my feet onto the things there.

"Let's roll," she said, releasing the brakes on the chair, and spinning it so we were facing back out toward the main area of the emergency room.

Missy pulled the curtain over, and held it out of the way as the nurse wheeled me out from where I'd been for the last however many hours, and toward the freedom I desperately wanted. She was holding the paperwork, and my purse had been left in the trunk of my car, so the only thing I really had were my keys.

"My car," I said, suddenly realizing it was still at the school.

"Don't worry," Missy said. "We'll stop and pick it up on the way home. You can ride with Alej, and I'll drive it home."

"Oh, good," I said. "One less thing I have to worry about."

"Of course," she said, squeezing my hand as we walked out the doors to the parking lot.

He was standing next to the car, holding the door open, and he came to me as soon as we slid outside.

"She's a little wobbly, still," the nurse said.

"I've got you," he said, looking at me.

She wheeled me up next to the passenger side of the car, then set the brakes. Instead of me standing up, though, Alej just reached down, and picked me up out of the chair, turning and placing me gently into the seat, careful of my head as he went through the door. Once I was sitting, he reached over, and grabbed the seat belt, wrapping it around me and plugging it in so I was secure.

"I can do it myself," I said.

"You don't have to," he replied, then kissed me softly. "Thank you," he said to the nurse as he shut the door.

Missy and he talked for a moment, then he opened the back door behind my seat as the nurse turned and went back into the hospital. When he climbed into the driver's seat, he looked at me, placing his hand on my cheek. I pressed my cheek into it, reveling in the connection we had.

"Missy is gonna give me directions to the school," he said. "Then she'll bring the car home. Once we're there, I'm going to get you inside and settled before I start dinner."

"She said you were cooking something yummy," I said.

"Mama's famous enchiladas," he said. "You're not allergic to anything, are you?"

"Not a damn thing," I said. "Except, apparently, my boss."

"Yeah," he said, and there was a steeliness to his voice. "We're gonna have to deal with that. But not until tomorrow."

I laid my head back on the rest, and closed my eyes, only for everything to start rolling again, so I opened them quickly, and just stared at the dashboard. Hopefully, this craziness didn't go on all night, because all I wanted to do was go to bed and sleep. If it kept going the way it was, though, closing my eyes might not be the best choice. Hopefully, the medication they gave me for the pain would knock me out, and I wouldn't have to worry about anything else, at least for the night. Tomorrow was another story, though, and not one I was looking forward to.

Missy was quietly giving Alej instructions on how to get to the school, and I was thankful they'd figured that issue out. I didn't exactly have the fanciest car, but it was all I had, and I didn't need it to get messed up. Not that it really would. Or at least I hoped it wouldn't.

"Hey, babe," Missy said, and I turned to look at her, regretting that decision as my vision went all wobbly. "I need the keys."

I reached into my pocket, and pulled them out, holding them out to my side. She opened the door, and the light came on. It was late enough that the sun was in its falling motion, so it was dark enough that the light was too much. I put my hand up over my eyes as soon as she took the keys, and Alej fiddled with whatever it was that made the lights turn on, so they went out.

"Thanks," she said. "See you at home."

"Thank you," I said, but couldn't turn to look at her.

When she shut the door, I was sort of startled, then put my hand to my head again.

"Hey," Alej said. "You okay?"

"Yeah," I said. "It was just too much light, then the slamming door was loud, and shook the car. Just not quite myself right now."

"Let's get you home," he said, and pulled out of the parking lot to head back to the house.

I desperately wanted to close my eyes, but every time I did, the world tumbled, and I was getting nauseous from it, which was even worse than the splitting headache I had going on. By the time we pulled up in front of the house, I was nearly ready to throw up, and I was not at all about to do that.

Alej opened my door, and helped me out of the car, then held me as we walked up to the house. Missy was already there, which I thought was a bit odd, but figured my brain was just playing tricks on me. When I got inside, Missy had the lights off, except for the one above the stove in the kitchen, and one lamp on a table next to the couch.

"You want to lie down?" Alej asked.

"I think so," I said, unsure whether that would help or hurt my brain.

He helped me down the hall, and into my room, walking me straight to the bed.

"Sit," he said, guiding me down.

Kneeling in front of me, he pulled the first one, then the other shoe off. I worked to get my jacket off, but it was entirely too complicated for me at that point, and I was just getting frustrated.

"I got it," he said, stopping my hands from their movements.

He undressed me slowly, taking care not to jostle me in any way. Once my jacket and shoes were off, he started to pull up my shirt, and I let him. Honestly, having him taking care of me was the absolute best.

"Hey," Missy said as she stuck her head in my door. "What did you want me to put the oven on?"

"Four hundred," he said.

"Okay," she said, then shut the door quietly.

They were both being so good to me, so quiet, and just taking care of me. It meant a lot, and before I realized it, I was crying. Alej pulled my shirt over my head, and then sat on the bed next to me, pulling me into his arms.

"I got you," he said, and just those three little words were exactly what I needed.

I let go, crying for everything that had happened in the last few hours. From my boss being an absolute jackass to the fact that I was summarily fired, to the fact that I would likely have a huge ass medical bill from having to be taken by ambulance to the hospital, to all the testing they had to do, to the broken phone, to just, everything.

The best thing that had happened in the last few days was Alej. He was so kind, so caring, just taking care of everything. How I'd lucked out in meeting him was beyond my imagination, and I just couldn't believe my luck. The fact that he'd stayed with me, and had come to me when I'd been broken, meant so much more than he'd ever know.

When I'd cried myself out, he let me loose, looking at me with so much concern it hurt. It almost made me want to cry all over again. He brushed the tears from my cheek, just above the bandage, and kissed my forehead.

"Oven's ready," Missy said as she poked her head in again.

"I'll be right there," Alej said. "Let's get those pants off and get you settled. Then I'll finish getting dinner ready."

"You don't have to baby me," I complained, even though I really did like the attention.

"I'm not babying you," he said, helping me stand. "I'm taking care of my wife. There's a huge difference between the two."

He undid the buckle on my belt, then undid the button and zipper, pulling them down slowly, making sure I was steady when he let go of me. Once they were down past my knees, he helped me sit again, then took them off the rest of the way. He pulled the blankets back on the bed, and I realized he'd made it up when he got up that morning, which impressed me more than he'd ever know.

After getting me up and into bed, he pulled the sheet and blanket up and over my lower half, then kissed my forehead again. I would never tire of that little thing he was doing.

"Be right back," he said, then went out the door.

Missy came in as he went out, and she said something to him, low so that only he could hear it. He nodded, looked back at me, then headed down the hall, presumably to get dinner going. She came into the room, looking both concerned and confused.

"What?" I asked, not wanting to try to guess what she had going on inside her head.

"I've never met anyone like him," she said. "I mean, Kenton is amazing, and I'm sure he'd be just as concerned as Alej is if what happened to you happened to me, but this is so amazing. I wasn't sure I was gonna like him, but he's proving quickly that he's a good guy."

"Yeah," I said, sighing a bit with relief. "I was afraid you were gonna complain."

"He's proven his worth," she said. "Besides, those enchiladas look amazing. Kenton's coming over after he finishes up at the office. His dad's being kind of a dick about something or other, and it's driving him nuts, so I think the distraction of good food, and watching Alej fawn all over you might do him some good."

"I'm sorry I'm such a pain," I said.

"On, no you don't," she admonished. "You didn't do this. That rat bastard at the school did. He's been a dick to you for entirely too long, and this was just the last straw. I say, live off Alej, and let him pay for everything."

"Missy," I said, my voice low so he didn't overhear. "I am not going to do that. I am not a gold digger, nor did I marry him because he's rich. I married him because I was drunk, but I'm staying with him because he's amazing. I will not be a kept woman."

"I'd keep you however you wanted," Alej said, and I snapped my eyes up to see him standing in the doorjamb, leaning against the frame, a sinful smile on his lips.

"I'm not doing that," I said, and it came out harsher than I planned. "I can't let you do that. I can take care of myself. I don't need someone to take care of me."

"I know that," he said, pushing off the frame and stalking over to the bed. "I meant that I would take care of you. I will do whatever you want, but you will accept some help from me for right now. I have some things in motion already because of this issue, and I want to make sure that you're cared for. If you try to argue, I'll win. I am a stubborn man, so don't try to fight me on this."

"Alej—"

"Nope," he said, shutting me down. "You are to rest, and you can't do that if you're arguing with me. We can talk about it later, but for right now, I want you to just relax. Let me take care of you. Please."

The look on his face told me I wasn't gonna win this argument, and it didn't really matter right that moment, anyway, so I smiled at him.

"For now," I said. "We'll table it. But we will have a talk about this kind of thing when I'm better. Promise you'll be open-minded, please?"

"I promise," he said. "We have about fifteen minutes or so until dinner is ready. Do you have a tray or something I can use to bring your food to you?"

"I can get up," I said.

"Nope," both Missy and Alej said in unison, and I honestly kinda loved that they were on the same page.

"You were instructed to rest," Alej said. "It's my job to take care of you. Now, do you have something?"

"I think there's something in her closet," Missy said, getting up and going to the door across the room.

She slid it open, and rummaged around in the darkened interior, then gave a triumphant chant before pulling out a sort of short-legged tray.

"This should work," she said, turning, and handing it to him.

"Perfect," he said, taking it from her, and kissing me again, before walking out of the room.

"You two are terrible," I said, but I was smiling.

"We're just taking care of you," she said. "I guess I should be thankful you're not milking it for all it's worth."

"Yeah," I said. "I don't do that sort of thing."

"Do you not remember junior year?"

"Don't remind me of that," I said.

I heard the doorbell, and Missy got up.

"That's Kenton," she said. "Stay in bed and don't get up. Promise me."

"I promise," I said. "And I'm not an invalid."

"You almost fell getting into the wheelchair," she reminded me.

"Fine," I replied. "Go let your man in. I need to get this bra off, though, so come back without him, and help me."

"Hang on," she said, then went to the door. "Alej," she called.

"I already let him in," I heard him say.

"Thanks," she said. "Helping Hailey with her clothes, so stay out there."

"You know that's just gonna make Alej want to come in, right?"

"He better not," she said, and I laughed, then held my head.

"Come on," she said, helping me to lean forward, so she could unhook my bra.

Once she'd done that, we pulled the straps from over my shoulders, and out the sleeves of my tank top, before pulling the whole bra through the hole to give me the relief I desperately needed. There was nothing better than taking your bra off after a long day, and today had been more than long enough.

Chapter Eighteen

Alejandro...

"Hey," I said as I pulled the door open.

"Alej," Kenton said as he stepped into the house. "How's she doing?"

"She's doing as well as can be expected," I said. "She's wobbly and has a concussion. Add the stitches and giant handprint on either of her cheeks, and it's ugly. Doc said she'd probably end up with black eyes, and lots of swelling."

"I guess you get to test that 'in sickness' thing early on," he said.

"Yeah," I replied. "Not how I wanted to do it, but here we are."

"Is she okay with all the attention?"

"Not at all," I said. "She's fighting everything."

"Alej," Missy called from the bedroom.

"I already let him in," I said.

"Thanks," she said. "Helping Hailey with her clothes, so stay out there."

"Like that's not an invitation for you," he said.

"Yeah," I said. "But I know she needs the help and is probably pretty uncomfortable. I'll let this go and take care of the rest of her clothes after dinner."

The buzzer on the stove went off, and I headed into the kitchen.

"Smells good," he said.

"My mama's famous enchiladas," I said, pulling them from the oven.

"That smells good," Missy said as she came down the hall.

"Is she ready for dinner?" I asked.

"She needs to go to the bathroom," she said. "I tried to help, but I think she needs you."

"On it," I said, having set the first tray onto the stovetop. "Put that other tray in, and set the timer for twenty minutes, please?"

"Got it," Kenton said, switching places with me, as I headed down the hall.

"It's stupid," Hailey said, as I walked into her room.

She was sitting on the edge of the bed, feet on the floor, but her hand was on her head. She looked over to me, and her eyes were full of tears again.

"Hey, baby," I said, going to her. "Heard you need your big, strong husband to help you out."

"I can't believe I can't even walk to the bathroom by myself," she said. "I hate this."

"I know," I said. "And you'll be fine when you are. Until then, though, I am your servant, here to do your bidding."

"Can you make my head stop pounding?" she asked as I helped her to her feet.

"If I could, I would," I said.

She swayed a bit, but I held her up, not too tight, but just enough that she knew I was there. She smiled up at me once she got her balance, then started to shuffle toward the bathroom.

"This has got to be the sexiest thing you've ever done," she said, sarcasm dripping from her words.

"There's nowhere I'd rather be," I replied.

We took the walk slowly, taking a few minutes for her to cross the small space between her bed and the bathroom. I didn't turn the light on, since she'd had issues with it earlier, and walked her over to the toilet.

"Get those panties off," I said.

"Wish it were for something way more fun than this," she replied, but shoved her underwear down.

Lowering her to the seat, I got her situated, then stood back.

"Want me to wait outside?"

"Yeah," she said, looking at her hands on her lap.

I kissed her forehead, then stepped out of the bathroom, closing the door so that it was just next to the jam, but not actually latched. While she did her business, I went back to the kitchen, and started plating up the enchiladas. I'd washed the tray off, as it had some dust on it from living in the back of her closet for a while. When I was making dinner, I'd also found all of her dishes, so I knew where everything was when I started cooking. The table had been set for two, and I had two plates on the tray, one for me and one for Hailey. I grabbed the silverware that I'd wrapped into a paper towel with me when I went back into the bedroom to check on her.

"You ready?" I asked through the closed door.

"Not yet," she said.

"Okay," I replied. "Don't try to get up on your own. I don't want you to fall."

"I know," she said, and sounded annoyed.

I set the silverware on the nightstand, then headed back to the kitchen. Kenton and Missy had finished plating the first tray of food, and they'd also thrown the salad together. I'd completely forgotten I'd picked that up at the store, so I was thankful they found it.

"I wasn't sure what you guys liked for dressing," I said. "I just got a couple of different ones, hoping something would work."

"These are great," Missy said. "Hailey actually loves this one, so you did good."

I had pulled out some small bowls for the salad when I was first getting things set up, so I grabbed a couple of those and filled them with the salad fixings, taking them into the room with me when I went back down the hall.

"Alej?" Hailey said from the bathroom.

"It's me," I said. "You ready?"

"Yeah," she said, and I opened the door.

Her smile was pitiful, but also adorable, and I walked over to her.

"I already flushed, but we need to light a candle or something in here," she said, not looking at me.

"I'll get that after I get you back to bed," I said. "Up you go."

I had my hands under her armpits and helped her stand. She'd grabbed her panties as she did so and pulled them up along the way. I helped her to the sink, where she turned the water on, and washed her hands, drying them on the towel that hung on the small ring next to the vanity mirror.

When she turned to walk back, she tripped on her feet, and if I'd not been holding her, she would have gone down. I scooped her up, and carried her back to the bed, not wanting to risk her falling at all.

"You don't have to treat me like a child," she said.

"I'm not," I said.

"You also don't need to treat me like I'm some porcelain doll or something, either," she added. "I'm not gonna break."

"Your face is contradicting you," I said. "Besides, I like doing this. Makes me feel strong and useful."

She smiled up at me from where I'd placed her on the bed. I pulled the covers up, tucking them around her waist, then handed her the bowl with the salad.

"Missy said you liked this kind of dressing," I said, holding the bottle out to her.

"How did you know?" she asked.

"Just a guess," I replied. "To be honest, though, I bought like five different kinds."

"Please tell me you got a blue cheese one," she said. "Missy loves that kind."

"I did," I said. "I wasn't gonna, because it definitely isn't my thing, but something told me to grab it."

She took the dressing after I'd opened it, and poured a generous amount onto her salad, then handed the bottle back to me. I set it on the nightstand and went to pour my own when I heard the buzzer from the oven.

"Be right back," I said, setting the dressing down next to hers.

When I got to the kitchen, Kenton had already pulled the second tray out of the oven.

"Anything else going in?" he asked.

"Nope," I replied. "Just the two things. Dessert is frozen. Speaking of which, I should probably pull it out so it has time to thaw a little bit so we can cut it."

Missy opened the freezer and squealed.

"Oh my God," she said. "Hailey," she shouted down the hall. "He's never allowed to leave you."

"I take it you approve," I said with a smile.

"It's her absolute favorite," Kenton said.

The cheesecake came out of the freezer, and Missy set it on the counter next to the tray with dinner for Hailey and me. I took the tray and headed back to the bedroom, wanting to spend time with her, just the two of us.

"What was she going on about?" she asked when I came in.

"I got cheesecake," I said.

"Oh, no," she said. "You'll never be allowed to go anywhere again."

"Sounds like it," I said. "Not that I'm planning on going anywhere. Except when I'm traveling for work. Speaking of which," I said, setting the tray over her lap on the bed. "What are you gonna do when I have to go to spring training?"

"You still have two weeks, right?" she asked.

"Yeah," I said. "Well, more like fifteen days, but yeah."

"I'll be fine by then," she said.

"The doctor..."

"Was an asshole," she said.

I was poised to sit on the other side of the bed, salad in hand having poured my own dressing on it, and just stared.

"What?" she asked.

"I didn't know you realized it," I said.

"Oh, yeah," she said. "He acted all high and mighty when he was trying to use these stupid big words to tell me I hit my head hard enough to rattle my brain. Going on and on with all of these medical terms like he was a genius or something. I said to him that I had a concussion, which I'd had before, and that I knew how to handle it. I also asked him to try to talk to me like I wasn't stupid, because I was well educated, and had more than a basic knowledge of the human body, having taken anatomy when I was in college when I first started. I was going to be a doctor, but the cost to get the degree wasn't something I wanted to deal with. Besides, I loved kids, and really wanted to teach, so I switched majors halfway through."

"You were gonna be a doctor?" I asked.

"Yeah," she said. "Specifically, a pediatrician, because kids."

"I think I love you more now than I did before," I said, then realized what words had just come out of my mouth and froze.

She'd stopped moving, too, a fork full of enchilada halfway to her mouth. I looked at her and she looked at me, both of us with that deer-in-the-headlights look on our faces, and I didn't know what to do. Then she smiled.

"You love me?" she asked.

"Yeah," I said. "I just wasn't sure if it was too soon."

"We're married," she said. "Probably should have happened before now."

"Well," I said as I settled on the bed next to her. "We've kind of been doing this whole thing backward, or at least not in the most traditional order, so it makes sense we haven't said it."

"I love you, too," she said with a big grin. "I didn't want to say it first, 'cause I felt like we weren't there, yet. I'm glad you said it, though."

"Me, too," I said. "I've been thinking it for a while, too, so glad it wasn't as awkward as I thought it was at first."

"Are you sure you're okay with this whole thing?" she asked. "I mean, it's been three days, maybe less, since we met, and we're all sorts of twisted up."

"I've never been known to do things the right way," I said. "Well, except for getting married. That I did right the very first time."

Her fork had gone back down to the plate, and she was just looking at me. I wanted to just throw the food on the floor, and make love to her, but I didn't want to screw anything up with her head and shit.

"I want you," she said.

"You've got me," I replied.

"No," she said. "I mean, I really want you."

"Oh," I said as her meaning dawned on me. "I want you, too. But I think you should eat. It'll be time to take a pain pill in a little bit, and they said not to have you take it on an empty stomach. After dinner, and your pain pill, if you're feeling up to anything, we can see. I just don't want to hurt you."

"I promise I won't break," she said.

"I know," I replied. "But I wouldn't know what to do with myself if I hurt you more. I just found you, and I plan to spend a hundred years with you. I think we can take it a bit slow for one night."

"As long as you don't stop altogether," she said. "Cause I will throw hands if you do."

"So feisty," I said.

"You ain't seen nothing yet," she replied, picking her fork up again, and stuffing a bite into her mouth.

The way she pulled the fork out, letting it come out slowly, her eyes getting hooded as she let the flavors explode in her mouth, it was like she was trying to kill me. Then she moaned, low and slow, and I couldn't even focus. All I wanted to do was watch her enjoy the food I'd made. When she'd finished the bite, she looked at me and smiled, knowing exactly what she was doing.

"You should eat," she said, pointing her fork at the one in my hand. "Your salad is gonna wilt."

I'd never eaten so fast in all my life, not even tasting the food I shoved in my mouth. All I could think about was her, and that's all I wanted. It was what I was hungry for, thirsty for, all that I desired. She had become the most important thing to me, and today I'd realized I never wanted to be without her. Come hell or high water, I was going to keep her.

Chapter Nineteen

Hailey...

The food was so good, but my head was pounding by the time it was time for another pain pill. As much as I wanted to, I knew I couldn't do anything with Alej. My brain was just being stupid, and the swirling and swimming of the room every time I shifted, just pissed me off.

He'd been so attentive, serving me in bed. Hell, even the fact that he'd gone out and gotten groceries, then made dinner, all before he came to the hospital to get me, was more than any other guy had done for me. By the time the food had been put away, after I ate way more than I'd ever eaten in my life, I was dying from pain.

"Here you go," he said, handing me a pill from the little orange bottle from the hospital.

He also handed me a glass of water and waited while I took the pill before setting the water on the nightstand. I wanted him to hold me, but I was afraid to lay down. Even the thought of it made my head hurt.

Missy and Kenton had headed to the guest room at the other end of the house, which I was thankful the house had been set up that way. They'd all done up the dishes, putting the leftovers into the fridge for tomorrow, and however long they lasted. The food was absolutely amazing, and I was thrilled to know that my husband could cook. It still felt weird to call him that, but it was the truth.

"Let's get you up and your bladder emptied before we settle down," he said, pulling the covers back from me, and helping me to move to the edge of the bed.

I held his hand as he helped me up, and I felt steadier than I had earlier. That made him smile at me, and just walk with me to the bathroom instead of holding my hand the whole way. When I turned to sit on the toilet, he stood and watched me, and I felt all sorts of awkward.

"Sorry," he said. "I just don't want you to fall."

"It's just weird," I said.

"As soon as you're down, I'll go out," he said. "Promise."

I pushed my panties down, and eased myself onto the toilet, landing a little harder than I intended, which caused him to hover. I glared at him, though, and he stepped back, then went out of the bathroom, and shut the door.

Thankfully, I only had to pee this time. God, it was so awful to have him walk into the bathroom, and have to help me off the toilet after I'd taken a shit. I don't know that I'd ever been so embarrassed before in my life. He'd been so nice about it, helping me stand and wash my hands, not saying anything about the stank I'd left in the room. Just polite and kind. Yeah, I really did love him. And he obviously loved me, too, if he could do that, and not mention of it.

I flushed the toilet after wiping, and he opened the door, standing there in just his boxers and nothing else. God, he looked delicious, and I wanted him so bad it wasn't funny. He helped me up, turned me to the sink, and waited while I washed my hands. When I opened the cabinet over the sink, I pulled out my toothbrush and the paste, wetting the brush before putting some of the minty paste onto it.

"I have spare brushes under the sink," I said. "If you don't have one, that is."

"I do," he said. "I'll wait until you're settled, then will come in, and take care of that sort of stuff for me."

"Okay," I said, then shoved the brush into my mouth.

I did my duty, getting each tooth as clean as possible while staring into his dark eyes. The way he was standing, just behind me, I could feel the heat coming off him. I could smell his cologne, the way it mixed with his own scent, and it just sort of helped me to relax. When I was done, I spit the suds out, leaning forward to get some water in my mouth when everything went sideways.

"I got you," he said, his arms around my waist.

"I need to rinse," I said.

"Sit on the toilet," he said, helping me over there.

He walked out into the room and returned with the glass from the side of the bed, handing it to me. The way my bathroom was situated, the toilet was right next to the tub, so I was able to rinse my mouth out, and spit it out into the tub without getting up off the pot. When I was done, I handed the glass back to him and he set it on the counter by the sink, taking my toothbrush from me and placing it back into the spot inside the cabinet where I kept it.

"Ready?" he asked, and I nodded, just enough to answer, and not so much as to make everything go sideways again. "Let's get you settled."

Helping me up, he walked with me to the bed, which wasn't that far, but seemed entirely too far for me to navigate on my own. I sat on the edge and he helped lift my feet under the covers, then he pulled them up and kissed my forehead.

After he was sure I was set, he went back to the bathroom and brushed his own teeth, doing a much better job at it than I did. When he came back, he smiled at me, and I melted. He walked around the bed to the other side and slid in beside me. With the light on his side the only one on, he was silhouetted. He reached over and pulled me to him, and I slid down some so that I was flatter on the bed.

By looking him in the eyes as I moved, my brain didn't go all over the place, and I was actually comfortable lying down. He looked at me questioningly, but I smiled at him, and scooted closer. His arms were around me, and his body was warm against mine. He pressed his lips to my forehead, and I closed my eyes, and to my surprise, the room didn't sway, didn't swirl, didn't do anything. It was like he was my anchor to keeping me safe in the harbor of his arms. I drifted off to the rhythm of his heartbeat, falling into the blackness beyond consciousness.

"Morning," Alej said as I rolled over. "Are you hungry?"

I looked up, and he was standing next to my bed, completely dressed, and freshly showered, if his wet hair was any indication.

"Starving," I said, then coughed.

My mouth had that cotton taste again, and I wasn't sure why my face and head hurt so much. Then reality came crashing back, and I sucked in a breath.

"I've got your meds," he said, holding the bottle. "And fresh water. I also made pancakes, if you want some. There are eggs and bacon as well."

"Where did all the food come from?" I asked.

"I went grocery shopping yesterday," he said. "Got everything we would need for the next few days so you wouldn't have to worry about it."

"Who are you?"

"Your wonderful, loving husband," he said.

"Yeah," I said. "But how are you so absolutely perfect?"

"Oh, baby," he said, and it was sweet if not condescending. "I'm far from perfect, and it'll show up at the most inopportune time. For now, though, I got you."

"I need to go to work," I said.

"Nope," he replied. "Doc said at least the rest of the week off. Missy called the school this morning before she left for work and told them. They want a copy of the doctor's note, but it can wait until next week. They've got a sub in already, so you're covered."

I sat up, my bladder screaming at me, and flipped the covers back, swinging my legs around to sit on the floor. I waited for the room to roll, but it didn't.

"You good?" he asked.

"I think so," I said, looking up at him. "Could use a little help getting up and to the bathroom, though. Just in case."

"At your service," he said, and I smiled.

"Yeah," I said as he helped me stand. "I'm gonna need some of that, too."

"Let's get you fed, first," he said as I walked to the bathroom.

I did my business, without an audience, thankfully, and flushed before washing my hands. When I came out of the bathroom, he was there, just waiting patiently, holding out a pill, and a glass of water.

"Do you want breakfast in bed?" he asked after I'd taken the pill. "Or would you like to head to the table?"

"Let's go to the table," I said. "But I need to get some clothes on. It's cold."

"Yeah," he said. "The furnace shows that it's off during the day. My guess is you set it up that way. I wasn't sure how to change it, and didn't want to mess it up."

"I'm surprised Missy didn't fix it," I said. "She usually does that if someone's gonna be home."

"She was a bit rushed," he said.

I was standing in front of my dresser, just staring at it, not really sure what I needed to do. My brain didn't want to function properly, and that just pissed me off.

"Pants?" he asked, and I looked at him. "Where are your pants?"

"Oh," I said, then pulled the drawer open.

I pulled out a pair of leggings, then went to the closet to grab an oversized sweater down from the shelf before walking back to the bed. He took my clothes from me, and set them down, then squatted in front of me to help me put my leggings on. I used his shoulders to hold myself steady as I did it.

I pulled the sweater on, not bothering with a bra since I wasn't going anywhere, and we headed out of the bedroom. Considering how out of it I was yesterday, I was glad I was stable now. It would be terrible if my balance had stayed all wonky like that. The closer I got to the kitchen, the more I could smell the food, and my stomach growled in hunger.

"You hiding a dragon in your belly?" he asked.

"I don't think so," I said. "But whatever is in there, it's starving, so we best get to eating."

"My pleasure," he said and pulled a chair out from the table.

I sat down and he went to the kitchen, opening the oven and pulling out a tray that was loaded with pancakes, and another that had a heaping pile of scrambled eggs next to an equally huge stack of bacon on it. I didn't know who he thought he was feeding, because there was no way I could eat that much. He'd set the table for the two of us, and set the trays onto towels he'd placed in the center. There was syrup and jam, as well as butter and the salt and pepper for the eggs, along with a bottle of tabasco sauce.

"You want to serve yourself?" he asked.

"Sure," I said. "I think I can handle it. Would you make a coffee for me?"

He turned from the counter with a mug that was steaming in his hand and smiled.

"Guess I read your mind," he said.

"Thanks," I replied, and saw that it already had cream in it, and looked to be about the right amount, too.

It was weird that he'd made it right. I took a sip, and it was absolutely perfect, so I looked at him, confused.

"I saw you only put creamer in it at the airport," he explained. "I guessed at the amount of creamer, figuring I'd err on the side of too little, but tried to make it match the color yours had the other day."

"Can I say I'm a little freaked out right now?" I asked.

"Did I overstep?"

"No," I said. "It's just weird that you can get this so right without even really knowing me. It's like we were made to be together."

"That's what I've been thinking all along," he said, kissing the top of my head before settling down with his own mug.

"It's weird, isn't it?" I asked.

"I mean," he said after taking a sip of his coffee. "It's not traditional, that's for sure."

"Oh, that I already knew," I said. "I meant this. Between us. How quickly we connected. Is it weird?"

"I kinda like it," he said. "But, speaking of traditional, my mama is pretty upset she hasn't met you, yet."

"How does she know?" I asked.

"Oh yeah," he said. "I forgot you didn't know. Someone posted a video of us coming out of the church. It's clearly us, and it shows us kissing, your ring very prominent on the side of my face."

"Oh, God," I said, closing my eyes. "Just what I fucking need. A scandal to go along with my shitty boss firing me."

"You're not fired," he said.

"Oh, Dick would disagree," I said.

"He's been replaced," he said.

"Wait, what?"

"Missy asked about it when she called the school this morning," he said. "She was told that he was no longer allowed on the property, and would be facing disciplinary action, as well as a sanction, and may end up losing his job."

"Seriously?"

"Yup," he said, stuffing a fork full of eggs into his mouth. "Eat up," he said after he'd swallowed.

I looked at my plate, and it just didn't look appetizing any longer. I should have just taken the hit, not kicked up such a fuss. But then I thought that it wasn't my fault he decided to be his namesake, an absolute dick. No, he started this by trying to bully me, and that was one thing I could never stay quiet about. Bullies were trash and needed to be put in their place. But getting him to lose his job? That was not what I wanted. I just wanted him to listen to me, and to not be so overbearing and horrible. He broke my phone for no good reason, hurt me physically, and all over something that wasn't even a thing.

"Hey," Alej said, rubbing his hand on my shoulder. "You okay?"

"I'm just pissed," I said. "I feel bad that he might lose his job, but it's his own fault, so I'm mad that I feel bad. Does that make sense?"

"It does," he said. "It's hard to watch someone else deal with the consequences of their own actions, especially when you were involved in their issues coming to light. From what you've said, he's not exactly a liked person."

"I mean," I hedged, not really wanting to talk bad about the guy.

"So," he said. "He chose to try to put you in your place or something, and you weren't having it. Am I getting the situation right?"

"Basically," I said.

"Then he chose to go over the top," he said. "Did you strike first?"

"No," I said, incredulous that he'd even ask.

"Didn't think so," he said. "Which means he fucked around, and now he's gonna find out."

"That's one of my favorite sayings," I said. "And when you put it in that context, I guess you're right. Still, is it right that he loses his livelihood over it?"

"If someone did that to Missy," he began. "Told her she was going to have to have whatever happened to you happen to her, and she said she wanted a witness, which is what you said you'd asked for, right?"

"Right," I said. "He was trying to have a disciplinary meeting without allowing me representation."

"Okay," he said. "This guy tried to go against the rules, then blocked you or pushed you or whatever."

"First he blocked me," I said. "Then, when I went to dial 911, he slapped the phone out of my hand. I told the secretary to call the police and picked up my phone. That's when he grabbed my phone and threw it against the wall, then shoved me down. After that, he slapped me, and I hit my face on the wheel of the chair. It all happened so fast."

"Hey," he said, turning, and pulling me to him. "I shouldn't have made you talk about it."

"That's not it," I said. "These tears are me being pissed at him. It's stupid, but I cry when I'm mad."

"Not stupid at all," he said. "I just don't want to make you relive it."

"You're right," I said. "He brought all this on himself. I need to stop feeling sorry for him, and just let him lie in the bed he's made."

"There's my girl," he said, kissing me hard. "You are one feisty woman, and I wouldn't have it any other way."

"You taste good," I said, licking the syrup from my lips he'd left from his pancakes.

"So do you," he replied. "And as much as I'd love to taste every bit of you, you need to eat. Those meds will tear your stomach up if you don't."

"Okay," I said. "But then maybe after, we can use that syrup for something else."

"You're a vixen," he said. "And you're all mine."

I dove into my plate, the promise of all sorts of things floating in my head, and my desire ratcheting up with each bite.

Chapter Twenty

Alejandro...

We didn't end up using the syrup, with me having convinced her that it would be entirely too sticky and hard to clean up, but we did have a delightfully calm lovemaking session after breakfast. Then, I helped her shower, taking care not to get her stitches wet in the process. After that, I got her bandage changed on said stitches before placing another one onto it, adding the antibiotic cream the hospital gave to me.

She'd wanted to do a bunch of stuff, but she was exhausted, so I tucked her into bed, and stayed by her side until she fell asleep. Then, I got up, and got some stuff cleaned up around the house. It wasn't my house, but I knew how to wash dishes, put food away, clean up after myself. I wasn't one of those guys who needed a woman to take care of him, and I wouldn't be that guy to Hailey. She was very capable, but if I could lighten her load, I would.

Once the house was clean, I decided to call my *abuelita*, and tell her why we didn't invite her to the wedding. It wasn't gonna be the truth, that's for sure. How do you tell your grandmother that you married the pretty girl just to fuck her? Not the kind of conversation I wanted to have with my eighty-five-year-old grandmother.

"Nieto," she said when she answered my video call.

"Abuelita," I replied.

"Your mama told me you were married," she said.

"I did get married," I replied. "She's wonderful. I think you'll like her."

"Rosie sent me the picture," she said, and I was confused.

"What picture?" I asked.

"The one she found on the internets that you kids use," she said.

"Oh," I said. "Yeah, we didn't share that. Someone put that up without our permission. I didn't want you to find out that way. I wanted to call and tell you."

"I don't mind so much," she said. "I just want you to be happy. Are you happy?"

"Very much so," I said. "She's everything I've ever wanted in a wife. She's beautiful, smart, a hard worker, and just all-around wonderful."

"You sound like your Abuelo when we first married," she said. "He was so silly in love with me. I'm glad you found someone who makes you silly in love."

"Me, too," I said.

"Oh," she said. "Is that the blushing bride?"

I turned around, and Hailey was standing at the end of the hallway.

"Hey, baby," I said. "You okay?"

"I woke up and you were gone," she said. "I heard you talking and wondered what was going on. I'll go and let you chat."

"No, no," I said. "Come and meet my *abuelita.*"

"Are you sure?" she asked, touching the bandage on her face.

"You're beautiful," I said. "Now, come on."

I was sitting on the couch, and motioned for her to sit next to me so my grandmother could meet her.

"Oh dear," *Abuelita* said. "Who has hurt you? Alejandro Luis de la Garza, what have you done to your wife?"

"It wasn't him," Hailey said. "I got hurt at work. He's been wonderful taking care of me."

"He better not hurt you," *Abuelita* said. "If he does, I'll come up there and beat him. He knows I will, too."

"Don't worry," I said. "The person who hurt her is in custody. I'm playing nursemaid until I have to go to work."

"That's my good boy," she said. "It's nice to meet you. My name is Carmen, but you can call me *Abuelita* if you'd like."

"It's nice to meet you," Hailey said. "I'm Hailey."

"What a beautiful name," she said. "Alej said you were a hard worker. What do you do?"

"I'm a teacher," she said. "I teach kindergarten at the local school."

"Oh, what a wonderful job," she said. "You must really like children."

"I do," my wife said. "Eventually, I'd like to have a couple. Not yet, but eventually."

"You need to enjoy just being a wife for a while," *Abuelita* said. "You know, the joy of knowing your husband, and the two of you enjoying the time you have together."

"Alej has made that part easy," she said, smiling at me.

"I'll let you go," my grandmother said. "It's good to see you, Nieto. Good to meet you, Hailey."

"Bye, *Abuelita*," I said, then disconnected the call.

"I thought your grandmother was going to be upset," Hailey said.

"My mama is upset, and she's the one who said *Abuelita* would be," I said. "Honestly, I wasn't sure."

"Is that why you called her?"

"Yeah," I said. "I didn't want to wake you, but I had done everything I could without talking to you, and didn't want to do something that would cause any friction, so figured a call to my grandmother would be a good thing to do."

"I'm glad I got to meet her," she said. "Even if it was just over the phone. And even though I look like a train wreck."

"You're beautiful," I said, kissing her temple.

"Whoa," she said, looking at my phone. "Is it really that late?"

I looked as well and saw it was late afternoon.

"I guess so," I said. "You slept longer than I thought you would."

"Because of the drugs," she said. "I'm never good on medication, especially anything that causes drowsiness. They knock me the fuck out."

"How do you feel?"

"Fine," she said. "But I'm still tired."

"Probably gonna be that way for a while," I said.

"I don't want to take any more pain meds," she said.

"Doc said to not let the pain get ahead of you," I replied.

"The nurse said I could do ibuprofen or Tylenol, too," she said.

"Fine," I said. "How about you take the prescription ones for the rest of today, and tomorrow you can switch to the over-the-counter type?"

"Okay," she replied.

"Hungry?" I asked.

"No," she said. "I just wanted to be with you."

I hugged her to me, kissing her head, and wondered how I was going to be able to leave when it was time for me to go to spring training. I guess I'd just have to figure that out when the time came. Until then, though, I planned to spoil my wife with as much attention as she could handle.

Some of it would be taking her to her doctor's appointment the next day and being with her when she went back to the school. I'd also contact the detective on her case to see if there was anything they needed from her that I could handle. If I could take things off her plate, I would.

I was also going to make love to her as many times as her and my body could handle. We had to stock up since I'd be gone for a month and a half before coming back to play our opening day.

145

"Opening day," I said, an idea dawning on me. She looked up at me. "You should come to opening day. Not with the kids and stuff, but just you. You can sit in the stands behind home plate with the other family members of the team and cheer me on. What do you think?"

Chapter Twenty-One

Hailey...

"You should come to opening day," he said. "Not with the kids and stuff, but just you. You can sit in the stands behind home plate with the other family members of the team and cheer me on. What do you think?"

"I do want to watch you play," I said. "But isn't it during the week or something?"

"Let me look," he said, then fiddled with his phone to look. "Here," he said, showing me his phone. "It's a Thursday."

"Yeah," I said, looking up at him. "That's not gonna work. I have to teach that day."

"Could you get a sub?"

"I could," I said. "But I'm already gonna be out for so long with this thing." I motioned to my cheek and the damage that had been done there. "Besides. Don't you want to concentrate on the game? Wouldn't I just be a distraction for you?"

"I'm gonna be thinking about you either way," he said. "It makes sense that you're there with me so I can focus just on the game, knowing I'll be in your arms sooner, rather than later."

"I still think it would be weird to be sitting there without anyone I knew," I said.

"So, invite Missy and Kenton," he said. "I can get tickets for them, too."

"I don't know," I said, still not sure I'd even feel like going. "I mean, my face is still gonna be messed up. Do you really want me to show up at your game looking like a freak? And what do I wear? I mean, I don't want to disrespect you or disappoint you or anything."

"Baby," he said, kissing my temple. "Nothing you do would ever disappoint me. I want you there because I love you and want to share you with the world."

"Yeah," I said. "Not willing to be shared."

"Not like that," he said. "I mean, I want my baseball family to meet you. I know Nick is gonna be pissed if you don't come. I can introduce you to his girlfriend, too. She's really nice."

"I'm just not so sure," I said.

"Why don't we table it for now," he said. "We can figure that out later. For now, though, what do you want to do?"

"Go back to bed," I said. "I want you to rock my world. None of this gentle shit, either. I want you to fuck me so hard I can't stand."

"I don't want to hurt you," he said.

I shifted on the couch, sliding my leg over his lap, and climbing on him. I put my hands on either side of his face, and looked into his deep, soulful eyes, and just kissed him. Pressing my body against his, my tongue seeking entrance into his mouth. When he opened for me, I slid inside, deepening the kiss to show him the passion I had running through my body.

He had his hands on my hips as I worked my body along his length, rubbing my pussy on him. It didn't take long for him to start getting hard, and it just pushed me that much further, grinding against him as his hands dug into my skin, pressing me down against him. I was in pajama pants, but didn't have anything else on underneath. My oversized tee shirt covered everything enough to be decent for the video call with his grandmother, but now it allowed him to easily access the skin underneath.

When he slid his hands off my hips and went under my shirt, taking a tit in each one, squeezing and massaging them in time with my grinding, I had to pull back and take a shuddering breath in.

"Oh, God," I whispered.

"You like that?" he asked.

"God, yes," I moaned, still keeping my movement along him somewhat steady.

He flicked his thumb over my nipple, and I arched into it, pressing my body toward his hand, my head going further back as he played me like some damn instrument. I could feel myself climbing, higher and higher, reaching for the apex where I could tumble into oblivion, and forget the rest of the world that was outside our two bodies.

Abruptly, he pulled his hands away. I whined, and looked down at him, confused as to why he'd stopped. That's when the door opened, and I whipped my head around to see Missy coming in.

"Sorry," she said when she saw us. "I can go."

"It's fine," I said. "How was work?"

"I swear," she said, hooking her keys onto the pegs we had by the door. "That manager is going to end up with a sexual harassment suit one of these days."

"What did he do now?" I asked.

"You remember Becca?" she asked, and I nodded. "Well, she's pregnant. She's been hiding it from work because she doesn't want any fanfare or anything. She's actually almost seven months along, and no one knew."

"Really?" I asked.

"Yeah," she said, hanging her coat up with her purse. "I guess good old Dale decided to out her to everyone with a big old surprise celebration. He got everything set up in one of the less used conference rooms, then sent an email out to everyone to come up for it. We all walked into blue and pink balloons, a cake, chocolate fountain, the whole nine yards. There were a bunch of wrapped gifts sitting on a side table. Everyone was just looking around, trying to figure out what was going on. When she walked in, he shouted his congratulations, and she turned right around."

"Oh, God," I said. "That's awful."

"But wait, there's more," she said, in that way those infomercials do. "I went to find her, and she was in the bathroom, crying in one of the stalls. I told her I was there, asked her what she needed, and she just kept sobbing. Finally, after I got her calmed down some, she told me she was raped. Turns out, one of her exes found her when she was out on the town with a couple of friends from college. They'd invited him, trying to get them to rekindle some sort of romance or something."

"Why do people meddle?" I asked.

"Exactly," she said, getting increasingly animated. "Anyway, this guy sort of followed her to the bathroom and raped her. She didn't say anything, just went home out the back door. Guy had always wanted to fuck her, but she wouldn't put out. That's why they broke up. She wasn't interested in hooking up, and had been very careful about who she was with."

"Please tell me she filed charges," I said.

"She did," she replied. "But all the friends backed him. Said she was flirting with him, encouraging him, all that shit that people say when they blame the victim. God, I couldn't imagine being that person. Because no one would back her story about her not wanting to be with him, because she'd stayed when he showed up, and didn't just leave, they didn't file charges. She doesn't want to put him on the birth certificate because she doesn't want him to have access to the baby."

"Is she gonna keep it?" Alej asked.

"She is," Missy said. "She just isn't sure what to do with the whole parental part of it."

"I might be able to help," Alej said. "I've got access to lawyer referrals, so we can find someone to help her force him to terminate his rights."

"She doesn't want him to know," she said. "That's why she ran out as soon as she walked in. She's afraid someone's gonna post it on social media, and then someone will tell him. It's just nuts. Besides, she can't afford a lawyer, anyway. She's barely gonna be able to handle dealing with having a baby, and being a single mom."

"Let me handle that part of it," he said, and I looked at him. "What?" he asked, seeing my look.

"Why would you do this?" I asked. "You don't even know this girl."

"Let's just say that I've seen how these things go down," he said. "If it were you, or Missy, or my sister. I'd move heaven and earth to see things right. No woman should have to deal with a rapist, and especially if they think they can have access to their child. She should get ahead of it before anything gets out, though. We all know how those silly social media posts can turn out."

"Yeah," I said.

"You, sir, are a hero," Missy said.

"Just proof that not all heroes wear capes," I replied.

"It's not that big of a deal," he said.

"Says the man who married my best friend because she wouldn't sleep with him," Missy said, and I burst out laughing.

"Touché," he replied, a smile on his face.

"I'm starving," Missy said. "Are there any of those enchiladas left?"

"I was just gonna heat the tray up," Alej said. "Why don't you two chat while I get on that."

He was up and moving, before I even realized it, and he placed me down on the couch gently before kissing the top of my head. When he disappeared, Missy looked at me and smiled.

"You two really are good together," she said.

"I'm stupid happy," I said, though I kept my voice low. "We

traded the words. It was funny, but also adorable. He let it slip accidentally, and I just had to let him know."

"Already?" she asked. "Kenton and I waited over a year."

"I also met his grandmother," I said.

"How? When?"

"He video called her when I was napping," I said. "I came out, so he had me meet her. She's really nice, and she knows what's what."

"How did she know about you guys?"

"Oh, yeah," I said, realizing that I hadn't told anyone. "Apparently, unbeknownst to either of us, someone took a video of us as we left the chapel. They caught us coming out, then kissing, and my ring was so obvious on my finger, that it was all very self-explanatory. I don't know who all knows, but his mom saw it, and sent it to his grandmother."

"It's out on social media?" she asked.

"Somewhere," I said. "I just wish it wasn't out there. I mean, I'm not embarrassed about it by any stretch of the imagination. I just wanted to tell people in my own time."

"Have you gotten any flack about it?" she asked.

"I haven't heard from anyone," I said. "To be fair, I've been a bit preoccupied with the whole face thing and my job. Alej says they can't fire me, but good old Dickhead said it, so I'm worried."

"Your job is safe," she said. "When I called them this morning, they had already gotten a sub for you for the rest of the week and said that if you needed more time before you came back, they'd understand."

"I forgot you called," I said. "Thank you for that."

"Of course," she said. "Why wouldn't I?"

"Still," I said. "I guess I should check my phone and see what is going on. Not like I have any family to tell or anything, except you guys, and you all know."

"I'm just sad we didn't get to do a bachelorette party for you," she said.

"Considering how well yours turned out," I said. "Maybe that's a good thing."

She laughed, and I was glad to see she was looking better.

"Seriously, though," she said. "We can still do something, just us girls, if you want to."

"Why don't you wait until I leave for spring training," Alej said as he stepped from the kitchen. "She's gonna need extra help with everything when I'm gone, and I'd feel better knowing her friends were around to do that."

"Extra help?" Missy asked.

"He means with this whole thing," I said, gesturing to my face. "He seems to be under the impression that I'm incapable of dealing with it all."

"I just want to make sure you're taken care of," he said.

"We'll be around," she said. "Speaking of which."

"What?" I asked after she stopped talking.

"It's girl's night," she said. "It's Wednesday night."

"Oh, yeah," I said, realizing that everything that had happened had only taken a few days.

"I can cancel," she said.

"No," I said. "We'll make it work. It'll be fine."

"I can head to my house," Alej said.

"Nonsense," Missy said. "Everyone wants to meet you, and they would be more than a little angry if you weren't here."

"Besides," I said. "You can watch us be stupid. It'll be a new side of me. See if you really want to stick around or not."

"You're not getting rid of me that easily," he said. "Should I make something extra for dinner?"

"No," I said. "We usually just order pizza."

"I do have this whole tray of enchiladas in the oven," he said. "They're almost warm. Will that be enough? I can throw together the rest of the salad, too."

"They are gonna love you," Missy said just as someone knocked on the door.

"I'll get it," I said, pushing up off the couch.

"Sit," Alej said, his hand on my shoulder. "I'll play butler and chef for the evening."

"Thanks," I said as he went to the door. "This is gonna be fun."

"Hey, Hai..." Emma said. "You're not Hailey."

"I'm Alej," he said. "Her husband. And you are?"

"I'm Emma," she said. "Kelsey's coming, so don't close the door."

"Come on in," he said, opening the door wide to let my friends in.

"Well, ain't you a tall drink of water," Kelsey said as she came through the door.

"Oh, honey," Emma said as she saw me. "What the hell happened? Did you do this to her?"

The way Emma turned on Alej was both comical and ridiculous. She was short, even by our standards, so standing near my husband, she just looked so mini it was comical. The fact that she thought she could take him on, especially after she saw my face, and thinking it was him that did it, just made me laugh.

"He didn't do it," I said.

"No," he said. "I would never hurt her, intentionally or otherwise. In fact, I'm pretty pissed I couldn't keep that from happening to her."

"Well, good," Emma said. "I don't know what I'd do about it, but I'm glad I don't have to find out."

"Come sit down," I said to her. "You're being ridiculous. And Kelsey, keep your hands to yourself. He's mine."

I loved my friends dearly, but sometimes they could be a bit much. Alej shut the door, throwing the deadbolt, then headed back to the kitchen.

"So," Kelsey said as she plopped down on the couch. "Who's ordering tonight?"

"No one," Missy said. "We've got Mama... What's his last name?"

"de la Garza," I said.

"Okay," she said. "We've got Mama de la Garza's famous enchiladas for dinner. I think he's throwing together a salad, too."

"What about dessert?" Emma asked.

"Hey, babe," I called. "Is there any cheesecake left? Or did Missy eat it all?"

"I did not eat it all," she said, slapping my shoulder.

"I got two," Alej said.

"You're a good man," Kelsey said. "If you get tired of Hailey, I'm single."

"Kelsey Renee," I said, glaring at her.

"Oh, my," she said. "Not into sharing? How strange?"

"You are ridiculous," I said, but I was laughing.

It was actually really great to hang out with them again. It hadn't been that long, but still felt like months. I was really glad they all seemed to like Alej, though, 'cause that would have sucked if they didn't. Not that it would change anything, but still.

Chapter Twenty-Two

Alejandro…

They were all just these wild girls, watching horror films and eating, while gossiping about people from their jobs. It seemed weird that I wasn't at all turned off by Hailey being this juvenile in some aspects. Still, I let them do their thing and headed into the bedroom to check some emails and figure out what the plan would be when I headed to Florida.

When she finally climbed into bed, I had been asleep for a while, and she tried to be quiet. I'd been in that half-awake half-asleep stage where I heard things, but they didn't always register as what they actually were. Her cool body cuddled up to my warmer one, and I naturally wrapped my arms around her, pulling her back to my front, smelling the citrus from her shampoo, and feeling perfectly at home.

"Baby," she said, just barely above a whisper.

"Mmhmm," I hummed.

"I love you," she said, and it was soft, like she was trying to see if I was awake or not.

"Love you more," I said, knowing it wasn't necessarily true, but the sentiment was.

"Thank you for everything," she said with a sigh.

"Anytime," I replied, kissing her temple before drifting back off to the dreamland that had somehow become filled with everything there was to my beautiful wife.

When I woke, she was still cuddled next to me, pressing her ass into my crotch, causing my cock to stir and rise to the occasion. Much as I wanted to just take her right then and there, I wouldn't do that. I'd told her before, and I meant every word of it, when I said that consent was sexy to me.

I nuzzled behind her ear, pressing a kiss right there, and she sighed and shifted herself just enough that I could get better access to her neck. I pressed my lips there, sucking a little bit of skin in, but not enough to cause a hickey, because those weren't sexy to me. Sucking in a bigger breath, she sort of rolled away from me, and turned her head to look at me.

"Morning beautiful," I said, brushing hair from her face behind her ear.

"Good morning," she said.

"How do you feel?" I asked.

"Pretty good," she said. "Just a little sore, but not the good kind. Wanna fix that?"

"I don't want to hurt you," I said.

"Then love me," she said, her hand reaching over to me and caressing my cheek.

I kissed her palm, pressing my lips to it, then slid up her arm a bit, kissing my way along her body toward her lips.

"My breath is probably shit," she said.

"Don't care," I said, pressing my lips to hers.

She hadn't moved from her stomach, so I scooted up and over her, straddling her legs, and reaching up to grab a condom from her nightstand.

"You good with this?" I asked, and she shifted, shoving her ass more up in the air. "I'll take that as a yes."

I was already worked up, but did want to make sure she was

ready for me before shoving inside her. Sliding back a bit, I slid my hand between her thighs, and even though I had them trapped between my own, she managed to shift enough to present herself to me, as if she were a gift. To be fair, she was the most precious gift I'd ever received, and I wanted to show her how much I appreciated it.

With my fingers between her thighs, I slid them up her slit, and felt how wet she was, already anticipating me, which made me smile.

"You're very wet," I said.

"You're very slow," she replied, looking over her shoulder at me. "I'm ready, willing, and able. Just need you to get a move on."

"So needy," I said.

"I am," she said, sort of shifting her hips up and down.

"Tell me what you want," I said, leaning over her body, my arms on either side of her shoulders, cock pressed against her ass.

"Fuck me," she said.

"Try again," I said, grinding against her. "What do you want?"

"You," she said, looking at me as I was over her. "I want you. All the time, no matter where I am, no matter what I'm doing, I want you. Now, in the shower, on the kitchen table, on the couch. Anywhere I can have you, I want you. Please."

Her begging was what did me in, and I shifted up, using a hand to guide me to her entrance. I eased into her, slowly, enjoying how much this position made her tight around me. It was one of those things that men didn't always understand. Women didn't loosen up, at least not in the sense that men seemed to think. No, women adjusted to fit what worked for them. It was the reason they could push an entire baby through the same place a cock would fit, and both of those would result in entirely different feelings.

Position, on the other hand, was something that could give you a different sensation, for both partners. She was definitely liking this new position, too, as her breathing became quicker, her body moving in time with mine as I slid in and out of her. The way she was laying, there really wasn't much I could do, especially with my legs on either side of her thighs. I could move, but that would change things too much, so I kept up with what I was doing, as it was definitely getting the job done.

"Oh, oh," she moaned out, pressing her ass up against me, her pussy holding me hostage, unable to move.

"Come for me, baby," I said, and she did, her pussy spasming around my cock, squeezing it in a pulsating sensation.

When she found herself again, she relaxed, and I was able to move again. I pulled back, intent on continuing with the position we were in, but she pulled forward, and I was completely out of her.

"Lay down," she said, patting the bed next to her.

I shifted, pulling my leg from the other side of her, and lying down on the bed as she'd asked. She pressed her hands into the mattress and sat up, moving over to straddle me. She slid her pussy up and down my length, stroking me in this beautiful way, then she shifted her hips, her palms on my shoulders, and I reached between us to hold myself up so she could slide down.

The slow and seductive way she moved down me until our bodies met, me pressed fully inside her, was so calculated, so perfect. With her weight forward on her hands, she lifted her hips, sliding up to nearly the tip of my cock before settling back down again. Her eyes were locked on mine, such an intense blue that it seemed there was a fire behind them.

I let her take the lead, my hands on her hips, not to make her move, but to steady her as she rose and fell above me. As her breathing increased, she licked her lips, her eyes rolling back as she closed them, moving to the rhythm only she could hear. Watching her dance above me was something I would likely never tire of. She was so full of life in every way.

She was more than just a beautiful woman, she was honest, trustworthy, and all the things any man would want in a partner. Her work ethic, the way she went about what she did, was what kept me knowing I would stay with her for the long haul. I think we'd both had hesitations, especially when she woke up the next morning, not remembering our wedding. I wondered whether she'd want to redo it, to have the bigger, grander, more luxurious event. I somehow doubted it, but I would offer it to her, because either way, I would keep her.

My mother would want that big thing, that's for sure. She had always dreamed of big weddings for both me and my sister. Bella had done that, filling the church we grew up in with flowers and family from all over the world. It wasn't something I was interested in at all, but if Hailey wanted it, I would give it to her.

Her movements had sped up, and she was becoming a bit more erratic riding me as she was, so I concentrated on her body, moving my hands up to cup her tits, their more than a handful size meant I couldn't wrap my hand completely around them, but found that she didn't need that, anyway. Instead, I slid my thumb and first finger up to her nipple, teasing the bud that had formed, pinching and pulling on it in the way she liked. Her mouth fell open, her head going back, and she rode me hard and fast, punishing herself with my cock as she found another release.

When she collapsed on top of me, my arms went around her waist, holding her to my body, the sweat she'd built up from her work cool on my skin. Her breathing slowed, her body still pulsing around my own, as she settled into the here and now.

"Holy fuck," she said on a breath. "That was intense."

"You looked beautiful above me, dancing to your own beat," I said, running my hand up and down her back.

"Did you..."

She didn't finish the question, and I wasn't sure if it was because she was embarrassed, or what.

"I will," I said, knowing I could take care of myself if she wasn't up to it.

"Now I feel bad," she said.

"Don't," I replied, pushing her hair back as she pushed up and looked down at me.

"But..."

I shut her argument down by pulling her down to kiss her, pressing my tongue through her lips and sliding it along her own. I was hungry, not just for food, but for her. She filled every need I had, and still had more left over. I shifted my hips, pressing up and into her as I held her against me. Her legs were on either side of my hips, her pussy at the right angle so that I could keep this up and get over the edge.

She held me tight, her hands on my cheeks, and worked her hips to help me, shifting them up and down in time with my own thrusts. I had my hand at the base of her spine, pressing her as she shifted, and it didn't take long before I got the tingling sensation, the tightening of my balls, and with one final thrust, I came, filling the condom inside her.

When I pulled my mouth away, we were both panting, and her eyes were glazed over as she looked down at me, a smile pulling on the corner of her lips.

"I'm going to need to wake up to that every morning," she said, then pressed her lips to mine in a chaste kiss. "Like, every single morning."

"That's gonna be hard for me if I'm not here," I said. "Do you have a stand-in husband you'll be using?"

"What?" she asked. "No. Not at all."

"Just checking," I said, but was smiling.

"You're horrible," she said, pushing up to a sitting position.

"Only sometimes," I said.

"I gotta get up," she said, shifting off me.

I reached between us to hold the condom on so it wouldn't spill all over, and she took her very fine ass to the bathroom. Pulling the condom off, I tied the top to keep the contents inside, then sat up to head to the bathroom myself. She walked out after flushing and washing, right past me. I slapped her ass as she did, and she turned around and slapped my own. Snatching her hand, I pulled her to me, devouring her in a kiss until she softened and wrapped herself around me.

"That's not fair," she said. "You can't use my sex drive against me like that."

"All's fair in love and war," I replied.

"As long as this isn't war," she said.

"Never," I replied, letting her go, and stepping into the bathroom.

Chapter Twenty-Three

Hailey...

ailey...
We'd spent the week doing medical appointments for my face, me meeting with Alej's attorney, and fucking like rabbits. Honestly, the first two things I could have done without, but that last item on the list was my favorite. The attorney said we definitely had a case against the principal for assault, but that it would likely be handled by the prosecutor's office. He did say that if the school took action to fire me, then we'd have a case for wrongful termination, too. Honestly, all I wanted was to get back to teaching the kids, back to normal.

Alej had asked if I wanted to come with him and stay at his house for the second week, so I decided to take him up on it. I let Missy know I would be out of the house for the week, and that she and Kelton could hang there or not, either was fine. I packed my bag and we headed to his place. It was weird being in there with him. I mean, I'd only seen it the one time when we first came back, but he had an amazing kitchen, with a fully stocked pantry. He ordered in some fresh groceries, and he was an amazing cook. I took my turn at making some meals, but he did the majority of the cooking.

It was weird not working for those two weeks, but I was definitely ready to head back when my doctor gave me the green light. Of course, it also happened to be right after Alej had to leave for Florida for spring training. We had made love so many times that weekend that I really was sore, and walking funny, but it was definitely worth it.

"Welcome back, Ms. Truitt," the kids said as I walked into my classroom.

"Aw," I said. "Did you guys miss me?"

"What happened to your face?" Bo asked.

"Bo," the substitute chided, but I interrupted.

"It's okay," I said. "I was hurt, but I'm going to be fine. It was why I was gone for so long. I had to wait until the doctors said I could come back."

"How did you get hurt?" Ayanna asked.

"I was pushed down," I said. "It was scary, but I'm okay now."

"Okay," she said, and that was the end of the discussion.

It was truly baffling that kids could ask such intrusive questions, then be placated with the simplest of answers. It was a wonderful thing, and I was glad I didn't have to go into great detail with them.

The day was spent with everything fun, and no more talk about the slice on my face that was in the healing process. By the time the last of the kids left from the morning session, I was exhausted. The school had kept the substitute on for the week, just to help out. They wanted to make sure I was comfortable before they let her go.

When the afternoon kids showed up, we had the same round of questions, I gave the same answers, and we moved on to the lessons we had for the day. Kids were resilient, but I was definitely worn out when the final bell rang, and they all headed home.

"You look tired," Mary said when I went into the office to gather some fliers.

"I am," I replied. "But it was a good day."

"I have a question," she said. "And you can answer it or tell me off if you want."

"Well, that sounds ominous," I said.

"I just noticed that you have a ring on your hand," she said. "Did something happen while you were away?"

I rubbed my thumb across the back of the rings, which only made them more obvious the way they reflected the fluorescent lighting in the office.

"It actually happened a couple of weeks ago," I said, still unsure how much I wanted to share.

"Congratulations," she said. "So, who's the lucky guy?"

"He's a pretty private person," I said. "We're trying to keep it on the down low for now."

"I completely understand," she said, but I knew she had no idea. "So, when's the big day?"

"What do you mean?" I asked.

"Your wedding day?" she asked. "When is it?"

"It was a couple of weeks ago," I said, and she looked confused. "I got married when I was in Vegas."

"I thought you were going for your friend's bachelorette party," she said, clearly confused.

"That's what it started out as," I said.

"Did he go with you on the trip?" she asked. "Or did you plan that the whole time?"

"It's kind of complicated," I said, not wanting at all to have this conversation with her. "I just want to make sure that it stays between us, okay? Don't tell anyone else, cause we're not ready to go public with it right now."

"Oh, for sure," she said. "I know how to keep things secret."

"I'm serious," I said. "This isn't something I want to explain to anyone else. For now, it has to be kept a secret. We're planning on when and how to tell people, but he had to go out of town for work, so we'll figure out how we're telling people once he's back in town. Can you promise me you won't say a word?"

"Cross my heart," she said.

"If someone asks me about it, I'll know where they got the information," I said.

"Hailey," she said. "I will keep this secret. I promise."

"Okay," I said.

I headed out of the office, then had to turn back around and go back in, because I hadn't gotten the fliers I needed to put into the cubbies. It was the whole reason I headed to the office in the first place. Mary was talking with another staff member when I walked back in, and she sort of shut up and looked surprised.

"I forgot the fliers," I said, pointedly looking at Mary with a look that clearly said I was disappointed in her betraying my trust.

"They're in your cubby," she said, pointing over to the wall.

The other staff member was someone I didn't know, but she was looking at me, clearly trying to figure out who I was, and what Mary was talking about. I completely ignored them both, grabbed the fliers, and headed back to my classroom. When I walked in, the sub, Liz, looked up at me from her phone and smiled.

"What's that for?" I asked.

"Mary is a gossip," she said. "It's all over the school already, so be prepared for questions, and suspicious looks in the next few days."

"Shit," I said, then looked around, making sure no parents or kids were still in the room. "What did she say?"

Instead of reading whatever it was, she showed me her phone. It was a message program that had a bunch of people in the group chat, some I didn't know, but others I recognized. I scrolled up and saw that the thread started the day I got back, just after I was taken to the hospital. Of course, Mary was the first note, and the sub was added after she came in that next day. I could see that she hadn't participated in the comments, but she didn't let me know, either.

"I should have told you," she said. "But I wanted to make sure that I could keep an eye on things until I had a chance to sit down with you. It was my plan to do that when you got back, but you sort of caught me with the new posts."

Looking over everything, Mary had told everyone what had

happened in the room, and that I was going to the hospital. She also seemed to be on the principal's side, saying he wasn't doing anything wrong by talking to me about the issue of me being gone an extra day.

Liz and I had been close since I first started teaching, and she was the sub I often called if I needed someone on short notice. We were more friends than just coworkers, so the fact that she'd held out on me was a bit sad.

"I didn't want to bother you while you were recovering," she said. "I should have, but I felt conflicted. I mean, you were hurt, had gone to the hospital, and then hadn't come back. I wanted you to have time to recoup, because what Mary said initially was that you were knocked out."

"I was," I said. "But she still had no right to share this."

The chat was bad. And it was full of shit that wasn't true. She said I went storming into his office, and started yelling at him, which was so far from the truth that it wasn't even funny. The latest shit was what really pissed me off. She said I ran off to get married, then came back to flaunt it in her face, knowing that she was going through a divorce. She was making all sorts of shit up, like I had been the affair partner of my now husband, and that I'd run off to get hitched as soon as he was free. When I saw the shit about me being loose, and likely having slept with most of the men on staff, as well as husbands of the women, I just lost it.

"I need to get screenshots of this," I said.

"I've been saving them," she said, taking her phone and switching apps. "I wanted to make sure nothing got deleted before I had a chance to do it. I was just taking more when you walked in."

"Can you send those to me by email?" I asked. "To my personal email, though. Not the one for the school."

"Absolutely," she said. "But I gotta ask. Did you get married?"

"I did," I said, showing her the ring.

"Damn," she said, drawing the word out as she looked at it. "Is he rich?"

"He is," I said. "But that's not why I married him."

"Tell me about him," she said.

"Let's get wrapped up here," I said. "Then, we can go have some drinks and I can give you all the details."

"Good plan," she said, grabbing the fliers from the desk and working to get them stuffed into the cubbies.

It didn't take long, and we had shaped the room up, getting the toys put away, the supplies back to where they belonged, and setting it up for the morning. When we were heading out, the vice principal, Jessica Moody, stopped us.

"Can I talk with you?" she asked me.

"Does it have anything to do with work?" I asked.

"It does," she said. "But it's not a performance review or anything like that."

"I still want someone present for the meeting," I said.

"Ms. McCoy can come with you," she said, looking at Liz.

I looked at her and she shrugged, so we headed to the office again. Once there, I noticed that Mary was gone, and so was the other staff person who had been there with her. We walked into her office and she sat behind her desk, not closing the door, which actually made me feel better.

"It has come to my attention that there has been some gossip going around," she said. "I wanted to find out whether anything was true, and if there was anything I needed to know."

"What have you heard?" I asked.

"That you're married," she said. "That you have been having affairs with staff or their partners, and that's how you got this position, and that you only married the guy because he had money, and you'd pressured him into it."

"I am married," I said. "But it isn't anyone that anyone here would know personally. I have not, nor would I ever, sleep with anyone I worked with, or their partners. We got married of our own free will, and it was sudden and unexpected."

I was not about to give her any additional information, because honestly, I didn't want anyone to know.

"That was my assumption," she said. "I was sure that the rumors were mistaken, and that whoever was spreading them was trying to gain clout."

"Honestly," I said. "The only person on staff that knows is Mary, and Liz. But I just told Liz before you walked into my class, and I told Mary when I was in the office picking up the fliers that are going out to students tomorrow. I also told Mary that I didn't want anyone else to know, and that if anyone did find out, I would know where they got the information. I'm guessing that's how you found out."

"It is," she said, and she seemed disappointed. "Mary was concerned that it would affect your ability to teach. That you were getting ready to abandon your position, just as you had after you'd been hurt a couple of weeks ago."

"I was pulled from work by my physician," I said. "I wanted to come back sooner, but he wouldn't release me. I spent the two weeks with my husband getting him ready to leave for work. I also spent the time going to medical appointments and meeting with an attorney."

"Why are you meeting with an attorney?" she asked.

"I'm not at liberty to say," I said, as the attorney said not to talk to anyone about it. "Just know that I will be working with the prosecutor's office regarding the assault, and everything else will be worked out privately with my attorney."

"Do we need to be worried?" she asked.

"Not if you follow the law," I said. "I'm sure it will all be fine, but there are some concerns I have about a chat group message that has been going around. I believe that many of the staff are in it, and they are spreading rumors and lies, specifically about me, and I want to know what is going to be done about that."

"That was actually why I brought you in," she said. "I overheard someone in the kitchen saying something about being shocked by what was being said. I don't think they noticed me, so they were freely talking about it, and what they said was appalling. When they noticed me staring at them, they shut right up. I wanted to get the information from you first, just to see what was going on, or whether there were any truths to the rumors."

"I've actually been in that chat," Liz said. "I've been taking screenshots throughout the last couple of weeks, so I'd have the evidence in case it was needed. I showed it to Hailey just before we were leaving, and we were going to go discuss it over dinner."

"Would you let me see it?" Jessica asked.

"I'd prefer if she emailed it to you," I said. "I've asked her to send it to me as well, because I need to get the information to my attorney."

"That would be fine," she said.

"I'll send it all over to you when I get home," Liz said. "I have to get some of the screenshots off my laptop, because I transferred them over there each night when I got home. I didn't want to risk losing them."

I didn't know if she was bullshitting, but it wouldn't surprise me. She was smart, and knew what she was talking about, so I didn't put it past her to actually have done that.

"That would be fine," she said. "I just can't believe the juvenile actions of these people."

"Everyone can be juvenile," I said. "Why do you think all those reality shows are so popular? People love gossip and titillating facts, the juicer the better. What could be better than me being the school..." I didn't want to say it, because it just made it that much more real.

"Exactly," Liz said. "And trust me, this isn't the only school that's like this."

"It's not even the only business that's like this," Jessica said. "Thank you," she said, looking at me. "I have scheduled a meeting with a few of the people who I know were involved, as well as a union representative for them. If you are interested in taking part in that meeting, I can get you the information."

"If you can get me the details, I will get it to my attorney," I said. "He will let me know whether I should attend, or if he wants to."

"I would hate to have to involve attorneys," she said, holding her finger up as I went to interrupt. "But I understand you wanting to protect yourself. I'll send you the information on the meeting now to your personal email address, not the one attached to the school. You can let me know whether you want to attend or not."

"Thanks," I said.

I got up, and Liz did as well, and we walked out of the office. When we got to our cars, I asked her where she wanted to go. She told me about a café close by, and we agreed to meet there. When I pulled up, it was pretty packed, but I figured we could find a place to sit and chat out of the way somewhere. We ordered and were sitting at a table when Mary and a couple of other women walked in.

"Shit," I said, shifting so they couldn't see me.

"I didn't even think about this," Liz said. "They've been doing happy hour here for a while, and I completely forgot. Let's get our food to go and find somewhere else to eat."

No sooner had she said it, and Mary walked up to our table.

"Mind if we join you?" she asked, sounding so sweet it was sickening.

"Actually," Liz said, gathering her stuff. "We were just leaving."

"I hope it's not on my account," she said, and I never wanted to slap someone more in my life.

Instead, I just picked up my stuff, walked away to the counter, and let the waitress know we were going to take our food to go instead. She looked between me and Mary, and seemed to know something was up, so graciously agreed, making a note so they would package our dinner up. I went ahead and paid for the food, giving a generous tip, and waited by the register for Liz to catch up.

"She's pissed," Liz said when she came over to me.

"Only because she got caught," I said, keeping my voice low enough that only my friend could hear me.

"For sure," she said.

"Here you go," the waitress said, handing us a bag with our orders.

"Thanks," I said, taking it. "Let's go to my place."

"Right behind you," Liz said, holding the door open for me to scoot out.

When I opened my front door, Missy was sitting on the couch with Kenton, and they both looked up at me.

"Sorry," I said, holding up the bag of food. "Intention was to eat at the restaurant. Unfortunately, the rats arrived, so we left. I didn't get you guys anything."

"Hold up, what?" Missy asked.

Liz walked in right behind me and I handed her the bag and pointed to the kitchen.

"There's a group chat at the school," I said. "Mean girls' style, where they're trying to figure out exactly what is going on with me. They know I'm married, but know nothing about Alej, and I'd like to keep it that way. The vice principal has called them to task, and is having a formal meeting with them, to include a union rep, and me if I'm interested. Liz got screenshots."

"Sure as fuck did," she said, poking her head out.

"I have to email it all to the attorney Alej got for me," I said. "Then ask if I should go to the meeting. With him, without him, with a union rep, or not at all. Not my idea of a good time."

"My God," Missy said. "Are they still in middle school?"

"Mentally, probably," Liz said, holding up the plates and forks she had with our food.

"Go and eat," Kenton said. "Don't mind us. We actually have reservations in about half an hour, so we'll be out of here then."

"Okay," I said.

"Have you heard from him?" Missy asked.

"Yeah," I said. "He texted me when he landed and got to the condo down there. He offered for me to come down if I wanted, and even said you guys could come, too."

"I wish," Missy said. "There is entirely too much to do around here before the wedding, and we're only a couple weeks out. Maybe next year we can go down for our anniversary."

"That might work," I said.

I walked over to the table and sat down with Liz, picking up my fork, and starting to shovel food in. I was famished, and I was annoyed. Liz and I looked at the screenshots she'd sent to me, and we talked about what was said outside of them while I was gone. Turns out, there were a lot of people thinking I had done some pretty terrible things in the year and a half that I'd been at the school. It made me wonder whether I even wanted to stay there, which broke my heart, because I loved those kids.

Chapter Twenty-Four

Alejandro...

"Are you fucking kidding me?" Nick asked.

"Nope," I said, then pulled out my phone to show them the pictures.

"Dude, that's fucked up," JP said.

"It's the best thing ever," I said. "Honestly, we were both hesitant. I mean, after she woke up the next morning and said she didn't remember. But now, we're good. Like really good."

"Prenup?" Nick asked.

"None," I said. "Don't even care. She can have everything I have, as long as I get to keep her, I'm good."

"That's some fucked-up shit," JP said.

"I mean," Nick said, and we both looked at him. "What? Charlotte and I are good. We're just not gonna get married. No need."

"Kids?" I asked.

"Nope," he said. "I mean, she has that one girl who works with her that has a baby, and her sister's kids, but that's it. Neither of us want any of our own."

"Don't your parents want you to have kids?" JP asked.

"My mom would love it, but she isn't gonna push," he said. "I told her I wasn't interested, so she's fine."

"My mama is hot about this," I said. "She's pissed she didn't get to approve of Hailey before we got married."

"Dude," JP said. "Does she know you didn't know her when you got married?"

"That is not a conversation I'm going to have with her," I said with a laugh. "If I thought she was pissed as it is, I wouldn't live to see another day if I told her that."

We laughed, knowing that they had actually met my mama and knew how she was.

It had only been a couple of days since I'd left, and I couldn't get Hailey off my mind. All I wanted to do was have her there when I went home after practice, but she was almost a thousand miles away. Besides, she was working, and I wouldn't make her stop if she didn't want to. Not that I couldn't afford for her to not work, but I didn't want to take anything away from her. If she asked, I'd have said yes, but she didn't. In fact, she'd been pretty insistent on staying at work.

Now that we'd been apart, I could tell that we would likely stay together. At least as long as she missed me as much as I missed her. I had called her each night, and we'd talked quite a bit, so when I headed home after practice, I was going to see if she'd be willing to do a video call. Maybe even have a little phone sex to get me by until I could actually hold her.

"Hello?" she said when she answered the phone.

"Hey, baby," I said.

"Alej," she said, and I could hear the smile in her voice. "I had a hell of a day, and I have to be quick because I am waiting on a call from the attorney."

"What happened?" I asked, my focus solely on her safety, and not my needs.

"Bunch of bullshit at work," she said. "Nothing you need to worry about."

"Baby," I said. "I'm worried. Are you safe? Do you need me to come home? Should I send someone to stay with you?"

"Alej, I'm fine," she said.

"Are you sure?"

"Yes," she said. "I'm a big girl, and I'm fine. It is nothing more than stupid gossip that went way too far, but I'm fine."

"Okay," I said. "Because you don't need to work if you don't want to."

"I'm not quitting," she said. "I'm fine, everything is fine, I promise."

"I miss you," I said.

"I miss you, too," she replied. "I do have someone here with me. She's my friend and the sub who filled in for me when I was out."

"Where's Missy?"

"Out with Kenton," she said. "I think they're finally feeling the urgency, what with the wedding being in just a few days."

"Oh yeah," I said. "I'm gonna need to see you in your dress. Well, and out of it."

"Yeah," she said. "Not sending any compromising photos. No need to make anything a potential target, because it would happen."

"Well," I said. "We could always do a video call after the wedding. Just you and me, in our respective rooms, sharing our enjoyment of watching the other get off."

"Was that a come on?" she asked. "Cause it sounded like you were coming on to me. I'm not sure my husband would approve of someone coming onto me like that."

"If it were any other man," I said. "I am absolutely sure your husband wouldn't be happy. But it's me, so it's fine."

"Yeah," she said. "Let's table that discussion. I gotta finish dinner, and I'm kinda being rude to my guest."

"Okay," I said. "But I'm gonna think about you when I shower tonight."

"I'll do the same," she said, and I could hear the anticipation in her voice.

"Let me know how it goes," I said. "Talk to you tomorrow."

"Talk to you then," she replied, then disconnected the phone.

Definitely was going to need a cold shower after all that, so I took my happy ass into the bathroom, stripped down, and climbed into the tub. Turning the water on, I let it get warm, then pulled the plunger to direct it out of the shower head. The blast of cold water hit me, and I reached under and turned the temp up. A cold shower sounded well and good until you got hit with that blast.

Closing my eyes, I imagined Hailey in the shower with me, remembering the first time she'd snuck in behind me at the hotel. I wasn't sure she would have come in, what with how thrown she was finding out we were married, but she had, and it was fantastic. Her hips were perfect, her tits were perfect, her mouth was perfect; every-thing about her was absolutely what I wanted in a woman.

It still boggled my mind that she'd even talked to me on that dance floor. The way she was moving, the number of men who were watching her, some had even approached her, but she'd ignored them all. When I walked up, I stood near her, and when she looked at me, her eyes were on fire, that blue flame just dancing the way her body was. She came to me, wrapped her arms around my neck, pressed up even farther on her toes, and pulled me down to her. My guess was that most everyone around assumed we already knew each other, but that wasn't the case. Still, when she'd asked me to take her to bed, I obliged without question.

Now, some three and a half weeks or so later, she was tempting my mind again, but this time she was farther away by a long shot. Still, remembering her, the way she felt in my arms, the ways she moved around me, it was more than I could take, and as I stroked my cock, all I could think about was her pussy wrapped around it, pulling me into her with her strong muscles, her body pressed against my own, her warm breath on my neck, and I lost it, shooting my load along the tiles on the wall. I had to press a hand against the same wall to keep me upright, my knees nearly buckling with the release.

When I was finally finished, and had enough energy, I showered, washed my hair and body from the day's activities, then sprayed the wall down to get my cum off it. When I was out of the shower, the water shut off, I could hear knocking on my door. Unsure who it might have been, I dried off, then wrapped the towel around my waist, and walked to the door, opening it.

"Dude," JP said, holding his hand up to block me. "Put something on."

"I just got out of the shower," I said. "What did you expect?"

"Not this," he said, his other hand waving up and down to indicate my near nakedness.

"Come on in," I said. "I'll get dressed and be right back."

He'd taken me under his wing when I first came up to the bigs, and he'd made sure I had someone to hang out with and ask questions of. We'd kept up with the dinners after practice ever since, sometimes bringing others along, but often it was just the two of us.

I walked into my bedroom, pulled the towel off, and got dressed in jeans and a tee shirt. I pulled my tennis shoes on, tying them tight, before heading back out to the living room of my condo.

"Anyone else coming?" I asked.

"Nick, Austin, and Brandon are meeting us there," he said.

"Cool," I said, shoving my wallet and keys into my pocket from the counter in the kitchen. "Let's go."

He got up from the couch and headed out the door, waiting for me to shut and lock it behind me, then we went down the two flights of stairs to the parking lot for the units. We both had condos in the building, and we usually carpooled to and from most everything.

"You're driving," he said. "I had to look at you, so you need to pay me back for that."

"Fine," I said, not at all minding. "It's not my fault you were early."

"Dude, I was late," he said. "I gave you extra time, knowing you were gonna call your girl. Didn't want to interrupt anything that involved the two of you."

"Good," I said. "I don't need that kind of interruption."

"You're whipped," he said, but he was smiling as we climbed into my old car. "How come you ain't bought a new car, yet?"

"It's on my list of things to do," I said. "Can't be taking my beautiful wife around in this old thing."

"Is she that pretentious?"

"Not at all," I said. "She was actually impressed that I didn't have a bunch of flashy shit. Felt like I was a real guy, not some player."

"You're a player," he said. "You just don't play the kind of games she was thinking."

"Never have, never will," I said as we pulled into the lot for the bar we were heading to. "Besides, don't need to. I just had to go find her on the other side of the country."

"Yeah, what are the odds you'd meet someone from home there?"

"Probably pretty high," I said. "But I guess she didn't think she'd meet anyone there like that, either. She was thankful I wasn't a serial killer."

"You sure you're not?"

"Dude," I said. "Give me a little credit."

"Okay, killer," he said with a laugh.

We climbed out of the car and headed in, pulling the door open, and letting the cool air rush around us. Growing up, I always wondered what it would be like to be cold. By the time I started playing, I was wondering why I didn't enjoy the warmth of Florida when I had it. Some of the cities we played in during the early months of the season were downright cold.

"Hey," Austin said as we walked up to the table they'd snagged.

"What's up?" I asked.

"Just waiting on you, princess," Brandon said.

They were two of the team's outfielders and seemed to really work well together. Austin had been with the team when I was called up three years earlier, but Brandon had just joined the team the previous season and had fit right in with the other two regular outfielders, taking his spot in right field next to Austin, who handled center field.

"I even gave him extra time, and he was late," JP said as he sat down.

"What took you so long?" Nick asked.

"He was talking to his wife," JP said. "He answered the door naked, and I had to see that. There are some things you just can't unsee."

"Dude," Nick said.

"I was not naked," I corrected. "I had a towel on. I had just gotten out of the shower. Something you guys might want to invest some time doing."

"Jackass," Austin said, and we all laughed.

"What'll it be, boys?" the waitress asked as she came to the table.

We went around the table, ordering our usual meals, not even bothering to look at the menus that were scattered across the table. She jotted down notes, then picked the menus up, and headed over to the bar.

"She's fucking hot," Austin said.

"Don't fuck where you eat," JP chided.

"Doesn't mean I can't look at the menu," the other player replied. "These images are definitely going into my spank bank."

"Gross," Nick said. "You're not thirteen, act like a fucking adult."

"Thank you," I said to him. "Sometimes I forget how childish these guys can be."

"Don't mock me," JP said. "Pretty sure you'd hit that if you weren't tied up."

"Not a chance," I said. "She's a nice woman doing her job, and her job isn't to be hit on by the assholes that come in here."

Just as I finished the statement, we heard a yip from near the bar. We all turned, and could see some fucker trying to grab her, his hand on her ass, squeezing it.

"The fuck he did," Nick said, standing up, and striding over.

I followed suit, going with him to back him up.

"Hey, dickwad," he said, grabbing the guy's hand, and ripping it off the waitress. "Keep your fucking hands to yourself."

"Fuck you, asshole," the guy said.

"You might want to rethink that," I said, backing Nick up.

"Oh, you think y'all are gonna be able to deal with me?"

"Dude," Nick said, twisting his arm a little further back. "I'd suggest you wander off, and crawl back from whatever rock you crawled out from under. This is a place for civilized people, not Neanderthals like you."

"The fuck did you just call me?"

"He said you're dumber than a box of rocks," Austin said, and I hadn't heard him follow us over. "Now, shut the fuck up, keep your hands to yourself, and let the lady work."

Said lady had walked away, so she wasn't in any danger, but it was nice that he thought of her.

"You're done," the bartender said, handing the guy a receipt, and his card. "I charged you the tip you weren't gonna leave, and if you challenge it, we'll bring the cops in here, and let them sort your shit out."

"You can't do that," he whined.

"And if you come back," the bartender said. "Let's just say, you won't be welcome."

"Fuck all of you," he said, yanking his arm out of Nick's hand.

He swiped his card up and walked out without a backward glance.

"Thanks," the waitress said. "I appreciate you all standing up for me."

"No problem," Nick said. "Ladies should always be treated with respect."

"We're comping your meal," the bartender said.

"No need," I said.

"Gonna insist," he replied, and the look he gave me said not to argue.

We walked back to the table where Brandon and JP sat. As we sat down, a pitcher of beer landed in the middle, along with enough mugs for us to all share. I turned to see who was setting it down, and it was an older man.

"You guys deserve this," he said. "I would have done it, but my bum leg keeps me less mobile. Appreciate you sticking up for the lady, so I'm buying you a round. Hope you like this kind."

"Thanks, man," Brandon said, and I looked over at him. "These guys do deserve it."

"We can share," Nick said, pouring a glass from the pitcher and handing it over.

"You all players?" the man asked.

"We are," I said. "Who's your team?"

"Gotta love my Manatees," he said.

"Well," Austin said. "You might find a soft spot for the Magicians."

"Ah, well, I might at that," he said. "You guys did pretty well last year."

"Not quite well enough," JP said. "This year, though, we got our eyes on the prize, looking to go all the way."

"If you can get past the Anglers," he said.

"God, ain't that the truth," Brandon said.

"Enjoy your beer," he said, then turned, and headed back to his own table.

It wasn't until he was heading back that I noticed the limp in his step, and the wobbly gait he had.

"Dude's a legend," the waitress said. "He fought in Vietnam. Moved here because of his injuries, said the sun and steam help him."

She set down our food from the tray she'd set on the stand, handing each of us our meals without missing a single one.

"Ketchup is there," she said, pointing. "Anything else you need?"

I looked around, and we all seemed to be doing the same.

"I think we're good," I said. "Thanks."

"Thanks for sticking up for me," she said. "Doesn't usually bother me, but that dick was awful."

"He comes in again, you call us," Nick said. "We live close by and can be here quick."

"It was the first time he came in," she said. "Geoff will watch out for him and make sure he doesn't come back. That, and Jerry over there is always on, so he'll make sure someone knows if he comes back in."

"Good," I said. "Hate to see you harassed like that. You got someone to walk you to your car after work?"

"For sure," she said. "Geoff will walk me out, no problem. Gotta get back to it. Enjoy, and let me know if you need anything."

"She's still hot," Austin said.

"And not on the list of toys you can play with," Nick said.

"God, I'm just looking," the younger player replied.

Chapter Twenty-Five

Hailey...

"Oh my God," I said, looking at Missy. "You look absolutely stunning."

"Are you sure?" she asked, turning in her dress, the train whooshing back and forth on the hardwood floor of the room we were getting ready in. "Does my hair look okay? My makeup? Shit, did I forget something?"

"Missy," Kelsey said, placing her hands on Missy's arms. "Everything is perfect. Nothing was forgotten. We got you."

"Yeah," Emma said, dabbing a tissue under her eye.

"Don't you dare," Missy said, a scowl on her face. "You start crying and I'm gonna cry. If I cry, then Hailey will, so you better stop that shit right this fucking minute."

Emma nodded, swallowing hard. She was our emotional friend, the one who cried at stupid commercials and everything. We had to change the channel or mute it if one of those abused animal ones came on, it was ridiculous. Don't even get me started on her crying while reading her romance novels. There was one book she read where a character died, and she threw the book across the room.

Literally threw it, then shouted at it that it better not have said what she thought it did.

We were all standing around her in our seafoam green gowns, each a unique style and fitting of our body types. Missy's dress was on another level. White for the most part, but the bottom of it was dyed this deep purple, and the way the color went from white to purple was whimsical and absolutely perfect. She'd had to have it made special, since her mother had ruined the previous one. It had been plain white, much more conservative, and exactly what her mother had wanted, but didn't really fit Missy. This one was absolutely all about her.

"You get the honor of being first," I said. "We'll all make sure it's perfect for you."

"Not the first," she said, looking me dead in the eyes.

"Yes, the first," I said. "Mine was on a whim and I didn't get to do all the fancy things, so it doesn't count. You're the first to have an actual wedding."

"Fine," she said. "I guess that's true. Still, we need to do something for you guys. We should plan something. When do you want to do it?"

"Missy," I said. "That's not something we need to worry about right now. Today is about you and getting you to that happily ever after moment of saying, 'I do.'"

"Okay," she said, and it sounded like she was disappointed.

"Good," I said, picking up the gloss off the table where her makeup was. "Now, shine those lips up so Kenton can't wait to kiss them."

She giggled, taking the tube from me, and pulling the wand out, swiping it across her lips. Just then we heard a scuffle outside the door.

"Oh God, now what?" she asked, and I could see she was worried.

"I got this," I said. "You guys get her finished."

When I opened the door, her mother shoved past me, wearing a white dress that resembled the one she'd shredded, storming into the room like a hurricane.

"I'm here, baby," she cooed, as if she had been expected and welcomed.

"Shit," I muttered as I watched all the color drain from Missy's face. "Mr. Baxter," I shouted out the door, then went to the woman who had made nearly everything about Missy's big day about herself. "Mrs. Baxter," I said, trying to get in between her and her daughter. "We need to talk."

"I'm not leaving," she said, glaring at me, and I could tell she'd already had entirely too much to drink. "My baby is getting married. It's a mother's job to make sure the day goes off without a hitch."

"Mom," Missy said, and the tears were filling her eyes.

"It's okay, baby," she said, patting her daughter on the shoulder. "I'm here now. Mummy will make it all better."

"Cora," Mr. Baxter said as he stepped into the room, Missy's brother, Mike, and one of the other groomsmen behind him.

"No," she shouted. "I'm here for my daughter. I will make sure she is perfectly ready for her big day."

"Mom, please," Missy said, but her dad was right there, reaching around to grab hold of his ex-wife, and take her from the room.

"No," she shrieked, digging her fingernails into Missy's shoulder, causing her to cry and try to duck and get away. "You won't take her from me. She's my baby."

"Cora, please," Missy's dad said. "Look at what you're doing to her. Do you really want to do that to her on her wedding day? Make her cry? Leave her with marks on her body? Think about what the pictures will look like."

It was a low blow, but calculated, as he knew that image was everything to Cora Baxter, and having her be the cause of it looking bad was something she couldn't live with. It was bad enough that she'd ruined the first dress and Missy had had to get a new one, but to ruin the wedding itself was definitely something she didn't want to do.

"Oh, yes," she said, stepping back. "Of course. We don't want to ruin things. This dress, though, won't do at all. I've brought one with me you can change into."

"Why don't we go get that," I said, helping to steer her out of the room.

Missy had laid down the law with her mom after we had dinner a couple weeks earlier, telling her that she was still invited to the wedding, but she had better mind her manners, not drink, and behave like a civilized person, or she'd have her kicked to the curb without any problem. Of course, she'd done everything she wasn't supposed to, including wearing white, which Missy had been completely firm about. She'd even gone with her to pick up the dress she was to wear.

We walked her out of the room, shutting the door behind us, and Mr. Baxter helped his ex-wife down the stairs, and toward the door to the outside. The venue had security, and we'd simply let them know that this woman was being removed from the premises and was not allowed to attend the event. It didn't actually take that long to get her out, and Kenton had come over to see what was going on, his mom there with him.

"She's drunk, wearing white, and trying to make Missy change her dress," I said.

"Oh, God," his mom said.

"How is she?" he asked.

"She's shaken," I said. "Might be a little delayed in starting. Just let folks know we're freshening her up."

"If she needs me," he said.

"I'll let you know," I replied. "But I think she'll be fine."

He hugged me, and whispered thanks in my ear before I headed back up the stairs to the room. When I walked in, Missy was a mess. Her makeup was streaked, she'd gotten out of her dress, and Mike was busy fixing the shoulder their mom had torn.

"Why does she hate me?" she cried.

"It's a *her* problem," I said. "She's gone and won't be back. Kenton said if you need him, he can come up."

"No," she nearly shouted. "I can't let him see me like this."

"Not a problem," I said. "We'll get everything fixed, and you'll be ready to go in no time."

She was sobbing, tears running down her cheeks, her hands shaking, and was just an all-around mess. I went over to the table where we had some snacks and drinks, poured some champagne into a glass, and took it over to her.

"I can't drink," she said. "I don't want to be drunk when I get married."

"One glass will not hurt you," I said. "Besides, it will help to calm your nerves. Just take a little sip."

She nodded, tried to hold the glass, but her hands were shaking so bad she nearly spilled it. I held it for her, tipping it up so she could get at least a swallow or two down, before lowering it. Her hair was still perfect, but her makeup would need to be completely redone. Thankfully, Kelsey was a genius when it came to makeup and fixing things. Once we got her calmed a bit, and Mike said he'd be able to fix the dress so that no one would know, we got to work on getting her back to her beautiful self.

I'd told her that everyone knew that we were delayed because of an accident, but that no one knew it was her who was falling apart. She tried to have me tell them it was all her fault, but I refused, reminding her that her mother had woken up and chose violence, and we'd shut it down. Finally, we had her presentable again, and her brother helped to get her into the dress after showing her his repairs. The dude was a master with a needle and thread, but give him more supplies, and he'd be a force to be reckoned with in the fashion industry.

"Okay," I said, holding up the gloss again. "Let's do this right."

She took it from my hand, swiped the brush along her lips, then stuck it back into the tube, and smiled.

"You're beautiful," I said, and the other two friends agreed.

"Sis, you are gonna slay out there," her brother said, his smile bigger than any of ours.

"Thank you for helping me," she said, giving him a hug.

"Where would you be without me?" he asked, but he was smiling. "You'd be getting married in a potato sack, that's where."

"But you'd make that sack look fine," she said, squeezing him again.

"Shut up," he said. "We better get out there or we're gonna have an angry mob on our hands."

He stepped back and opened the door. Her dad was standing just outside, and when he saw her, he beamed.

"Look at you," he said. "More beautiful than any bride in the world."

"Don't let Helen hear you say that," she said.

"I think she'd agree," he said. "Besides, it's a different kind of beauty when it's your baby girl."

"Thanks, Daddy," she said, taking his arm as he walked her down the stairs.

We all followed behind them until we reached the ground level where she turned into a side room to await her grand entrance. The planner came to us, and made sure we were all ready, then lined us up so we could start the ceremony. Mike was walking down with Emma, who had her tissues ready. Then it was Kelsey with John, and Kenton's best friend, Jason walked with me.

When we got to the front of the room, Kenton looked at me, asking without words whether she was fine. I mouthed that she was great. Then I said she was beautiful, so Jason had smelling salts for when he passed out from seeing her. That made him laugh and cut the tension just enough that when the music began. The crowd stood and I watched Kenton fall in love with my best friend all over again. Seriously, if I'd had a camera to capture his reaction, it would have been the best thing in the world.

Everything was beautiful. From the words that the officiant said to the vows they shared with each other, and even her grandmother tearing up in the front row. The only thing that would have made it better would have been to have Alej with me. It had only been a week, and I missed him terribly. So much so that I thought about taking some time off and going to where he was in Florida. But with everything that was going on with the school, and the principal being a dick, like his name indicated, to the school board coming down on us with questions about exactly why it went so far, I wasn't sure it was the best time.

"By the power vested in me by the state of Louisiana," the man said. "I now pronounce you husband and wife. You may now kiss to seal the deal."

The crowd laughed at that line, but it was special to them both. It was something they said to each other often, making sure that it was taken seriously, whatever the agreement was. Besides, they both hated the fact that it was the man's job to kiss his bride, and not the other way around.

When they finally met, the whole room erupted in cheers, clapping, hooping, and all-around merriment. It was really a special moment, and I found myself tearing up just a little bit.

"Ladies and gentlemen," the officiant said once they'd ended their kiss. "I would like to introduce you to the newlyweds."

There was a loud pop, then a scream, and we all looked around, confusion everywhere.

"Oh, God," someone from the back shouted. "Someone call an ambulance."

Chaos erupted all around, and Missy looked at me, completely confused. Kenton wrapped his arm around her and ushered her toward the stairwell that was at the end of the room where we were. The rest of the bridal party headed right behind them, going up the stairs to the rooms we had used to get ready.

"What's going on?" Missy cried. "What happened?"

"Don't worry about it," Kenton said, but I could see complete horror on his face.

"Let's get you guys settled," I said. "I'll go see what happened."

"I'm going with you," Mike said. He looked like he knew what was going on, so I let him.

Once we had the two of them in the bridal suite, Mike shut the door and looked at me.

"What do you know?" I asked.

"Come on," he said, grabbing my hand, and leading me toward the front of the building.

I'd known this kid since he was little, before he was even in school, and I'd never seen him this shook. Following him down the stairs, we ran into a wall of bodies, both guests of the wedding and police and firefighters. Whatever happened, it was bad. I could sense the eeriness in the air.

"Mike," Mr. Baxter shouted, and worked his way through the crowd toward us. "Stay back. You don't need to see this."

"I saw," he said, and his voice was hollow. "She always ruins things."

I looked between the two, their appearance so similar, and knew exactly what they were saying.

Chapter Twenty-Six

Alejandro...

"Slow down, baby," I said, trying to understand the words over the video call. "Are you safe?"

"I'm fine," she said, though her face told me otherwise. "I might need to stay here for a while, so I didn't want you to worry if I didn't answer. My phone is dying."

"Do you want me to come home?" I asked.

"There's nothing you can do," she said, then I heard a male voice say something, and she turned away from the phone. "I gotta go. I'll call you when I get home. I miss you and love you."

"I love you, too," I said. "If you need me, call me."

"Okay," she said, then was gone.

"What's going on?" JP asked.

"I don't know," I said. "She was at her best friend's wedding, but something happened."

"You gonna go to her?"

"I want to," I said. "But she said she was fine."

"But is she?"

"I don't know," I said. "God, I want to be there, but it's a ten-hour drive at best."

"So fly," he said. "Just go. Coach won't mind. Say it's a family emergency."

"I can't do that," I said.

"Why the fuck not?" he asked, and the look he gave me was serious. "Seriously, what the fuck are they gonna do? You're under contract. You have a family emergency. Your wife is in distress. Just fucking go."

"I don't know," I said.

"You don't go, she's gonna be pissed," he said.

"She'll be pissed if I do," I said. "She's not some damsel in distress needing to be rescued. She's shown me that already."

"Let me ask you this," he said. "If you had a choice, would you be here worrying or there?"

"There," I said. "In a heartbeat."

"Then go," he said. "I'll cover, just send the email, book a flight, and go home."

"Fuck," I said. "Okay."

"Good boy," he said, slapping me on the shoulder. "Want me to pack for you?"

"I got it," I said, pulling my laptop out. "If anyone asks, just tell them I had to take care of my wife."

"I got you," he said. "Now, get to it."

I didn't argue, just logged onto my computer, pulled up my email, and shot one off to the manager. Then I went to the airline website and found a flight that was leaving in a couple of hours, giving me time to get a bag packed, and to the airport. Once that was accomplished, I checked in for the flight, packed up my laptop, went to my room, and threw some shit into a duffle bag before coming back out.

"I'm driving," JP said. "You're too stressed. Just get an Uber when you get there."

"I will," I said, pulling my suitcase behind me, my laptop bag over my shoulder.

We went down the stairs and climbed into his Jeep after throwing my bag in the back. We were at the airport shortly, and I was out and into the security line. Since the airport was tiny, and it was pushing ten at night, it didn't take long to get through and to the gate. I sent a text to Hailey letting her know I was coming home, and that I'd meet her wherever she wanted, just to text me when she knew. If I didn't hear from her, I'd head to the house and go from there.

You don't need to come home.

Her text came through as I was getting on the plane, so once I was situated, I replied.

My wife is in distress, I'm coming home. Where should I meet you?

I knew it was stubborn, and that she might be pissed, but she needed me. She said she didn't, but I could tell. Her voice was off, and the look on her face was that of shock, so something must have gone down. I just didn't know what.

I'm still at the venue. When will you be here?

I told her the time my plane was scheduled to land, then waited for her to let me know where to meet her. She sent me the address of a hotel right downtown, so it must have been where everyone was planning to stay after the wedding. I told her I'd come right there from the airport, then had to shut my phone off for the flight.

The entire time, all I kept thinking was that I would see her soon, and she could tell me what happened. Whatever it was, it was definitely not a good thing. Unsure what I was gonna roll up on when I landed, I tried to get a little sleep on the plane, but my mind kept going to the worst-case scenario, and I just couldn't deal with it.

As soon as the plane landed, I turned the phone back on, and waited for it to bring in any messages that might have been sent while I was in the air. I got an email response saying I could take as much time as I wanted, just to let them know. A couple of the guys also sent me texts to let me know they were thinking of me, and to call them if I needed anything.

It's awful. I'm sorry. I need you.

Hailey's text was more than I thought I could handle.

I'm on my way.

It was like the entire world was moving in slow motion, everything getting in my way, and the universe was conspiring to keep me from her. When I got off the plane and up the walkway, I took off, heading toward the exit. I'd ordered an Uber, and would be meeting them as soon as I got out of the airport.

"Hey," the guy said.

"Sorry," I replied. "Family emergency, so as fast as you can get me there, I'd appreciate it."

"No problem," he said, having shut the trunk with my bag in it.

He climbed into the driver's seat, and we took off, heading into the heart of downtown. It was a Saturday night during the work up to Mardi Gras, so everything was packed. He got somewhat close, but cars were at a standstill.

"I'll just get out here," I said when we were relatively close to the hotel.

"You sure?" he asked.

"Yeah," I replied, and he pulled over to the curb, popping the trunk so I could grab my bag. "Thanks, man," I said and shut the door.

I got onto the sidewalk, and headed down the congested street, holding my bag in front of me, and sort of shoving people out of the way with it. When I reached the hotel, I pressed into the lobby, and pulled my phone out of my pocket. I called her, not sure where she was in the hotel.

"Alej?" she answered, and her voice was hoarse.

"I'm here," I said. "In the lobby."

"Oh, thank God," she said. "I'll be right down."

She disconnected before I even had a chance to respond, so I headed toward the elevators. When they chimed, the door opened, and she stepped out and right into my arms.

"I got you," I said as she broke on a sob. "I'm here."

"I'm so sorry," she choked out.

"It's no problem," I said. "I'm here now. Let's go upstairs."

She nodded against my chest, then pulled back a bit. I tucked her under my arm, and grabbed my bag from the floor, and stepped onto the elevator. She pressed the button for the third floor, and the doors closed, shutting the world out. When the doors opened again, we stepped out, and she led me down a short hallway to a room that had the door slightly ajar.

"Hey," one of the women said, her face a mess.

"Hi," I replied.

"Sit," Hailey said, pressing me toward the bed on the far side of the room.

I walked over and sat down, her following me and sitting next to me, wrapping her arms around me as she tucked herself into my side.

"Wanna tell me what happened?" I asked the room.

Both of her other friends were there, the two who had come over for a movie night a few weeks earlier. I couldn't remember either of their names, but knew they were all part of the whole pack of women my wife was part of.

"It was all going great," the second woman said. "The guy had just pronounced them married and told them to kiss..."

She choked up, covering her mouth with her hand, tears streaming down her face.

"It was her mom," Hailey said, and I looked down at her confused. "We heard a shot, then someone shouted to call an ambulance, but it was too late."

"I'm confused," I said. "I thought her mom had been told not to come to the wedding."

"She had," the first woman said. "But she showed up anyway, drunk off her ass, trying to make a scene."

"Thank God Missy's dad was there," the other woman said.

"Yeah," Hailey said. "He just sort of took control."

"Don't sell yourself short," the first woman said. "She told mummy dearest that she needed to make sure that everything would look good for the pictures. That's what convinced her to get out of the room."

"That, and the fact that I said I'd help her bring in the new dress," Hailey said.

"Didn't her mom shred her dress?" I asked.

"The first one, yeah," one of them said.

"Kelsey," Hailey said. "Do you have the pictures of Missy on your phone?"

"Maybe," Kelsey said, turning and grabbing her phone from the nightstand between the beds.

I hadn't remembered the other women's names from that night, so I at least had one of them now. Eventually they'd say the other name, and I'd be good to go. Kelsey switched to sitting beside me on the bed we were on and turned her phone to show me.

Missy was stunning in her dress, and it was a completely different one from the one her mother ruined. I wondered whether this was more her style, and she was able to pick it out without her mother's influence. From what I'd noticed about her in the couple of weeks I'd been with Hailey, this was definitely more what she would choose.

"I'm glad we got some pictures before," Kelsey said, moving back to the other bed.

"Me, too," Hailey said.

The third woman was crying again, and it appeared she hadn't really stopped.

"Emma," Kelsey said, and I finally knew the last woman's name. "You're gonna be a mess if you keep this up."

"I'm already a mess," she choked out.

"Okay," I said, trying to piece together what actually happened. "Her mom came before the wedding?"

"Yeah," Kelsey said, holding Emma.

"And her dad helped get her out of there?"

"Me, too," Hailey said. "I just wanted to get her away from Missy so she'd stop crying."

"What happened to her, then?" I asked.

"We don't know," Emma said, beginning to calm more. "Just that she was escorted out of the building, and security was told she wasn't to come back."

"But she did," I said.

"At the very end," Kelsey said. "We don't know where she got the gun..."

"It was Missy's dad's gun," Hailey said.

"How do you know?" I asked.

"Mike told me," she said. "His dad told him when we came back down."

"I take it she's gone," I said. "Missy's mom."

The three women all nodded.

"How's Missy?" I asked.

"We know she's messed up," Kelsey said. "But Kenton's with her."

"He's such a good guy," Emma said.

"I thought so," I said. "At least the little time I spent with him."

"He's a fucking saint," Hailey said. "The shit her mom pulled; I'm surprised he didn't run for the hills a long ass time ago."

"They were so made for each other," Kelsey said. "Like, you couldn't find a more perfect couple. He's her rock in the storm, her quiet place when the world around her is raging."

I sort of squeezed Hailey, letting her know I was that for her, whenever she needed. She looked up at me and smiled, snuggling in closer.

"I gotta get some sleep," Emma said.

"Same," Kelsey said.

They were all still wearing their bridesmaid dresses, and they all looked like their makeup and hair had been through a hurricane. It was amazing they were still awake, what with it being well after midnight, pushing into the early morning hours.

"I can let you guys get settled," I said, standing up. "I'm going to grab a drink downstairs. If anyone wants anything, just let me know."

"You don't have to go," Emma said.

"You guys need to change," I said. "I'll give you that privacy. Seriously, though. Food or drink, I'll go grab something if you want."

"Can you go find some beignets?" Hailey asked.

"And some cocoa?" Kelsey added.

"Oh, yeah," Emma chimed in.

"Your wish is my command," I said with a bow, then kissed Hailey before walking out of the room.

I took the elevator down to the lobby and walked up to the desk to ask where the closest place was to get the treats the women wanted. He directed me out and down the road just a bit, so I stepped out the door, and followed his directions. It was pretty easy to find, and the crowd wasn't so bad that I had a problem getting a couple of bags of the sugary treat along with four large cups of cocoa, figuring two of the beignets each would suit just fine. By the time I was back on the floor, the door was slightly ajar, and I was able to push my way in, finding the women snuggled into their beds in pajamas, the lights low, and talking softly.

"Here we go," I said, sliding the cups onto the nightstand and handing one bag to Hailey, and the other to Emma, who was closer to me on the other bed.

"Thank you so much," Emma said, and Kelsey added her thanks as well.

"Thank you, baby," Hailey said, pushing the covers back so I could get into the bed.

"Let me just get something else on," I said, grabbing my bag, and taking it with me to the bathroom.

I didn't own any pajamas, but I figured some workout shorts would suffice for the night. I closed the bathroom door and changed, shoving the clothes I had on into the bag, and taking care of my bodily functions while I was in there.

Shutting the light off, I opened the door, and walked back into the room, setting my bag at the end of the bed I was going to share with my wife. Each of them had a steaming cup in their hands, the covers pulled up to their bodies, leaning forward, and dunking the pillows covered in powdered sugar into their cocoa. It was the absolute right way to eat them, and I was glad they all knew that.

I slid into the bed, pulling the blankets up, and over my shorts. I'd kept my shirt on, not wanting to be too indecent for the women who I didn't know very well. Picking my own cup up, I took the top off, setting it next to the others on the nightstand, before turning to Hailey, and taking the beignet she offered me. There was sugar everywhere on the covers, and I sort of felt bad for the housekeepers who would have to clean it up. I made a mental note to leave a tip when we all left in the morning.

We all enjoyed our treat, the sounds of the city that was alive, and celebrating, filtering in through the closed window next to us. It was weird to think about how much activity was going on just a few floors down when the room I was in was full of sadness. They'd watched their friend get married, which should have been one of the best things in life, except for the actions of a selfish person who took that joy and marred it with tragedy.

"You're thinking awfully hard there," Hailey said, and I turned to her.

"Just trying to wrap my head around how something so wonderful can be turned to horror with just one action," I said.

"Yeah," she said. "I wish I could fix it."

"Me, too," I said. "Me, too, baby."

I heard the soft crying and looked over to see Emma's face filled with tears, her cup nearly forgotten in her hand, the other lying empty on the covers, sugar covering her fingers. I set my cup down, slid off the bed, and took hers, walking it, and my own over to the dresser across from the beds. I went back, and Kelsey and Hailey handed me theirs as well, then they closed the bags up before passing them to me, as I came back for the last load.

Walking to the bathroom, I took one of the washcloths and got it wet, then did the same with a second one, and took them both, along with a hand towel, out to the room. I handed one to Hailey, the other to Kelsey, who was sort of holding Emma as she cried. When Hailey was finished, I handed her the hand towel to dry off, taking the wet cloth from her.

Kelsey was using the cloth to wipe away Emma's tears, so I took the one that Hailey handed me, and washed her hands, being as gentle as possible, but ensuring she didn't end up with sugar in the bed, or in her hair. When Kelsey was done, she handed me the wet cloth, taking the dry one to repeat her actions before handing it off to me.

"Come on, babe," Kelsey said, shifting down into the bed and taking Emma with her. "Let's get some sleep."

Hailey was looking at me like she wanted to ask me a question, and I figured she wanted to join the other two, making sort of a sandwich, with Emma surrounded by her friends to hold her while she mourned. I nodded my head, shifting it toward them, and she got up and climbed in behind Emma, the three of them scooting together to find comfort in each other. I took the towels back to the bathroom, setting them on the counter, before walking back to the bed. Climbing in, I shut the lamp between the beds off, then scooted back toward the wall.

I figured Hailey would either join me at some point, or I'd wake up in the empty bed. Either was good with me. As I drifted off, I could hear Emma sobbing, the other two women speaking softly to her with comforting words, and I couldn't help but fall more deeply in love with my wife. The way she was caring for her friend was more than anyone could ask, and she was doing it willingly.

Chapter Twenty-Seven

Hailey...

The fact that he flew home for me meant more than he'd ever know. I'd never really had anyone who put me first. I mean, my friends were all there for me, but they had families and shit, so I was brought along as more of an afterthought. But not Alej. No, he left his job, got on a plane, and flew home. Willingly.

When I woke up a few hours after we all fell asleep in a puppy pile, and Kelsey always called it, I was cramped and nearly falling off the edge of the double bed. I slid out, almost hitting my head on the nightstand, and got up to go pee. When I came back, I climbed in bed with Alej. There was more room, plus, I kinda wanted him to hold me.

I hadn't cried. At least not really. I mean, sure, there had been tears. But I hadn't really let it all go. I was the strong friend, the one that everyone leaned on. The stable one who could hold the others as they all fell apart. It wasn't that I was mad about it. No, it was nice to be able to do that for them. But right now, I needed someone to be there for me.

He pulled me to him when I climbed in, and I got as close as I could, holding him for dear life. That's when it started. The tears were there, running down my face when I climbed in, but the full body shakes took over. I wasn't a loud crier, because that was a good way to get your ass beat or harassed in the system. I'd learned early on that being weak was a way for others to take advantage of you, and I was not at all about that.

"That's it," he whispered in my ear. "I got you. Let it all out."

And I did. I wept in a way I had never done before. Not just for the absolute shit show that happened the night before, but for everything leading up to it. All the way back to when I first realized that I was disposable, that I wasn't worth anything unless it was for me to give to someone else. First my mom, who left me in our shitty apartment with a box of Pop Tarts, half a jug of Sunny Delight, and nothing else. When I ran out of food, I tried to get out of the apartment, but she'd done something on the outside of the door so I couldn't open it. If it weren't for Mrs. Appleton in the apartment next door, I probably would have starved.

Mom was so pissed when she came back and had to deal with the cops and social services that she just signed me away. The last thing she said to me was good riddance. That she never liked me anyway, and I wasn't worth her stupid stretch marks and saggy tits. I mean, who the fuck says that to their own child? Especially someone who is literally dependent on you?

After that, I was passed around from house to house, trying to find someone who would keep me long enough for me to settle in. It wasn't until the Thompsons showed me that I wasn't worthless that I actually started to do anything worthwhile. The first thing they did was buy me a suitcase; one I picked out for myself. Then, they let me pick out some clothes that I could put into it, along with one special toy that I didn't have to share with anyone.

The stupid thing was never unpacked until I moved out. Oh, sure, the clothes got swapped out for things that actually fit me, but still, it was never empty. I found that I loved to learn, and was really actually good at it, too. They're the ones who instilled in me a sense of pride in myself, and I would forever be grateful for them. It fucking killed me when they died.

Now, I was dealing with the death of another parent. True, she wasn't my mom, but I'd known her for a long time. Hell, we all had. But she was selfish and needed to run the show, no matter who it hurt. Well, I guess she got to fuck her daughter one last time on the way out.

Alej was warm, his body a firm foundation, and I planned to build a good life with him. It had started weird, and was not at all the way it should have, but my God did I fucking luck out. He was not just a beautiful man, but he was kind, caring, and overall, just wonderful. And he was all mine.

Pressing my lips to his shoulder, he sucked in a breath, nuzzling against my ear.

"Your friends," he said.

"They can sleep through anything," I whispered back. "I need you."

My hands went to the end of his shirt and shoved it up, giving me access to his body. I ran my hands up his chest, feeling the muscles bunch as I touched them, and it just made me want him more. He pulled the back of my shirt up, then shoved his hands down into my panties, pulling me close to him. He was definitely ready for me, and I loved that I could get that reaction from him.

I pushed against him, rolling him onto his back as I shifted to shove my pants down. He helped me rid my body of the offending garments, then shoved his own shorts down, his cock springing free in the dark of the room. The city outside was still alive, the sounds filtering up through the walls and windows, and I loved that I was choosing life over the death that had come to us.

Slipping my leg across his body, I straddled him, sliding my pussy up and down his length, feeling it against me as I let myself go, let myself get washed away in the beauty and safety of this man. Rising up, I raised him so I could slide down, and he helped me by holding himself up so my hands could hold me steady. When he was fully inside me, stretching me, I sighed. This was my happy place, being held and loved by this man, and it did wonders to put my shattered heart back together again.

I eased up, pulling away from him, then settled back down. I wasn't in the best position to do much of anything else and knew it would take a long time to get either of us where we needed to be, but that was okay with me. It would just be that much longer that he could keep my demons at bay. Over and over again, I rose up and fell, his cock sliding in and out of me in such a magical dance, and I could finally feel that slight building within me.

Leaning forward, I pressed my lips to his, his arms wrapping around me to hold me tightly to his body, and I just let myself settle there for a moment. His hips picked up the rhythm, pulling back and forth to keep us moving while staying so tightly bound together.

Without warning, he shifted, rolling us over so he was on top. I made a sound, but he swallowed it with his kiss, and then he was in control, his hips surging forward and back, pounding into my pussy with his cock so hard I was losing my mind. He kept his lips on mine, taking each moan and cry into his mouth, ensuring that we wouldn't wake up the girls in the other bed.

It was hotter thinking that they might catch us, and all it did was push me closer and closer to that cliff, that peak that I wanted to reach, so I could tumble into nothingness and everything all wrapped together. And it came without warning, the orgasm ripping through me in a tidal wave of feelings, some I had no name for. I felt him falter just a bit, then he found his own release, pumping into me and leaving bits of himself there.

When he finally let up, pulling his lips from mine, I sighed, feeling more content than I'd ever felt in my entire life. He completed me, filled me in ways no one else ever had, and made me feel alive and worthy all at the same time.

He slid out of me and climbed over my leg to lay on his back next to me, his breathing somewhat ragged as he did. Once there, he reached over and pulled me next to him, holding me close and kissing my forehead before whispering in my ear.

"You are the most wonderful thing I've ever experienced. I never want to be without you."

"I'm not going anywhere," I said quietly, pressing my lips to the hollow on his chest where his collar bones met. "I can't exist without you. I need you in my life."

We lay there, both catching our breaths, as we came back to the mortal plane of existence, a place that seemed boring and uneventful. I was nearly back asleep when he shifted.

"You need to go pee," he said. "Don't want you to get an infection. Besides, I should clean myself up, too."

I let out a little groan, then rolled over to get up, grabbing my panties and pajama pants to take with me. Padding into the bathroom, I pushed the door so that it was almost shut, then sat to pee and wipe. He was right in that I was a mess, but it was one I enjoyed. We should probably stop going without a condom, but I had my IUD, so I figured we were safe occasionally. Not that I would be all that upset if a happy accident happened.

There was a tap on the door, so light I almost didn't hear it, then he stuck his head in, and smiled. I was pulling my pants on, but still sitting on the toilet. He had his shorts on, so I assumed he used some tissues or something to clean himself before pulling them up.

"You almost done?" he asked.

"Yeah," I said, standing and pulling everything up. "I just didn't want to fall over while putting them on. That would definitely wake the girls up."

"I think we did," he said with a smirk.

"Fuck," I said, moving out of his way so he could use the toilet. "I'm gonna go out and see if I can smooth things over."

"Okay," he said. "Be right there."

I slid out of the bathroom, closing the door behind me, and made my way over to the bed.

"What time is it?" Emma asked.

"No clue," I replied, then picked up my phone. "Seven," I said when I got the screen to light up.

"When's checkout?" she asked.

"I think eleven," I said. "Go back to sleep."

"Gotta pee," she said and moved to sit up.

Just then, Alej came out of the bathroom. He came to me as Emma got up and went in. He kissed me, then climbed in behind me, settling under the covers. I looked at Kelsey who was still sound asleep and wondered how Missy was doing.

Alej reached out and rubbed my back, and I turned and looked at him over my shoulder. I had gotten so lucky with him, and I honestly couldn't imagine what would be happening right now if he wasn't in my life. Just a few weeks with him and my whole life felt like it was so much better.

Kenton had proven himself to be a solid guy, and I hoped he'd been able to keep Missy from spiraling out of control. She would do that when we were in school, go off the deep end after something her mom had done, and we would all rally around her and make sure she was settled before we left her alone.

It was fucked up to say it, but with her mom gone, her life would likely get exponentially better. The way Missy was wound up and freaked out any time she had to deal with her mother, this would likely be good for her. The fact that she wouldn't have to have that toxicity in her life would be a blessing once she got over the fucked-up way she was relieved of it.

"Hey," Emma said, and I looked up to see her standing in front of me. "You okay?"

"Yeah," I said. "Just trying to still wrap my head around everything."

"Have you heard from Missy?" she asked and I looked at my phone.

"No," I said. "No messages at all."

"Should we check on her?"

"I'm hoping Kenton kept her busy last night," I said. "And that she's sleeping it off right now. They're staying another night here before they head out for their honeymoon, so no need for her to have to get up."

"Let's hope so," she said.

"Shut up," Kelsey said, and both Emma and I started laughing. "I'm not kidding," she barked again. "Either shut up or get out. I need sleep."

"Sorry," I said.

Kelsey was the absolute worst in the morning. Seriously not an early bird in the least. To be fair, we'd all been up for quite some time, so the fact that she was upset made sense. It had only been a few hours, not nearly a full night's sleep, since we finally shut the lights out.

Emma climbed back into her bed and I set my phone down and did the same, snuggling close to Alej, who pulled me into him, my back to his front, his arm wrapped around my waist, holding me close. I hoped I never got tired of that, but worried that it would get old not seeing him for long stretches of time. When I thought about it, my break would be right in the middle of his work time, and he would be off when I was ramping up. I wondered whether we would ever have much time off together outside of the end-of-year holidays.

"Stop thinking so much," he mumbled in my ear, and it made me smile.

"How'd you know I was thinking?" I asked.

"Because you're stiff and not relaxing," he said, sort of jostling me a bit. "Relax and go back to sleep. Whatever it is will keep."

He was right. We had plenty of time to figure out the rest of our lives, and nothing would change in the next few hours. When he pressed a kiss to my neck, I sighed and relaxed, falling quickly to sleep.

Chapter Twenty-Eight

Alejandro...

We were standing in the lobby waiting for the newly-weds to come down for breakfast. They'd scheduled a late brunch type thing, and we weren't sure if that was still on or not. With everything that had happened the day before, I wondered if Missy would be up for anything festive.

Her dad and brother had been kind when they met me, thanking me for coming back in the middle of the night to help out. It was weird that they were so kind and protective over Hailey, but I figured it was because she'd been around for so long.

His parents and younger sister were also there, and introductions were made there as well. They seemed like decent people, and I could see how Kenton had ended up being such a nice guy with the way they were.

"Hey," Missy said as she stepped out of the elevator. "Are we all ready for brunch?"

The mood she was in concerned me, but I wasn't sure if that was her normal response to trauma, so I didn't say anything.

"We weren't sure you still wanted to do it," her dad said.

"Why wouldn't I?" she asked, as if it were the dumbest question in the world.

"Just checking," Hailey said. "You look amazing."

She went and hugged her friend, then hugged Kenton as well.

"I'm starving," she said, then grabbed her new husband's hand and pulled him toward the door.

We all followed behind her, and Hailey looked at her dad with some confusion. To be fair, Missy did look amazing, and not at all like I anticipated her to look when she came down. I anticipated red and puffy eyes, sloppy clothing, or not coming down at all. But she was so put together you'd never know anything at all had happened.

"Is she gonna be okay?" I asked as we stepped out of the hotel.

"She will," Hailey said. "She does this compartmentalization thing. I know she has a regular therapist, so she'll probably either go see them or do some sort of video conference to figure out how to handle her emotions."

"As long as you think she's okay," I said.

"I think so," she replied. "Thanks for being concerned."

"She's become family," I said. "Friends are the family you choose."

Hailey squeezed my hand and smiled up at me, and I knew that what I'd said was what she needed to hear. We walked down the street to a small café, stepping in and finding the room that had been set up for us to enjoy a buffet brunch with everything you could imagine available.

"Oh my God," Missy said as we stepped into the room. "I didn't know you were coming. It's so good to see you."

She walked the few feet from where she was standing over to us as we stepped through the door.

"Glad to be here," I said, as she reached out to hug me.

"I'm really glad you're here," she said with a sad smile.

I hugged her, and when she stepped back, she had a tear running down her face.

"None of that," I said, brushing it away with my thumb. "Today is about celebrating you and Kenton. Speaking of which, where is he?"

"Alej," I heard from behind me and turned to see him. "Glad you could make it."

"Glad it worked out," I said. "Gotta head back tonight, though."

"You're here now," he said. "That's what matters."

The food was amazing, and we all had more than enough to fill us all up. By the time things were winding down, I'd met Missy's dad and brother, as well as Kenton's parents and siblings. I was full and felt like it was a good day spent with good people. I wished I could have stayed longer, but I needed to head back to Florida.

"You wanna drive me to the airport?" I asked Hailey.

"Can we swing by the house first?" she asked.

"Sure, why?"

"Thought we could..."

She didn't finish the sentence, but that was likely because we were in the middle of a crowd of people.

"I'd love that," I whispered in her ear before kissing her temple.

"Good," she said, squeezing my hand.

We climbed into her car and headed out of the center of town and toward her house, which was closer than mine. When she pulled into the driveway, she shut the car off and looked at me.

"Thank you for coming," she said.

"Of course," I replied. "Why wouldn't I?"

"Because you had work," she said. "And because you had to fly out here and come and rescue me."

"I didn't rescue you," I said. "I just came to comfort my wife. Something any decent man would do."

"Still," she said. "It was a lot of work, and I appreciate it."

"Wanna show me how much?"

"Get your ass in the house and I will," she said, opening her door and racing for the front door.

I climbed out and followed her at a slower pace, but likely just as excited as she was.

Chapter Twenty-Nine

Hailey...

I opened the front door and turned around to see him coming through it. He wrapped his arms around my waist and shut the door with his foot while simultaneously pressing his lips to mine, pulling me against him, and lifting me off the floor. He took a step in my direction, and pressed me against the wall, one hand on my ass, the other at the back of my neck. I couldn't help but wrap my legs around his waist, pulling him to me when I did.

It was so much passion my brain couldn't keep up. Between his hips surging against me to his tongue sliding along my own, the way his fingers dug into my ass, it was almost too much. When I pulled back to catch my breath, I looked into his dark eyes, so full of everything I ever wanted to see, and everything I was likely reflecting back from my own.

"We have too many clothes on," I said.

He stepped back, setting me on the floor before pulling his shirt over his head, and tossing it off to the side. It was like we were in a race, seeing who could get undressed faster. His hands were working on his pants while he shucked his shoes. I worked on my own clothes, yanking my shirt off and shoving my pants down. I had more clothes on than him, which was a normal thing, but it seemed to take me entirely too long to get them off, and he ended up helping me with my pants as I finished unhooking my bra and dropping it on the pile of clothes at my feet.

"Better?" he asked, and I nodded. "Good."

With him already on his knees, he slid a hand between my thighs, running his fingers across my sex, and I leaned back against the wall, pressing my hands to it to hold me steady.

"You're so wet," he said. "You been waiting for me for a while?"

"My whole life," I said.

"I'm not going anywhere," he said, then pressed a finger inside me, and damn did it just give me that rush.

He lifted my leg, setting it atop his shoulder so he had better access to my pussy. He pressed his lips to my sex, slipping his tongue out to taste me, and all of it just was everything I needed. His finger slid in and out, doing that come hither motion that scratched that spot just inside me, making me want to fall into bliss, but not quite getting there with just what he was doing. He made a valiant effort, sucking my clit, rubbing my pussy, stroking that spot just the right way, but it wasn't quite enough.

"I need you inside me," I said, my panting breaths making me sound sultrier than I intended.

Taking his mouth from me, and pulling his finger free, he stood up and kissed me, and the taste of myself on his lips was amazing. He wrapped me in his arms and picked me up, my legs going around his waist again, and carried me to our room. As soon as we were in there, he set me on the edge of the bed, then pulled out the drawer where we kept the condoms open to grab one.

As I laid there, I watched as he removed the slippery disc from the foil pack, and slid it down his cock. The way he looked at me while he did it was more than just sexy, it was so fucking hot I damn near came from the look alone. He leaned down, his hands going on either side of me, and I opened my legs for him, waiting for him to fuck me, wanting him so much that it almost hurt.

"Scoot up," he said, and I did as he bid, sliding closer to the head of the bed. "Good girl. I want you so bad right now."

"I want you, too," I replied. "Come to me."

I reached out my hands, and he crawled up the bed on his hands and knees, settling himself between my thighs, his body pressing me down into the mattress. He kissed me again, this time slow and sensual, taking his time tasting every bit of my mouth, mimicking what he would soon be doing with his cock, and I was desperate for that.

His body was against mine, firm and strong, but his cock was out of reach, which sort of pissed me off. I shifted my hips, pressing up toward him, but he kept himself just out of reach, in completely the wrong position for me to work to get him into me. I let out a bit of a whine, and he smiled against my lips.

"Am I frustrating you?" he asked.

"Yes," I said, shifting my hips again to try to get his cock where I wanted it.

"Do you want me?"

"More than anything," I said.

"Is this what you want?" he asked as he shifted just enough to find purchase and slide into me and my God, did it do everything I wanted.

"Yes," I sighed, moving in time with him.

He slowly stroked in and out of me, long, even, and so disappointingly slow. I wanted him to fuck me, hard, fast, and get me over that edge. He didn't do that, though, and the buildup was excruciating. I felt like it would take forever to get me to where I needed to be, and he was just prolonging the torture. His arms were wrapped around me, holding me where I was, not giving me any way to speed things up, and it felt so good, but it wasn't enough.

"Faster," I whispered, and he began to increase his speed.

"Faster," I said again, hoping he'd get to the hard fucking that I craved.

Shifting, he took my leg and raised it up, changing the angle at which he entered me, and that just did what it needed to do, sending me tumbling into the brilliant explosion I wanted. I tumbled up and out and over everything and everyone, fire burning through me in the most beautiful way, until I was gathered back in his arms and he held me as I found myself again.

"Damn, baby," he said when I opened my eyes and looked up at him. "You were so beautiful when you came. I don't know that we'll beat that one, but I will strive every day to do so."

"You are everything I need," I said, and meant it with my whole self.

"Come with me to Florida," he said, and I looked at him.

"I can't," I said. "I have to work."

"You don't have to," he said, but I stopped him.

"I know you can pay for everything," I said. "That isn't what I meant. I worked hard to get to where I am, and I'm not going to give it up."

"Okay," he said. "Just know that I'll take care of you."

"Of course you will," I replied. "But this is something I have to do."

He slid out of me, holding the condom tight to his body, which told me we had come together. Shifting, he laid down next to me, and I turned to look into his eyes. He'd pulled the condom off and tied it off, but there wasn't a trash can in the bedroom, so he set it on the side of the bed.

"Do you know what's happening with the principal?" he asked.

"He pled guilty," I said. "The District Attorney's office called me earlier this week to tell me that he had done that, and that he had agreed to the plea deal they offered. They also said that they have put a permanent restraining order in place against him, so I should be fine."

"Good," he said. "I was worried that you'd have to see him again."

"Nope," I said.

There were a million things we needed to talk about, but none of them mattered so long as he was lying next to me in my bed. I wanted to take him up on going with him, but it just wouldn't work. My job was too important to me, and I never wanted to give that up. The fact that I did it on my own, without the help of parents or other people really meant something to me, and I felt it would be a disservice to myself if I walked away from it.

"You sure are thinking," he said, and I blinked and smiled.

"Just trying to figure out how we're gonna make this all work," I admitted. "It's absolutely unconventional, but I really do love you, and can't imagine my life without you."

"Same, babe," he said, pressing his lips to mine.

"When do you leave?" I asked and heard the sadness in my voice.

"Not until tomorrow morning," I said. "I booked a flight back when we were eating. I should go tonight, but I don't want to leave you yet. It was hard the first time, but it'll be harder this time."

"It was hard when you left," I said. "I almost took you up on following you."

"Really?"

"Yeah," I said. "But I had too much to do leading up to Missy's wedding. Plus, I'd just missed a couple of weeks for the stupid injury, so I didn't want to press my luck."

"Besides weekends, when do you have off next?"

"I'd have to check my calendar," I said. "I'm not really sure off the top of my head, and with the way you've blown my mind, it doesn't surprise me."

"I blew your mind?" he asked, almost as if he wasn't sure I was telling the truth.

"So much," I said. "Let me know when you're ready to go again, though, cause I'd love to see if you can do it to me one more time."

"Oh, I'll do it again," he said, pressing himself over me, and kissing me.

Chapter Thirty

Alejandro...

We'd gotten two more rounds before I was just unable to continue. Biology could fuck things up sometimes, but she was well and truly satisfied. When her alarm went off, she groaned, slapping her phone to snooze it. I cuddled up to her, pressing my front to her back, hoping we'd have time for one more before I left.

"You better be quick," she said, not even bothering to hide her enthusiasm. "I might need a shower before I go to work."

"Then let's get in the shower," I said, kissing her shoulder.

She flipped the covers off herself, grabbed her phone, presumably to turn the alarm off, and was heading to the bathroom before I even rolled over to get out of bed. When I heard the water turn on, I snagged a condom from the drawer, and headed in after her.

Stepping into the tub, she was under the water, getting her hair wet. I grabbed the shampoo, pouring some into my palm, then went to her to work it into her blonde locks. Her hair was always so soft, and I loved running my fingers through it. Some guys would probably think that was weird, but I couldn't help it.

While my hands were busy in her hair, hers were on my cock, stroking me slow and easy, twisting as she came to the head before going back to the base.

"Keep that up and you won't get any," I said.

She smiled, then tipped her head back, rinsing the suds from the top of her head. I leaned down, taking her nipple into my mouth, and she arched against me, pushing further into my mouth. I sucked her in, pulling back a bit, setting my teeth just to the bud that was extended from her, holding her in my mouth. Her moans echoed off the tiles as she set her hand on the wall, grabbing the safety bar that was set into it.

Instead of slowing down, I reached a hand down, sliding it between her thighs, stroking along her pussy lips, and she opened for me so beautifully, giving me free access to her most intimate parts. I slid a finger into her, but the angle was awkward, so I wasn't able to get much motion. Instead of continuing, I let her tit pop out of my mouth, pulled my hand away, and moved her around so she was facing the wall. She bent forward, her legs spread, her ass aimed right at me, and I reached back to grab the condom from the shelf where I'd set it, opening it up and sliding it on.

Sinking into her, she moaned, pressing back and into me. I began to move, slowly at first, but her hips were persistent in their need for more, so I sped up, holding the safety bar with one hand, her hip with the other, and began to fuck her hard and fast. I'd learned that she liked that a lot, so I gave it to her whenever I could. While I didn't mind it, I also liked the slow and steady love making we'd done much of as well.

I felt the telltale signs of impending release, and knew I wouldn't last long, so slid my hand that was on her hip around and began to stroke her clit, working the cluster of nerves in an attempt to push her past the final hurdle and to send her into that blissful space. It didn't take long, and she was squeezing me, pulling me into her as I worked to try to find my own release. She was crying out, calling my name, and it sent me flying. I held the safety bar for dear life as we both plummeted into oblivion before coming back to the here and now.

"I am going to miss you so much," she said, her breath coming in fast pants.

"Same," I said, trying to remember how breathing worked.

I pulled out of her, holding the condom, and then let it fall to the floor of the shower as I gathered her into my arms. The water was still warm, so I grabbed the soap and worked a lather over her body, washing her with care as she settled back to find herself. Once she was washed and rinsed off, I turned the water off, opening the curtain to grab a towel from the bar.

Wrapping it around her, I rubbed the soft fabric over her skin, drying her off. Her hair was still dripping, so I pulled the towel up and worked on her hair the way she'd shown me, more patting it than rubbing it, to get it dry. She reached over and grabbed the second towel, handing it to me and taking the one I'd been using. Bending forward, she wrapped her hair up in that turban style that women did, then leaned forward and kissed me.

"Thank you," she said.

"My pleasure," I replied as I toweled myself dry.

"I meant for coming home," she added.

"Of course," I said. "I want to be there for you every chance I get."

"I just hate that I had to pull you away from your work," she said.

With her standing naked in front of me, it was hard for me to concentrate on much, but I did my best to keep from ogling her, and instead listen to what she was saying.

"I promise, it's not a problem," I said. "I will come home if I can, and this time I could. I'm glad it worked out this way. Not the reason for me coming home, obviously, but for being able to be here for you."

"You don't know how much that means to me," she said and leaned into me, pressing her body against mine.

I wrapped my arms around her and held her there, loving the feel of her entire body against my own. The way her curves fit against me, her head just under my chin, even with the towel wrapped around her head. She really was my everything, and I was sad I had to leave her.

"I wish I didn't have to go back," I said.

"I know," she said. "And I wish I didn't want you to stay, as selfish as it is. I just don't know how we're gonna make this work. You were only gone a week, and I missed you so much."

"We'll figure it out," I said. "Many other guys get this figured out, so I'm sure we can do it. We're both smart, so it should be doable."

"I just wish it would be easier," she said, then pressed her lips to my chest and leaned back to look up at me. "I have to get dressed and go to work."

"Yeah," I said. "I need to get to the airport. I've got an Uber coming, so don't worry about me."

"Okay," she said, still holding me. "I wish we could stay here for a longer time than we have had."

"Me, too," I said.

"But, alas, duty calls," she said, letting her arms down and stepping away from me.

I let her go and finished drying myself off before heading in to get dressed and pack up the couple of things I'd brought with me.

"You should come down for a weekend," I said as I was putting my shoes on. "You could meet my parents."

"Are you sure your mom wants to meet me?"

"Doesn't matter," I said. "My dad seems excited about meeting you, though."

"He does?" she asked.

"Absolutely," I said. "In fact, he's suggested that we do a big family dinner before the season starts so you can meet everyone."

"Yeah, that sounds terrible," she said. "Big crowds, plus meeting the in-laws, plus being in another state, plus all my anxiety about how we met: that's just a recipe for disaster if you ask me."

"We can start small," I said. "You figure out a weekend that would work for you to come down in March and I'll make a plan to have dinner with just my parents. I won't tell them you're coming, so they won't be able to make a big deal about it."

"Isn't that sort of lying by omission?" she asked.

"Let's call it self-preservation," I said. "You'll get the initial meeting done without all the fanfare, they'll get to see what an amazing woman you are, and it will be over and done with in just one meal."

"I think I can pull that off," she said. "As long as you promise it won't be more than just them."

"I'll enlist my *abuelita's* help," I said. "She loves you already, so she'll help me make it work. Besides, she thinks my mom's gone over the edge with all her issues with us."

"I do like your grandmother," she said.

"I can't wait for you to meet her in person," I said. "She's a really cool lady. She's planning on coming up during the All-Star break, so I'm sure we can arrange for you to meet her then."

"When is that?" she asked.

"July," I said. "Usually the second week or so. I'd have to check the schedule for the actual dates, but that's the ballpark of when it is."

Her phone started going off, and she looked at it confused, then shut the alarm off.

"Guess I'm gonna have to order in for lunch," she said. "I gotta go."

She came to me, kissing me hard, and I wrapped her up, and held her to me.

"I miss you already," she mumbled against my lips.

"Find a weekend," I said. "We can count down to then. Besides, we can video call, and have phone sex if you want."

"Not the same," she said.

"I know," I replied, then kissed her again. "I love you."

"Love you, too," she said with another kiss.

She looked at me, then squeezed me hard, and turned to leave. I couldn't be sure, but I swore there were tears in her eyes, and I had to wonder what that was about. I didn't have time to think, though, because my app alerted me to the fact that the car was here to take me to the airport.

I grabbed my bag and headed out, locking the door behind me after I closed it. I climbed into the car, and the driver said hello before pulling out and onto the streets to make his way to the airport. He dropped me off, and I said my thanks before heading to security. When I got to the gate, I sent Hailey a text telling her I missed her, and that I'd let her know when I landed.

I miss you so much it hurts.

That text just killed me, almost making me want to just turn around and head back. I didn't because I knew my job needed me, but it still felt like a gut punch.

Pick a weekend and we'll be back together soon.

It was the only thing keeping me in check, the fact that we'd made plans to have her come down for a weekend. I wanted nothing more than to spend the rest of my life in her arms, but that wasn't how life worked. I shut my phone off, not wanting to be tempted to call her and demand she come with me. It wouldn't do any good, and would only make her more upset, so I held off.

By the time I got back to my condo and dropped my bag off, it was almost too late for me to head to the game, but I went, knowing that it would keep my mind occupied when nothing else would. I missed her so much, and I wasn't sure that the small amount of time we'd spent together would hold me over until she came down. It had to, but it would be a hard thing.

"You okay?" Coach asked when I got into the locker room.

"Yeah," I lied. "Had a big tragedy in my wife's life, so had to hold her while she got herself put right."

"If you need more time..."

"I'm good," I said, not wanting him to tempt me in any way.

"Okay," he said, obviously realizing that I needed him to not ask. "You good to play, or want to ride pine?"

"I'd love to play," I said. "Get my mind off everything."

"Completely understand," he said.

I was glad he did and changed into my uniform to head out to the field and get warmed up. JP saw me and I gave him a head nod, same with Nick and Austin. My guess is they knew I needed to get out of my own head and into something that didn't really require thought, so they let me do my own thing getting ready for the game.

Coach had put me fifth in the lineup, so I had a minute to get my brain into gear on the field for a couple of innings before coming up to bat, but then the rest of the guys decided it was gonna be a hitting game, and I was up in the bottom of the first with the bases loaded and nobody out.

Before I stepped into the box, I closed my eyes and thought about Hailey. Her beautiful body, the way she looked the night before when she completely shattered under me, and how she looked at me when she walked out of the house to head to her job. If I could get through that, I could figure out a way to hit a fucking ball with a bat.

I stepped around the catcher and walked up to the plate, digging my foot in the back of the box before taking a couple of swings and stepping fully in. Waiting for the pitch, I watched everything around me, letting my mind go to what needed to happen, not anything else.

I focused on the pitcher, who had shaken the catcher off a couple of times before the coming set. He got into the wind up, rocked and threw, and the ball just sat there, right at the perfect height, as if it was on a tee, and I swung, the reverb rippling up my arm to my shoulder as I watched the ball sail up and up until it went over the wall.

"You wanna run?" the ump asked, and I looked back at him, realizing I'd been watching my shot.

"Sorry," I said, and headed toward first, dropping the bat on the ground on my way.

I slapped the first base coach's hand as I went around, then kept the jog going around second, and giving the third base coach a high five as I rounded that base as well, coming into home and the guys who were on base all congratulating me. It was always surreal, that first big bomb of the year, and with the way the last few days had gone, it was even weirder. Hopefully, the rest of the week would go well, and Hailey would tell me she was coming down the next weekend.

Chapter Thirty-One

Hailey...

As much as I had wanted to stay home, and stay with Alej, I knew I needed to work. It helped that I also knew I wouldn't have to deal with good old Dick, and his shit. Still, I had only worked a week before the chaos that was Missy's wedding. Now, though, she was off on her honeymoon, and hopefully Kenton would be making her forget about everything but that.

They'd posted a picture of them at the airport, and the caption had said they were turning their phones off, and would be out of commission until their return in a week and a half. I envied the ability to simply step away from the insanity, and simply exist with just the two of them. It was something I wanted to do with Alej, but we'd kind of fucked that up by getting married before we even knew each other.

He'd said he wanted me to meet his parents, but that gave me all sorts of anxiety. I didn't have a family I could introduce him to, save my friends, and he'd met them already. How was I supposed to act around his parents? Should I shake their hands, or give them a hug? What if they hated me? How would I act if they were outright hostile? I wanted to meet them, but was terrified at the same time, and I wasn't sure whether it was a good thing or not.

I'd promised to check the schedule and see when I could get a weekend to head down there, and I really wanted to, but my job was kind of nuts, what with having missed a couple of weeks due to the injury. I'd only been back a week as it was, and I didn't really know whether I could find a time that would work and not make me any more insane. Not that the work was nuts or anything, because how crazy can a group of five-year-olds get?

But then again, there was the whole thing with Dick, and his dicking around. He accepted the plea and there was a restraining order in place, but would he adhere to it? Instead of worrying about it in class, though, I let myself get lost in the little kids, and all their antics.

"Ms. Truitt," Ginny said. "Can we get pretty rings like yours?"

"Oh, no," I said, realizing that she was looking at my wedding and engagement rings. "These are special, given to me by someone very important to me."

"Oh," she said. "Mommy said that good girls who do what they're told get pretty rings like that. Are you a good girl to get that ring?"

That was such a loaded question, and I wondered what her mother did to get pretty rings. I didn't want to assume she was anything other than a doting parent, but wasn't sure, because how did I know what went on behind closed doors.

"It was because someone loved me," I said. "Now, let's finish coloring this picture."

Vague enough to be ambiguous, simple enough for a child, and divert the attention of said child away from my jewelry, and back to the task at hand. Thankfully, each tactic worked, and Ginny was back to coloring her picture.

By the time the first class headed home, I was exhausted and ready to be done for the day, but that wasn't what was going to happen. Instead, I headed to the teacher's room, and grabbed my lunch.

"There she is," one of the other teachers said as I walked in.

"Hey, Hailey," another teacher said. "Is it true that you're married?"

"Why?" I asked.

"Mary was saying something about you being married to someone really rich," the first teacher said. "She said that you got a fancy lawyer and were suing the school district after what happened a few weeks ago."

"Well," I said, trying to figure out the best way to answer this question without giving anything away. "Mary was there when everything happened. She saw firsthand what went down, and if she wants to talk about anything, that's her business. I, on the other hand, am simply looking to eat between classes."

"Geez," the second one said. "No need to bite our heads off. We were just trying to figure out what happened."

"Not biting your heads off," I said. "I just prefer to keep my private life private."

With that, I grabbed my lunch, and headed out of the room. I'd have to make a point to ask Liz if these teachers were in the group chat she was in that were saying all sorts of shit about me. It wouldn't surprise me if they were. They were all between five and ten years older than me, and they seemed to have already been a group when I started. I'd never wanted to push into a group or anything, so I let them have their clique and just stayed in my own lane.

"You saw the ring, right?" one of the teachers asked, as I walked out.

I wanted to call them out, bitch at them for making my life their gossip chain, and talking shit behind my back, but I didn't want to throw Liz under the bus. She was my inside man at this point, and I wanted to have that information available should I need it in the future. Hopefully, these busybodies would find something else to hold their attention, and I could be left by the wayside, a forgotten relic in their past. Thinking about it more, I really wanted to shove it in their faces that yes, I was in fact, married. I'd been married for a while, and they'd never get as good a man as I had. They were probably still with some losers from their high school or college days.

It sort of made me laugh to think about that. If I were still with the boyfriend I had in high school, I'd probably be three kids in, living in a trailer, with some drunk ass dude who didn't know how to wash a dish or change a diaper. The guys from college were a bit better, but it still wasn't exactly top-notch material. No, I had definitely married up the food chain.

I headed right to the vice principal's office, figuring I could find a weekend that would work for the school with her, instead of hunting up the school's calendar online where we normally did our requests. I wanted to get the okay first, before requesting the time off, so that when I did, no one would be able to kick me off that time.

"Ms. Truitt," she said after I knocked on her door frame.

"Got a minute?" I asked.

"Sure," she said. "Come on in."

I thought about closing the door, but that would likely make anyone who walked by curious, and give them reason to eavesdrop, so I left it standing open, and went in to sit down in one of the chairs. She'd been moved to acting principal and would likely take the spot officially once dear old Dick was canned.

"I need to find a Friday and Monday that I can take off in the next couple of weeks," I said, jumping right in. "I am meeting my husband's family, and this is the best month for that to happen."

"Your husband?" she asked.

"Yeah," I said, not elaborating. "His family is in Florida, and he's currently there for work, so it makes sense that I go to him, instead of all of them coming up here. It will be a weekend trip, but I'd like to have the buffer days so that I can avoid anything like what happened last time I went out of town."

"I'm sure whatever weekend works for you will be fine," she said. "Did you have any specific date you wanted?"

"I just wanted to get the okay from you before I submitted my official request," I said. "I know that isn't how this normally goes, but I didn't want to end up with any issues after the fact."

"Then let's pick a date now," she said, pulling up what I assumed was the calendar on her computer. "I wouldn't want to do it this weekend, but maybe the next one would work. We have testing that will happen at the end of the month, so if we can avoid that, it would be better. Otherwise, it looks totally open."

"Great," I said. "I'll ask my husband what weekend works best and let you know."

"I'll go ahead and block both weekends between this upcoming one and the last one for you," she said. "Then, we can just take one of them off the calendar."

"I really appreciate this," I said, standing up.

"If anyone tries to give you grief," she said. "Just send them to me."

"Okay," I said and walked out.

I damn near ran over Mary, who was standing right outside the office, which meant that she had been listening to my conversation. How much she heard, I didn't know, but honestly, I didn't give a single fuck at this point. She'd shown me who she was, so I was gonna believe her.

"I heard you say your husband," she said.

"I have to go," I said, trying to get around her.

"I just want to find out about your husband," she said, stepping in front of me.

"Mary," I said, raising my voice so that Ms. Moody could hear me. "I am not interested in discussing my private life with you. I have a class I need to get ready for, so please move."

"Mary," I heard the vice principal say behind me, and Mary's eyes went big. "Can I speak to you, please?"

"Of course, Ms. Moody," she said, then glared at me.

I moved to the side so she could get past me, then continued on my way to my classroom. I didn't need to know what was going on with Mary, or anyone else, for that matter. When I got to my classroom, I sent a text to Liz to ask her if she was open either of the week-ends I'd saved. She was my go-to when it came to substitutes, and if I could make sure she was open for the dates, I would do that for her. She worked when she wanted, and didn't always say yes to my vacan-cies, but I liked to offer it to her before going to the pool of substitutes we had.

She sent me a message that she was open both weekends, so I sent a text to Alej, letting him know that I could do either weekend and to let me know so I could solidify the dates with the school. I hadn't expected to hear back from him, but he sent an almost immediate response that the second weekend would be fine. I sent an email to Ms. Moody to let her know both the dates I would be gone, but that I had already lined up a substitute for them. I also texted Liz with which weekend I was going to be gone.

With that settled, I got back to my day, playing and teaching my students, who were entirely too adorable. I hadn't wanted kids when I was younger, and figured I could just have the kids in my classes as my substitute ones, but the more I taught, and even as far back as when I was doing my student teaching, I found myself longing to have my own. My upbringing was rough, but I had promised myself that if I ever did have kids, they'd be cared for, and nurtured with love and understanding. I'd even thought about fostering kids, but wasn't quite ready for that big of a dedication. At least not yet.

Now, though, I looked at the kids and could see bits and pieces of each of their parents, how they looked like their mom sometimes, and their dad others. Some kids were mirror images of one parent, but seemed to have the personality of the other. It was interesting to see how the genetics worked. There was a set of twins in my afternoon class who were identical, except in personality. They never dressed the same, which I was thankful for, but even if they had, I could always tell which was which.

My afternoon was wild and rambunctious, but full of so much fun that I was sort of sad to see the day end. The kids all gathered up their bags, and I made sure that they each got a flier to take home that was about the upcoming book fair we were having. Those were always my favorite days at school when I was little. Not that I was able to get books, but the fact that I had a whole bunch of new things I could peruse through. My books came from the library, at least until I got older, and was with one family permanently.

Now that I had my own house, it was filled with all the books I wanted to get when I was younger, but couldn't because I didn't have any money to purchase them. It had started small, in my college years, where I would add a book or two to my library each year, and when I bought my house, I asked folks to give me either books from a selected list, or gift cards for me to use toward them. Of course, my friends had all been more than generous and I had a whole bookshelf full of books. Most of them were much more geared toward younger ages, but they filled me with warmth knowing I could pick them up, and read them any time I wanted.

Taking the leftover fliers to the office, I stepped in, and saw that Mary was not at the desk. In fact, no one was there, which was quite odd. I stepped past the front desk toward the breakroom and heard several voices.

"...and she thinks she's hot shit," I heard Mary say. "That bitch of a vice principal called me into her office and read me the riot act about sticking my nose into someone else's business where it didn't belong. Honestly, I'd be fine if Dick came back and really fired her. She's a mess and a pain in my ass."

I couldn't believe what I was hearing. I pulled out my phone, turned on the camera, and started videoing while I was standing outside the room. I stayed out of the eyeline of the door, just around the corner, where I could still hear the conversation, but where they wouldn't see me unless they actually came out.

"She does seem a bit high and mighty," one of the others in the room said. "She took that extra day without even asking. Something about a flight mix up, but her flight came back fine. She just took a later one."

"And did you see her ring?" someone else asked. "It's fucking huge. There's no way that isn't worth at least ten grand, probably more. My guess is she found a sugar daddy, and she's working on taking all his money so she doesn't have to work anymore."

"She doesn't work now," Mary said. "Believe me. I've been by her class, and she's always just playing with the kids, not doing anything that's actually teaching. She might as well be considered a glorified babysitter for all she's worth. I wouldn't be surprised if she didn't even have an actual license for teaching and she's been hired on through some sort of brown nosing or something. Bet she's sleeping with the vice principal, and that's why they get on so well."

I'd heard enough, and had recorded enough to get them all fired, so I kept the camera going, and walked into the room, making sure I got everyone who was in there onto the screen at some point as I panned around the room.

"It's good to know what you all think of me," I said, then turned around, and walked out, stopping the video, and locking my phone.

"You fucking bitch," I heard Mary say, but I headed straight to the vice principal's office.

"Ms. Morris," I said as I stepped to her door.

"Hi," she said.

"She's lying," Mary said as she pushed past me into the room.

"Mary," Ms. Morris said. "I'm not sure what you're talking about."

"Whatever she says, it's a lie," she said, glaring daggers at me.

"Ms. Truitt hasn't said anything," she replied.

I watched as Mary looked between the two of us, her eyes widening, nostrils flared, like she was trying to figure out a way out of the situation she'd just caused.

"She's gonna tell you that I'm badmouthing her," Mary said, trying to cover her tracks. "I heard her saying something to someone that she was trying to get me fired. I just want you to know that I don't do that sort of thing."

"Ms. Truitt," Ms. Morris said, looking at me.

"Hold on," I said, opening my phone and pulling up the video, sending it to the vice principal. Once it was sent, I said, "You should be getting an email with a video attached. I'll let you handle whatever has to happen next. I need to head home. I'll talk to you tomorrow."

With that, I turned around, and walked out of the office and headed toward the door. Mary came flying out behind me and shoved me from behind, nearly knocking me over, and I yelped. Others had come out of the breakroom, and were standing around watching, not doing anything to stop her. Ms. Morris came out of her office, likely when she heard me, and I could see she was not at all happy with what was going on.

"Mary," she nearly shouted.

"She's trying to get me fired," Mary said.

By this point, I was back against a wall, Mary in front of me looking like she'd like to kill me. I did not at all feel safe, and all I could think about was what had happened when I first came back. I had that fight-or-flight feeling going, and I was not going to go down without a fight.

"Stay back," I said, and my voice was so calm, it was unbelievable. "I don't care what happens to you, but you will treat me with the respect I deserve."

"You're a fucking whore," she said, and lunged toward me.

I ducked just as she would have hit me, and she ended up punching the wall behind me, which was brick and did not at all give. I heard a crack and wasn't sure if it was her hand or the impact, and didn't really care. I shuffled from underneath her, and moved toward the vice principal, hoping to find some safety with her presence.

"Mary," Ms. Morris said. "The police are on the way. If you continue to act this way, I will have to subdue you until they arrive. I suggest you sit down, and patiently wait."

Her calm demeanor belied the heightened stress in the room, and I wondered whether she was bluffing or not. Mary seemed to believe her, and sat down on a chair right next to the door, all the air deflating out of her.

"The rest of you should have a seat as well," Ms. Morris said without turning around.

One by one, the rest of the women walked past us, and sat in the lobby area of the office, none of them looking at me, or Mary, for that matter. They sat, heads hung low, like naughty children. It would have been comical if it weren't so bizarre. It was like high school, or rather middle school, all over again. Mean girl shit that was so useless it wasn't even worth remembering.

Within moments, a couple of police officers walked into the office, so I guessed it wasn't a bluff from the vice principal. She really had called them. I assumed that since what happened to me a few weeks earlier, she wanted to be extra cautious, and make sure that safety measures were at the forefront.

"Good afternoon," Ms. Morris said as she walked over to the police. "Could I chat with one of you while the other stays out here and watches these fine folks?"

"Of course, ma'am," one of the officers said and followed her back toward the back end of the office.

"Who'd like to tell me what's going on?" the other officer asked as we all waited for them to come out.

"I think it best that Ms. Morris discuss that with you," I said. "She's the one who called, so she's the one who has the most information."

"True," the officer said. "But it's good to hear everyone's side before we make any decisions."

"Fucking whore," Mary mumbled under her breath.

"Ma'am," the officer said to her, and she looked up, surprised she'd said it out loud.

She sort of waved the words off, as if she could brush them from the air, then looked back at her lap. The officer looked toward me, and I just shrugged and shook my head, not wanting to say or do anything to set anyone off.

"I'd like to speak to Mary," the officer who had gone back with Ms. Morris said as he stepped back into the room.

No one moved, and I assumed that they were not wanting to throw a friend under the bus, no matter how toxic she was.

"She's the one sitting there," I said, pointing at her.

Mary glared at me, promising me so much pain and unpleasantness with her gaze, but I just stood there, no emotion on my face, trying my best to stay under control. That was something I'd learned at an early age, how to control my face, make it look like I didn't care at all, when inside I was collapsing or falling apart or whatever. It had really come in handy when kids would do something that was so funny, but also so completely wrong. All I wanted to do was laugh, but knew if I laughed, it would only encourage them to continue it, so I had to keep that amusement to myself.

"Fine, whatever," Mary said as she stood up. "Might as well get this over with."

She walked back to the vice principal's office with Ms. Moore and the officer, and her friends didn't say a thing. They simply sat and looked at their laps. I wanted to leave, but I also wanted to see this through.

"Ladies," the officer who was still with us said, and one of the women looked up. "Can you tell me what is going on?"

The one who had looked up just shook her head, then looked back down. None of the others would even look up. It was like they were caught and sitting in middle school waiting to talk to the principal themselves, like they'd been caught bullying someone and didn't want to put anyone out by accepting responsibility. It was absolutely atrocious and I didn't want anything to do with any of them.

I texted Liz to let her know what had been going on, and she walked in when she arrived, which was a surprise.

"Hey," she said, walking right up to me to give me a hug. "I sent you screenshots, they're going down, they know it, and they're trying to make a game plan."

She'd whispered the last in my ear so no one else would hear her.

"Ma'am," the officer said. "Can I ask what you are doing here? Do you work here?"

"I was coming in to see what you might need for the future substitution coming up," she said. "I usually come earlier, but I had a class I was teaching, so didn't get out in time to be here during the day."

"I'm going to ask that you not talk to these women right now," he said. "We're conducting interviews, so need to make sure they don't get stories straightened out that are false."

"Totally understand," she said, putting on her best smile that could knock even the most hardened person down to a swooning idiot. "Should I go wait in my car? Or can I sit here until y'all are done?"

Liz was a knockout, so the fact that she could turn on the charm so easily made her the best kind of ally to have, especially in this type of situation.

"You can stay," he said, pulling at his collar a bit. "But I'll ask that you don't talk to anyone."

"No problem," she said, sauntering over to one of the chairs in the middle of the other women.

That was one of her other qualities; the ability to be petty without it looking like she was doing it on purpose. It was why she was so good at being a teacher, and a substitute at that. She could tell you to go to hell in such a way that you actually looked forward to the trip. I was glad she was on my side, because if she wasn't, I wouldn't have had all the insider knowledge and facts.

My phone pinged, and I pulled it out to see who was sending me a message, but the officer came over to look as well.

"I'm going to ask that you not communicate with anyone at this time," he said. "We need to make sure we get honest answers from everyone."

"Okay," I said. "It's my husband, though, and he's gonna want to work out our travel arrangements for when I go to see him soon. Would it be all right if I texted him that I'm in a meeting, and that I'll call when I'm out?"

"Let's hold off," he said, giving me a look that said he'd already told me what was going to happen, and I better not argue.

"Okay," I said, then shoved the phone back in my pocket. "Can I sit down?"

"Sure," he said, so I pulled my own petty move, and went and sat in Mary's chair behind the counter. I did it as more of a display of dominance than anything else, but the movement wasn't lost on the other women. One of them opened their mouth, as if to argue, but then shut it when I simply smiled at her.

Today was going to be long, and all I really wanted to do was talk to Alej and have him tell me everything would be all right. I knew it would but hearing him say it just made it feel more real.

Chapter Thirty-Two

Alejandro...

I'd sent a text asking her if she wanted me to work on getting flights, and to see when she would want to come down specifically, as in, what time of day and such. When she hadn't answered, after having been pretty communicative, I wondered if something was wrong, but didn't want to add to her stress, so dropped it.

Spring training had been going well, and even though I'd missed a couple of games, I was still feeling like I would be ready to go come opening day. Nick had blended in seamlessly with the core group of players, and the other new members of the team had found their places as well. It was always interesting when the new season started, because there were always roster moves during the off-season, and we had to get accustomed to the new group.

Now that we'd been at it a couple of weeks or so, we were getting into fine form, readying ourselves for the full season, which was a marathon, not a sprint, and we had to be able to endure all one hundred and sixty-two games that came our way, along with any post-season games we could get, which was the ultimate goal.

I was still in my early career, but felt like I was doing well, and when my time came to renegotiate my contract in a couple of years, I hoped I'd be able to do so with a good foundation of wins and playoff experience under my belt. Of course, I also hoped that I'd be able to have a family started by then, but wouldn't push on Hailey, because we both had the same, or at least similar plans, when it came to adding to the family.

Mama had been wild when I first went to see her when I got to Florida, asking why my wife hadn't come with me, why she hadn't been introduced before we were married, and when we were going to get married for real, in a church, like proper folks. Papi had tried to keep her under control, but we all knew that when Mama decided something, she was going to get it, no matter who stood in her way.

That was one of the reasons why I'd suggested the later dates for Hailey to come down. I didn't want her to have to deal with Mama and her tirades, at least not right away. I knew it was gonna be a lot, just wanted to push it off for as long as possible, maybe make some headway in the department of her calming down some. Whether it would work or not, I wasn't sure, but I had to do something. I didn't need Hailey being accosted as soon as she landed.

It wasn't until after the game was well underway that I thought again about what had held Hailey up. She was pretty attentive to my texts unless it was actually during class time, so the fact that I'd texted her at the end of her day, and hadn't heard back from her before the game started had made me a little nervous. I was sure it was nothing, but I still wondered if everything was fine. By the time I was pulled from the game in the fifth, I asked the coach if I could check my phone for messages. He knew I'd been working to get her down, so he said it was fine.

"Hey," Nick said as I passed him coming into the clubhouse.

"Hey, yourself," I said. "You look intense."

"Just got some news," he said, cryptic as ever.

"Don't share," I said with a laugh and headed to my locker.

"Hadn't planned to," he replied, but smiled up at me from where he was sitting in front of his locker.

I pulled my phone out and turned it on, hoping to have a message from Hailey.

Sorry about not responding. Something came up at work and I couldn't.

Crisis averted for now. Yes, please plan the flight. I don't want to have to think about that right now. Too much to text, so call when you can.

I looked at the time, adjusted for the difference in time zones, and called her.

"Alej?" she asked as she answered.

"Yeah, babe," I said. "What happened?"

"Would you believe another ridiculous thing at school?" she asked. "Because, yeah, it was nuts, but I think I'll be good from now on."

"I'm not sure I like the sounds of that," I said. "Want to talk about it?"

"Just mean girl shit with busy bodies," she said. "It really isn't a big deal, other than the fact that it fucked my afternoon up."

"I'm sorry, baby," I said. "Can I do anything to make things better?"

"I'd say come fuck my brains out, but that's not feasible right now," she said with a laugh. "I'm just sitting at home wishing you were here. I think we're planning a girls' night tomorrow, though, so that'll take my mind off this."

"Sounds good," I said. "So, what time do you want to fly out here? I didn't want to book early in the morning if you wanted later in the day. Also, do you want to fly out Friday, or come Thursday night?"

"I could come Thursday night?" she asked.

"You can come anytime you want," I said. "You give me the date and I'll make everything work out."

"Then I should come Thursday," she said. "That would give us another night together. Oh, wait. Don't you play games at night? Will you be able to come get me?"

"We actually don't play that day," I said. "I already checked the schedule to make sure. I'll be able to come get you at the airport, and we can go straight to my condo."

"How many houses do you have?"

"Hailey," I said. "I have one small condo here in Fort Myers for spring training, and when I want to be here with my parents, and a home in New Orleans where I would much rather spend my time."

"This is weird," she said. "I don't know anyone who has more than one house."

"It's only weird because you're not used to it," I said. "A ton of guys have condos down here. We sort of own most of the building. It's not that unusual, considering we spend several weeks here every year. Saves on renting places, and it means we don't have to worry about finding something if we forget."

"I guess," she said. "I mean, logically, it makes sense, I just... I don't know. It seems almost frivolous or something. Like you're showing off."

"Do you want me to sell it?" I asked. "Because I will if you want me to."

"What? No," she said. "I just didn't think about it, I guess."

"We haven't exactly had a lot of time to have these kinds of conversations," I said. "There are gonna be some weird things that come up. I'm sure there will be more, too."

"Yeah," she said. "We really did this backward, didn't we?"

"I'm not mad," I said.

"Me either," she said, and I could hear the smile in her voice. "I miss you."

"I miss you, too," I said. "Just a couple of weeks, though, and you'll be down here, and we'll be together."

"Yeah," she said. "And I get to meet your mom."

"I'm working on her," I said. "I've been trying very hard to make sure she knows to be on her best behavior while you're here."

"Is she really that bad?"

"Well," I said, thinking back over my life. "My first girlfriend lasted all of ten minutes of interrogation before she ran out screaming. I kind of had a reputation after that, so it was pretty lonely. It's one of the reasons I never told her about my other girlfriends until we were established. It's what I wanted to do with you, you know. Give us time to really get settled in our relationship before I brought her into it."

"Best laid plans of mice and men," she said.

"Exactly," I replied. "If I ever figure out who it was that posted that video, I'm gonna have words with them."

"You should really have words with your sister," she said. "She's the one who sent it to your mom."

"Oh, you're right," I said, having forgotten that tidbit. "I'm gonna have to seriously remind her what Mama is like. Of course, she never had that issue. Mama loved everyone my sister brought home. Even the assholes."

"Hey," Nick said, looking over at me. "You eat with that mouth?"

"Sorry," I said, but he shot me a shit-eating grin that told me he was fucking with me, so I flipped him off.

"I gotta go," she said, suddenly sounding distracted.

"What's up?" I asked.

"Someone just rang the doorbell," she said.

"Are you expecting someone?" I asked, suddenly concerned.

"No," she said. "But I'm sure it's fine."

"Hailey," I said. "Don't answer the door until you know who's there. And stay on the phone until then, please?"

"You're so worried," she said. "But fine, I'll stay on the phone with you."

I could hear her shuffling around, so figured she was heading to the door.

"What the fuck?" I heard her say.

"Hailey," I said, my concern heightened.

"Oh my God," she said, and it was a surprised voice, not one of concern. "Get in here you goof."

I could hear another woman's voice in the background, so I felt a bit more comfortable.

"It's my substitute, Liz," she said.

"Okay," I said, sighing in relief. "You had me freaked out for a minute."

"Sorry," she said. "I'll talk to you tomorrow, okay?"

"Okay," I said. "I'll get your plane ticket booked so you will have everything ready to go."

"Thanks," she said. "Love you."

"Love you, too," I said, and she disconnected the call.

"What was that all about?" Nick asked.

"A friend came over, but she didn't know they were coming," I said.

"So, she's good?"

"Yeah," I said. "I gotta book a flight for her to come down and meet my parents."

"Oh, yes," he said. "The whole meeting the family bit. I was fortunate in that it's just my mom, and she loved Charlie. Her family seemed a bit standoffish, but once they saw that I was fine financially, they softened up."

"Yeah," I said. "Mama is a bit overprotective of me."

"Does she pull the, 'he's my baby boy,' routine?" he asked.

"So many times," I said. "It's why I wanted to wait to introduce them. But then we got caught, so it was a bit out of my control."

"These people who post shit about celebrities don't understand that we have private lives, too," he said. "It's like they think all we're good for is looking pretty, and giving them whatever entertainment value we can. Not like we have actual lives or families or anything. God forbid we try to keep things on the down low."

"Exactly," I said. "We're for their amusement alone, otherwise we are useless."

I grabbed my shower kit and headed in to get cleaned up. There was still an hour or so left in the game, and I wanted to get this out of the way so I didn't have to deal with the rest of the team fighting for space. Not that we really fought, but since we were still working with an expanded list of players, including guys who would likely be with the lower levels of the team come opening day, I didn't really feel like dealing with the numbers.

Once that was done, I pulled out my phone, and went to work getting a flight for Hailey to come down and see me. I did miss her terribly, which was a weird thing for me. We'd only been together for a month at most, so the fact that I felt like she was missing was new, and it was not lost on the fact of the novelty of it. Hopefully, though, as the season wore on, we'd find a groove and be better at missing each other without having to be near one another the whole time. It would definitely be a work in progress, and one I was willing to do whatever it took to make work.

Chapter Thirty-Three

Hailey...

"Thanks," I said. "Love you."

"Love you, too," he said, and I disconnected the call.

"Was that him?" Liz asked.

"Yeah," I said, and could feel my face flush. "He was worried since I hadn't responded to his text earlier."

"Aw, that's adorable," she said. "Is he always like that? I mean, it's still new, but is he?"

"Honestly," I said. "He's been so sweet and attentive to my needs it's almost nauseating. But in a good way, you know? Like, he's always making sure I'm good with whatever is going on, that I get to get off before he worries about himself, which let me tell you, he's great at that."

"Okay, TMI," she said with a laugh. "I mean, good for you, but I do not need to hear about your sex life."

"Yeah, sorry," I said. "I just haven't ever had anyone that has been so kind and considerate to me before. He just does everything for me, and not just in bed."

"Don't need to know where you're getting your rocks off," she said.

"That's not what I mean," I said. "He just makes sure that I'm taken care of. When I got hurt, he was so nice, and helped me so much. Said he'd pay for whatever I needed, would stay home with me if I needed him to, in spite of his need to head to spring training. He's offered to pay off my house, let me live with him and rent this out, or whatever I want. He really is just an all-around great guy."

"Well, then, I'm glad you got this," she said. "To be fair, your picker was sort of broken at one point."

"Don't even get me started on that," I said. "I was notorious for picking the absolute wrong guy, and it showed in the way that I freaked the fuck out when I figured out I'd married Alej. I thought I was gonna be fucked up completely, but it didn't turn out that way."

"So, you're good now?" she asked.

"Definitely," I replied.

"Great, then I can ask you for a favor, right?"

"Is that why you're here?" I asked.

"Guilty as charged," she said, and at least had the decency to look embarrassed.

"Okay, spill," I said. "What's this big favor you need that you couldn't just come out and ask me for?"

"My brother got into some hot water," she began. "He did something stupid, and he knows it, but I don't want it to fuck his whole life up."

"Then he shouldn't have done something stupid," I said.

"I know that, you know that, and he knows that," she said. "Thing is, he was in with a couple of dicks who talked him into something he would never do. Now he's the only one facing consequences for his actions, since the other two guys come from money, and their parents bailed them out by hiring big time attorneys for them. Unfortunately, Billy's the odd man out, so he's gonna end up with all the consequences, and the other two are gonna get off with slaps on the wrist at best."

"I don't know what I can do," I said. "I'm not a lawyer, or even rich, so how am I supposed to help him?"

"I know that," she said. "You said he'd be willing to pay for stuff for you, so I thought I'd see if I could do a longer substitution for you, maybe you take a longer trip than you originally planned? We would be fine if we helped him, but it would dip into our savings a bit, and if I could work some extra days, especially with your class, 'cause you're stupid organized, then I could make enough to cover some of that. Defer the funds in the interim, so we could cover his attorney."

"It's not that I don't want to help you," I said. "I just have to think about my career, too. I've been gone a lot in the last month, some of it totally not my fault, but I still feel bad bailing."

"You're not bailing," she said. "I'll be there. I promise I'll be the best sub you ever had. I just really need to do this for my brother. It isn't fair that the guys he got hooked up with bailed on him. I don't want to do the same thing."

"Let me talk to Alej," I said. "I'll see what he says and then let you know. What did your brother do, anyway? I know Alej will ask me."

"It's stupid," she said.

"Don't care," I replied. "If I'm gonna help, I need to know."

"You know that park?" she asked.

"Oh yeah, that one," I said, sarcasm dripping from my voice.

"LaFreniere Park," she said.

"Oh yeah," I said. "It's a great place."

"Except if you're drunk and your friends talk you into skinny dipping in the pond," she said.

"No," I said. "Please tell me it was dark and there weren't any children there."

"It was dark," she said. "But someone saw them and called the cops. Of course, the two assholes he was with saw the person on their phone, got out and got dressed, but didn't tell Billy, who was so drunk he was lucky he didn't drown. Cops show up, pull them all in for questioning, and my dumb as fuck brother couldn't be bothered to keep his mouth shut, and spilled everything."

"Did they give him his rights?"

"They say they did, but he was drunk," she said. "I think there's something that you have to sign away your rights, but you can't do that if you're high or drunk or something, and he was definitely drunk."

"Yeah," I said. "I got you. Let me ask Alej if he has someone we can get for his case."

I dialed Alej, putting the phone on speaker, and hoping he was still by his phone, so I didn't have to explain it a ton, and lucked out.

"Hey," he said when he answered.

"Got a proposition for you," I said.

"I'm open to damn near anything with you, baby," he said.

"This isn't about sex," I replied.

"Damn," he said, but was laughing. "What's up?"

"Remember the substitute I told you about?" I asked.

"Yeah," he said. "Does this involve naughty teachers?"

"Alej," I said, but Liz was laughing.

"Am I on speaker?"

"You are," I said.

"Could have warned me," he replied.

"Anyway," I said, drawing the word out. "Her brother was an idiot and got arrested. I promise it's not something horrible, but we need to find an attorney for him."

"What did he do?" he asked.

"Hi," Liz said. "I'm Hailey's friend, and sister to the dumbass who got himself locked up."

"Nice to meet you," Alej said.

Liz gave a rundown of what happened, and Alej listened without interrupting, giving her all the time she needed to get her story out. Once she was done, she asked, "Do you know someone?"

"I don't," he said. "But I'll make a call and see who I can find. What's your price limit?"

"She's gonna work until she can pay it off," I said. "I'm going to give her some extra days so she can save up the money."

"How about I put the retainer down and then you pay the rest," he said. "Once everything is settled, we'll work on a way to repay the retainer. Sound like a plan?"

"You really don't have to do that," Liz said.

"You're a friend of Hailey, which makes you important," he said.

"He's really big on family," I said. "And chosen family is just as good as blood relatives."

"Sometimes better," he said.

"I feel like I'm taking advantage of you," Liz said. "I really do, but I would very much appreciate the help."

"Good," he said. "I'll make a few calls, then give Hailey the information. In the meantime, make sure your brother doesn't say anything to anyone until he has someone to represent him."

"Afraid that ship already sailed," I said.

"He was drunk," Liz said. "And when he's drunk, he likes to share absolutely every detail of everything."

"Let the attorney know that he was intoxicated when he was interrogated," Alej said. "That might mean something. I have no idea, but it should. Like, you can't consent to sex when you're drunk, so how can you consent to being interrogated?"

"Good point," I said.

"I'll get you a name," Alej said. "Until then, tell your brother that he is not to talk to anyone, even you, until we get an attorney for him."

"Thank you so much," Liz said. "I don't know what I would do if he ended up in this mess without someone to help him."

"Just make sure he knows he's lucky to have you as a sister," Alej said.

"Oh, he knows," she said.

"So," I said. "About that trip. Should we make it longer?"

"Let me do some checking," Alej said. "We'll figure it out."

"Okay," I said. "Love you."

"Love you, too," he replied, and I disconnected the call.

"I don't know how to thank you," she said, and there were tears in her eyes. "He's such a good kid, but he's just dumb sometimes. He's a follower and will do damn near anything to get a laugh. It's one of those endearing qualities that ends up fucking him in the ass sometimes."

"I get it," I said. "I could have easily ended up doing dumb stuff, especially with how I was brought up. Thankfully, I've found people who remind me to be smart."

"You're way smarter than me," she said.

"I don't know about that," I replied. "You've got some serious smarts, like screenshotting that chat to save my ass. That was brilliant."

"It wasn't a big deal," she said. "You'd have done the same thing."

"I would," I agreed. "But that's beside the point."

"I'm just glad I could ask you this," she said. "I'm going to owe you so big."

"I may take you up on that," I said. "Now, since you're here, we should eat. But I don't know what I have in my kitchen."

"Sounds good," she said.

It was a good night, and I was glad I was able to help my friend. It was the least I could do, considering all she'd done for me in the last few weeks.

Chapter Thirty-Four

Alejandro...

It had been a while since we'd decided when she was coming down, and the flights had been booked, and I was anxiously awaiting her arrival. We talked every day after my games, and each time I saw her on the screen, I wanted to climb through and hold her. It wasn't just about missing the sex, because that was there, too. No, I wanted to spend time with her. Go look at things, enjoy each other's company, get to know her better than I already did. We had essentially been strangers when we got married, so we were working backward now, doing the things normal couples did on their first dates. We just had the bonus of getting to have sex whenever we were together.

Mama and Papi were anxious to meet her, and I knew it was coming up much sooner than I wanted, but it had to happen. I had planned a dinner out with them, but hadn't told them I was bringing her with me. I also invited my sister, her husband, and the kids, so everyone was going to be there. We'd talked about it a few times on our video calls, and I could tell she was nervous. I wondered whether

I should have done the meetings with them differently, just the parents, then my sister's family, but it was all set up, now, so I guess we'd just have to grind our way through it.

She'd shown me about a dozen different dresses, asking which one would be best for her to wear to the meeting, and honestly, she could wear whatever she wanted. I'd told her that, too, but she really wanted to impress my parents. I gave her my opinions, picking three different ones that looked the best on her, and said she should ask her friends for the final pick. She wanted to go with something a little less revealing, but I told her that whatever she wore would be fine, and meant it. I also told her that if anyone said anything about it, I would be shutting that down hard and fast.

It was finally the day she was scheduled to fly out, and I was a nervous wreck. I had been doing well on the field, getting myself into season shape so I could make it through the grind. My hitting was coming back nicely, and I had a handful of home runs for the spring. I also had gotten a lot of practice with Nick around the bag, both of us working on our double play turns so we could do them without even thinking. We had taken care to make sure we were on the same page throughout the practices, and I felt like we were ready to go for the season.

"She's coming tonight, right?" he asked as we were wrapping up some batting practice.

"Yeah," I said. "I can't wait."

"Well, put it out of your mind during the game," he said. "If you're thinking about her, you're not thinking about the diamond, and that's where your head needs to be while the game is going on."

"Oh, I know," I said. "I'm just looking forward to being done and picking her up."

I wished she was here already, but I couldn't make that happen, so I had to settle for waiting through the day to see her again. She'd texted that she got on the plane, and I knew what time it was set to land. She hadn't been surprised that I got her a first-class ticket, but she was pleased with it.

The game seemed to drag on, and our fielding was miserable, especially mine. I made a stupid mistake, letting a ball get past me that I shouldn't have, and felt like I was just playing badly all around.

"Hey," Coach said when we came off the field. "You got something going on?"

"Just waiting for my wife to come into town," I said.

"Ah," he said, a knowing smile on his face. "Can you keep your head in the game? Or should I let one of the kids go in and get some reps?"

"I need to be able to focus," I said. "I'm trying, but something feels off. Can't put my finger on it, but I just feel like I'm missing something."

"Okay," he said. "Hit the showers, check your phone, and I'll let Finley get some work."

"Okay," I replied.

I really hated having to leave a game, but it was clear I needed to adjust my brain, and staying out there wasn't doing anyone any good. I walked down the tunnel toward the clubhouse, figuring I'd hit the showers, then check my phone, but I was drawn to the electronic device, and just needed to see what it was.

If you're planning on introducing your wife to Mama and Papi at dinner, you might want to skip that.

My sister's text was odd, and not something she would normally send. It was cryptic, and I didn't like the vibe it gave off.

What do you know? What aren't you telling me?

I set the phone back in its box, and headed to the showers, figuring I'd give my sister some time to respond. After I'd showered and dried off, I headed back to my locker, and pulled the phone out.

Mama is sure you're bringing her.
She said she's gonna do an intervention.
I don't know what she meant by that, but she's asked that I not tell you about it. I think she's bringing Abuelita up for this, too.

Fuck, I thought.

Call me when you can.

I set my phone down to start getting dressed, and it rang.

"Hey," I said when I answered it.

"Mama is raging," Bella said. "She is sure that you got married to a harlot, and she's gonna save you with this intervention. I don't even know what to do right now."

"It's kinda your fault," I said.

"How is it my fault?" she asked. "I'm not the one who went and got married."

"You're already married," I said. "And you're the one who showed Mama that picture. If you hadn't shown her, I could have done the introduction on my terms. Now, though, I have to figure out how to do it without screwing up my marriage."

"Is your marriage really that fragile?" she asked.

"That's not what I mean," I said. "Mama tends to scare people, which is not what I want to happen with Hailey. Besides, if *Abuelita* is coming up, then I think things will be fine."

"How do you figure?"

"She already met Hailey," I said. "Well, not in person, but by video chat."

"She did?" she asked, and I could hear the confusion in her voice.

"Yeah," I said. "A few weeks ago, actually."

"What did she say?"

"Who?"

"Abuelita, of course," she replied, as if it was obvious.

"She was glad to meet her," I said. "She asked if I was treating her well, and whether we had plans for our future past the honeymoon phase. Asked about her work, and all the usual questions. It was actually a great call."

"Did she tell Mama?" she asked. "Because if she did, then that may be why Mama is on this crazy train."

"I don't know," I said. "I don't even remember if I told Mama that I'd called *Abuelita*. I mean, I told her I was going to call her, but that was about it. It's been kind of a whirlwind, to be honest, so the days are all mixed together."

"I'd say to be ready to leave at a moment's notice from the restaurant," she said. "If Mama is right, and she's gonna stage some sort of intervention, whatever that means to her, then you should be ready to run. Your wife, too."

"Pretty sure I can stand up to Mama," I said, and she laughed.

"When was the last time you stood up to her?" she asked.

"When she called me screaming about getting married without her there," I said. "That conversation was wild, but I held my ground and told her she wasn't in charge of my life. That I was an adult and could make the decisions myself, and this had nothing to do with her."

"But that was on the phone," she said. "In person is way different. She's gonna blow a gasket, cause a scene, and try to get you to do what she wants. You've seen her do that before."

"And she's never done it to me," I said. "She's gonna figure out really quickly that I am no longer a little boy, but a man who can make his own decisions."

"Mama will always see you as her little boy," she said.

"I know that," I replied. "But she needs to change that attitude, especially if she wants to have a relationship with me, my wife, and any kids we may have."

"Is that why you married her?" she asked. "Is she pregnant?"

"What?" I asked. "No, she's not pregnant. We didn't even have sex until we were married, so that isn't why we got married."

"Then why did you marry her?" she asked.

"Bella," I said, not sure how to answer the question, and definitely positive I didn't want to give her the truth. "My life is my own, and the reasons why I do things make sense to me. Do you think I'm some kind of idiot?"

"It's just weird that you've never mentioned her before," she said. "You just all of a sudden end up married. It seems a bit odd, don't you think?"

"What's odd for you is perfectly normal for me," I said. "Hailey and I are perfect for each other. She's perfect for me, and we work really well together."

"So, why haven't you introduced her to us yet?"

"It's complicated," I said. "Look, I gotta go, okay. I'll see you when we have dinner."

"Okay," she said. "But be warned, Mama is gonna go off, so you better prepare your wife for that inevitability."

"My wife can charm anyone," I said. "She's wonderful. You'll see."

"I hope she's got thick skin," she said. "See you tomorrow."

"See you then," I said, then disconnected the call.

"That sounded intense," Austin said, and I jumped.

"Geez," I said. "Warn a guy before you scare the shit out of someone."

"Sorry," he said. "I didn't know you didn't see me. I mean, I've been sitting here for a while."

"Like you said, it was an intense phone call," I replied, setting my phone down.

I heard the rest of the team coming down the tunnel, so I finished getting myself dressed.

"Did we win?" I asked Austin before he walked to the showers.

"Yeah," he said. "Not that it matters in the grand scheme of things, but we did."

"Good," I said.

He walked off to get cleaned up as the rest of the team filtered in to do the same.

"You get your shit straightened out?" Nick asked.

"I did," I said. "Although, tomorrow night is gonna be a bit much."

"Why's that?" he asked as he pulled his shirt off.

"Family dinner," I said. "First time they'll meet Hailey."

"Oh," he said, drawing the word out. "Those are always fun."

Sarcasm dripped from his words, and I couldn't help but laugh. It helped me to see that not everything was so important that the world would end because of it. I finished getting dressed, then checked my phone to see whether Hailey's plane was gonna be on time or not. Thankfully, it was showing that it would land in about an hour, so that gave me enough time to finish up here, then get to the airport to get her. I couldn't wait to see her, too.

Chapter Thirty-Five

Hailey...

Sitting in first class was definitely a new experience for me. I'd done it on the way back from Vegas with Alej, but that was the only other time I had flown that way. Normally, I just sat in the cheapest seat available. Not that I flew that often, but the handful of times I had, it had been pretty much at the back of the plane, either squished against the window, or between two strangers. The only time it wasn't was my flight out to Vegas with the girls. We'd booked the aisle and window seats, and, fortunately, we'd been able to not have anyone sit between us.

As the plane touched down, the brakes pulled to come to a stop, I gripped the arm rest between me and the guy sitting next to me. I still didn't like landing, but at least it didn't bounce or anything, so that was a bonus. The crew said we could turn our phones back on and out of Airplane Mode, so I turned mine on, waiting for it to boot up. I hoped I'd see something from Alej, letting me know he was already at the airport and waiting for me.

Let me know when you land. I'm in baggage claim waiting for you.

It was so sweet that he came in. He hadn't needed to; I could have made it out to the parking lot on my own. I wasn't a complete idiot in that regard.

I just landed, but we haven't gotten to a gate yet.

I wanted to call him. I wanted to hear his voice. I wanted to see his face. Doing that while still on the plane seemed rude, though, so I just had to hold on until we were released from this metal tube and back into the real world.

I can't wait to see you.

The feeling was mutual, and I texted him as much. Unfortunately, the pilot came over the speaker saying that we had a bit of a wait to get to a gate to unload. Something about another plane still being there. Hopefully, they'd figure their shit out and we could get out, but I would just have to wait and see.

After entirely too long, although it was probably only about fifteen minutes, we were moving again, and pulling into a gate. I was so ready to get out of this seat it was ridiculous, and as soon as the plane stopped, and we heard the pilot do their checks over the intercom, everyone was getting up.

I was fortunate, in that I only had the small bag under the seat in front of me, and the small carryon bag in the overhead compartment. It had been a struggle to get it up there, but the guy next to me was kind enough to help.

"You want me to pull your bag down for you?" he asked after he'd pulled his own down.

"If you wouldn't mind," I said. "Thank you."

He pulled my bag down, setting it in the aisle, then stepped back to let me out of the seat and to walk ahead of him.

"Thank you," I said again, stepping into the aisle, and pushing my bag in front of me to the front door and off the plane.

Once I was out there, I switched to pulling it behind me, going up the walkway toward the terminal and out into the setting sun coming through the windows. Looking at the signs, I followed the arrows to where the baggage claim was. I didn't have anything to pick up but guessed that was the easiest place for Alej to meet me, so I just kept on going. The airport was small, and it didn't take me long to get out of the secure area and head to the place where I would finally see my husband.

"Hailey," I heard him call, and looked around to find him coming toward me.

"Alej," I said, walking faster toward him myself.

I let go of my suitcase as soon as he was in front of me, and reached up to wrap my arms around his neck, just as he wrapped his own around my middle, pulling me up to kiss him. We collided in a tangling of tongues, teeth, lips, and arms, and everything just everywhere. I couldn't touch enough of him, and it seemed he felt the same way. Finally, we pulled apart, and he set me on the ground, his hands sliding up and cupping my face, staring into my eyes.

"God, I've missed you," he said.

"I missed you so much," I replied, equally enamored with just drinking him in.

"This all you have?" he asked, reaching for my bag.

"Yeah," I said.

"Good," he said, taking the handle and pulling it behind him, tucking me into his side. "We're going to my place."

"I'm glad," I said, and walked with him out of the airport.

While I'd never been to Florida, it felt like home did, so much humidity that my hair curled tighter, my body glistening with sweat, and it was hard to breathe. I'd never liked the heat, and always thought I'd move to somewhere cooler, but home was home, and I'd stayed in New Orleans. I didn't even go anywhere for college. The fact that I got grants and scholarships to the college where I was from helped with that, though.

We got to his car, and he opened my door, letting me climb in before popping the trunk, and putting my suitcase in there. He climbed into the driver's seat and turned to look at me. It was like he was trying to memorize me or something, and I felt something niggling at the back of my brain that something was off.

"What's wrong?" I asked.

"My mama," he said. "She's kind of trying to stage an intervention."

"What are you talking about?" I asked, fear curling in my gut.

"It doesn't matter," he said. "She thinks she knows best, but she can't dictate anything to me. You and I are good. I promise."

"You're kind of freaking me out right now," I said.

"I know," he said. "I didn't want to say anything, but I didn't want to blindside you, either. All I want is to take you home and love you. Dive into you, and never come up for air again. That's all I really want right now. Everything else can wait."

"Why does she hate me?" I asked.

"She doesn't know you," he said. "She thinks that she can decide who is right, that she has to approve of you before we can get married for real."

"We *are* married," I said.

"I know," he said. "And nothing is going to change that."

I stared at him, and felt the tingling of tears in my eyes, stinging at the edges, trying desperately to escape.

"Baby," he said, reaching over. "You mean everything to me. We're gonna be fine. She has no say in my life, and if she tries to pull something, I'll shut her down. I promise you; I *will* protect you."

I sniffed, trying my best to keep from actually crying, but it wasn't working. He pulled me to him, actually pulling me over the center console, and into his lap, and held me tight while I just fell apart. This wasn't like me, but this situation was nuts, so the fact that I was overreacting made some sense.

Once I'd gotten the good cry out, he pulled back, and kissed me, soft and slow and so sweet it hurt.

"I love you," he said, and his eyes showed me that he would be my protector, my savior, my everything I needed him to be.

"I love you, too," I said, pressing my lips to his again.

"Let's get home and we can show each other how much we care," he said and I laughed.

"I'm gonna need you to swing through a pharmacy, and pick up more condoms," I said. "I don't know if we have enough."

"Yes, ma'am," he said as I slid off his lap, and back into my seat.

I pulled my seatbelt on as he started the car, and we pulled out of the parking lot, and headed out to wherever it was he was taking me.

"ALEJ," I gasped, flying over the edge of the cliff I'd been climbing again.

"That's it, baby," he crooned in my ear, driving into me hard and fast.

I'd lost count of the number of orgasms he'd given me, but it was entirely necessary. It kept me from worrying about meeting his family, and that was precisely what we'd been working toward. His body tightened, pressing into me, and then I felt him fill the condom, spasming and pulsing with each thrust. He collapsed on top of me, breathing hard like I was, and we both simply worked to regain ourselves from the bliss we'd just entered.

"Oh my God," he gasped out, each word taking a full breath to be released. "That was absolutely amazing."

"Yeah," I agreed, pressing my hands up on his shoulders.

"Oh, I'm sorry," he said, reaching between us to grab the condom before rolling off me.

"I need a shower," I said, not moving an inch.

"Same," he replied, staying where he was as well.

"Is it bad that I don't want to move?"

"Only if it's bad that I don't want to, either," he replied.

We stayed there, both still panting, the sweat cooling on my skin in the air-conditioned room. His condo wasn't huge by any stretch of the imagination, but it was perfect. There was a combination living room and dining area with a small kitchen on the side. Then there was a small hall that led back to a couple of bedrooms, a powder room to the one side, and a full bath in the master bedroom. The other bedroom had a desk set up in it, so I assumed he used it for an office of some sort.

"Gotta pee," I said, rolling over and off the bed.

"Good girl," he said, and I looked back over my shoulder at him and smiled.

"You trying to get me in a good mood?" I asked as I stepped into the bathroom.

"I thought I already did that," he said with a laugh, and I heard him moving to get up.

I sat on the toilet and peed, then wiped and flushed before turning the faucet on to wash my hands. The door wasn't shut, but it was just not quite open, so he knocked before opening it.

"Why do you do that?" I asked.

"What?"

"Knock," I said. "I'm fine if you just come in."

"Just being polite," he said. "Sort of a warning that I'm coming in, and you can stop it if you want."

He lifted the lid and seat on the toilet and peed, and I just laughed.

"What's so funny?" he asked.

"You let me know you're coming in, but you don't warn me you're gonna take a piss?"

"I didn't think you minded," he said, and sounded upset.

"I'm totally yanking your chain," I said. "As long as you don't go taking a shit while I'm in here, then I'm good."

"Yeah, no," he said. "I don't want to end the honeymoon that quickly."

"Good," I said.

He finished himself, then stepped over to the tub, turning the faucet on. He stuck his hand under the water, waiting for it to get to the right temperature before pulling the plunger to get the shower started.

"Your shower awaits," he said, holding a hand out to me.

I stepped over the lip of the tub and into the water, moving forward enough for him to have room to get in behind me. Turning around, I tipped my head back, letting the water run over my hair, running my fingers through the curls as they got wetter and wetter.

"You are beautiful," he said, and the reverence in his voice made me open my eyes. "I can't believe I get to keep you forever."

"Well, that sounded creepy," I said.

"You know what I mean," he said.

"I do," I said. "Still sounded creepy."

"Well, I plan to tell you every day that I want to keep you forever," he said. "I don't want to share you with anyone. Well, at least until we have kids, because then I kinda have to share you with them."

"We're gonna have to come up with a better phrase for you to use," I said. "Otherwise, it sounds like you're gonna stuff me and mount me on the wall or something."

"Oh, I plan to stuff you and mount you," he said, a smile curving his lips. "I plan to do that as much as humanly possible."

"Are you a middle schooler?" I asked.

"Just a man in complete love with his wife," he said, then pulled me to him and kissed me soundly.

I could feel his cock stir, but I was worn out, and didn't think I could handle another round, at least not right then.

"See what you do to me?" he said, pressing his cock into my stomach. "I just can't get enough of you."

"I'm afraid I'm gonna have to call a truce," I said. "I don't know if I can do another round right now."

"That's fine," he said. "I don't know that I can, either. I just don't want you to think you don't turn me on."

"The feeling is very much mutual," I said, my arms around his shoulders, clasped behind his neck. "But right now, I need to wash the airport and humidity off me."

He kissed me one more time, then stepped back and grabbed a bottle of shampoo, turning it up and letting some of the liquid fall into his palm. When he had enough, he set the bottle aside, then turned my back to him and began to wash my hair, his fingers massaging my scalp as he worked the suds through my locks. Every time he washed my hair, I felt amazing, like he was more than just in love with my body. No, he took care of me, even in this mundane task, and did it without complaint.

His hands slid from my hair and he turned my back to the showerhead, using his finger to tilt my head up so I could rinse the shampoo out of my hair. While I did that, he took up a cloth, got it wet, then squirted some of the body wash on the shelf onto it, getting it all sudsy as well, then began to wash my body. Each stroke of his hand inside the cloth pressing against my skin, swirling around and around on my skin, the rough texture of the cloth with the slow movements making me relax even more.

My shoulders, my chest, my stomach, down my arms, and over my hips. Then he knelt in front of me, washing from my thighs down to my feet before pressing the cloth between my legs to wash my sex. Even that wasn't anything that was more than just doing something for me, no motive at all. He stood and turned my front to the spray and did the same along my shoulders, down my back, along the globes of my ass, cleaning me completely.

I rinsed my front as he washed my back, then he turned me back around to rinse my back again. It was all movements, no talking, just being in each other's company, doing something that had to be done while sharing a space. When I was clean, he moved me around himself, and tipped his own head back under the spray. I handed him the shampoo and he washed his hair while I rinsed the cloth out to wash his body. Following his lead, I scrubbed him from shoulder to toe down the front, then did the back after he'd turned around. This simple thing we did together meant so much to me. It felt more intimate than the sex did, which said a lot about how it resonated within me.

When he was rinsed, he shut the water off, pulling the curtain back and pulling one of the towels from the rack to wrap around his hips. He handed one to me for my hair, then wrapped the third around my body, rubbing me with the soft material to dry me off. Once I was mostly dry, he helped me out of the tub and onto the stone mats that were next to the tub. They were cool, but not cold, and I noticed as I stepped off them, they dried almost instantly.

"Those are cool," I said.

"Found them online," he replied. "They seemed logical, so I thought I'd try them out. They work well."

"I should get some for my house," I said.

"I'll order you some," he said.

I finished drying myself off, hitting my lower legs and feet, before stepping out of the bathroom and back into the bedroom. The air was cool, but not so cold as to be a bother. My hair was wrapped up in the towel, and I wanted to put on a tank top and some panties before I ran my comb through it with the leave-in conditioner he had in the bathroom.

"Why are you putting clothes on?" he asked, and I turned to look at him.

"I want to do my hair," I said. "It's just easier if I have something on."

"Oh," he said, but I could tell he was disappointed.

"I can take them off when I'm done," I said. "If you ask me nicely."

"Or I can pull them off you," he said, a devilish look on his face.

I just shook my head and finished putting them on. Walking back into the bathroom, I grabbed the bottle of conditioner spray and, after pulling the towel off my hair and throwing it over the shower curtain bar, I started to spray it into my roots. I got some out toward the ends, but I knew it would naturally work its way down there with my combing.

Grabbing my comb, I started at the tips and worked the knots out of each section, slowly so as not to tear any of the hair. I continued around my head; each section being worked at an even pace. Finally, I had all the tangles out, and I was able to pull the comb from my scalp to the tips, combing each portion several times to make sure there weren't any hidden knots.

When I walked out of the bathroom, Alej wasn't in the bedroom, so I headed toward the larger part of the condo, but stopped just before the end of the hall when I heard another voice.

"She's finishing up," Alej said. "But I can tell her you want to meet her."

"Oh, I do," a woman said, and I wasn't sure who it might be.

I went back to the bedroom and pulled on some leggings, and an oversized tee shirt, something that would definitely cover my body and make me much more presentable to guests than just the panties and tank top. I was just finishing pulling on the tee shirt when Alej came into the room.

"Oh," he said, seeing me dressed.

"I heard someone," I explained. "Figured I'd at least cover up a bit to be more presentable."

"Yeah," he said. "It's my sister. She wants to meet you before you meet the parents. That way she can feel you out or something."

"I get it," I said. "I'm some unknown quantity, so she wants to know what to expect."

"You don't have to," he said.

"It's fine," I replied. "As long as she knows this isn't how I normally look."

"I told her she interrupted us," he said.

"She thinks we were having sex?" I asked, incredulous.

"No," he said with a laugh. "I told her you were just finishing up your shower."

"Okay," I replied. "I guess we should get this over with, then."

"You're sure?"

"Alej," I said, placing my hands on his cheeks. "I love you, and that's all that matters. I'm sure your sister will be fine."

He leaned down and kissed me slow and soft, just enough to help me relax just that much more, before pulling away and wrapping his arm around me. We walked down the hall, barely able to fit both of us in it, but we did it. When we stepped into the main section of the condo, I saw a woman standing with her back to us, looking at something that was on the counter in the kitchen.

"Bella," Alej said, and the woman turned around.

I don't know what I expected, but she was gorgeous. Her long dark hair, that had been down her back, all the way to the waistband of her jeans, was so shiny it literally reflected the lights from the ceiling. She had dark eyes like Alej, but her face was nearly porcelain, much fairer than his. Their eyes were the same shape, and her lips were fuller than his, but not by much. She was taller than me, too, but not quite as tall as my husband.

"You must be Hailey," she said when she saw me. "It's so nice to finally meet you."

She walked toward me, her hand out in front of her. I took it in my own, meeting her halfway across the room.

"You're Alej's sister," I said. "It's really good to meet someone else from his family."

"Who else have you met?" she asked.

"Well," I said. "I didn't meet her in person, but I talked to your grandmother over a video call a couple of weeks ago."

"Oh, that's right," she said. "Alej told me about that."

"It really is good to meet you," I said again.

"I just wanted to make sure that you weren't crazy like Mama insisted," she said. "I know you're gonna meet her and Papi tomorrow. And you'll meet my husband and kids as well. It should be an interesting dinner."

"I've told Mama she has to be on her best behavior," Alej said.

"You told them I was coming?" I asked. "I thought it was going to be a surprise."

"I decided that I didn't want Mama to ambush you when we walked in," he explained. "Besides, this way she knows and won't throw quite the temper tantrum."

"Oh, those are legendary," Bella said.

"Sounds interesting," I said, unsure exactly how to react to that.

"What about you?" Bella asked. "How did your parents react to Alej?"

"Bella," Alej said, his tone serious.

"It's fine," I said. "I'm actually not in contact with my parents, or any family, really. Don't really know who they are. My foster parents passed away shortly after I graduated college, so it's just me and my chosen family, which were all..."

"Pissed that we got married," Alej said, interrupting my sentence.

"Only because they weren't there," I added. "And because Missy was supposed to be the first one married."

"Oh," Bella said, and she looked between us, like she was trying to figure something out.

"You should probably get home," Alej said, obviously figuring out whatever it was that Bella was thinking. "Wouldn't want hubby to be pissed at me."

"He's fine," she said. "Besides, I thought we could go out and have some drinks or something. You know, really get to know each other."

"I have to play tomorrow," Alej said. "And she just got here, so we need to get some rest."

"I see," she said, and I wasn't sure I liked the tone of those two words.

"Bella," Alej said, and I heard the warning in his tone.

"I'm just looking out for my baby brother," she said.

"I'm not a baby," he replied.

"I can see that," she said, and her tone again held something I didn't particularly like.

"I'll see you tomorrow," Alej said, moving to the door.

Bella followed him, but looked over her shoulder at me before finally walking out. Alej shut the door behind her, then threw the latch and let out a sigh.

"I take it this is normal?" I asked.

"She's Mama-lite," he said.

"I see," I replied. "Well, she's pretty and smart, so she probably thinks I'm just some dumb blonde who stole her baby brother."

"Which you did," he said, a smile crossing his lips. "And I wouldn't have it any other way."

I smiled at that and reached out to him. He came to me, pulling me into his arms and holding me against his chest, my ear resting over his heart, which was pounding rapidly behind its cage.

"I love you," I said.

"I love you, too," he said.

"Good," I replied, then pulled back a bit. "I'm also starving."

"Oh my God," he said, looking at me. "When did you eat last?"

"Right before I got on the plane," I said. "I mean, I ate some stuff on the plane, because they feed you in first class more than just those pretzels and biscotti things, but still, not a ton."

"Do you want to go out or should we order in?"

"If we leave, and your sister sees us, will that be a problem?"

"Let's order in," he said, making the decision. "What are you in the mood for?"

"What's good here?"

He pulled his phone out and pulled up a food delivery app, giving me free rein to choose whatever I wanted. I settled for a burger joint that had decent reviews. Once the order was placed, Alej put his phone away, and pulled me back into his arms.

"We've got half an hour," he said. "Should we try one more time before the food gets here?"

"Really?" I asked.

"I mean, I'm a guy, so yeah," he said, and I laughed.

"I don't think I have it in me right now," I said. "Between the flight, you starving me, and then meeting your sister, I'm worn out."

"Sorry about that," he said. "She kind of ambushed me. So, for tomorrow. I do have to play, and you can't really come with me initially, but I can leave you my car and have tickets available at will call for you to come watch if you want. Or, you can take the car and run around to do whatever you want in town, too."

"I'd really like to come watch you play," I said. "I don't know the last time I went to an actual live game. I know it's been years, that's for sure."

"Great," he said. "Let me put the address into your phone so you can map yourself there. I'll have JP drive me to the game, you can come later, like an hour or so before the start time, and then we can go straight from the game to dinner."

"Wait, directly from the game?"

"Sure," he said. "Isn't that okay?"

"I mean," I hemmed. "I thought I'd have a chance to shower and change, maybe do my hair and makeup before going out. I don't have to, but I do want to make a good impression, so..."

I let the word sort of hang in the air.

"You could leave before the end of the game," he suggested. "Then you'd have time to come back here and do all that, and JP can just bring me home, and then we can go. If you want to do that instead."

"Let me think about it," I said. "I'll let you know either way in the morning."

"Perfect," he said.

Just then there was a knock on the door.

"That was fast," I said as he went to the door to open it.

"Dude," a guy said from the other side of the door.

"JP," Alej said, pulling the door open further and letting the man in.

"Oh, sorry," he said when he saw me. "I thought we might hit the bar. Guess you're in for the night, though."

"Yeah," Alej said. "But since you're here, let me introduce you. Hailey, this is JP. JP, I'd like to introduce you to my wife, Hailey."

"It's an absolute pleasure to meet you," JP said, coming over to shake my hand. "Don't let anything this guy says scare you. He's really a cool guy, just slightly crazy."

He winked with the last that he said, and I couldn't help but smile.

"It's nice to meet you," I said as I shook his hand.

"Well, whatever he's told you about me, it's all lies," JP said with a laugh. "Unless it's good stuff. That's all true."

"You're actually the first friend I've met," I said. "Besides his sister and *Abuelita*, you're the first person from his life I have been introduced to."

"You met Bella and survived?" he asked, his eyes going wide.

"You make her sound like a monster," I said.

"I mean, she's nothing like his mom, but yeah, she's a lot," he said.

"Anyway," Alej said, drawing the word out. "You've got a bar to corrupt and we've got dinner coming, so..."

"I guess I'll see you around," JP said with a smile, then turned back to the door. "See you in the morning."

"Yeah," Alej said. "I'm gonna need you to give me a ride so she's got the car. You cool with that?"

"Sure thing," he said just as another knock fell on the door.

Alej opened the door and took the bag of food from the delivery person, then let JP out. When he shut the door, he turned and looked at me with this sort of odd grin on his face.

"What's that look for?" I asked.

"Nothing," he said, but I didn't buy it.

I also didn't really need to know, so I let it go as he set the food on the little table he had for us to eat. I really was starving, so we dug in right away.

Chapter Thirty-Six

Alejandro...

"You're sure?" I asked her when I was getting ready to leave. "Because I can just get a ride back with JP and you can do whatever it was you wanted to after the game."

"Alej, I'm fine," she said. "Trust me. I can make this work. I'll just wear my dress to the stadium, and duck into a bathroom as soon as it's over to touch up my makeup. It'll be fine. I promise."

"As long as you're sure," I said, watching her reaction.

"Will you please go to work," she said, shoving on my arm. "I will be fine. I'm gonna get showered and ready to go see you, and I'm excited for it, too. But I can't do anything if you're still here fussing."

"Okay," I said, holding my hands up in surrender. "Just call or text me if you change your mind. Text is best, cause the phone will be in the clubhouse."

"Would you get out of here already?" she asked.

There was a knock at the door, and she looked at me. I knew it was JP, so I just turned around and answered it.

"Let's roll," JP said, his shades on his eyes, likely recovering from his night out drinking.

"Bye," she said, kissing me.

"See you soon," I replied after the kiss.

I walked out the door and down the hall in the direction JP had gone. He was already in his Jeep when I walked outside, so I climbed into the passenger side as he started it up. He was quieter than usual, so I wondered what was going on, but didn't want to bother him. He was one of those guys who would work a problem in his head until he couldn't figure it out. Then he'd come to someone and get insight that he might not have thought of.

By the time we pulled into the parking lot at the stadium, he was settled more, so he must have figured out whatever it was he was thinking about. I didn't need to know and. Honestly. didn't care. I was still worried about the dinner I was taking Hailey to tonight. I wondered whether Bella had told Mama about Hailey, but didn't want to ask her directly. Whatever happened, I would protect Hailey, even if it meant confronting my mother.

When I walked into the clubhouse, I went straight to the manager's office to let him know I needed a ticket left for Hailey.

"That's your wife, right?" he asked.

"Yeah," I said. "But she hasn't changed her name, so it needs to be under her maiden name."

"No problem," he said, then grabbed a sheet of paper. "Write it down and I'll give it to Peggy. She's the one that does these now."

"Sure," I said, taking the paper and writing her name on it. "Where will she sit?"

"In the family section," he said.

"Okay," I said.

I wasn't sure if I wanted her mixed in with all the families, but there really wasn't much I could do. I shot a text off that there would be a ticket for her, and that she'd be sitting with the family for the teams. Honestly, I wasn't sure who all would be there. We had a handful of married guys, along with the coaches' families, but there were so many single guys on the team I wondered whether there would be one-night stand women, or hookups that randomly ended up there.

There wasn't any doubt she could hold her own, but I didn't want to make her any more uncomfortable than she already would be. Besides this being the first time she'd be seeing me play, she was also going to be meeting my family, and both of those in combination seemed like a whole lot. I felt bad that I hadn't planned this out more, but then again, I hadn't been the one to spill the beans about our marriage. No, that fell squarely on Bella's shoulders, after, of course, the dick that posted the video he took of us coming out of the chapel.

"What's up?" Nick asked as I was standing in front of my locker. "You look like you're a million miles away."

"Who do we talk to when it comes to PR stuff?" I asked.

"What's going on?" Nick asked, his voice low and serious.

"It's just," I began, unsure how to word what I wanted to know. "So, I got married in Vegas, and someone took a video of us as we came out of the chapel. They posted it online, and that's how my family found out about it. I wanted to be the one to tell them, wanted time for them to get to know Hailey, but because of the video, it all came out early."

"I mean, you can't put the genie back in the bottle," he said.

"Yeah, I know that," I replied. "I just want to know what I can do about the video being leaked without either of our permission. The dude should face some repercussions of some type, right?"

"I think that's gonna fall under something like freedom of the press, but I could be wrong," he said. "You were in a public space, right?"

"Yeah," I said. "We were on the sidewalk outside the chapel."

"Then they had the right to take video," he said. "If it had been from the chapel itself, like inside, then there might be something you could do. Outside, though, I think you're fucked."

"I guess I'll have to go find the actual video," I said. "I remember something Mama said about it being a stupid little chapel and also something about Elvis, but I could totally be wrong and misremembering, too."

"Find the video," he said. "After that, you can decide what you can and can't do."

"Good plan," I said.

"Now," he said, slapping me on the shoulder. "Forget everything else and let's go play."

"Let's go," I said, and we headed out toward the field to get our practice in before the actual game started.

Chapter Thirty-Seven

Hailey...

"It should be under Hailey Truitt," I said to the woman at the ticket window. "But he may have used his last name. I don't know."

"Nope," she said. "I found you. Just the one, right?"

"Yeah," I said.

"You have your ID?" she asked.

"I do," I said, pulling my license out of my wallet and handing it over to her.

"Perfect," she said. "Have you been to a spring training game before?"

"I don't even think I've been to a baseball game before," I confessed.

"Oh, you're gonna love it," she said. "If you have any questions, just ask one of the people with the name tags. We're all here to help you out."

"Thanks," I said. "Which way do I go?"

"Just over there," she said. "Show them the ticket, they'll scan it, and give you directions to your seat."

I walked in the direction she pointed and saw that there was a line to get in. I started to go to the end of the line, but someone shouted, and I turned to look.

"You're with the family," the woman from the window said. "You go in right here."

She was standing in a door that was near the gate everyone else was going in. It felt a bit weird going in before the rest of them who had been standing in line, but I guess I needed to get used to that, especially if I ever went to a game back home.

"Your ticket," the man at the door said.

I held it out and he scanned it with a handheld scanner thing and I heard a ping before he moved aside and let me through the door.

"Yeah," the woman said. "I should have been a bit clearer, sorry about that."

"It's no problem," I said.

"Go check with him," she said, pointing to a man in the same sort of uniform she and the guy who scanned my ticket were wearing. "He'll be able to tell you how to get to your seat."

"Thank you so much," I said.

"I can tell you're new at this," she replied. "I like to make sure the new ones who are actually nice, and will probably stick around for more than just one game, know the lay of the land. You'd be amazed at how many hoes walk through here, pardon my French."

I laughed at that, realizing that I may have ended up in that category if I hadn't insisted Alej marry me before we had sex.

"Who's your husband?" she asked, her voice pitched low. "We're not supposed to ask, but you seem like a nice woman, and I'd hate to see you hooked up with one of the assholes on the team, again, pardon my French."

"Alejandro de la Garza," I said.

"Ooh," she said, drawing the word out longer than it needed to be. "He's one of the nicest guys on the team, so you picked a good one."

"I think so," I said.

"Well," she said, sort of tucking herself back into her little building. "You go on and find your man, and give him a big kiss from me. I mean, don't tell him it's from me, but yeah, kiss him good."

"I will," I said. "What's your name?"

"Oh, girl, I'm Penny," she said. "My brother always said it was 'cause I wasn't worth more, but I showed him when I ended up doing just fine on my own."

"I'm Hailey," I said. "It was really a pleasure to meet you. Thank you so much."

"Git," she said, shutting the door and leaving me to find my own way.

I walked over to the man she'd pointed to and showed him my ticket, asking where I should go to get to my seat. He gave me directions, and I headed that way. I thought about getting a souvenir, but then wondered whether that would be tacky, so I decided against it, figuring that I could get something another time.

Walking up the stairs toward the seats, I wasn't sure what to expect, but when I got high enough to see out onto the field, I had to stop and stare, moving slowly until I was fully at the top of the staircase. The field was broad and bright green, the white lines crisp along the edges. There were men on the field, doing whatever it was they did to get ready to play, but it didn't detract from the sheer beauty of the field itself. I wasn't sure where to look first, because it was all just awe-inspiring. I don't think I'd ever seen anything so beautiful in all my life.

"Excuse me," someone said, and I moved to the side so I wasn't in the path of others coming up the stairs. "Hey, you look familiar. Do I know you?"

I turned to look at a woman I didn't recognize.

"I'm sorry," I said. "I don't think I know you."

"You just look really familiar, and I'm not sure why," she said.

"Sorry," I replied, then moved further out of the way so she could go past me.

"I swear you look like a celebrity or someone I've seen online somewhere," she said, still staring at me. "Oh, I got it. You just married one of the guys on the team."

She said it so loud that several other people in the area turned to look at us.

"I'm not sure what you're talking about," I said, trying to lie my way out of this, and find an escape.

I began walking toward the section that was indicated on my ticket, but the woman was following me.

"I'm sure it's you," she said. "Didn't you just get married? In Vegas?"

I kept walking, hoping she would get the hint that I wasn't interested in talking to her, but she just kept going. On and on about how she saw the video online, saw me actually get married, and that she was sure I was the one in the images. I finally stopped in my tracks, and she nearly ran me over.

"Ma'am," I said, trying my best to sound older than I was. "I don't know who you are, don't know why you're hassling me, and don't know what you're talking about. I am simply here to watch a baseball game, so if you don't mind, I'd like for you to leave me alone. Do I make myself clear?"

"Whoa," she said, holding her hands up. "You don't need to be such a bitch about it."

"Apparently I do," I said. "Because my simple ways of shutting you down didn't seem to be working, and you just kept going on and on. I will now demand that you leave me alone before I call someone from the security team to handle you."

"Good God," she said, and her tone turned ugly. "Just because you're married to a player doesn't mean you can be a bitch to the fans. We're the ones who pay their salary and give you the lifestyle you enjoy."

"Listen here," I said, turning fully to her and raising my voice. "I am very much an employed woman. I pay for everything I have, including my tickets to this game. Just because you think I look like someone doesn't give you the right to bitch at me, hassle me, and dump your insecurities on me. If you can't figure that out, then I'm not sure there's much help for you. Now, I will ask you for the last time, leave me the fuck alone."

"Is there a problem here?" one of the ushers asked.

"Yes," I said. "This woman won't leave me alone, even though I've asked her several times."

"Ma'am," the man said, looking at the woman. "I'll ask that you go find your seat, please."

"I'm going to my seat," she said, throwing her nose up in the air.

"Can I see your ticket, please?" he asked.

"It's with my boyfriend," she said, sort of shuffling.

"Then I'd suggest you go find it so you don't get thrown out of the stadium for not having a ticket, and for not being in your own section," the man said, clearly calling her bluff. "If you had your ticket, I would let you cross through this section. But since you don't, I'm afraid I'm going to have to ask you to go back that way," he said as he pointed the opposite direction. "And find your way to your section."

"Why don't you ask this bitch where her ticket is?" she barked.

"Mine's right here," I said, holding the ticket up.

The usher looked at my ticket and said, "She's in the right section."

"Thank you," I replied, turning away from the woman.

"Fucking bitch," she said, and I felt her hand on my back as she shoved me.

Luckily, she didn't get a chance to push too hard, because the usher got between us and kept her away.

"Security," I heard the man say, and turned to see that he had a hold of her hand with one of his, the other on a walkie talkie. "I have someone who needs to be removed from the stadium."

"Fuck you," the woman said, yanking her hand away.

She took off toward the stairs, then headed down them. I didn't really care what happened to her, as long as she left me alone.

"Shit," the usher guy said. "You good?" he asked me.

"Yeah," I said. "Thanks."

"I'm sorry about that," he said. "Normally folks are really chill here, but some get it up their ass that they own the players, and by extension, anyone in their families."

"I'm beginning to see that," I said.

"Do you know where you're going?" he asked.

"That way," I said, pointing in the direction I was going.

"Yeah, you're gonna want to look for section..." he paused, like he was trying to remember. "Well, it's on your ticket, so look for that section. You'll have to show your ticket to the usher there, and they'll direct you down. It's the family section, so that's why I knew you were connected."

"Thanks," I said again. "I just don't understand people."

"People are crazy," he said. "Go on, now, and enjoy the game."

"Thanks," I said. "I intend to."

He turned back to the direction the woman went and headed down the stairs. I continued on my way to the section on my ticket, and once I got there, showed it to the usher. I was hopeful that would be the last interaction I had that was nuts, but guessed it wouldn't.

"Now batting for the New Orleans Magicians, Alejandro de la Garza," the announcer said, and I cheered, clapping and shouting for my husband.

The game had been amazing. I wasn't really a sports person, but watching the guys out there, doing what they were paid big money to do, was astonishing. Alej had said something about the kids coming to a game, or some of the players coming to the school, and the more I watched, the more I wanted that to happen.

Their athleticism was so incredible, the way they moved so easily, and in such a short time, that they were able to catch the balls, or get them from the field, and then know exactly where to throw it, just blew my mind. I wished I'd gotten to know the game better before coming today, but there wasn't really time. Besides, baseball was a summer sport, so I'd have had to start before I even met Alej, which wouldn't happen unless I went back in time, which, yeah, I hadn't figured that out, either.

Alej was standing next to the plate, a term I'd learned while sitting here, and was waiting for the pitch to come in. I worried about him being hit with the ball, but he was very quick, and when a ball came close, he was able to back away before it getting to him, which was another thing that was amazing. It took absolutely no time for the ball to go from the pitcher's hand to the plate, and yet, he was able to not only know it was coming, but figure out it was coming toward him, and move out of the way.

The next pitch was further out, and he swung and hit the ball hard, over the head of the guys on the inside of the field, the place where he played. He tossed the bat and ran down the line to first base, then turned like he was going to go to second, but then came back to first. It was all so fast that I didn't know where to look. Did I watch the ball and who had it? Did I watch Alej and what he was doing? Or was I supposed to watch something else? It was all so confusing, but the people around me were kind and helped me to understand what was going on out there, so I wasn't completely lost.

It was the fifth inning, and I saw someone come out of the dugout, another term I'd recently learned, and go to where Alej was on first base. I guessed that they were switching spots, but wasn't sure why, so I asked the person next to me.

"They want to let the younger guys, the ones who may not make it onto the starting day roster, get a chance to see some live action," she said. "During the season, this won't happen unless they want someone with more speed on the bases. Spring training doesn't matter that much, though, so they're just letting some of the other guys play."

"Oh," I said. "So, he didn't do anything wrong."

"Oh, no," she said. "Totally normal. Don't worry, he'll be good to go come opening day."

"Good," I said. "Thanks for helping me today. I don't really know the game at all, so it's all new to me. This is actually my first ever game."

"How did you guys meet?" she asked.

"It's kinda awkward," I said, and I could feel the blush rush to my cheeks.

"Blind date?" she asked. "Met online? What?"

"It's really not that big of a deal," I said, not wanting to share our story. "I'd rather not talk about it, actually."

"You're safe, right?" she asked, seriousness in her eyes.

"Oh, yeah," I said, realizing that she might think I was being abused. "We just met in a weird way, and got married pretty quick, so I don't want people thinking I'm a gold digger or anything. I actually didn't know what he did when we met."

"Honey," she said, and I could hear that she was gonna drop some wisdom on me. "Everyone is gonna think you're a gold digger. It's the nature of the beast with this kind of thing. I think it's good that you didn't know what he did. Means you fell for him for the right reasons, not because of his money."

"I honestly didn't know much of anything about him when we met," I said. "It was kind of a whirlwind thing, so we've been getting to know each other better over the last few months."

"So, you're a newlywed," she said, her eyes brightening. "Oh, that's great."

"It really is," I said. "Only problem is we haven't done most of the normal things you do when you start dating, like meeting the family and such. I'm actually meeting his parents today after the game."

"Are you pregnant?" she asked.

"What? No," I said. "No, we're waiting to have kids."

"Oh," she said. "I just thought that you got married so quick because of that."

"No," I said with a laugh. "That is most definitely not the reason we got married."

I didn't want to elaborate, because, who wants to say you got married because your drunk ass thought it would be funny to tell the guy you wanted to sleep with that you wouldn't do it unless you got married. Yeah, that's not the story I wanted to tell people. I mean, my friends knew, but they were there, sort of. Thinking about it, though, I had no idea what he had told his parents, or what the story was that we were going to go with. I probably should have thought of that before, but it really didn't matter. At least until now. No, now I just had to keep my mouth shut about it all and wait until we devised a plan.

The rest of the game went by without me paying it much mind, not that I understood anything that was going on. We won the game, so at least that was good. I'd texted Alej. letting him know I was here, and for him to tell me where to meet him so we could go to dinner. Tonight would either be amazing or an epic failure, and I wasn't sure which terrified me more.

Chapter Thirty-Eight

Alejandro...
 I'm here. Tell me where to meet you when the game is over.

I was glad she'd stayed for the whole game. Hopefully she'd seen the good things I did, like the couple of hits, and the three double plays I'd helped turn.

Meet me outside the locker room.

I also texted her where that was, so she didn't get lost, and told her to show them her ticket so she could stay inside the gate even after the rest of the crowd had to leave. I was already done with my shower, so I just had to wait a few while the crowd dispersed before I went out there. Didn't need her to see me get mauled by the rabid fans, not that I entertained any of them. Mostly, it was just autographs that were wanted, but there had definitely been some bullpen bunnies that were in the crowd, and I avoided them like the plague.

"You got a ride?" JP asked.

"Yeah," I said. "Hailey's waiting for me."

"And you're not going out now because?" he asked.

"Fans are crazy," I said. "Have you not noticed that?"

"I noticed," he said. "I just ignore them. Put on that air of self-importance and the fact that I'm better than them and they tend to leave me alone."

"Yeah," I said. "I can't do that. I've been taught to be polite my whole life, so I tend to overdo it."

"Gonna have to knock that shit off now that you're married," he said.

"I never crossed the line," I said.

"Of course you didn't," he said, but had a knowing grin on his face.

"What?" I asked. "Seriously, never done anything with a fan after a game, or before."

"Yet you somehow managed to marry a fucking knockout," he said, and it was the first time I'd heard his impression of Hailey.

"Somehow, I did," I said.

"You must give good dick or something," he said. "Because she is way out of your league."

"Don't think I don't know that," I said. "I'm actually surprised it's worked out and she hasn't figured out what an absolute trash panda I am."

"Meh, you're a nice guy," he said.

"And nice guys usually finish last," I said. "Which is why I'm trying my hardest to keep from fucking this up. I like her, love her, and don't want to do anything to end this relationship. It's too important to me."

"Well," he said, pulling his jacket over his shoulders. "Keep her away from your family and you should be fine."

"Very funny," I said, but laughed anyway, because he was right.

We both headed out the door, and Hailey was standing there, sort of hugging herself. It wasn't cold, or even that cool, even though it was March. Something seemed off about her, and it put me on edge a bit, JP's words coming back to me about her being out of my league.

"Hailey?" I said, and she turned to me. "Hey, what's wrong?"

"I'm sorry," she said, and there were tracks down her cheeks from her mascara running. "I tried to be kind, but I think I fucked it all up."

"Woah," JP said as he came out the door behind me. "Who fucked up?"

"I did," Hailey said, a sob coming out.

"Come here," I said, pulling her to my chest. "Nothing's wrong, you're fine. I got you."

She sobbed against my chest, her arms around my body as I held her. I watched as a security guard came up to us.

"You good?" he asked, indicating my wife against my chest.

"Yeah," I said.

"What the fuck happened?" JP asked the guard.

"Someone was thrown out," he said. "They attacked her, started throwing insults, and ended up being escorted out."

"Okay," I said, not understanding why Hailey was still so upset, unless it had just happened. "When did this happen?"

"Before the game," he said.

"I'm sorry, what?" JP asked.

"There's more," he said. "Turns out she had some friends in the stands with her, so she let them all know what she looked like," he said, pointing with his head to Hailey. "What she was wearing, all that. When she came down after the game, they sort of all went after her. It was kind of a mad house, but we got her away from the crowd."

"Hey, baby," I said, sort of leaning back to give her space to look up at me. "Wanna talk about it?"

She shook her head, then tucked it back against my chest. Seeing her so broken just fucked something up inside me, and I was seeing red.

"Did you get the information on them all?" JP asked, and thank God he was here, because my brain was going way too many directions to think clearly.

"We identified the woman," he said. "And the rest of her party that was on the same ticket reservation, and they've been permanently banned from the stadium. It's not something we usually do, but this was a pretty extreme case."

"Do we need to see a doctor?" I asked.

"No," he said. "I mean, I don't think there was actually a physical altercation beyond a little bit of shoving. We were there pretty quickly, so it was shut down almost as soon as it started. I just wanted you guys to know what was going on so you could take whatever precautions you might need to make sure you're safe."

"Thanks," I said, still holding Hailey. "Let's get you home."

"But dinner..." she began, but I cut her off.

"Dinner is postponed," I said. "I'm taking you home to get you settled. I'll text Mama and let her know so she won't worry."

She sniffed a bit, then nodded against my chest, squeezing me around the middle.

"You want an escort to the car?" he asked.

"I think we'll be good," I said.

"Nah," JP said. "We want an escort. No sense in chancing anything."

"Okay," I agreed. "You got the keys?" I asked Hailey.

"Yeah," she said, reaching into the pocket of her dress and pulling them out.

"Thanks," I said. "Do you remember where you parked?"

She shook her head, so I wasn't sure what we were gonna do.

"We'll go to my Jeep," JP said. "I'll drive you around the lot to find your car."

"I'm sorry," she said, and I just held her.

"Nonsense," JP said. "Some jackass decided to show their entire ass, so it makes sense you're not quite all together."

She turned and looked at him, and he winked at her and she laughed. It was a good sound, and I was glad he was with us.

"Let's get you guys to the car," the security guard said.

"Thanks," I replied, then turned to Hailey to walk beside me.

JP came to the other side of her, wrapping his arm around her as well, basically cocooning her between us. Her one arm was around my waist, and she put her other around his, which I was surprised about, but not at all bothered by. We followed the security guard out the gate and to the lot where the players parked. There were a handful of people out there, but no one bothered us as we got to JP's Jeep and climbed in. I sat in the back, letting Hailey sit up front. She tried to insist, but I just put her in the seat and pulled the belt around her, not giving her any room to argue.

He started it up, and the rumble made her jump and yelp, and I put a hand on her shoulder, but JP put his on her thigh. I sort of gave him a look, and he shrugged, then moved it off her, putting the Jeep in gear. We took off toward the other lot, the one that fans used, and he drove toward my car, which was pretty obviously one of the last ones in the lot. There were a few people in this lot, more than the other, but I didn't think they'd do anything, as they were all standing around what I assumed were their own cars.

My friend pulled up beside the car, putting Hailey's side next to the passenger side of mine, so I climbed out, then unlocked the door, before getting Hailey out and into the car.

"Watch out," JP said, and I looked up to see a bunch of folks coming toward us.

He got out of his car after turning it off, and stood between his door and mine, trapping Hailey inside, and everyone else out. I went around the front, but had to push the seat back to where I could get in. I finally got in and locked the doors, starting the car up. Hailey's eyes were wide, staring out the windshield at the oncoming people.

"Are we safe?" she asked.

"We will be in a minute," I said, putting the car in gear and heading out of the spot and away from the crowd.

I knew the lot well, so headed toward the gated area we'd just come from, and the guard there let us through so we could go out the exit that wasn't covered by fans. I'd heard JP start his Jeep up as we were pulling away, so knew he was going to be getting out of there, too. Pulling onto the street, I turned away from the condo and started toward downtown, hoping that if anyone was following us, I could spot and lose them. I didn't need people knowing where I lived, or worse, where Hailey might be if I was at the stadium and she was home alone.

I turned down several streets, going in circles and backtracking, and finally, after about fifteen minutes, I headed toward the condo. When we pulled in, JP's Jeep was parked in its spot and he was leaning against it, sunglasses on and looking sort of smug.

"Are we safe?" Hailey asked.

"We are," I said, turning the car off and getting out.

I walked to the other side just as JP opened the door. I sort of gave him a look, and he shrugged again, helping Hailey out of the car, shutting the door behind her. We walked into the building and headed up the stairs to the second floor and my condo. JP kept pace with us, just behind us on the stairs. I wasn't sure what he was all about, but I didn't share what was mine, at least where Hailey was concerned. And especially not today. She'd been through enough.

We got to my condo, and I opened the door, letting Hailey in. When I went to shut the door, JP's foot was there, blocking it.

"Dude," I said.

"She's upset," he said. "I just want to make sure she's okay."

"That's my job," I said, with more force than I probably should have used. "If we need anything, I'll let you know."

"Anything at all," he said. "I'll be here in a moment."

"See you tomorrow," I said, then shut the door, turning the lock and turning back to Hailey.

"What was that all about?" she asked.

"He just wanted to make sure you were okay," I said.

"Did you have to be rude?"

"He wanted to comfort you," I said, looking at her pointedly, hoping my look was enough to get the intentions he had across.

"Oh," she said, drawing the word out. "Do you do that kind of thing?"

"No," I said. "And even if I did, I wouldn't right now, or until we'd had a long conversation about it."

"Yeah, not my thing," she said. "Not that it's wrong, just not something I would think I'd enjoy."

"Me, either," I said. "I want you all to myself."

I stalked toward her, pulling her to me, and kissing her soundly. She gasped, which I took as an invitation to invade her mouth with my tongue. Her arms went around my neck, her leg lifting to hook on my hip, and my hands went down to her ass, picking her up, and pressing her to the wall behind her.

She was so responsive, like the fear or whatever it was, pushed her to need me, and I was going to be happy to oblige her in any way she wanted me to. With her legs wrapped around my waist, her body pinned to the wall, I used one hand to undo my belt and button, undoing my zipper down before shoving my pants and boxers down, freeing myself so I could indulge in her.

When I reached up under her dress, I realized she wasn't wearing any panties, and that just made me all the harder. Gripping myself, I shifted so that I was at her entrance, then let her down slowly so I went inside her, her pussy pulling me into my base, and the way she wrapped around my cock just did everything for me.

We hadn't stopped kissing, and she was using her heels to pull me closer to her, effectively creating the rhythm I was using to fuck her. The heels of her shoes were somewhat sharp, and the contrast to the pleasure I was feeling from my cock inside her to the pain she was eliciting with her heels in my ass, was something I wasn't used to, but definitely was enjoying.

I kept my motion going, pounding her into the wall with each thrust, and she was beginning to breathe hard, pulling away from my mouth so she could get more oxygen into her body. Her eyes were fluttering, mostly closed, but occasionally opening in a heavy-lidded fashion to stare into my own.

"I love you," I said, punctuating each word with a thrust.

"Oh, God, Alej," she said, panting with each word. "Just like that. Oh yeah, keep going."

I kept going, just as she'd asked me to, although I was starting to feel the burn in my thighs, the way they were working to both fuck her and hold her. I wanted to get her off once before I let her down and took her to bed. Finally, when I thought I was going to have to give in, she gasped, squeezed my cock with her pussy, and pressed her heels into my ass, her fingernails into my shoulders.

"That's it," I said, encouraging her to continue on as long as she could. "Come for me, baby. Come all over me."

Her pulsing pussy was nearly my undoing, but finally, she eased up, giving me a reprieve to hold out a little longer.

"Oh, God," she said, her head falling to my shoulder.

I shifted her up and off me, setting her on the floor, holding her until she had her balance. She looked up at me, the tears streaking her face almost beautiful.

"Thank you," she said.

"For what?" I asked.

"For this," she said, waving a hand between us. "For taking care of me, protecting me. You don't know how much it means to me."

"I promise to continue to do it until you kick me to the curb," I said.

"I never want to let you go," she said, pressing up on her toes to kiss me softly. "Now, can we go to the bedroom and do this again?"

"After you," I said, moving back as much as my trapped ankles would let me.

She slipped past me and headed to the bedroom while I leaned over and pulled up my pants enough to walk. When I got in there, she'd kicked off her shoes and put them off to the side, and I caught her pulling her dress up and over her head. She was completely naked in front of me, and all I wanted to do was marvel in her beauty. When she turned to look over her shoulder at me, she smiled, then turned fully toward me, allowing me to see everything she had to offer, at least physically.

"God, you are beautiful," I said, and she shrugged.

"I think you have too many clothes on," she said, her smile turning wicked. "Should I help you get out of them?"

"Whatever you want," I said. "I am yours for the taking."

"Good," she said as she sashayed that fine ass toward me. "I plan to take you as many times and as many ways as I can."

"From your lips to God's ears," I said, letting go of my pants and boxers.

She started with my shirt, unbuttoning it so slowly it was almost painful. When she saw some skin, though, she pressed her lips to me, laying kisses down my chest as she opened my shirt. When she reached the bottom, she shoved it back and over my shoulders where I took over and shook it off to let it fall on the floor.

Kneeling in front of me, she reached under my pants to get to my shoes. I braced myself on the doorframe and lifted first one, then the other foot, allowing her to pull my shoes, socks, pants, and boxers all off, almost at once. Before I knew what was happening, though, she was up and pulling my cock into her mouth, her velvet tongue sliding along the bottom of it as she nearly swallowed me, the head hitting the back of her throat.

"Oh, God," I moaned, holding on to keep myself upright. "If you keep that up, I won't be able to hold back."

"We've got all night," she said after letting me fall from her lips. "I plan to keep you very busy, so don't worry about it."

With that, she slid around me once again, sucking me into her mouth, sliding up and down, giving a twist at the end, her tongue swirling around my head. With one hand, she had my balls, not quite squeezing them, but more massaging them, holding them in her warm hand. Her other hand was on my hip, but slid around to grab my ass, pulling my cheeks apart some. I wasn't sure what her intention was until she slid her finger along the crack, pressing against my asshole. I bucked, pulling out of her hand and mouth, my eyes wide.

"Sorry," she said. "Wanted to try something new. It's okay if you don't want to, though."

"It's just not something I've done," I said truthfully. "I wasn't prepared."

"Let's hold off, then," she said, but her face told me she wanted to do it.

As much as I wanted to give in to her wishes and desires, that was beyond my comfort level, so I decided that we could explore that when emotions weren't quite so high. I told her as much, and she again told me it was fine.

"Come on," she said, getting up and walking to the bed.

I got right behind her, holding her standing, but pushed her body over the bed so she was bent at the waist, her ass up in the air and inviting. Instead of fucking her, though, I knelt and licked her from clit to slit, shoving my tongue into her pussy, and she moaned, a heady sound from deep within her. The fact that I could elicit such a noise from her was a boost to my ego, one she'd sort of hurt a bit just a few minutes earlier. Instead of dwelling on the bad, I decided to push the good as far as I could, continuing my work on her pussy, sucking in her clit, and sliding my face enough to shove a finger inside her. Her pussy spasmed around the intruding digit, and I knew that I had her moving in the right direction, toward that cliff we all loved to tumble over.

Working my finger around, I found the rough patch just inside her, and began to scratch it with the tip of my finger. Again, I elicited a moan from her, and I couldn't help but chuckle, which caused her to moan again. She was so responsive, even more so now that we'd known each other for a while. Every time she showed me with her body and her noises how much she appreciated my work, I felt bigger and better than anyone in the world.

Doing my best to keep everything moving, I felt her squeeze my finger, which told me how close she was. I set my teeth into the bundle of nerves I was working, biting just enough to add pressure, but not cause too much pain, and worked that patch fast until she fell apart in my hands, her body pulsing at its release.

Once she was back to the here and now, I pulled my finger free, kissing her ass as I stood up, and helped her into the bed. She was languid, like liquid fire, her body so warm to my touch, and I just wanted to feel her all over me in any way I could. I reached for the nightstand to grab a condom, which we'd only been good about using about half the time, and she grabbed my wrist before I could take hold of the package.

"I want to feel you," she said. "Just you and me, nothing between us."

"You're sure," I said, knowing she'd let me know if that changed.

"I need you," she said, and the way her eyes looked at me, I knew I would never refuse anything she asked of me.

Climbing up onto the bed, I moved my body between her thighs, settling there, my arms holding my upper body over her, caging her in with them. She reached between us, finding me and guiding me to her center, and as I slid in, she sighed. It was something I'd never tire of hearing, and I just sort of let myself stay there, in that moment, feeling her all around me. Her hands came up to cup my cheeks, and she looked deep into my eyes, conveying all the love she had for me in that moment, and I drank it in, absorbing it into my very soul.

I began to move, slowly at first, but as I did, her hips came up to meet me, and at her urging, I increased my speed until I could hear her breathing, mine, and the sound of our bodies slamming into each other. It was hard and fast, and she pulled me down to her, wrapping her legs around my waist, leaving just enough room for me to maneuver, while she kissed me deeply. The collection of feelings, and knowing just how much I meant to her, pushed me over the edge and I fell, filling her in the process, as she held me and kissed me.

Chapter Thirty-Nine

Hailey...

"You're sure?" he asked for probably the hundredth time.

"Yes," I said, for just as many times.

"Because we can totally skip it if you want," he said.

"Would you shut up so we can go?" I asked.

"I don't want to push you," he said.

"Babe," I said, looking him in the eye. "We're gonna be late if you don't go now."

I'd come to watch the next game, and this one didn't end in me crying or anyone pushing me or nagging me. It was actually really pleasant to sit with other family members in the stands and watch him play. I had figured out a few things, but knew I'd be picking up a book on baseball and all its rules at some point in the next week or so before the actual season started. There was so much to learn, and even though it wouldn't be learned quickly, I had faith in the fact that I could figure this complex game out.

He finally started the car, and we pulled out of the parking lot, and headed back toward town to where we were set to meet his family for the replacement dinner we'd missed the night before. He'd told me that if I felt at all uncomfortable, to just let him know and we'd leave. I was sure I'd be able to handle everyone, after all, I'd pretty much held my own with his sister the day I arrived.

I'd be lying if I said I wasn't nervous, but I was actually looking forward to meeting the rest of the family, at least the ones that were here in Florida. When he pulled into the parking lot of the restaurant, my stomach did a little flip, but I figured it was just my nerves trying to get the best of me. In the last five or six weeks, so much of my life had changed that it was a wonder I was able to keep track of everything. Still, I knew Alej loved me, and I loved him, so other than the two of us, no one else's opinion mattered.

"You ready?" he asked after he'd shut the car off.

"Yeah," I said.

"Nervous?"

"A little," I replied. "Just the normal nerves, though."

"You give me the word, we're out of there," he said, then leaned over and kissed me.

"Keep that up and I'll make you take me home," I said as I pulled away.

He went to put his key back in the ignition, but I stopped him with a laugh. He got out, came around the car, and opened my door, helping me from my seat to stand in the parking lot. My head swam just a bit, making me feel dizzy and a little nauseous.

"It's just nerves," I said, more to myself than to him.

"We can leave right now," he said, holding me in place. "I'll text and tell them you're sick."

"I'm not sick," I said, settling myself to my full height, all five foot two that it was. "Let's go. Don't want to make them wait any longer."

"If you're sure," he said, and I could see concern in his eyes.

"Don't be ridiculous," I said, play swatting his arm. "Now get me food so I don't starve."

"Yes, ma'am," he said, shutting the door behind me, and offering me his elbow.

I hooked my hand in it, and we walked toward the door to the restaurant. It was somewhat crowded, but we had reservations, and he'd gotten a text from his family that they were already there, so we just gave our name, and told the hostess we were meeting someone who was seated.

"Of course," she said, looking at her podium to see where we needed to go. "Follow me," she said as she stepped out from behind it and showed us where we were to sit.

"Alejandro," his mother said. "I'm so glad you're here."

"Welcome," his father said, standing to take his hand.

His mother had gotten out of her chair and came around the table, pulling him into a hug that lasted entirely too long for my liking, and then proceeded to try to kiss him right on the lips.

"Mama," Alej said, holding her at arm's length.

"What?" she asked. "You won't let your mama kiss you now?"

"Mama," he said, his tone firm. "You haven't kissed me in years. Don't pretend this is normal."

"You crush me," she said, dropping her head.

I wasn't sure if it was performance art or something else, but I didn't like the possessiveness she was showing.

"You must be Hailey," his father said, coming around them to shake my hand. "It's a pleasure to meet you, finally."

"It's nice to meet you, too," I said, taking his offered hand in my own, and giving it a good shake.

"Come now, Mama," his father said. "Let's sit and let them sit. Alej has been playing all day and is probably hungry."

"Oh, yes," she said, looking me over with a judgmental stare. "He needs to eat to keep his strength up for his job."

She went with her husband and sat on the other side of the table. His sister wasn't there, and neither was anyone else, so my guess was that Alej had asked that they not come, or something came up so they couldn't. Either way, it would be nice to not meet so many people all at once. Alej pulled my chair out and helped me to sit before taking his own chair.

"So, tell me, Hailey," his father began. "What do you do for a living?"

"I'm a teacher," I said. "Put myself through college to get my degree. I wanted to give kids what I was given when I was growing up, which was a good education. Sometimes that's all that stands in the way of staying where you are, and going someplace better in life."

"I bet you love children," his mother said, her eyes brightening up. "Are you going to have children soon with my Alejandro?"

"Mama," Alej said, his tone clearly warning.

"What?" she asked, trying to act innocent.

Thankfully, Alej had told me exactly what his mother was likely to do during dinner. He said she'd either try to run the entire conversation, and not let me get a word in edge-wise, try to make me look like I was a fool or stupid, or that she would try to get us saddled with a dozen kids before dinner was even over.

"We've talked about this," Alej said, looking at her pointedly. "My family planning is not your business. We will decide if and or when we have children, how many we have, and what we will name them. You will be allowed to be a grandmother at our choice, and if you overstep, you will be turned into the grandmother we do not see."

"Alejandro Luis de la Garza," she said, pulling the full name out. "You will not speak to me in such a way."

"Mama," he said, clearly done with her shit. "If you say one more word that isn't polite and simple conversation, we will leave. Do I make myself clear?"

She sputtered, but finally nodded, then glared at me. It was so uncomfortable, but I endured it because I knew it would just make her happy if she'd scared me off, and I didn't want to give her that satisfaction. Instead, I sat there, with a polite smile on my face, waiting for my turn to say something. Not that I needed permission, but more that I was being overly polite just to show her exactly who was the biggest bitch at the table.

"So, tell me," his father said once the dust had settled. "How did you two meet?"

Oh shit, I thought. We hadn't even talked about what story we were going to tell anyone, so I let Alej take the lead.

"It's boring," he said, and I smiled, because it was about the most un-boring story I'd ever thought about. "Let's just say it was love at first sight, and we couldn't wait to get our lives together started."

He moved his hand to my thigh, and gave me a squeeze, and I slid my legs open a bit, hoping he would give me something interesting to think about rather than this conversation with his parents. Not that I was willing to fuck him in front of them, but more that I needed something to keep my mind busy instead of thinking about everything going on around me. We were sitting close enough that he could likely get his hand to my pussy without much effort, but I wasn't sure if he'd go that far. When he turned to look at me, I could see that I was getting to him, and all I could do was smile. He shifted in his seat a bit, which told me he was uncomfortable, at least within his pants, so I smiled even bigger.

"Are you at least Catholic?" his mother asked.

"Agnostic," I replied. "But that doesn't mean I'll stop Alej from choosing whatever religion he wants to follow."

"But your children will be baptized in a Catholic church, right?"

"Mama," Alej warned.

"What am I supposed to talk about if I can't ask these questions?" she said.

"You can ask about her job," he said. "Ask about her favorite color, or what she had for breakfast. Just don't push."

"Those won't tell me what I need to know about my future grandchildren's mother," she said, and Alej stood up.

"Come on," he said to me, pulling my chair out, and helping me to stand.

"Where are you going?" his mother whined, and that's what it actually was—whining. Like a petulant toddler who wasn't getting their way. It was almost comical if it weren't so horrifying.

"We're leaving," he said, turning me away from his parents, and toward the entrance.

"But we haven't even gotten to know her," his mother whined more.

"And until you can act like a decent person, you won't," he said.

Putting me in front of him, he walked us to the entrance, passing waiters who looked a bit confused. By the time we got to the front, the hostess was back at her podium.

"Was there a problem?" she asked.

"Not with the restaurant," Alej said. "Just with the company we had."

"I'm sorry," she said.

"Completely not your fault," I replied.

We left the building, Alej with his hand on the small of my back, guiding me to his car. I almost expected his mother to come running out, but she didn't. I wasn't sure whether it was from shock, or if her husband had contained her. Either way, I was glad we were out of there and away from her.

"Let's go home," Alej said, his lips close to my ear, his breath rushing along my skin. "Then I can do to you what you were hinting at in there."

"Yes," I said, my voice low. "I can't wait for that."

He opened my door and helped me into the car, then shut it after I was inside. His walk to the other side of the car was swift and sure, climbing in quickly, and starting it up. He backed out of the stall, then pulled ahead to get out of the lot. His phone began to ring, but he pressed the button on the side to silence it. Either he knew who it was, or wasn't interested in talking to anyone. It took nearly no time, and yet entirely too long, to get back to the condo, and when he pulled into the parking spot and turned off the car, he turned to look at me.

"I'm sorry," he said. "I didn't intend for them to ambush you, and I don't want you to feel like you have to live up to some sort of specific standard to fit in with my family. You're my chosen family now. and all I care about is making you happy."

"You don't need to apologize for your family," I said. "They're adults, and are capable of doing that on their own, if they feel it necessary."

"Well," he said, unbuckling his belt. "My mother is never wrong, according to her, so it'll be a cold day in hell before she apologizes."

He leaned over, gave me a quick kiss, before opening his door and getting out of the car. By the time I had my belt off, he was at my door, opening it for me and helping me out. We didn't say anything as he led me up to his condo, and I didn't mind. It gave me some time to think about what to expect in the next few years, at least where his mother was concerned. I wasn't sure if it would be a good thing or not, but he seemed fine with the way things turned out, so I wasn't going to argue.

When he opened the door, he let me in first, then came in after me, pulling me to him after shutting the door, and pressing his lips to mine. My arms went up and around his neck as I raised up on my toes. He scooped me up, his hands under my ass, and carried me to the bedroom where he plopped me down on the bed.

"I'm ready for my dessert," he said, shoving my skirt up and diving under it to get to my pussy.

"Oh, God," I moaned as he slid his tongue along my seam.

I'd gone without panties again tonight, knowing that I wanted him to have access if he wanted it, and didn't want to have to deal with them once we got home. The plan worked out well, too, since he was able to get in there and stroke me, licking and sucking me, causing me to writhe under him as he took me up and up and up, higher and higher, until I reached the stars and exploded among them. Absolutely shattered to a billion pieces, only to be brought back together again by his careful hands, easing himself into me in slow and even strokes.

Everything this man did to my body was perfect, and I would take advantage of everything he gave to me. And he gave to me over and over, several times that night, until we were both so spent we ended up just falling asleep in each other's arms, holding tight to the most important thing in the world.

Epilogue

Three and a half months later...

Hailey...

"You're sure you're fine?" he asked me.

"Alejandro de la Garza," I said. "I am not a fragile piece of porcelain, but a human, a woman, and moving swiftly to becoming a mother. I will not break, and going on this trip is absolutely something I want to do now, rather than after the babies get here."

"I just don't want to put too much pressure on you," he said.

It happened in Florida. All that sex without protection, even with my IUD, led to us ending up starting our family much sooner than we'd anticipated. But it wasn't an unwelcome surprise. In fact, I was rather glad that it happened when it did. When he came back to New Orleans after spring training was over, we decided to go ahead, and move into his home. He thought it was a safer neighborhood, even though mine was perfectly safe. His first road trip to the West Coast ended up seeing me hurling all day long, missing several days of school because of it, and sure I had the flu or some other bug I'd gotten from one of the kids in my classroom.

When I finally ended up going to the doctor, she asked if I thought I could be pregnant. I was sure I wasn't, but she wanted to do a test, just to make sure, and there we were. When it came back as definitely pregnant, she sent me for an ultrasound to figure out how far along I was, and to see if the IUD had slipped or shifted, or was in any way an issue with the baby. Turns out, it had moved itself down and out of my uterus and was just gone.

I freaked out, though, knowing that we wanted to wait, and not wanting to cause him to just come home and deal with whatever was going on, so I lied to him. It was the only time I'd done it, and I still, even this many months down the road, and every apology I'd given him, and every time he'd told me he understood, felt guilty. Now, though, he was just so overprotective it was getting old.

"I just don't want you to push yourself too much," he said. "You know what the doctor's said, right?"

"I know," I replied, getting angry. "Because there are two, it may mean I have to be a bit more careful. That doesn't mean I need to be stuck in a room without moving for the rest of my pregnancy. We talked to the doctor, and she said it was fine for me to go, so we're going. And if you don't knock it off, I'm gonna tell *Abuelita* what you're doing, and you know she's gonna get on your ass about it."

"Okay, I surrender," he said.

We were in the car on the way to the airport, and were going to be flying down to the Dominican Republic. It would be my first time out of the country, and I was looking forward to meeting his *abuelita* in person. We'd done several video calls over the months, and she was the first person we told that we were expecting. His parents still weren't talking to us, which was fine by me, because that meant I could avoid the whole insane mother-in-law bombardment of the baby rabies I expected from her.

I was technically due around Christmas, but they figured that I'd have the babies early, so we were looking at a Thanksgiving birth. It was terrifying to say the least, because I didn't really have anyone I could talk to about being pregnant and giving birth. It was honestly the hardest part about the whole thing. Sure, it was hard when he was gone, but I managed just fine. We decided that I wouldn't be going back to teaching, at least not until the babies were here, so I finished out my year about a month ago, and we had been doing all the planning, and preparing to get us ready for these two little ones to get here.

He wanted to find out what we were having, but I wasn't sure, so when they did the ultrasound to figure out the genders, they turned the screen above the bed off, and shifted the machine so it wasn't pointing at me, that way neither of us could see what they were. They did get genders, put the information into an envelope, and made us promise that we wouldn't open it without the other's consent. I'd given it to Missy to hold on to, and she promised she wouldn't look until we asked her to, or until we decided we wanted to do a gender reveal.

The closer we got, the more I wanted to know, so we decided that we would take the envelope with us when we went down to see his grandmother. We would let her open the envelope and be the first, besides the technician, to know whether we were having boys, girls, or one of each.

I'd asked the doctor why I ended up with twins, and she said that it was likely in one of our family histories, but Alej said he didn't have any twins in his family at all that he knew about, and since I was an orphan, I didn't know my family history. We assumed it was on my side, and when we saw that they were likely fraternal, we knew it was my fault we ended up with two at the same time.

We were flying first class, because Alej insisted that we needed to give me the best of everything, and I wasn't going to complain, because I had gotten used to flying this way, and it was hard to give up that luxury. Besides, it meant I was close to the bathroom on the plane, and I had been going so much it was ridiculous.

Now that we were finally on our way, though, I worried that

something would happen on the flight down, or after we landed. Alej assured me that we would be in a very safe place, but I had my doubts. That is, until we actually landed, and I saw the beautiful area around the airport. He'd rented a car, so he could be in control, and drove us down the highway along the water, and I wanted to cry because it was so pretty.

When he pulled up to a gated area, I was relieved that we would be safe behind a fence. We were only going to be there for a couple of days, and now I wished we'd had longer. Unfortunately, during the summer, Alej had to work, so that meant we had to go during the All-Star break, when it was the hottest time of year, or after the babies came, which I wasn't quite ready to agree to.

As the gate opened, he inched us inside, and it closed behind us as we pulled down a long driveway. I wasn't sure what to expect, but the huge house wasn't it. The building was so big I couldn't even see the whole thing through the windshield. I must have let out some sort of noise, because he laughed beside me.

It was built out of that stucco that I expected, white walls and giant pillars in the front, with a circular driveway that pulled up under a canopy by the front door. He pulled in, put the car in park, and shut it off.

"Stay put," he said as he got out of the car.

I did as he said, knowing it would only cause him to be upset, and that wasn't anything I ever wanted to do. Instead, I waited patiently for him to come and open my door, then help me out of the car. We walked up the few steps to the big door, and he pressed the button on the side of it. I heard the chimes come from the other side of the door, and it was a beautiful melody that I didn't recognize. The door opened, and a young woman stood there in what I would assume was a maid's uniform of some sort.

"Señora Barrera," the woman shouted, and then pulled the door open further. "Come," she said. Her accent was thick, but I could understand her fine.

"Come on," Alej said, helping me into the house. I wasn't too big, yet, but was definitely bigger than I anticipated I'd be when I ended up pregnant.

"*Nieto*," a woman said, and I recognized the voice.

"*Abuelita*," Alej said just as she rounded the corner and came down the hallway.

"Oh, my," she said, looking at the two of us. "You are so incredibly beautiful. Even more so in person. Come, come, let's have some lemonade."

She held my hand, and we walked back the way she had come from, Alej leaving me in her care as he went to bring in the bags.

"You must tell me everything about you," she said. "I want to know all there is to know, so that when my little great-grandchildren get here, I can help them to know their mother."

She was so sweet, the way she just chattered on about nothing, that I just wanted to stay there forever. By the time Alej was back in with the suitcases settled into a guest room, I was on my third glass of lemonade, and in desperate need of a bathroom.

"Alej," I said when he stepped into the sunroom we were in.

"Abuelita," he said, then came to me.

I looked at him, hoping he could see what I needed, and he did right away.

"Come with me," he said, helping me up from the chair I was in.

"Oh, no," *Abuelita* said. "I should have thought of that."

I knew she knew what I needed, so I let her feel a little bad, but only because I didn't want to be rude. Alej took me to the restroom and let me handle myself. When I came out, he was leaning against the wall, waiting to take me back to his grandmother.

"Are you doing okay?" he asked.

"I am," I said, with a sigh of relief. "This is just what I needed. The chance to get away from everything and everyone and just relax."

"You've been here for half an hour, and you're already relaxed?" he asked.

"Your grandmother is a gem," I said. "I could sit and listen to her chatter on for days on end."

"Are you ready to find out?" he asked, and I nodded.

We walked back into the sunroom, and he helped me sit down, then sat next to me.

"Abuelita," he said, holding out the envelope.

"What's this?" she said, taking it from him.

"This is the results of the ultrasound," he said. "It says whether the babies are boys, girls, or one of each."

"We wanted you to be the first to know," I said.

"Oh, my," she said, holding a hand to her mouth. "Are you sure?"

"You have been so kind," I said. "We wanted you to have the honor."

"Do you know?" she asked.

"We don't," Alej said. "The only other person who knows is the ultrasound technician who did the testing."

"Do you have a guess?" she asked, looking at me.

"I have no idea," I said. "And it doesn't really matter. So long as they're healthy, I'll be happy."

"Should I look?" she asked. "Or is this for me to see after you leave?"

I looked at Alej, and he looked at me, then we both looked at his grandmother.

"We'd like to know," Alej said. "We have some ideas for names, but it would be helpful if we knew the genders so we could decide for sure."

"Back in my day, we had to wait till the baby was born," she said, sliding her finger under the flap that was sealed on the back of the envelope. "This is so exciting, though. And to know before they are here, so you can prepare everything just for them is wonderful."

It was almost like she was stalling, the pace at which she worked the glue loose on the envelope before pulling the sheet of paper out. She unfolded it, reading it carefully, then smiled up at us.

"Looks like I have a couple of new great-grandsons to welcome," she said, and I beamed.

"Both boys?" Alej asked, and almost seemed a bit upset.

"Two wonderful sons," his *abuelita* said. "You will be a wonderful father, and I'm sure Hailey will be the perfect mother."

"Not perfect," I said. "But I'll do my best."

"Two boys," Alej said again, then looked at me. "We're gonna have a couple of baseball players on our hands."

His face beamed at the thought of bringing his sons into the game he loved so much, but I wanted to temper his enthusiasm just a bit.

"Unless they decide that they want to be teachers like their mother," I said.

"Or something completely different," he said, his smile growing wider by the moment. "I'm gonna be a dad to two boys."

There were tears in his eyes, and they began to slide down his cheeks, as he came to me, kneeling in front of the chair I was sitting in. He kissed my belly, then leaned up, and kissed me.

"Are you happy?" I asked.

"Happier than I could ever be," he said. "Unless we end up with two daughters after this."

"Let's wait until they're born before we start planning the next ones," I said with a laugh.

"There's plenty of time for more," *Abuelita* said.

She was right. We were still so young, and we had all the time in the world to have more kids, or not. Either was fine with me, so long as I got to do it with Alej.

Note from Author

Images and Blurbs available upon request.

I would ask that you obtain high quality headshots and cover art images directly through me, rather than taking them from either my website or Amazon, however, blurbs are readily available through both places.

About the Author

Born and raised in the Pacific Northwest, CM Kane was fed a steady diet of sports, particularly baseball. Having this love of the game instilled in her at an early age, she found that nothing was better than getting lost in the game. Storytelling was another gift that was encouraged in her youth, and she's taking to the written word to explore a new aspect to the game she loves.

Social Media and Website Links:

Website:
https://www.authorcmkane.com

Facebook:
https://www.facebook.com/AuthorCMKane

Instagram:
https://www.instagram.com/authorcmkane/

Amazon:
https://www.amazon.com/author/cmkane

BlueSky:
https://bsky.app/profile/authorcmkane.bsky.social

Also by C.M. Kane

Seattle Cascades

1. Extra Innings

2. Caught Stealing

3. Backstop

4. Power Hitter

5. Double Play

6. Find a Gap

7. Sweet Spot (Coming Soon)

8. 7th Inning Stretch (Coming Soon)

New Orleans Magicians

1. Choke Up

2. Caught in a Pickle

3. Brand New Ballgame (Coming Soon)

4. Fan Interference (Coming Soon)

5. Flashing the Leather (Coming Soon)

Austin Aces Hockey Club (Shared World)

Power Play

Anthologies

Unnerving: Eclipse

Street Justice (Limited Time)

Fooling Around (Coming April 1, 2025)

Neon Lights & Country Nights (Coming June 1, 2025)

Stand Alone Titles

A Switch in Time